L.A.D 12/4/18 I

_SIDE VERDUN

Erziehung vor Verdun

A novel from the First World War

OUTSIDE VERDUN

Erziehung vor Verdun

A novel from the First World War

ARNOLD ZWEIG
Translated by Fiona Rintoul

FREIGHT
BOOKS

First published in the UK May 2014

© Aufbau Verlag GmbH & Co. KG, Berlin 1957
First published in Amsterdam in 1935 by Querido, Amsterdam

Freight Books
49-53 Virginia Street
Glasgow, G1 1TS
www.freightbooks.co.uk

A CIP catalogue reference for this book is available from the British Library

ISBN 978-1-908754-52-3
eISBN 978-1-908754-53-0

Typeset by Freight in Plantin Std
Printed and bound by Bell & Bain Ltd, Glasgow

  The translation of this work was supported by a grant from the Geothe-Institut which is funded by the German Ministry of Foreign Affairs

the publisher acknowledges investment from
Creative Scotland toward the publication of this book

Arnold Zweig (10 November 1887 – 26 November 1968) was a German writer and anti-war activist. He is best known for his World War I tetralogy of which *Outside Verdun* is part. Zweig volunteered for the German army in World War I and saw action as a private in France, Hungary and Serbia. He was stationed in the Western Front at the time when Judenzählung (the Jewish census) was undertaken. After World War I he was an active socialistic Zionist in Germany. Following Hitler's attempted coup in 1923 Zweig went to Berlin and worked as an editor of a newspaper, the *Jüdische Rundschau*. Zweig would later witness the burning of his books by the Nazis. When the Nazis took power in 1933, Zweig was one of many Jews to go into voluntary exile, first to Czechoslovakia, then Switzerland and France and finally Palestine. In 1948, after a formal invitation from the East German authorities, Zweig decided to return to the Soviet occupation zone in Germany where he became a member of parliament. He was President of the German Academy of the Arts from 1950-53. He died in Berlin in 1968.

Introduction

As the historian David Reynolds emphasises at the beginning of his recent book, *The Long Shadow*[1] , it is chiefly through literature that we remember the First World War. That has a number of implications. The publication of literary depictions of the war has depended to a large degree on the readiness of the general public to read and think about the subject, and it is a remarkable fact that the best-known literary memoirs of the First World War in English, for example – those by Robert Graves, Edmund Blunden and Siegfried Sassoon – only appeared some ten years after the war had ended. In the German-speaking world, following the defeat of 1918, inhibitions against literary accounts of wartime experiences seem to have been so strong in the 1920s that when the Ullstein publishing house launched Erich Maria Remarque's *All Quiet on the Western Front* in 1928, its marketing strategy was built around the notion that some kind of taboo was being broken. The newspaper serialisation began precisely on the tenth anniversary of the armistice, and Remarque's novel was presented as the work that finally told the truth about the war, the truth that had hitherto been denied to the reading public.

In the German context, the memory of the war remained a hotly contested issue. On the one hand, the nature of the war was radically de-heroicised by writers such as Remarque and Arnold Zweig. But around 1930 there was also a strong reaction from authors who were keen to have the war remembered as Germany's supreme effort to assert itself as a nation, heroically and against great odds[2]. The favourite setting for these nationalist war novels was the Battle of Verdun, the attempt of the German High Command in 1916 to 'bleed France white' by attacking the French line at its strongest point. It

---

1   David Reynolds, *The Long Shadow: the Great War and the twentieth century*, London 2013.

2   See David Midgley, *Writing Weimar. Critical Realism in German Literature, 1918-1933*, Oxford 2000, chapter 6: 'Remembering the War'.

was a strategy that notoriously misfired, producing almost as many German casualties as French and a total casualty list probably in excess of 600,000. Arnold Zweig's *Outside Verdun*, first published in 1935, is a reckoning with both the human cost of that campaign and the subsequent mythologisation of it by the nationalists.

Arnold Zweig was born in 1887 and grew up in Silesia, a province of the German Reich with a strong literary tradition of its own. His Jewish descent and his lower middle-class background (his father traded in grain and leather goods) were no obstacle to his receiving a very good education – although Prussian legislation in 1896 that required the army to buy its supplies direct from the producer effectively drove his father's business into bankruptcy. Zweig's literary interests were well nurtured during his schooldays in the industrial town of Kattowitz (now Katowice, Poland), and between 1907 and 1914 he was able to study German literature, philosophy, psychology and the history of art at a variety of universities that included Munich, Berlin and Göttingen. Already before 1914 he had established his reputation as an author of narrative fiction characterised by psychological sensibility and a refined sense of style. He had also engaged powerfully with a notorious instance of central European anti-Semitism, the persecution of a Jewish community for alleged ritual murder in Hungary in 1882, and his drama on that subject (*Ritualmord in Ungarn*) was awarded the prestigious Kleist Prize in 1915. In April 1915, however, Zweig was conscripted into the German equivalent of the Army Service Corps, as a common soldier not bearing arms on account of his poor eyesight. He served in this capacity in Belgium, Serbia and in the vicinity of Verdun until the summer of 1917, when he was transferred to the Press Division of the Army High Command on the eastern front, in Lithuania. Here is the biographical background to the story of the trainee lawyer Werner Bertin as Zweig tells it in *Outside Verdun*.

Wartime experiences, a daily routine under military discipline shared with other common soldiers, undoubtedly sharpened Zweig's awareness of the oppressive potential of Wilhelmine society. He emerged from the war as a radical pacifist, a fervent socialist and a committed Zionist. For several years he concentrated his efforts on political essays and the robust confrontation of anti-Semitism, which had become acutely politicised in Germany in the course of the First World War. His investigations of the social and psychological roots of anti-Semitism, which drew strongly on the insights of Freud, were published in 1927 as a book with the title *Caliban* (he saw the figure of the savage in Shakespeare's *Tempest* as an epitome of the antipathy that one human group may develop for another). When he returned to literary writing in the mid-1920s his style, too, had become more robust. From now on his narrative idiom is often close to that of the serving soldier: stark, down-to-earth, and characterised by the low irony of the undeluded, whose main hope in life has been reduced to mere physical survival. And the driving force apparent in his major novels is a passionate commitment to the exposure of injustice and inhumanity.

The vivid and powerful nature of his writing meant that Zweig was among the very first German war novelists to attract attention in English translation towards the end of the 1920s. Already before the publication of *All Quiet on the Western Front*, Zweig had earned widespread critical respect with *The Case of Sergeant Grischa* (1927), a work that distinguishes itself from the generality of war novels because, in the entirety of its conception, it adopts perspectives that are independent of the exigencies of military action. Sergeant Grischa is a Russian prisoner of war who escapes captivity in the spring of 1917 and tries to make his way home. Arrested while carrying false papers, he is condemned as a spy and eventually shot, despite the best efforts of those who have helped to establish his innocence. Around this scenario Zweig builds a penetrating exposé of the mentalities and the material interests that determine human actions at this late stage of the war. The figures he depicts range from the soldier on guard duty who knows that only the punctilious execution of orders will prevent him from being sent to a murderous section of the front, to the general and the industrialist whose strategic calculations set the goals to which individual lives are subordinated. Grischa dies because, in the political circumstances of 1917, any situation that might nurture thoughts of insubordination among the German troops must be promptly eliminated from those calculations.

In *Outside Verdun*, too, what is at issue is not so much the carnage – the arbitrary nature of which is made plain enough – but the impact of the war on fundamental understandings of morality and humanity. Werner Bertin, as we encounter him in the first chapter, is someone who acts on humane instinct, offering water to a column of captured Frenchmen as they are led away from the battlefront, an act that makes him a target for recrimination and victimisation, someone of whom his superiors can make an 'example'. His exposure to more glaring iniquities begins when he is befriended by a young NCO, Christoph Kroysing, who has discovered corrupt practices at work within his company, but who conveniently falls victim to enemy artillery fire before he can effectively testify about them. These experiences set in train a gradual learning process that will transform Bertin's life, his apprehension of what the war is about, and his sense of who he is. And as he learns to adjust his expectations to the circumstances in which army life has placed him, he comes under competing influences. On the one hand the class-conscious workers in his company, Wilhelm Pahl and Karl Lebehde, who already know what they can expect from Prussian military discipline, would like to harness his intelligence to their cause. On the other hand the brother of the dead NCO, Lieutenant Eberhard Kroysing, is a born warrior who would like to help him escape from the ranks of the oppressed by joining the officer class.

When *Outside Verdun* was first published in 1935, Arnold Zweig was living in Palestine. As a Jew and a prominent socialist writer, he had been forced to flee Germany when Hitler came to power. In the novel he can be seen to take account of various factors that had arguably contributed to the installation of the Nazi regime. When we find Bertin's company commander, Captain Niggl, for example, imagining that the source of his misfortunes is a conspiracy of Jews and freemasons, then we are being given a pretty clear reminder of the scapegoating impulse that lay at the roots of Nazi ideology. And in his accounts of battlefield experiences Zweig systematically undermines the myths that had grown up in post-war publications and in public memory around the Battle of Verdun in particular and around the notion that the German army had been undefeated in the field. But true to the spirit of his psychological investigation of anti-Semitism in *Caliban*, Zweig does not caricature the human types that he recognises as posing a threat to civilised standards of behaviour. Instead he tries to understand their personality and motivation. In Eberhard Kroysing and his loyal and resourceful corporal Süßmann, he depicts two figures who have, to all appearances, successfully adapted to the physical conditions of the war of attrition, and it is the precise ways in which they have adjusted their attitudes and expectations to the conditions of the battlefield that contributes most to the process of disillusionment undergone by the idealistic intellectual Werner Bertin.

The town of Verdun on the Meuse was protected by an elaborate system of outlying fortresses. When the Germans advanced from the north in the closing days of February 1916, one of these forts, the Douaumont, fell into their hands. It had been left lightly defended because the French command was not confident in its ability to withstand the most powerful German artillery fire, and the tiny group of German sappers who found their way inside it had advanced more rapidly than either side had expected and took the defenders completely by surprise. The German success, then, was a piece of sheer good luck, as Süßmann explains to Bertin in Zweig's novel, but it was publicly celebrated as a grandiose military exploit nevertheless. Moreover, the legend of the Douaumont grew over time because it became a major forward operational base for the Germans in their turn and therefore came under repeated heavy bombardment over a period of months until the French succeeded in recapturing it in October 1916. Aerial photographs of the time show it to have been progressively reduced to a flattened ruin.

This is the terrain to which Kroysing and Süßmann have adapted their lives and their outlook. They can laugh at the heroic legends put about by the Supreme Command, as they do at the naive insistence of Bertin – a Parsifal in squaddy's boots, as Kroysing calls him – on inalienable principles of justice. The experiences of battle have stripped Kroysing of any illusion that official bulletins will be anything other than a tissue of lies, and he does not hesitate to have an entire company of service corps transferred to the Douaumont, to his patch, in order to take revenge on those he holds responsible for his brother's death. Outside Verdun we are truly 'on the fringes of humanity', as Zweig puts it in his title for Book 4.

Just as in *The Case of Sergeant Grischa*, where Zweig had explored the social dimensions of a modern nation at war, here too he presents the socially conditioned mentalities that have been imported into wartime situations from civilian life in Wilhelmine Germany. It is above all the nature of *industrialised* warfare that he progressively exposes through the experiences of his protagonist, a form of war that is dependent on the continual supply of goods and armaments to railheads near the front, on an extensive labour force that attends to the physical and practical needs of the military forces, and on a substantial bureaucracy that organises and oversees the distribution of material and labour. The petty officiousness to which Bertin finds himself subjected thrives most readily among the military bureaucrats, epitomised in the figure of the retired civil servant Captain Niggl and the battalion commander Major Jansch, by profession a journal editor and nationalist ideologue. For Niggl, and for others who are numbered among Bertin's oppressors, the war has brought enhanced status, as well as enhanced pay, and the opportunity to lord it over others, without apparent restraint.

The system of oppression to which Bertin finds himself exposed makes those moments when he can escape from it all the more enticing. His naïve belief that, despite all indications to the contrary, his army service must be helping to support a just cause is supplemented by a boyish spirit of adventure, which comes to the fore when he is allowed to roam in the landscape behind the front and to visit Kroysing and Süßmann in their quarters. What ultimately strips away his illusions is not the conversations that he has with them about the vicissitudes of military fortune, but the first-hand encounter with the reality of the battlefront that they also enable him to experience. Bertin is allowed to accompany Kroysing's sappers when they move up to the front line and to witness the conditions in the forward trenches for himself, and Zweig's description of his responses is worth quoting here verbatim. Peeping over the breastwork as the artillery barrage builds, Bertin experiences a moment of elation at the destructive potential unleashed around him. But when he ducks into the dugout where the crack troops are resting, he also makes a discovery that thoroughly undermines the heroic expectations he has brought with him thus far. It is the discovery that being on duty here is much the same as being on duty in his own company of military labourers:

The faces of the sappers, gunners and Saxon riflemen made him feel almost sick. Until now he had garlanded them with splendid delusions, draped them in noble titles. But no illusion could hold out here. The men in this boarded clay grave were just lost battalions, the sacrificed herds of world markets, which were currently experiencing a glut in human material. Crouched on a plank under the earth 200m from the enemy and yawning suddenly from exhaustion, he saw that even here the men were just doing their duty – nothing more than that.

The earth rumbled above him, chunks fell from the walls, dust rained down from the timbers and as the infantrymen calmly carried on smoking their cigarettes, he wondered hesitantly how he had come to see this truth. It hurt! It robbed you of the strength to endure life. Surely it couldn't be the same everywhere else as in his own company.

The rest is attrition. The Douaumont is vacated under French pressure, Kroysing vanishes temporarily in the fog of war while vainly attempting to rally troops for a counteroffensive, and in the aftermath of that episode Bertin is confronted with a series of unnerving horrors: a blinded man mechanically addressing an imaginary doctor, a devastated field battery, and the corpse of a schoolfriend. In the course of his duties he is at the mercy of the institutionalised malice of his superiors and is assigned to the dangerous and fatiguing task of searching for unexploded shells. Progressively the novel registers the arbitrary destruction of the people Bertin has come to know. Both Pahl, the character most closely associated with the possibility of resistance against the war, and Kroysing, a defiant warrior and a fervent nationalist to the last, are killed in an air raid on the hospital where they are recovering from wounds. Süßmann, meanwhile, has died a particularly pointless death as a result of an accident during weapons training, and his last message makes clear the dichotomy between fond illusion and disillusionment that remains difficult for Bertin to resolve to the very end of the novel. Tell my parents it was worth it, Süßmann says, and tell Kroysing it wasn't.

There are other novels in which Zweig explores the social and political dimensions of the First World War. He shows us the life of the home front in the early months in *Young Woman of 1914* (1932), focusing on the situation of the fiancée that Bertin left behind with an unwanted pregnancy, and the political machinations in occupied Eastern Europe in *The Crowning of a King* (1937). Indeed, he continued to add volumes to the cycle he called 'The Great War of the White Men' after the Second World War in East Berlin, where he settled in 1948 and where he died in 1968. But it is in *Outside Verdun* above all that he brings his reader face to face with experiences that challenge and undermine any attempt to glorify the war. It contains his most penetrating depictions of the effects of protracted warfare on the personalities and the outlook of the people directly involved, and it allows the reader to accompany the naïve young protagonist Bertin on his journey to deeper self-knowledge as well as to an awareness of the conflicting aspects of human nature that the war has brought into the open.

Not that *Outside Verdun* brings the reader to anything as neat as a firm conclusion. On the closing pages, Bertin is shown to be still wrestling with the conflicts he has witnessed and with the question of how he should position himself in relation to them. The date of the final scene, in which he and his wife have come to visit Kroysing's grieving parents, is June 29th, 1919, the day after the Versailles Treaty had been signed – with all the associations of subjugation that that event carried in the eyes of the German population, and thus also the associations of betrayal on the part of the politicians who accepted its terms.

For his readers in 1935, Zweig did not need to spell out the poignancy of that moment. But here, too, his novel distinguishes itself from the common expectations we might have of a war novel. By contrast with Remarque, who tells us how the life of his protagonist was snuffed out on a day when it was reported that 'all was quiet' on the western front, Zweig takes leave of Bertin in a post-war world in which he, and all of German society with him, will be facing difficult choices.

Professor David Midgley, University of Cambridge

BOOK ONE

In the woods

CHAPTER ONE

Turning off a tap

THE EARTH WAS a disc flecked yellow-green and drenched in blood. Above it, like a mousetrap, hung the unrelentingly blue sky, imprisoning humanity within the misery its animal nature prescribes.

The battle had been at an impasse since mid-May. Now, in mid-July, guns were still pounding the valley between the village of Fleury and Fort Souville. Volleys of explosions rolled back and forth; billows of poisonous smoke, dust clouds, pulverised earth and flying chunks of stone and masonry darkened the air, which was riddled with steel splinters and whistling bullets. At night, the area behind the front blazed and roared with gunfire; by day, the blue skies throbbed to the rattle of machine guns, bursting hand grenades, and the howls and whimpers of lost men. Time and again, the summer wind blew off the dust from the assaults, dried the storm troopers' sweat as they climbed from their dugouts, eyes and jaws fixed, and carried away the moans of the wounded and the last gasps of the dying. The Germans had been on the attack here since the end of February. This war between Europeans, which had been raging for two years, might have originated in the south east of the continent, but it was nonetheless France – her people, her land, her army – that bore the brunt of the devastation. There might be bitter fighting at this very moment in Bukovina, on the rivers Adige and Isonzo, but the combat was at its wildest on the banks of the two French rivers, the Somme and the Meuse. And the battle that raged by the Meuse was about possession of the fortress at Verdun.

Escorted by Bavarian infantrymen, a troop of French prisoners marched along the main road leading from the former village of Azannes to a surviving train station at Moirey. It was hard to march between fixed bayonets as prisoners of an opponent who had shown just how cheap life was to him – his own as much as the enemy's – during the invasion of Belgium and France. In Germany, people were starving. Everyone knew that. In Germany, prisoners were maltreated. It said so in the all the newspapers. For the French it was terrible to think that they should have fallen into the hands of the Germans precisely now, at the eleventh hour. Soon the Germans would have to call the whole thing off, because the force of the Franco-British attack on the Somme would knock the stuffing out of them. Still, these prisoners had escaped from hell fire with limbs intact. If they behaved themselves, they'd get through a few months in prison too, even if it did make them want to puke to be led away like a herd of cattle. The ravines and what had once been woods, now a mass of shell craters, were behind them, as were the Meuse hills and the descent to Azannes. The landscape here was still in one piece, so to speak. Beneath them to the right flowed a stream. Around them rose the rounded, green hilltops of the Lorraine countryside. If only they could have a drink. Heat, dust and sweat tormented the 40 or 50 marching men from the Fourth Infantry in their blue-grey tunics and steel helmets or twin-peaked caps.

As they turned a corner on the left side of the road, they spotted two big troughs, each with a jet of clear water gushing into it. Men from the German Army Service Corps (ASC) were washing pots and pans there. The Frenchmen raised their heads, straightened up and quickened their pace. The Bavarian guards knew about thirst too. They'd give them time to drink or fill their canteens. Both armies were really only bitter enemies in battle. In any case, word had long been out among the French that the ASC men were unarmed non-combatants, reservists from the Landsturm too young or too old for battle, harmless folk.

On the slope above the road, black against the blue sky, was an extensive hutted encampment with steps leading down. Waves of ASC men ran over. They wanted to see the spectacle, and it was lunchtime. Well, the more hands, the quicker everyone would get a drink. A blue-grey clump of thirsty men surrounded the troughs. Brown faces, all bearded, reached up; dozens of arms stretched out; there were mugs, pots, pans. Men dunked their faces in the translucent water, which shimmered and rippled at the bottom of the troughs. This French water, the last they'd swallow for a long time, tasted so good in their parched throats. It restored them. The ASC men understood immediately. They filled their pots and pans and helpfully took them down the line. German and French aluminium and tin clinked amicably together; white and pale grey fatigues framed the Frenchmen's dark tunics.

'Look lively,' shouted the NCO in charge of the platoon. 'Get a move on!' This was an unplanned stop. But he wasn't really serious. No one was in a hurry to return to their unit at the front if it was dug in at Douaumont. The men who'd quenched their thirst moved slowly away from the trough, dried their dripping beards and reformed in the middle of the road. Their eyes shone more brightly now. After two years of war, a certain mutual respect, liking even, had built up between the Germans and the French at the front. It was only to the rear, beginning with the lines of communication, that considerable numbers of people laboured to whip up hatred and anger lest the human material get infected with war weariness.

An ASC private named Bertin, recognisable from a mile off by his full, shiny, black beard, watched with satisfaction as one of his NCOs, a book seller from Leipzig called Karte, offered one of the Bavarians a cigar, holding out his trench lighter and pumping the Bavarian for information in his Saxon dialect. Hauling a container of water, Bertin pushed through the swarm of men, shouting a word or two to his comrades Pahl and Lebehde, and trotted to the end of the line, where people were vainly trying to elbow past those in front. Like drifting brown animals, a herd of strange yet familiar creatures, the men swore and pleaded in guttural tones, their necks straining from their open coats. They greeted the three men who'd come to take care of them with grateful eyes.

'Come on, make room,' Bertin shouted, coming away from the trough with a field kettle balanced in one hand and a full pan lid in the other. Suddenly, there was danger: officers had appeared up by the barracks and were watching what was happening. Fat Colonel Stein, his huge belly protruding over his bandy legs, hastily stuck his monocle in his eye and took it all in. On his right, he was flanked by his adjutant, First Lieutenant Benndorf, on his left by the company commander, Acting Lieutenant Graßnick, while Acting Sergeant Major Glinsky wryly watched the goings-on down below from a respectful distance. The colonel waved his riding crop indignantly at the dripping faces of those who'd cooled off in the trough. How long had this been going on? Three minutes or four? The four men absorbed all the details.

'Bloody shambles,' snarled the colonel. 'Who told them they could drink here? They can stick their bloody snouts in water somewhere else.' And, with one hand on his moustache, he shouted down the command: 'Sergeant, move on!'

Colonel Stein was commander of the ammunitions depot at Steinbergquell, which stretched up across the hill. First Lieutenant Benndorf was his adjutant. Graßnick was only a second lieutenant in the labour company attached to the ammunitions depot. All three men had seen action in 1914 and been wounded (Benndorf still walked with a stick and limped) and were now in charge here.

Colonel Stein could therefore expect obedience.

But without a favourable wind, the human voice obviously doesn't carry very far out in the open. There was at first no response to Colonel Stein's order, though this was against the natural order. Sergeant Major Glinsky rushed over to the balustrade, his backside wagging up and down, and, leaning half over, roared: 'Stop that, fall in, move on!'

Glinsky knew the right tone. The Bavarian sergeant's hand moved up involuntarily to the hilt of the bayonet hanging from his belt. Unfortunately, there were epaulettes glittering up there on the hill – otherwise that dirty Prussian pig would have got a few choice greetings in Bavarian. As it was, the sergeant turned sharply to his troops: 'Fall in, form up.'

It's as well if prisoners understand even what they don't understand, and some of the guards spoke a smattering of French. Slowly, the first infantrymen pushed forwards. The ASC men pushed between them with greater determination to make sure they all got a drink. The column reformed peacefully.

The colour rose in Colonel Stein's face. People down there were going against the spirit of his order. Down at Moirey train station, looking like tiny toys, the wagons were already rolling up that would take the prisoners away and then return as quickly as possible with gas ammunition. Time enough for the men to drink at the station. 'Stop this nonsense!' he ordered. 'Sergeant Major, turn the water off!' Everyone there knew the two brass taps near the feed trough that cut the flow of water to the lead spouts. Glinsky jumped to it.

Those ASC men who happened to be nearby heard this order with a grumble, a grin or a shrug, but it pierced one man to the heart. Bertin blanched under his black beard. He didn't think about the tap at Moirey train station. He felt the agony of having to carry on past the trough without drinking almost as if it were his own. He had just filled his canteen. He should now empty it into the dust, as some of his comrades were doing: that docile little chap Otto Reinhold for example, or Pahl the typesetter. But Bertin knew there was still a number of thirsty men waiting at the rear. They were shuffling past the troughs, barely moving, with three Bavarians behind them. No one would now dare to fill their cupped hands or mugs.

'Nowt we can do. They're turned off.' Private Lebehde, an innkeeper, pointed to the two taps, which were running dry.

'Now I've seen it all,' grunted Halezinsky, a gas worker, 'and they call themselves human.' And shrugging his shoulders he showed the last

Frenchmen his empty field kettle.

Bertin's canteen was made of aluminium. It was battered and black with soot on the outside but snow-white on the inside and full of delicious water. As he moved along the edge of the column – conspicuous because of his shiny, black beard – he calmly distributed the water. To a gunner who, with anguished eyes, had only reached out cupped hands he handed the full lid. To another man he gave the water from his canteen, holding it to his lips himself.

'Prends, camarade,' he said, and the gunner grabbed hold and drank his fill as he walked. Then he gave the canteen back.

All going well, Bertin, who was training to be a lawyer, had every prospect of living to be an old or at least an elderly man. But he would never forget the look that came into those brown eyes, which were shadowed black with exhaustion and set in yellowy skin grimy with artillery smoke.

'Es-tu Alsacien?' the Frenchman asked the German.

Bertin smiled. So, if you behaved decently towards a French prisoner, you had to be from Alsace. 'Certainly not,' he answered in French. 'I'm a Prussian.' And then by way of goodbye: 'For you, the war is over.'

'Merci, bonne chance,' replied the Frenchman, turning to march on.

Bertin, however, stayed put while the ASC men slowly slipped off up the steps. Satisfied, he watched the blue-grey backs with a warm glow in his heart. If those people were now sent to Pomerania or Westphalia as farm labourers, they'd know they weren't going to be eaten alive. He could and would defend his actions. What could they really do to him? All he need do was lie low in the barracks for the next quarter of an hour or until he was next on duty. Wrapped in a pleasant afterglow, Bertin climbed up the wooden steps with his canteen, from which Frenchmen had drunk, dangling all nice and clean from a crooked finger. Deep in thought, he strolled past Pahl the typesetter and didn't even notice the long look of amazement Pahl gave him.

Pahl let him pass because he wouldn't like to be seen with this particular comrade that day. He'd often taken him for a spy who stuck close to the workers in the company to get information and pass it on. But this man wasn't a spy. No. He was the opposite: rashness personified. If Wilhelm Pahl knew Prussians, this man was for it – but he didn't seem to care. Pahl the typesetter, by contrast, cared a great deal. He stood in the sun, a kind of big gnome with thick shoulders, overly long arms, a short neck and small, pale grey eyes, and gazed after the man who had followed his heart – in the Kaiser's army.

CHAPTER TWO

Inspection

DURING THE AFTERNOON'S work on that memorable day, an order swept through the sprawling park with its turfed ramparts, huts, tents and stacks of grenades: inspection at six o'clock! Inspection? How come? Hadn't there been four inspections in the past fortnight – with boots, underclothes, fatigues, tunics and neck bands? Hadn't the nearby gunners, sappers, radio operators and railwaymen been poking fun at this enormous labour company of 500 men for ages because they liked to play soldiers? Everyone knew they were the army's forgotten children: old people doing sterling work, being treated like new recruits in the middle of France. Quite a circus. Admission free. Annoyance and cursing, then, by the field railway wagons and tracks, ammunition tent and grenade stacks. But nobody connected the order with the events at lunchtime.

In the elaborate parlance of the German army, inspection means the ceremonial assembly of a company of men in its entirety in the barracks yard. Anyone who can move has to be there, even clerks from the orderly room and those from the 'sick bay' who are only a little ill. At 10 to 6 precisely, then, the company filled the empty space enclosed by the barracks, forming a horseshoe comprised of three columns. The roll call ceremony took place. Everyone was there – except the company commander, who kept them all waiting.

The ASC men were meticulously arranged and ordered according to size, with the giant Hildebrandt on the far left of the first column and tiny Vehse, Strauß and Naumann II furthest to the right, but an essential something was nonetheless missing, and Lieutenant Graßnick could never quite get over it. Their tunics spoiled the picture. It had started in Küstrin in Brandenburg – heavy Prussian Army Litevkas in dark grey with red lapels. Then came several dozen milky grey tunics made of a coat fabric meant for military officials. In Serbia, they'd received a batch of greyish brown infantry tunics, red about the seams from repeated delousings. Then finally in Rosenheim in Bavaria, on the way here, the depot had splashed out on a few dozen artillery tunics made of a greenish material with black piping. When the men were at work or marching, it didn't matter. But these kinds of colour games were too risky for the parade ground... The grey field caps and blue cord epaulettes made no difference. More than half a million German men were running around like this: Landstrum reservists with no weapons, workers, salesmen, intellectuals. Not in great physical shape, but with a little military drilling. The combat units' work slaves. Soldiers and yet not soldiers. A pitiful joke and essential troops rolled into one.

'Attention! Company – eyes left!'

The company froze. Acting Lieutenant Graßnick, whom the men nicknamed Panje of Vranje after the small town in the Serbian mountains where he'd spent his best days, approached at an easy pace. The company tailors had done everything in their power to make a proper officer of him. His tunic hugged his back perfectly, his high grey cap with its silver cockade was perched impressively above his red face and his epaulettes looked almost as good as a real lieutenant's. But to the actual officers he was still just a jumped-up sergeant major, and so he wafted about in a lonely void somewhere between the promoted men and the ruling class.

'At ease!' he croaked. 'Listen up, everyone.'

He received the communications, accepting a piece of paper from Herr Glinksy, to whom it had in turn been handed by the clerk Sperlich, rigid with obedience, and read what was on it: a Fifth Army brigade order. The men learnt that the great attack planned for 5 May had been betrayed by Alsatian deserters, and that this had now been confirmed by French prisoners. They were reminded of their duty to be discrete even when chatting to one another, on the train or writing home.

The men stood there, trying to keep a straight face. For God's sake, they thought. The silly French naturally hadn't noticed that the German army planned to shower its princely leader with successful attacks and captured trenches for his birthday. Obviously, no one over there had any idea that the crown prince was born on 6 May. General Pétain had to rely on deserters – and from Alsace to boot – to alert him to the forthcoming attacks. There were two Alsatians in the company, one young, one older, both exceptionally good workers and popular comrades. 'Alsatian traitors' thus sounded particularly tactful. Yes, the Prussians had imbibed tact in spades. But it looked like Panje of Vranje was finishing up now in his croaking lieutenant's voice. God help him. Amen.

But no. 'Unfortunately,' Herr Graßnick continued, flapping his hands excitedly, 'unfortunately, an unprecedented lapse occurred right here in my company this afternoon. Private Bertin, step out 30 paces. Forward march!'

A twitch ran through the company, like a horse or a dog pricking up its ears. Watch out, it said. This concerns us. Such a huge body of 500 souls is very sensitive to matters of honour and shame, and in certain circumstances one individual represents the group. It took Bertin a second to grasp what was happening. He blushed, then blanched under his black beard. Only then did he move. He hadn't expected to be plucked from among his comrades like a frog in a stork's beak. But a soldier should be prepared for anything, as Herr Graßnick was about to teach him.

'Didn't you hear?' he trumpeted into the profound silence that always descended when someone was to be punished. 'By the rear – march!'

Obedient as a well trained dog, the trainee lawyer Bertin turned, marched round the right wing of his, the third column and breathing heavily came to halt back in his place.

'Private Bertin, 30 paces, forward march!'

In his neatly blackened boots, Bertin sprang forward again. After 30 paces, he took position diagonally to the right of the company commander. Graßnick gave him a wry glance, looked him over and ordered him to: 'About turn!' The soldier swung round. Sweat ran down his glasses. Perhaps the blood was pounding in his eyes. The company rose around him like the three walls of a room under construction, the rows of his comrades in their different greys topped by a reddish strip: their faces caught in the sunlight. It was hard to feel so many eyes upon him, but there was nothing to be done about it. Why hadn't he followed Karl Lebehde's advice and shaved off this bloody beard that stood out like black Sauerkraut? Now he was going to pay for his obstinacy. But that fellow Graßnick could rattle on as much as he liked. What Bertin had done was right by both military and human law. Comforting prisoners was in the Bible, as was giving the thirsty to drink. It didn't matter what happened now. He was at one with himself and the moral code in his heart. Still, he couldn't stop his knees shaking slightly. Good that his wide trousers hid it.

'This man,' crowed Herr Graßnick with a forced snarl, 'this man here had the effrontery to allow French prisoners to drink from his canteen, although the colonel had expressly forbidden it. I leave it to each of you to decide what to call such unworthy conduct. One can only describe such a man as a stain on the company.'

'Am I in the pillory here?' wondered the black-bearded soldier, unable to stop his nose and forehead turning a sickly grey. His sticky-out ears felt like they had when he was at school and Herr Kosch the teacher pulled them. But because he was at peace with himself, he was able to feel sorry for the superior officer to his left. A town clerk from Lausitz disguised as an officer. The ruling class would never take him seriously, and yet he had to stand there blaring on in his staccato voice, trying to sound convincing between long pauses. He was about as well suited to this as spinach to a grater. Yes, he heard Graßnick croak, Bertin's behaviour was all the worse because he was an educated man of whom better might have been expected. He'd set a bad example to his comrades. Fortunately, his example did not extend to the whole company. The company's morale was good. Those in higher places were well aware of that. Drastic measures to put a stop to these kinds of incidents once and for all would therefore not be necessary.

Can you put a stop to an incident? wondered Bertin but he was breathing more easily. A couple of curious gunners from the ammunitions depot staff were now watching this carry-on at the labour company scornfully. A light wind from the west carried the scent of hay. On the other side of the stream, some emaciated artillery horses were being nursed back to health in a big tent. The drivers were cutting the tall, sweet grass in preparation for winter. For a moment, Bertin almost lost himself in this illusory peaceful world – framed by the dull thud and clash of the artillery battle on the other side of the horizon. *So, these are the kinds of things our company is worrying about at the siege outside Verdun*, he thought. *Why would a man like me worry about this rubbish?* There he stood, black-haired and pale, heels together, hands on his trouser seams, letting the clatter of Graßnick's closing remarks wash over him. Hopefully he realised that he deserved a court martial for what he'd done, Graßnick said. However, as his behaviour to date had been passable, justice would be tempered with mercy – and he'd better remember this favour. 'Fall out!'

Could've been worse, the company thought, and Bertin thought so too, as he bounded back to his place between docile little Otto Reinhold and Pahl the typesetter like a terrier let off the lead. Reinhold nudged him with his elbow and gave him an imperceptible smirk.

'Company – attention! Fall out!'

Four hundred and thirty seven men about turned and stomped off to enjoy their free evening. No one wasted a word on what had just happened. They had underwear to wash, trousers to mend, dinner to eat, letters to write or cards to play. They could do what they wanted now. Be human, free. Werner

Bertin strolled back to the barracks more slowly than the rest. Perhaps he felt a bit down-hearted. He decided to lie down for half an hour and then take his beard over to Naumann (Bruno), the barber. Off with it. Enough of standing out – basta.

From among the group of NCOs still standing together, Herr Glinsky's expressionless, bulging eyes fell on Bertin. To the right, above the hills at Kronprinzeneck and forward towards Romagne hung sausage-shaped captive balloons, shining gold in the evening light.

CHAPTER THREE

A glimmer

THE JULY NIGHT lay heavy on the 3rd platoon's barracks where some 130 men slept after a hard day's graft. Stacked three high on wire netting and sacks of wood shavings, they rolled from side to side, groaning, sweating and scratching themselves without waking. The company was riddled with lice. The men had left the delousing station at Rosenheim clean and as if new-born, and before they moved into the grimy barracks here they'd cleaned up Prussian style, jettisoning cartloads of their predecessors' rubbish. But the yellowish lice had waited patiently in the seams of the yellowish sleeping bags for their moment – and this was their moment. Lice are like bosses and fate: you can fight them but in the end you pretty much have to come to terms with them.

From the outside, the long barracks seemed to be cloaked in darkness. Dr Bindel, a civilian doctor in uniform, had got the company carpenter to install ventilation flaps in the roof, using plans drawn up by Private Bertin and Schnee, a medical NCO. Non-soldiers would probably have thought it impossible to sleep there and wake refreshed. But they would've been wrong. It was possible to sleep there, as 130 men proved. The rats that zipped happily along the passageways could confirm it too, for they never woke anyone, except when they bit into their big toe. In any case, the rats preferred to be under the barracks rather than up in the land of the living. It was safer below.

There were two glimmers of light in the barracks. Bertin was still reading, and by his head a stearin candle stuck on a tin holder burned, protected by his tunic, coat and rucksack. Some four men away and one level up, Pahl the typesetter was smoking a cigar. He smoked in order to think undisturbed, and his thoughts centred on Private Bertin.

The comrade down below wasn't reading because he wanted to. He had to play the writer again and was reading proofs. The first galleys of a new book that was being printed in Leipzig had arrived for him in the field post that evening. He'd shown the wide-margined columns of print, set in a clear font by reputable printers, to his comrade Pahl, who after all was in the business.

Evenings and nights were the only times Bertin could check his text for printing errors and mark them up with the traditional squiggles in the margins. He'd thought he wouldn't be able to concentrate after the stupid business with the inspection earlier, but he'd be getting a delivery like this every day now, so he'd reconsidered. Pahl knew only too well how important commas and colons were to writers, and how they chased down unnecessary repetitions. Bertin was quite right to keep his sentences in order, although he had other demands on his time now. The Germans were avid readers at the moment. They even read young authors – especially those. There hadn't been so many new writers for more than a century. Bertin's novel *Love at Last Sight,* which was typeset in the lovely Breitkopf font, had been unexpectedly reprinted that spring, and the royalties had greatly helped his wife. That much Pahl the typesetter knew from dinnertime chats. Pahl was very interested in the technical side of printing: the familiar names of the typefaces, whether it was better to set type manually or use a machine, the correction process. But he was much more interested in the author – admittedly for his own very particular reasons. As he lay there puffing on his company cigar, he mentally evaluated his comrade Bertin's aptitude for the boxing match that surely lay ahead of him. Before bedtime, Pahl had received a hint from Sergeant Böhne, an affable type who'd been a postman before the war and was a Party sympathiser, as to what might happen the following morning. Pahl's thoughts moved slowly one step at a time. It had awakened something within him to watch his comrade standing all alone at the centre of the company in the barracks yard with Graßnickian phrases raining down on him. Karl Lebehde was right. Bertin had shaved his beard off just a few hours too late – trust an innkeeper to understand the ways of the world. But it didn't do to scoff at a typesetter's musings either. For they drew on a thorough knowledge of the military order, which was based on a thorough knowledge of the social order...

In Pahl's view, the whole point of human society was to ensure that there were always enough workers available at the lowest possible wages, so that the workers didn't share in the profits of their endeavours and couldn't themselves sell what their skills produced, but were nonetheless loyal servants of the manufacturing process. To achieve this in peacetime, various conditions had to be put in place and maintained. In wartime, things simplified themselves nicely: anyone not working full out ended up in the trenches and had a hero's death to look forward to. Pahl had grasped this early on and resisted all attempts by the newspaper house back home to claim him back. He'd stood down in favour of married colleagues, having carefully weighed up whether the comparative freedom of the labour company was more tolerable than the slavery of the newspaper house. Let someone else pump out the dirty stream of lies to the nation that helped prolong the war.

Wilhelm Pahl saw himself as a product of the pressures and counter pressures of the class system. He'd come into the world with an ugly body and a squashed face. That's fate, although mountain sunshine and exercise – that's to say, wealthy parents or better social welfare – might have improved his physical condition. He was one of six children of Otto Pahl, a turner. He finished primary school – a royal Prussian primary school in Schöneberg – where his smart mind attracted attention early on. With his aptitude for thinking and learning, he could have gone far if he'd had wealthy parents or if social provision had been better. But being Pahl the turner's son, he left school at the age of 14, and an apprenticeship at a printers was the best that a good reference from his teacher could secure for him. He couldn't become an explorer or a natural historian, so he turned his attention to the circumstances of his own existence early on. It was too late to change his parents' financial position; he therefore joined those who wanted to reconstruct society. He went to the Workers' Party school and became a conscious component of the masses to which the future (due to the pressure being exerted by the masses) must inevitably belong. To keep the masses fenced in, society used them. Every year, in Germany and elsewhere, hundreds of thousands of society's have-nots were shoved into uniform and drilled, building on the work done in schools, to make them useful and ready to shoot *themselves* in the shape of other workers – entirely against their own interests. In peacetime, this was just a possibility; in wartime, it was a ghastly and shockingly stupid reality. It goes without saying that Pahl the typesetter hated the army and everything it stood for. He despised war, which he saw as the spawn of the masses' endless stupidity. At the same time, he understood war. It was essential to society's struggle for world markets. It allowed tensions within states to be redirected to the outside and meant that armies of proletarians, who might rise up against the ruling classes tomorrow, were busy slaughtering each other on the field of honour today.

Pahl the typesetter closed his eyes. He would've liked to go to sleep but couldn't just yet. The truth of his theory excited him. The slightest sign that the proletariat saw through the clever differentiation created by uniforms and manners of speech made the military machine nervous. The devil alone knew what they'd made of that harmless sheep Bertin. In any case, the performance earlier clearly demonstrated that they intended to use his example to proscribe fraternisation with French prisoners. But Bertin had acted purely out of good heartedness, out of a decent, perhaps slightly sentimental sense of comradeship. He hadn't been trying to condemn war itself. He was far too much the product of a higher education for that. Karl Lebehde had guessed that too. You had to hand it to Comrade Lebehde.

Now there would be nothing left for 'comrade' Bertin but to become a real Comrade. Wilhelm Pahl saw that, which was why he couldn't sleep. He wanted to promote this outcome. Sergeant Böhne had confided to him that a new commando was to be sent forward early the following day. Two long-range guns were stuck in a valley between Fosses wood and Pepper ridge. They had to be removed the next day so that a new (Bavarian) howitzer battery could be installed there. Front-line commandos were normally drawn from the strong men in the first and second platoons, but tomorrow's commando, unusually, was to be made up of the small, weak men in the 9th, 10th and 11th platoons, who had worked in the ammunitions tent until now. The recent offender, Bertin, belonged to the 10th platoon, Pahl to the 9th, and the sergeants and corporals who would have to go forward with them were the three platoon leaders.

'See anything unusual in that, Pahl?' Böhne had laughed. 'If you were a veteran soldier, you'd spot it.'

Wilhelm Pahl wasn't a veteran, but he'd spotted it anyway: this was an example of group punishment. The Prussian military sometimes liked to inflict disadvantages and unpleasantness on a whole group when one of its number was guilty of misconduct, so that the group would turn against the guilty party and make his life a misery. That was why Herr Glinksy had assembled the NCOs after the inspection.

In normal circumstances, for example at work, punishment wipes the slate clean. In the abnormal circumstances that pertain in the army of the class state, however, punishment marks the start of a man's suffering. From now on, Bertin would always be in the wrong, slipping from one awkward situation to the next. It would be a gradual process, possibly with the odd break along the way, but however uneven the delivery of the knocks, as surely as copulation leads to reproduction they would teach Private Bertin that life is harsh. Until now, he hadn't fared badly in the company, as he himself admitted. It was part of his idealism to want to be like any other ASC private, and idealism, as Wilhelm Pahl knew, was one of the subtlest lures used by society to prevent

gifted men furthering their own interests and to seduce them into serving the interests of the ruling classes for no wages other than glory. If the men in the company and the officers in charge of the depot assumed a Jewish writer and future lawyer must be a socialist, then they were smarter than Private Bertin himself and understood his true nature and the meaning of his feelings and impulse towards solidarity better than he did. Deep down, Bertin obviously knew the score. But not consciously. Consciously – and he'd often made this point – he believed that wars were necessary and Germany's cause was justified. As the majority of the Party thought the same way, he could hardly be criticised for this. Nonetheless, the default approach with all such lads was to adopt a certain entirely understandable mistrust until they'd shown by their actions which side they were on. In this particular case, however, it was highly desirable to bring the man into the fold.

There Bertin stood in the bright sunshine, in the pillory, a servant of the ruling class, still thinking the stupid things he'd been told to think. It just showed what an important and powerful force education was. But now Bertin really was going to get an education. Glinsky, Graßnick, Colonel Stein and the entire machinery of the army would see to that. He, Pahl the typesetter, would make sure this education had the right spin; he was the man for the job. A man such as Bertin could be invaluable to the working class. He was a writer who was having a book published right in the middle of the war. Wilhelm Pahl had never read anything by him, but he'd heard him talking. It was obvious the man could put anything he wanted across in words, even in front of an audience. Pahl recalled speeches Bertin had given to 40 or 50 highly sceptical ASC men when they were working in Serbia. By contrast, he, Wilhelm Pahl, preferred not to express his views in front of more than one or two trusted friends. He was aware of his ugliness, his hunchback, his short neck, his squashed nose and piggy eyes, and this held him back from appearing in public. And yet nothing was more important to further the cause of the working class. If the gifts of Bertin the lawyer and the thoughts of Pahl the typesetter could be combined that would be no mean weapon. If the hatred in Pahl and his indignation at class injustice could be made to burn in Comrade Bertin's breast, if Bertin's natural courage and disregard for personal danger were turned in the right direction, then they really could start something. It was something to work on. Maybe even during the war. Definitely afterwards. At the moment, all the power was in the hands of the ruling class. The owning classes, from which the officers came, had 70 million Germans at their disposal. They controlled their

thoughts, deeds and desires. Only idealistic sheep such as Bertin believed they would ever willingly give this power up. But there was no need to decide how to wrest it from them just yet. No, Wilhelm Pahl would have time enough to work it out clearly in his own slow way. He certainly didn't want to go to the Party majority with questions of how, what and when. The company hadn't honoured him with the nickname 'Liebknecht' for nothing. His opinion of those who had passed the war credit bills was exactly the same as that lonely man's. Liebknecht had paid for his courageous protests in the Reichstag and on Potsdamer Platz on 1 May with a prison sentence. In some places, comrades had risked a strike because of it. Not a bad sign. But at the moment the battle for Verdun and the costly campaign to control Europe – the world even – had eclipsed all else.

Pahl's cigar was burning down. He was pleasantly tired now. Sleep would come quickly and do him good. Those, then, were his 'War Thoughts' – quite different, admittedly, from those that appeared in the newspapers, penned by venerable, patriotic professors. Wilhelm Pahl had earlier consigned one such column to the underworld, tossing it down to the rustling maggots in the latrine. The big 42cm gun 2km away in Thonne-le-Thil, which had roared so loudly it made the barracks shudder, was also quiet now and had been since the day before yesterday. The story was that a squib round had wiped it out – it and its entire crew. No doubt they were surprised when the shell, which was as big as an eight-year-old boy, burst in the gun's barrel and ripped it open, spewing out a craterful of fire and steel – but not on to the French. What was this war for? A gigantic undertaking organised by the industries of destruction, involving extreme mortal danger for all concerned. You didn't even need the French pilots, who were getting cockier by the day, to finish a gun off... There: Bertin had put his light out. Pahl's cigar stub fell sizzling into a tin. A little water stopped it stinking the place out. Pahl snuggled down in his wood-fibre bag, pulled his blanket up and rested his head on his folded-up tunic. Bertin, he happened to know, used a fine latex air cushion as a pillow. *May sleep bring balm for your nerves, my boy*, he thought. *You're going to need it.* For the first time, Pahl felt a kind of grim sympathy for his comrade.

The snoring in the barracks was louder than the guns outside. Or had they gone quiet? Had society muzzled their iron jaws? Had the typesetting machines at the front stopped clattering? Were the printing presses no longer rolling that had flattened thousands of men into the letters of a new alphabet describing the future? No more trams on Schöneberg high street. Time for Sunday rest.

Christoph Kroysing

'SUPERB!' SAID PRIVATE Bertin the next morning. The dew sparkled in the sunshine, and the cross-country march took the Böhne commando away from the company commanders, and the men hated being near them. Yes, Bertin was responding rather differently to his despatch to the front than Herr Glinsky and his like had anticipated. For Bertin, this march provided an excursion into life proper. He positively quivered with joy at the thought that he was at last about to experience something. His whole being was as receptive as a dry sponge and pushed impatiently forwards, as if he were on an invisible lead. He was all eyes and ears that morning, totally alert.

There were several routes to the front from the Steinbergquell ammunition depot, which was tucked away at the junction of the Flabas to Moirey station road and the Damvillers to Azannes road. The shortest route was in Fosses wood and passed through a village called Ville, which had been shot to pieces and had gaping holes in its roofs and walls. It was still nice and early, and the sun slanted down behind the marching men. Pear tree leaves and laundry hung out to dry by signals men and flak gunners in their billet yard flashed in the morning light. The billets were all in the cellars. Ville was now a town of cellars, full of technical troops and infantry.

In the green valley, which they turned into as the road changed direction in the hills, they came upon the first dead. They lay under rust red tarpaulins, watched over by a sapper in a steel helmet. For a few minutes afterwards, the ASC men stopped talking. Then they found themselves in a green beech wood. Light shone through the young leaves on the treetops against the bright sky; a clear stream gurgled towards the men; drivers brought bareback horses to drink and carried full buckets of water up the hill on broad wooden shoulder yokes, disappearing behind black barracks where smoke billowed from narrow kitchen chimneys. The wood was practically untouched by shells, but the trees had been thinned and it was crossed by paths heading in different directions uphill. The further forwards the Böhne commando pushed, the more ripped and truncated trees they found lying on both sides of the valley. The red wood of the beeches stood out in the wild green tangle of creepers, foliage and brambles. Hazel bushes and wild cherry trees formed a thick undergrowth. Smooth, silvery grey beech trunks thrust upwards, hemmed in by dozens of younger saplings, pushing up branches as wide as a finger or arm to get as much light as possible and avoid being choked by the predatory tops of the older trees. Slanting light glimmered through the wild tangle, and birds called. As the valley turned southwards, all the trees were suddenly truncated, their bark hanging in loops. There were exposed white rocks everywhere, split open by shells, and a mass of creepers and shrubs sprawled round the edges of the huge blast holes, half submerged in the loam. Later – it must've been about eight o'clock – they crossed a plateau riddled like a sieve with shell holes, many of them as big as craters. The abused land stretched southwards: a desolate, brownish wasteland. Without warning, columns of smoke suddenly rose up, and a loud blast threw the ASC men into the nearest shell hole. Nobody knew which direction was which or if they were taking cover on the wrong side. The young man in Bertin felt great joy at that moment. This was how things should be. He was 27, but his heart beat like a boy's, perhaps that was his good fortune. He pushed on and before the next blast came he was lying beside the detachment leaders, Sergeant Böhne and Sergeant Schulz, the ammunitions expert. For the first time, splinters and clumps of earth hurtled over the shocked ASC men. They regrouped at the edge of the field and advanced in the pauses between explosions. No one was hurt. Still, they looked pale by the time they arrived at the light railway tracks in the next valley, screened by wire netting interlaced with foliage. At that very moment, the whirr and clatter of the German counter bombardment howled past above their heads. Further down, they met a couple of gunners from the heavy batteries, who grinned at them unperturbed and asked how they liked the pyrotechnics. Bertin felt almost ashamed of his comrades' blotchy faces and deathly pale noses.

'Get a move on!' said Sergeant Böhne, hustling his detachment down the pathless valley slope, pitted with shell holes and covered in footprints. Down below, a gunner was riding around. He inspected the edge of the wood and disappeared into a Beech copse. He clearly belonged to the battery that was to be installed there. In the valley, the barrels of two long-range guns stretched skywards like telescopes. Around them swarmed groups of small men. The light railway lines ended halfway up the shielding ridge. A new railway track needed to be laid between them and the guns so that the small locomotive could haul the barrel and mount of the first gun to the rear that night. Herr Böhne explained this to the young Bavarian NCO who was waiting for them. Bertin liked the look of the young man's agreeable brown face and his warm eyes under his visor. He was obviously a 1914 volunteer who had acquired an Iron Cross, Second Class, a wound and his stripes in the space of a year, and was now in charge of a detachment. Bertin had gone to university in the south of Germany, and he loved the man's dialect, which made him feel more homesick than his native Silesian. The work plan was simple. There were some piles of rails. The Prussians were to lay a new line to the guns, while the Bavarian's men dismantled the two monsters, removing their mounts from their bedding. They'd have to be gone by midday or the Frogs would rain on their parade. He knew the score, because he and his men were dug in as a standby detachment in the ruin up the hill known as Chambrettes-Ferme. Every morning, the Frogs, who knew the area like the backs of their hands, battered the line to pieces. The Bavarian's men then crawled out of their holes and laid new rails – and so forth. He had 30 men and two medical orderlies, because every now and then one of the men didn't duck quickly enough and got hurt.

As he spoke, he shaded his eyes, squinting at the captive balloon. He said he could tell from its pale colour that the other side was out of action for the time being because of the ground mist and the morning sun in their eyes. And so the work began. Some of the men levelled the ground with picks and shovels, while the main group brought over the rails and stuck them together like a child's model railway, fixing the sleepers into the ground with small clips. The hill ridge towered above them, a bleak yellowy brown dotted with grassy clumps between the shell holes, occasional thistles, camomile and dandelion leaves. At every step, they had to watch out for steel splinters, which came in all different sizes. The ground was covered with them, and they could damage the leather uppers of their boots. Perhaps there's been shooting here, Bertin thought, as he chipped away with his pick at the front of the group. The sun felt strong on their backs. They'd ditched their tunics long ago. Sergeant Böhne watched them out of the corner of his pale eyes, which were sunk in wrinkles. Swinging his walking stick, he paraded up and down, rather pleased with the excursion, which might get him an Iron Cross, and with the work of his men, who, to the Bavarian's astonishment, were making good progress. Yes, thought Bertin, who heard them discussing the topic, workers from Hamburg and

Berlin get through it quicker than others. And was he mistaken or was the young Bavarian with the blue and white cockade deliberately hanging about in his vicinity? The Bavarian had given him a searching look earlier. Or did people tend to imagine such things when they liked someone?

Behind the work party, first one then soon a second wagon were lowered in a flurry of screeching and braking. In just an hour, they had reached the guns. With much cursing, the heavy steel equipment and the barrel and mount with their wooden spars, wedges and baulks were heaved on to the groaning wagons. Then 30 straining men pulled the wagons uphill on long cables. Each man had a cable cutting into his left or right shoulder. Like Chaldean or Egyptian slaves, they panted up the hillside, heading for the far-off station, which, amusingly enough, had the same name – Hundekehle – as the tram stop for a well-known Sunday pub in the Grunewald area of Berlin. Suddenly, a lieutenant rode up with a camera. He made the struggling men stop on the hillside and took a snap of them strung out along the cables like a line of smoked fish. Then the typical builder's call to breakfast rang out: 'Take fifteen!' The Nissen huts up above, which had a telephone as well as an unfortunate name, had received news that it wouldn't be possible to supply a wagon for the second gun that day. Plenty of time, then, for a slug of water from the canteen, a piece of bread and a cigarette.

The wide hollow, yellowy green against the blue sky, was filled with a shimmering heat haze. 'That's Fosses wood,' Bertin heard the young Bavarian say, as he prowled round the gun positions in search of shade, gesturing expansively with his left hand. Bertin looked down on a ragged, grey slope covered in half-uprooted tree stumps. Small green leaves still sprouted from the splintered white and ochre timbers, and some of the trees still resembled chopped-down beeches, but most were tattered stakes, scarred by bullets and shell splinters, that looked more like skeletons. Unexploded cylindrical shells lay among the plants, some with their round ends sticking up towards the light. The grey fingers of ancient root systems thrust into the massive shell holes. Huge trees had been knocked to the ground and lay rotting, their earth-covered roots rising up like umbrellas, their crowns long since trodden into the ground. The destruction was a picture painted in three colours: the white of the chalky cliffs, the dark brown of the scattered soil and the irrepressible green of the foliage. In a few months, man had eradicated what nature had taken generations to produce.

In the odd protected corner of the embankment, one or two remaining whole trees provided shade. Bertin lay under one of them, the back of his head resting on his cap, his legs in a dry, crumbling shell hole. He idly watched the wind playing in the tree's dark, shining leaves, wondering how much longer the sun and moon would shine on this scrap of nature and creation on this slope in Fosses wood and on the smooth, green-flecked columns of beech. No doubt the new battery would see to it that the surrounding desolation of tree trunks, earth and shrubbery engulfed this last little patch of growth too. What a shame, Bertin thought, oddly not considering the people who would be destroyed along with it.

A light west wind carried on it the whip of individual shells, the rat-tat-tat of machine gun fire. But for a young man like Bertin the sun, shade and landscape were more meaningful and exciting than shrapnel or Tetanus bacteria. His was an essentially musical nature, in thrall to and moved by impressions, sensuous experiences and emotions. Right then, he was playing with a roaming cat that had appeared soundlessly in a bramble bush. Her bottle-green eyes were fixed on the sausage end lying on a piece of greasy paper near Bertin's left hand. The sausage emitted a wonderful smell of curing and select cuts of meat. Of course, a cat that knows her business needn't starve in wartime. The place was teeming with rats, and the cat's fur was thick and glossy across her iron muscles. But this smelt like something tasty: she could jump over and bite the man's hand, stick a claw in the sausage tip, then bolt up the slanting beech trunk into the high-forked branches... But she was a feral house cat, who understood how the locals operated these days. They no longer threw stones. Instead, they sent something that went pop whipping through the air from sticks with sharp, shiny ends. She crouched uncertainly among the creepers and brambles, tense one minute, relaxed the next. It was a rare treat for a soldier to be alone. Bertin loved it and he loved animals even more. He eyed the cat through the rims of his glasses. How beautiful she was in her wild composure! He remembered all the cats he'd ever had and lost as a boy in Kreuzberg – you never knew how. (Silesian people considered cat skin to be the best remedy for Rheumatism.) Nonetheless, he dithered about whether he should keep the sausage end to eat himself that evening. I've already sunk pretty far, he thought, if I'm weighing up whether to eat the scrap of meat in this sausage end or give it to a cat. No, he decided, she'd only get the skin. He flipped the sausage paper round the end of meat. The cat jumped back in alarm and spat.

'That was a nasty shock for her,' said a voice from above, an agreeable young voice that Bertin already knew, and two legs in grey-green puttees dangled into the shell hole opposite Bertin's legs. Instinctively, he straightened up, because a sergeant is still a sergeant and deserves respect, even in the lunch break. According to the clock it was 11am, according to the sun midday, and you could feel that. The two young men seemed to be the only sentient beings hereabouts. The cat crouched three paces away, invisible between two roots as thick as arms that had the same grey-on-grey flecks as she did. The two young men scrutinised each other and liked what they saw. The sergeant asked if Bertin wouldn't rather lie back down, and Bertin said no. You could sleep anywhere. He wanted to feel alive here, to open his eyes and smoke his after-lunch pipe. From his haversack he pulled a delicate pipe, which was made of meerschaum and amber and was already filled. The Bavarian shielded the sputtering lighter with his cap – a special cap, nicely worked. Bertin saw the letters CK embossed on the leather edging. Yes, this young person came from a good home. His neatly parted hair, broad forehead, and narrow wrists and fingers gave the game away. The Bavarian asked the Berliner how he had come to be here, lighting a cigarette himself. Bertin didn't understand the question.

'I'm on duty,' he answered, surprised.

'What? Just like anyone? Couldn't they find a better use for you?'

'I don't like the air in the orderly room,' Bertin replied with a smile.

'I see. You'd rather work outside and be photographed,' the Bavarian smiled back.

'Exactly so,' said Bertin, and the acquaintance was made. They exchanged names. The sergeant was called Christoph Kroysing and came from Nuremberg. His lively eyes scrutinised Bertin's face, almost sucking information from it. For a moment, they were silent. A couple of metallic strikes – did they come from Hill 300 or 378? – reminded them what time and space meant. Then young Kroysing shook himself. In a neutral undertone, he asked Bertin if he would like to do him a favour.

Nobody in the vicinity paid any attention to the two men. The root system of an enormous Beech, knocked over as if by a lightning strike, reared up to shield them. Neither of them even noticed how the cat, familiar with the ways of brainless bipeds, sloped off with the precious sausage end and paper in her teeth.

Christoph Kroysing told his story. For nine weeks, he and his men had been living in the cellars at Chambrettes-Ferme, and if it was up to retired civil servant Niggl and his orderly room, he would remain there for the rest of his days. He had committed an act of gross stupidity. He explained that he had joined the war during his first university term, been quite seriously wounded and then promoted. He'd been sent out with the Reserve division for now because they needed every educated man they could get, but he was due to start officer training in the autumn and should get his commission next spring. However, he had the bad luck not to be able to tolerate the way the NCOs abused the men's rights. The NCOs had set up their own kitchen where they scoffed the best bits from the men's rations: fresh meat and butter, sugar and potatoes, and above all beer. Meanwhile, thin noodles, dried vegetables and tinned meat were considered good enough for the men, who did heavy work on niggardly leave. This stuck in his craw, said Kroysing, due to family tradition. For a century, his forefathers had supplied the state of Bavaria with high-ranking officials and judiciary. Where there was a Kroysing, there was justice and fairness. And so he was stupid enough to write a long letter full of grievances to his Uncle Franz, a big noise at the Military Railway Administration (MRA) in Metz. The censors were naturally very concerned about what a sergeant said to the MRA head. The letter was sent back to the battalion with an order to court-martial its author. When Kroysing heard about it, he laughed. They only had to ask and he would talk, and he certainly wasn't short of witnesses. However, his brother Eberhard, who was at Douaumont with his sappers, took a different view. He came and gave him a hard time about his youthful folly, and said no one would speak up for him if the court martial got to them first. In any case, he'd said before he left, he wouldn't be able to do anything for Christoph. Everyone had to make their own bed, and now Eberhard's post would also be gone through with a magnifying glass.

They'd not had a good childhood together. The big brother was five years older than the younger one and always felt disadvantaged, something he bitterly resented, as is normal among brothers.

But the company wanted to avoid an investigation at all costs. They were clearly very anxious about it, and so, most unusually, the court martial didn't get in touch. 'That's why they've put me at Chambrettes-Ferme,' finished Kroysing. 'They're hoping the Frogs will do them a favour and consign the whole business to the files. For nine weeks, I've been watching every single face that fetches up in this lousy hole...'

Bertin sat there, his face shadowed and flecked by the beech leaves above him. Something inside him laughed with joy. It was good that he had come here. Here was someone about to be mired in brutality, and he could reach out a hand and pull him out. 'So what can I do?' he asked simply.

Kroysing gave him a grateful look. He just wanted him to transport a few lines, which he would give him next time, to his mother. 'Your post is above suspicion, isn't it? When next you write home, put my letter inside yours and then get it put in a postbox at home. My mother will then telegraph Uncle Franz and the ball will be set in motion.'

'Done,' said Bertin. 'We'll soon know when we'll be back here again. That sounded like an announcement. Did you hear it?'

'Fall in!' came the call from below.

'Better we're not seen together again,' said the Bavarian. 'I'll sit down and write the letter immediately. Thank you so much! Hopefully, I can pay you back sometime.' He shook Bertin's hand, and there was a gleam in his brown, wide-set, boyish eyes. Stiffly, he touched his hand to his cap and then disappeared between the trees, nearly stumbling on the cat, which was prowling around in the irrational hope of a second sausage end.

Bertin stood up, stretched his arms, inhaled deeply and looked happily around him. It was wonderful here. The felled trees were beautiful, as were the white shell holes, the limestone, and the terrible high-calibre shell splinters, which were stuck in the ground like serrated throwing knives. He ran like a young boy down to the solitary gun, where his comrades were already standing in their tunics and haversacks, and Sergeant Böhne was lining the detachment up to march off. Bertin had found someone like himself, had forged a bond, perhaps even a friendship. He laughed off muttered comments from his comrades, who said there would be trouble on the way back just because he had slept so long. They said they'd keep a better eye on him when they came back the day after tomorrow. The day after tomorrow, then, Bertin thought, taking his place for the count off.

The Bavarian sergeant was also lining his men up to march off. He waved and shouted, 'See you the day after tomorrow.' His greeting reached everyone, but Bertin knew whom it was really meant for.

CHAPTER FIVE

Sometimes things happen quickly

IN THE MIDDLE of the night, Christoph Kroysing ducked out of the entrance to the dugout, which had once been the Chambrettes-Ferme cellars, straightened up and took a couple of steps. His silhouette was slim and boyish against the light sky. His hands were in his pockets and he didn't have a belt or a cap on. His lank hair, still neatly parted, flopped across his right eye. He was entirely used to the dreadful Walpurgis Night that howled above his head. Steel witches hurtled towards the ground; long-range guns rattled and banged like trains; every four or five minutes, tonnes of metal from the heavy mortars ripped the air with a desolate gurgle. The screech and whistle of small field grenades mixed with the roar of 15-centimetre shells, which, being the army's main weapon, arched steeply through the air from three or four different types of gun. And in response came the banging, roaring and pounding of the French 7.5s, 10s, 20s and the dreaded 38s, which spat at the flank of the Germans' positions and trenches from the impregnable Fort Marre on the other side of the Meuse. It must be all go at the front. In the small section just about visible from Hill 344 behind the Douaumont ridge, the fighting divisions had been trying to exterminate each other with hand grenades, machine guns, and bare steel, and the aftermath was now subsiding. The Germans had advanced a few paces between Thiaumont and Souville, but the French had held firm, and the German artillery was now hammering their position, and they in turn were hammering the German artillery to give their infantry a break. It was the normal back and forth of the fronts, and Christoph Kroysing often thought that there would be no end to it until the last German and the last Frenchman limped out of the trenches on crutches to finish each other off with pocket knives or teeth and finger nails. For the world had gone mad. Only an orgy of madness could explain this stamping on the spot amid squirting blood, rotting flesh and cracking bones. They had been taught in school that people were rational beings, but that idea was a pedagogical swindle that should be buried – together with the bearded gentlemen who had the cheek to teach school children and who ought simply to be clubbed to death with human bones. 'Love thy neighbour as thyself.' 'God is love.' 'The moral law within us and the starry heavens above us.' 'It is sweet and honourable to die for the Fatherland.' 'Justice and law are the pillars of the state.' 'Glory to God in the highest, and on earth peace to men of good will.' Well, he'd always been of good will and now he was here.

If you wanted to look south and west, you had to be prepared to take a small risk. Kroysing knew of a hole in the Ferme's ramparts, a kind of seat, which he called his loge. It took scarcely a minute to scramble through the brickwork, but he might of course get hit. So what! He ran over and was soon squatting in his lair, where he caught his breath and laughed a little.

The vague brightness of the moonless, starry night was becoming ever more transparent, and his ear gradually adjusted to the myriad sounds of war. The gulleys towards Douaumont were under heavy attack. Rifle and machine gun fire whipped the length of the Pepper ridge. On the rubbish tip that was the village of Louvemont red flames flew up and died down, and only then did the detonation come. Out of sight down below, field kitchens were trying to come through, as were ammunition trucks and working parties with rolls of wire, posts, entrenching tools – horses, lorries, men. No, the Frogs were no longer scrimping on ammunition. In the valley to the left, dark red bushes of fire had broken out. A few hundred metres further on, where you couldn't see anything, was a much used field track that led to Herbe Bois.

On the southern edge of Vauche wood, where the military road ran up to Douaumont, a chain of little volcanoes thundered and flared, new ones erupting all the time, and over Douaumont itself, over his brother Eberhard and his men, hung a great clinging red mist – the never-ending belching of the chimney that was Verdun. The army's backbone was being pounded to bits there. Red and green flares flew up on the horizon, turning the infantry's cries for help into a jaunty fireworks display. The French army's white star shells floated slowly down, spreading a soft light – excellent for shooting each other by. Christoph Kroysing knew it all well: the Chemin des Dames, the Loretto Heights, the sugar factory by Souchez – all the sweet things associated with the war of 1914-15 when he was still an infantryman, putting his life on the line for the Fatherland. Now he was more inclined to watch. His little, rat-infested loge here in the shattered brickwork suited him just fine. The great arc of the horizon spread out before him, flashing and flickering, lighting up like a bolt of lightning and going black again. Despite the natural dampening caused by distance, the full ferocity of the roaring and clamouring reached him, overlaid by the thunder of German guns. The Fosses wood, Chaûmes wood and Vavrille batteries were working at full strength. Half-naked gunners, support troops, observers in the trees, telephonists at their apparatus: this was the night shift. He knew them all, those bloody shell-smiths. The next day, the new battery would settle in nearby, drawing French counter-fire into this quiet valley. Shame about that scrap of wood that was still standing. Shame about all the men who would meet their end here. Shame about Christoph Kroysing himself, who, at 21, was forced to accept that man's brutality and his instinct for survival were as vital as war and harder to escape. He leaned on a ruined wall, half crouching, half sitting, his hands cupping his lean, boyish face, which was framed by floppy hair. This is what it looks like outside Verdun, he thought. In all these weeks, things have hardly changed. The front line has been pushed forwards slightly, and we could cover the ground we've won with corpses. But that was what it was like at the Somme too, where the French and British were stage managing the same kind of hoax. There was a sudden boom on Hill 344. Bright lights flashed, fiery red on smouldering white. Perhaps it wasn't a good idea to sit outside much longer. At least he wouldn't go to sleep feeling as hopeless as he had the night before, haunted by the scum who snooped through his post, checking what he'd written to Mother and Father. No, he was alive again. He had his bottle back and he felt clearer in his head than ever before. They hadn't reckoned with the camaraderie of decent men in the army. Tomorrow or the day after, his comrade Bertin would return. The letter he had written that afternoon with his trusty fountain pen was already crackling in his tunic pocket above his heart. He'd have to be very careful for a couple of days. Then a mighty hand would reach down and remove Christoph Kroysing from this rat hole. Because even if the gods had abdicated and those who ran the world seemed to have turned into clockwork maniASC, there were men everywhere in the German army, individuals and groups, who wanted to put an end to injustice, who would be incandescent with rage if it were proved to them that brutality, self-interest and treason began right behind the foremost trenches.

As he stood up, his leg muscles aching, he thought how heavily the dew was lying and how clearly the stars shone in the sky. Did the same nonsense go on up there as on Earth? You could depend on it. Same old matter and spirit up above and down below. In the half light, the rats were dashing about on the ground like thin cats; they should definitely shoot a couple of dozen of them the next day. The rats could have got much fatter nearer the front, but they never deserted the ruined stables where they were born.

Tired and heavy-headed but confident, Christoph Kroysing climbed back into the dugout where his comrades were snoring. It stank more than a little among the damp brickwork, but tender currents flowed from the letter in his breast pocket and washed away all his unease. And as he folded his tunic and laid his head on it, as he did every night, young Kroysing smiled in darkness.

In the early hours, the Frogs fired their usual morning greeting at the light railway tracks: booming bursts of shell fire, drifting splinters, crashing steel and clumps of earth. As soon as it was over, the Bavarians emerged from their rat holes to assess the damage. The bastard French had knackered two whole sections straight off, miserable gits. They created nowt but work. A French plane circled up above in the morning haze, then disappeared to the east.

A fabulous summer day, thought Christoph Kroysing. He felt good today, better than he'd felt in ages. Blue sky – air to make you feel like flying away! Perhaps he'd first pay a visit to Hundekehle station to see if they were going to send a truck today to remove the second gun. Carefully, he trotted uphill, sticking close to the sections of track or jumping from sleeper to sleeper. From time to time, the Frogs spat over a little reminder – crumps the Germans called these kinds of shots, because they were there before you heard the gun fire. This part of the valley was much too well disposed to artillery observation, but today Kroysing felt immune to danger. He had the advantage of having been in the same place for 60 days. That meant you got to know it like the back of your hand whether you wanted to or not. Also, for the first time, he noticed flowers growing again at the edges of the shell holes: purple lady's smock, summer cornflowers, very blue, and a red poppy, like a swaying fleck of blood.

In Hundekehle, a heat haze still shimmered over the corrugated iron station building. There were no trucks there, so the second gun wouldn't be collected today, which was a shame. On the other hand, half a dozen infantrymen and a junior MO were taking the opportunity to sit and sleep in the shade of the railway hut, backs pressed to the metal, legs stretched out in front of them, completely covered in dust and earth. Their collapsed posture spoke of a superhuman exhaustion; inside, a young lieutenant, who had to stay awake and be responsible, was nonetheless making a phone call, wanting to know how he could move two machine guns and his men's gear to the rear. Blinking, he stepped out into the glaring sun, scrutinised the Bavarian sergeant, offered him a cigarette and asked what he was doing there. The lieutenant decided he should wake his men. Once they'd started sleeping, they wouldn't stop in a hurry, and as long as they were hunkered down in this accursed place, they'd needed to be awake, ready to scatter and take cover if there was an armed attack, even if they were relaxing now and enjoying the quiet. They'd come from Pepper ridge and been relieved about two in the morning. Their main contingent had taken the normal route via Brabant and been scattered by gunfire. He, Lieutenant Mahnitz, and his junior MO, Dr Tichauer, had been clear from the start that it was better to stumble through shell holes and cut across country to the rear than to come under heavy fire, especially as they were already dreaming about leave. He laughed cheerfully. They'd had a terrible time, but things would calm down now. The Germans and the French were both busy with the battle at the Somme. They richly deserved some peace, and they wouldn't say no to some hot coffee either.

Christoph Kroysing immediately decided to invite the lieutenant and his men for some freshly made ground coffee. Glad that his hint had been taken, the lieutenant selected a corporal who'd fallen asleep again to take the men's gear and the two guns back to Steinbergquell depot on the next empty train and await new orders there. Then the men set off, plodding along the section of track with sore feet and sagging shoulders. They chatted quietly, wondering if they'd be able to get a wash at the ASC men's billet or at least some breakfast. They were seasoned soldiers familiar with the conditions in this zone, and their slack amble and faded uniforms symbolised that. They always had one ear cocked in case the unhoped for happened. It was half eight in the morning. The Frogs couldn't see much from their captive balloon, but you couldn't be too careful, as they said in the army. So that the coffee would be ready when they got there, Sergeant Kroysing ran on ahead, telling the comrades from Hessen – for the men he'd picked up were from Hessen – to follow on slowly. There was no danger. 'He' had never fired at this hour.

What date was it that day? Immaterial. It wasn't a good day for Christoph Kroysing. After a great deal of toing and froing, the French high command had agreed, much against its will, to a request from the foreign office to allow neutral, foreign journalists to make a short visit to the front at Verdun. Axel Krog, a diligent and respected correspondent for important Swedish newspapers, was now standing in the French battery position opposite, which had never fired a shot at this inopportune time of day. His visit aroused mixed emotions: hostility, mockery, welcome. Herr Krog was a long-time member of the Swedish colony in Paris and a great admirer of France, the accompanying officer from the General Staff press office explained. 'He should join the Foreign Legion then,' muttered Gunner Lepaile, in purest suburban Parisian argot. But the French artillery was the best in the world – and not just in the days of Napoleon, the only gunner to make commander. The press office wanted to give Herr Krog an opportunity to publish an impressive article in Sweden, where the Germans were shamelessly spreading their propaganda. Accordingly, he was put in the care of an observation officer and given a field glass through which to witness a bit of sharp shooting: a few Germans being picked off with slim shells. Did Herr Krog know that there was a light railway over there? Units on the Pepper ridge were being relieved that night, and the Boche was moving troops back through this valley. The gunners despised what they read in the newspapers. They spat on those who wanted to prolong the war as much as those who wanted to end it. Furthermore, the gun would now need to be cleaned again. However, at the of the day, it was a matter of honour to show how well the 31st brigade could shoot. Guns one and two were ready and trained on their target: the human game 2.5 km away that would soon appear in the field glass.

Christoph Kroysing trotted down the tracks, jumping boyishly over the shell holes. When things took a turn for the better, they didn't do so by halves. Now he could choose whether to give his letter to this nice lieutenant or wait until the morning and give it to his comrade Bertin. In this remarkable way, the law of alternatives proved itself to be true. As he thought this, he came to the open valley floor. A light brown wasteland stretched out before him. Seventy or 80 metres before he'd reach cover.

What was that? Kroysing swung round. But even as he looked round, the burst of an explosive, the hot steel of a thudding missile crashed at his back. Pale and scared but miraculously unhurt, he made two leaps and disappeared into the next shell hole. But now the second gun chipped in. Roaring, yellow on black, the shell exploded in front of Kroysing, spun him round and threw him to the ground. *God, God, God*, he thought, fading from consciousness as the point of his chin hit the iron rail. *Mother, Mother, Mother.*

The Swedish journalist standing next to the French observer turned pale and said thank you very much. Amazingly artful shooting, but he'd rather not see any more. The men from Hessen were now speeding down the railway track at the double, the lieutenant at the front. They'd seen at once that the young Bavarian was no longer used to the fray or he would have thrown himself behind the rails immediately after the first explosion. You didn't mess with crumps. They crouched round Kroysing's lying body where blood was pooling. The junior MO Trichauer bent carefully over him. Nothing to be done. A morphine injection was all he could offer him now. The shell splinters had hacked through his shoulder blade and arm joint like a meat cleaver, severing his arteries and probably the lobe of his lung as well. There was no point in bringing him round. As astonished sappers and ASC men appeared above, asking why the Frogs were shooting at this unusual hour, and the group below gestured frantically for them to come down, Lieutenant Mahnitz looked with a sick heart on the creature laid out before him, with whom he'd been having such an enjoyable conversation less than five minutes before and who now began to groan like a suffocating animal. Half lying and propped up on his elbow, speaking to himself but also loud enough for his band of speechless, dirty men to hear, Mahnitz said: 'I'd just like to know when this bloody shit will be over.'

CHAPTER SIX

To Billy

THE NEXT DAY, as the ASC men approached the front line, taking the route round the Meuse hills this time, there was talk about how lucky they'd been to be at home the day before, because there had been an armed attacked in this area and a couple of men had been seriously wounded and transported to Billy. Bertin was sceptical about these excitable rumours; he was already looking forward to seeing Kroysing. Would he come today or later? Was he already stuck down below at the gun position? In contrast to the day before, that day's division of labour brought Bertin and his spade near to two Bavarians who were hacking away at the clay by the new track to make it easier to drag the track later.

'Where's your Sergeant Kroysing?' Bertin asked the nearest one, a freckly red head with a particularly large Adam's apple.

Without lifting his head, the Bavarian asked Bertin what he wanted with Kroysing. Bertin said he didn't want anything in particular; he'd just found Kroysing appealing.

'Well, lad,' the Bavarian said, battering away at a lump of clay, 'our Sergeant Kroysing won't be appealing to anyone ever again.'

At first Bertin didn't understand. His confusion lasted so long that the Bavarian lost his temper and asked him if his ears were blocked. Kroysing had stopped one, he said. He was a goner. He'd bled like a stuck pig in the truck that took him to the military hospital at Billy. Bertin didn't reply. He stood clutching his spade. The colour drained from his face and he cleared his throat. Strange, strange. And here he was standing about stupidly, not screaming, not lashing out... *That's war for you. Nowt you can do about, lad.* Had the Bavarian said that? He had. He was spitting it out, making his voice clear. It had happened the morning before. The explosion had smashed up Kroysing's left shoulder. You today, me tomorrow. They wouldn't be seeing Kroysing again.

They worked on. 'Did you know Sergeant Kroysing from before?' the

Bavarian asked after a pause, looking up, his face dripping with sweat. Bertin said that he had known Kroysing before, that he had been a friend of his and that if there were more like him in the army, the world would be a better place. Yes, the Bavarian replied, blue eyes solemn in his farmer's face. 'You're right there, lad. You won't find another sergeant like him however hard you look. Even if some people are pleased that he's out of the picture after yesterday afternoon...' With that he drew his face down into his open collar as if he'd said too much. Bertin told him he could speak freely to him, that he knew what was what. But the Bavarian demurred. 'It's fine,' he said, turning away.

But during the break the Bavarian appeared again in the company of a smaller, younger ASC man with a thin face and black, almost startled eyes. Both had their tunics open and their caps cocked over one ear. Casually and seemingly innocently, they came either side of Bertin, making it look like they were three ASC men strolling into the shade, bunking off in the hope of a nap. Between the bushy, truncated tree stumps, the remnant of a heavy shell or mine, blown off during the detonation, stuck in the soil like a small table. Its plate-like surface faced skywards, balanced on a steel leg as broad as a hand and thick as a finger. *Bugger me*! thought Bertin. This was their world – a world where men like Kroysing bit the dust.

This man here, the Bavarian told Bertin, was Kroysing's buddy. He had helped to cut his tunic off his body when he was being bandaged up. Something had fallen out from the bloody tatters that no one in their detachment wanted to keep. If Bertin wanted it, he could have it. It was a letter. Bertin said he would gladly take it. He was oddly moved by this bold manifestation of the will of the dead, or almost dead. Gingerly, the Bavarian ASC man handed him a swollen rectangle of brownish red material. It was almost still sticky and looked like a thin bar of chocolate. On it shimmered fudged, blue-black writing. Bertin turned pale, but he took this last greeting and commission and put it in the side pocket of his haversack. When he slid the solid bag of blue-grey linen back over his hips, it seemed to have got heavier. He felt a certain chill, a light shudder, run through his body. He thought he'd found a friend and now he had a commission to fulfil that was both unclear and full of potential complications. Poor little Kroysing! The grey cat suddenly appeared in front of Bertin like a root come to life, gazing at him insolently with her bottle-green eyes, and he was suddenly overcome with fury. Cursing, he hurled the nearest shell splinter at her, missed her of course and saw the Bavarian looking at him in astonishment. She was alive. A creature like that was still alive.

EARLY IN THE afternoon, a man stood doubtfully in front of the company orderly room. Anyone not ordered to present himself there, usually saved himself the trouble, as things only ever went well for Glinsky's favourites; decent men gave the place a wide berth. Nonetheless, Bertin from the ASC stood before the tar paper-covered door, crooked his finger, knocked and stepped inside, assuming the prescribed posture. It was clear from the rigid expression on his face and and the little crease above the bridge of his glasses that he had something on his mind. But with his officer's stripes on his Litevka, a cigar between his thick lips and a dead look in his protruding eyes, Herr Glinsky didn't allow such things to trouble him and hadn't for some time. He'd spent too long in civilian life pandering to the emotions of those he insured in order to make a living as an insurance broker. Now there was a war. The state was looking after him. It was payback time, and he took his dues. He had never realised (though Frau Glinsky had) how much it had cost him to become that unctuous individual each day. Life now was therefore all the sweeter...

Private Bertin: that was the one with the water pipe who shaved his beard off. For the moment, Glinsky concentrated on the latter description, though the former would certainly come up during their conversation. In the hot and somewhat musty air of the orderly room, he asked: 'What on Earth does that soldier with the shaved off beard want?'

The soldier with the shaved-off beard asked for a leave pass to go to Billy and return after the curfew. The connection was unreliable, and so he might have to come back in the evening.

The two clerks grinned to themselves. In exceptional circumstances, a soldier did of course have the right to such a pass after a tour of duty. After all, a soldier is not a prisoner with chains round his feet. But power is power, and favour is favour, and whatever this comrade imagined, nothing would come of it. He wouldn't be going to Billy today.

Private Bertin knew the two clerks. Sperlich, good-natured but stupid, had been some kind of office worker before. Querfurth, who had a goatee and wore thick glasses for long-sightedness on his squinting eyes, had been a draughtsman in the Borsig Works at Tegel. Under the previous sergeant major, they'd been pleasant enough, but mud sticks and their dealings with Herr Glinsky had corrupted them. He sensed that the three men were against him and that it would be hard for him to claim his rights. In a friendly enough way, Glinsky asked what he wanted in Billy. Bertin said he wanted to look for an acquaintance who'd been seriously injured the day before and taken to the hospital there. Remembering the blow he'd had, he swallowed hard two or three times and his voice quivered imperceptibly.

'Is that so?' said the venerable Glinsky airily. 'A wounded soldier in the hospital? And here was I was imagining a washer woman or a whore.'

Bertin heard a couple of fat flies buzzing round a fly paper hanging from the low ceiling. The company knew he was recently married; they'd expect a protest, a flash of indignation. But he didn't even think of it. He wanted to get to Kroysing and he would, and when you want something badly, you don't let someone like Glinsky rattle you. He gazed quietly at Glinsky's pasty, indoors complexion and prying nose and said nothing – and that was smart. Bertin's silence seemed to satisfy Herr Glinsky. He sat back comfortably in his chair and asked who the distinguished gentleman intended to honour with a visit. A French prisoner presumably. Bertin smiled instinctively. He'd expected that. No, he explained. It was a volunteer soldier, the leader of the standby detachment at Chambrettes-Ferme, Sergeant Kroysing. He'd been seriously wounded the day before.

Grey-skinned Glinsky's eyes and mouth fell open in delight. The story of the court martial had done the rounds, and a man like Glinsky naturally sympathised with all the Bavarian comrades who were threatened by it. But he pulled himself together lightning-fast: 'You can save yourself the journey. That man's been dead for some time. He was buried this afternoon.'

Bertin grasped that Glinsky was lying. Ordinarily, the 1/X/20 orderly room had no contact with the Bavarian labour company. NCOs from the two units swapped news and got to know each other when they met by chance at the big supply stores in Mangiennes and Damvillers. But it was hard to respond to the lie; he couldn't very well say that he wanted to visit the dead man's grave.

'I see,' he said hesitantly. 'Dead and buried?'

'Yes,' said Glinsky firmly, 'and now you can return to your duties and show me your back, Mr Water Tap Man. Dismissed!' Bertin swung round and left, while Glinsky hurried to get in touch with Sergeant Major Feicht from the Bavarian company and congratulate him on the resolution of a matter that had been hanging over his head.

Bertin stood outside in the sun, pensively putting one foot in front of the other. If he couldn't go to Billy on a leave pass, he'd go without one. But first he'd take advice from someone who understood the situation. Sergeant Böhne was passing at that moment, rubbing his hands together. Behind him the former innkeeper Lebehde, who belonged to Böhne's squad, was carrying a pot of extra-strong coffee, which he intended to share with Böhne and a couple of others over a celebratory game of skat. For the depot had given orders that all front-line commandos were to remain off-duty when they got back, and the company couldn't countermand those orders. Böhne's small, bright eyes became serious when Private Bertin explained in an undertone what was going on. Böhne was a father of two, and the young Bavarian's accident affected him profoundly. Karl Lebehde just shrugged his shoulders at the orderly room's decision, saying there were many ways to get to Billy.

In the meantime, the barracks door had closed behind them. There were only a few men around, and the long room was quiet. At a table in the right-hand corner, Corporals Näglein and Althans were already waiting for their coffee and game of skat. Time to take action, said Althans, if the Prussians had given up on *esprit de corps*. As they all knew, *esprit de corps* was one of Acting Lieutenant Graßnick's catchphrases. If Corporal Näglein, a farmer from the Altmark in Saxony-Anhalt, was rather a timid man, then Corporal Althans made up for it with his cheek. Althans was a thin Reservist, who hadn't been away from his infantry regiment for long. He'd been with them during the February attack in this area and had taken a heavy ricochet shot between the ribs, as a result of which he'd lain for months in bandages. He enjoyed showing anyone who'd look the deep hole under his chest. He performed a kind of courier service between the battalion in Damvillers and the company, without actually doing duty as an orderly. As such, he had a permanent pass that gave him permission to be out and about at any time – and it was made out to the holder, not in his name. He told Bertin he kept it in the cuff of his tunic, and that his tunic was hanging on a nail behind him. Understood?

A few minutes later, Bertin was trotting over the board walks and short cuts to the park, past columns of men unloading and hauling ammunition. He had a good cup of coffee inside him and he now had something else in the cuff of his tunic. The ammunitions expert Sergeant Schultz and his two assistants always knew of ways to get to Romagne, Mangiennes and Billy.

CHAPTER SEVEN

The older brother

'SERGEANT KROYSING, YES. He's going to be buried at half five.'

Bertin was pointed in the direction of some steps that led underground. In the white-washed cellar, three coffins waited, one of them open. In it was visible the one part of Christoph Kroysing's remains that was still presentable: his quiet face. The room was cooled by hanging wet linen cloths and a whirling fan, though it was still hard to breathe. But Bertin quickly forgot that. Here he was standing by the coffin of his newest and unluckiest friend. *A youth, and ruddy, and of a fair countenance,* he thought in the words of the Bible, and then, feeling solemn: *Oh, Lord, what is man, that thou art mindful of him? Or the son of man, that thou visitest him?* For man was like a blade of grass, blooming and withering like a wild flower. In Kroysing's sallow face, his long eyelashes and widely spaced eyebrows rose like musical notes from the dead ovals of his cheeks. His tightly closed lips bent bitterly downwards, but the broad curve of his brow rose imposingly from his temples beneath his soft hair. Kroysing, thought Bertin, looking at the noble countenance of this boy, this man, why did you do them this favour? Why did you let yourself get caught? Mothers hope their prayers may be of some help, to say nothing of fathers' hopes and of future plans. In a corner, there were further supports for yet more coffins. Shaking his head, Bertin went over to one and sat down on it to think by the whirring fan. He was back among the green-glinting beech leaves and the damaged tree trunks that looked as though they were made of corroded copper; he and Kroysing were sitting at the edge of the shell hole, a pair of field boots beside a pair of puttees, rusting shell splinters half buried in the earth, and the grey cat with the bottle-green eyes was staring hopefully at Kroysing's hand. That was past, as irrevocably past as the sound of Kroysing's voice, which Bertin could nonetheless still hear: 'You're the first person I've been able to speak to about these things for 60 days, and if you want, you can even be of great help to me.' If Bertin wanted to be of help! And where did helping a person lead? Here...

Bent over, he sat there, still shaking his cropped head, his small eyes filled with reflections on the strange ways of the world.

The door gently opened and another soldier entered the cellar. He was lean and so tall that he practically had to duck. Blonde hair, parted on the left, not wearing brads under his soles. His uniform was shabby, and Bertin didn't at first realise that the man in front of him was an officer, because his epaulettes and sword knot were such a dull grey. Bertin jumped up and stood to attention, hands on his trouser seams.

'For God's sake,' the man said. 'No need for that performance at the coffin. Are you from his unit?' And, walking to the foot of the coffin: 'So it's come to this, Christel.' *You always were a handsome boy*, he thought to himself. *Well, be at peace. Sooner or later we'll all be laid out as you are, only not as comfortably.*

Bertin had seldom seen brothers who were less alike. Eberhard Kroysing, a sapper lieutenant, folded his bony hands over the peak of his cap and didn't try to hide the two tears that fell from his eyes. Bertin withdrew quietly, giving the dead boy's face a last tender look, himself now choked up with sadness and letting it show.

'Stay, stay,' boomed Lieutenant Kroysing's deep voice. 'We needn't drive each other away. In any case the lid will be closed in a minute. Have a look and see if the pall bearers are coming.'

Bertin understood and turned round. The lieutenant kissed his little brother on the forehead. *Got a lot to apologise to you for, little fellow*, he thought. *It wasn't very easy growing up next to me, under me. And how come you, the baby of the family, got to look so much like our mother, while I only looked like Papa?*

Outside, there was the sound of approaching boots. Two orderlies walked in. They were used to their work and didn't observe the niceties at first, but they quietened down a bit when they saw the lieutenant and took the other two coffins away first – rough boxes made of spruce wood. Bertin helped them through the door and up the stairs to give the brother some time alone.

When the strangers were outside, Eberhard Kroysing took his small cigar cutter from his trouser pocket and cut a lock of hair from his brother's temple – for his mother. He carefully hid it in his flat wallet. He didn't want to break off his dialogue with the little one. 'Did you really have to be so jealous of my stamp collection?' he asked. 'Did we have to quarrel constantly? Perhaps we could have had a decent adult friendship? *Behold, how good and how pleasant it is for brethren to dwell together in unity!*' he said, quoting Dr Luther's translation of the Bible. That was a pious wish. 'Our family has been unlucky. No one will visit the beautiful family grave in the protestant cemetery in Nuremberg. You'll be buried here in catholic soil, and I'll most likely be eaten by the rats after the last shell has burst. Allons, let's shut this hut up, so we can perform our final duty to you, my boy.' And, choking on dry sobs, he kissed the little one once again on his cold mouth and on the dark fluff of his beard, and then fit the lid over the long box and screwed the corners down with practised fingers. When Bertin came back with the two orderlies, an officer, cap on head, strode stiffly past them into the land of the living where the slanting sun beat down.

The burial was a mundane affair, cloaked in a certain solemnity. The three fallen heroes were blessed by an army chaplain, whose cassock barely covered the uniform he normally wore. Delegations from the affected units led by sergeants had been drafted in. The Bavarian ASC men brought a wreath of beech twigs – a last greeting from the standby detachment at Chambrettes-Ferme, none of whom had been given leave to attend the funeral. The three coffins were placed on top of each other, and Bertin caught himself sighing with relief; little Kroysing was lowered in last and wouldn't have to bear the burden of others even in death. As the other two dead men had been artillery drivers hit on their way to the ammunitions store, their comrades' carbines fired a last salvo over the grave for all three. Then the funeral party hastily dispersed among Billy's canteens to seize the rare opportunity to buy chocolate and jam, and raise a few glasses.

A hospital sergeant came up to Lieutenant Kroysing. The company had asked for his brother's effects and had already collected them, and he gave him a list, which Kroysing glanced at absent-mindedly and put in his pocket. In the few seconds that this took, Bertin struggled with and made a decision. He walked briskly towards his friend's brother and asked to have a word with him. Eberhard Kroysing gave him a rather scornful look. These poor ASC men exploited any contact with an officer to ask advice about their petty concerns or air a grievance. This one here, who was obviously an academic sort and a Jew, would no doubt want to pester him about leave or some such. 'Fire away, man,' he said, 'but make it snappy or you'll get separated from your comrades.'

'I don't belong to that unit,' said Bertin carefully, 'and I would like to speak to you alone for 10 minutes, Lieutenant. It's about your brother,' he added, seeing Kroysing's dismissive expression.

Billy had been shot to pieces and patched up badly. They were both silent as they walked through the streets, both thinking about the freshly dug gave. 'It was nice,' said the lieutenant at length, 'that you sent him the wreath.'

'It came from his men at Chambrettes-Ferme, where he died. That's where I got to know him – early in the morning the day before yesterday.'

'You only knew my brother for such a short time and yet you came to his funeral? I really must thank your sergeant major.'

Bertin smiled weakly. 'My orderly room refused me leave to come here. I came off my own bat.'

'That's a strange state of affairs,' said Kroysing, as they went through the door of the officers' mess, a kind of inn for officers with soldiers serving.

Several gentlemen in shiny epaulettes looked over in surprise as the sapper lieutenant and ASC private squeezed in opposite each other at the table for two in the window alcove. Such fraternisation between officers and men was undesirable, forbidden in fact. But the poor bastards in the trenches didn't always behave in line with orders from the administration behind the lines. At any rate, the tall lieutenant with the Iron Cross, first class didn't look like he would appreciate a lecture.

Indeed no. From Bertin's first words, Eberhard Kroysing's face looked rather set. Bertin asked if he had known that his brother had problems at his company. Certainly, said Kroysing, but when you were stuck in the sapper depot at Douaumont, under daily fire from the French, you weren't overly interested in minor squabbles among NCOs at another company. The wine here was excellent. Bertin thought so too. He drank and asked if it had occurred to Lieutenant Kroysing that there could be a connection between those squabbles and Christoph Kroysing's death. At that, the lieutenant's eyes widened. 'Listen,' he said in a low voice, 'men fall here every day like chestnuts from a tree. Imagine if everyone tried to find connections...!'

'In connection with this case, might I explain how I got to know your brother and what he told me in confidence?'

Eberhard Kroysing looked into his wine glass, twirling it lightly between his fingers, while Bertin uttered one considered phrase after another, his eyes on Kroysing's face. Bertin's chest pressed against the marble table, which was a little too high for the low seats. He sensed that the young man opposite wasn't convinced, but he couldn't stay quiet. The main part of the room echoed with the booming laughter of boozers.

'To be blunt,' said Kroysing eventually, 'I don't believe a word you've said, sir. Not that I think you're lying. But Christoph was an unreliable witness. He had an over-active imagination. He was a lyrical soul, you know, a poet.'

'A poet?' repeated Bertin, taken aback.

'So to speak,' confirmed Kroysing. 'He wrote verse, pretty verse, and he was working on a play, a drama, he called it, a tragedy — what do I know? Such people quickly become obsessed by inconsequential things. Prejudices. Suspicions. But I, my dear chap, am a man of fact. My subject was engineering, and that precludes such fantasies.'

Bertin scrutinised his companion. He found it perplexing that Kroysing was so sceptical about someone whose personality and tone Bertin had immediately found convincing.

'I don't mean,' continued Kroysing, 'that my little brother was an idiot or a blabbermouth. But you men in the rank and file are prone to persecution complexes. You fancy everyone is bad and wants to make things difficult for you. You'd have to come up with some proof, young man.'

Bertin considered. 'Would a letter from your brother count as proof, Lieutenant? A letter that my wife was supposed to send to your mother? A letter in which the case is set out, so that your uncle in Metz may finally intervene?'

Eberhard Kroysing looked up, fixing his hard eyes on Bertin. 'And what is my Uncle Franz's involvement to be in this matter about which you're so well informed?'

'Set the wheels in motion for a court martial and cite Christoph at the hearing.'

'And how long was the boy in the cellar at Chambrettes-Ferme?'

'Over two months with no break and no let-up.'

Eberhard Kroysing drummed his fingers on the table. 'Give me the letter,' he said.

'It's in my haversack,' said Bertin. 'I couldn't know that I'd meet you here, Lieutenant.'

Eberhard Kroysing smiled grimly. 'You were right to doubt it. The news came to me indirectly from our battalion headquarters, and if the Frogs hadn't been unusually quiet, I might have missed my connection. But either way, I must have the letter.'

Bertin hesitated. 'There's something I must tell you. The letter was in his pocket when he was hit. It's soaked in blood and unreadable.'

'His blood,' said Eberhard Kroysing. 'So there's still something left of him above ground. But that doesn't matter. There are simple chemical processes that can deal with that. My sergeant Süßmann can do them in his sleep. It would seem,' he said, and his brow darkened, 'that I didn't look after the little one as well as I should have done. Damn it,' he shouted, suddenly angry, 'I had other concerns. I thought the court martial had given its opinion long ago and put everything in order. The idea that brothers look out for each other is just a fairytale. Often they fight and hate each other. Or have you had a different experience?'

Bertin thought for a moment then said no, his experience was no different. He usually only had news of his brother Fritz from his parents. The boy had been serving the whole time with the 57s, first in Flanders then in Lens, in the Carpathians and on the Hartmannsweilerkopf, and now, more was the pity, in the worst part of the Somme battle. Who knew if he was still alive? Brotherly love was just an ingrained figure of speech. Brothers had always fought for favour and position in the family, from Cain and Abel to Romulus and Remus, to say nothing of German royalty, who enjoyed blinding, murdering and exiling each other to monasteries.

'Let's go,' said Kroysing. 'The drivers here have organised a car for me, so I'll be back in my hellish cellar by tonight. We'll go via your park. And if I get the proof I need, then I'll put it before the court martial. And then we'll see. I'm not vengeful. But if those gentleman really did spirit little Christel away from my mother in order that he should end up awaiting resurrection on the third shelf of that grave, then it's time they made my acquaintance.'

They waited for the car in front of the mess. Above the hills towards Romagne, known as the Morimont, the sky was a diaphanous green. Bertin was hungry. He was counting on someone from his platoon having kept some dinner for him. If not, a ration of dry bread was enough for a man who had furthered a dead friend's cause. No one was better placed than Eberhard Kroysing to bring those responsible for his brother's murder to account.

The army driver in his leather jacket drove the open car over the white roads like a man possessed because he wanted to reach the firing zone, where he had to drive without lights, before dark. Less than half an hour later they pulled up by the water troughs at the Steinbergquell barracks. Bertin ran over and came back a short time later. He handed the lieutenant what looked to be a piece of stiff cardboard, wrapped in white paper. Eberhard Kroysing clasped it carefully in his hand.

A few nights later, Private Bertin had a remarkable experience, which he only believed the following noon when he saw the evidence with his own eyes.

Like many short-sighted people, Bertin relied on his hearing to interpret the blurry, threatening world around him. As people also hear when they are asleep because from the time of the glaciers and forest swamps danger has approached by night, he'd had some difficulty adjusting to communal sleeping. It was a sweltering July night in the valley, which cut between Moirey and Chaumont like a butcher's trough and was permanently filled with swamp fog from the Theinte. The moon was nearly full, and in its pale, milky glow the night seem deceptively clear. Nice weather for flying. The wakeful would do well to keep watch.

Shortly after one, the machine guns at the Cape camp began to rattle furiously a few kilometres beyond Thil wood; anti-aircraft guns croaked red sparking shrapnel up into the air. They were coming! It wasn't unexpected. Men of a very cautious disposition – a couple of gunners and a few ASC men, including Pahl the typesetter – had been sleeping in the old dugouts by the roadside for a week. The phone at Moirey shrilled with calls from the Cape camp. The Frogs wouldn't be flying over at one in the morning to distribute biscuits. One of the telephonists at Steinbergquell sped over to see the on-duty sergeant. A bomb attack on a depot currently holding 30,000 shells of which 5,000 were gas shells – and the company was asleep in its barracks! The sentries rushed around, while from the south (the ammunitions depot was at the north end of the encampment) the gentle mosquito drone of the French engines began to build in the dormitories: 'Air attack! Everyone outside with gas masks! Lights out! Assemble behind the kitchen hut!' Behind the kitchen hut, the ground fell gradually away so that a flat mound of earth curved up between it and the dangerous ammunition.

A lot of ASC men slept in their lace-ups; no one needed more than a couple of seconds to wake up, slip into their boots, coat or tunic, and underpants or trousers, and leap on to the wooden floor with a crash. The barracks stood open and empty in the pale grey of the night. The clatter of hobnailed boots was drowned out by defensive fire from the MGs and the artillery. The white antennae of searchlights slunk across the sky to help drag down the mosquito swarm: three planes, or maybe five. They were flying so high! Spread out along the damp grass and hard, clayey soil of the southern slope, the defenceless ASC men listened breathlessly and looked up to the sky where the storm would soon start. Yes, they were for it. A fine whistle was unleashed up above, two-voiced, many-voiced, getting stronger, and then the valley filled with flashing and roaring, and a dull thunder crashed. For a second, the Earth's fiery interior seemed to gape open were the bombs had hit; then the valley was engulfed in black. The valley roared under fire nine times; then the French had flown the loop that allowed them to escape the anti-aircraft fire; the planes flew off to the west, perhaps to launch a further attack on the other side of the Meuse.

'Well,' said Private Halezinsky in a quavering voice to his nearby friend, Karl Lebehde, 'another successful strike.'

'Think so? asked Lebehde, lighting a night-time cigarette with remarkable sangfroid. 'I'd venture to suggest they were after the railway station, August, which did take one hit. They'll sort us out next time.'

It was tempting to wander over there now. There would be hot shell splinters and fuses in the fresh bomb holes, and they could be sold for a good price. By early the next morning, the railwaymen would have nabbed them all. But the sergeants were ushering their men back to bed.

The barracks had been aired in the meantime and had cooled down. It was half past one, so they could still easily grab four hours' sleep. Halezinsky went to his bed and shone a light to check for rats. The electric light fell on the bed to the left of his. Someone was actually lying there sleeping. 'Karl,' he called quietly in utter astonishment, 'look at this. He must be a sound sleeper.'

The two men looked at Bertin's sleeping form almost reverently. He'd slept through the alarm, the attack and the bomb explosions that had destroyed a railway track and the fields 70 or 80 metres across the road. The next morning, he would be the only one who didn't believe the reports of the night before, who thought he was being taken for a ride. He would sacrifice some of his lunch break to go and see the bomb holes that had appeared overnight in the green fields and were big enough to accommodate a telephone box. He would bend over to touch the rails that had been blasted apart and check for freshly filled shell holes between the two rods. That was how completely his sleeping self had pushed aside the world of war, where a demise such as that of Kroysing was possible. A couple of kilometres ahead, machine guns were sweeping the ripped up ground under the limelight of flares; several thousand men, covered in earth, riddled with shell splinters, mangled by direct hits and poisoned by gas, huddled in bomb holes or behind ramparts to escape the fire bursts as the guns picked off flying shells. But only a mile and half away, a man of around 30 with good hearing had been able to sleep through a bomb attack, plunged into the deepest sanctuary and safety known to man, akin to the oblivion of the grave.

BOOK TWO

Resistance

CHAPTER ONE

A turning point

THE GERMANS WERE using all the smaller and larger settlements in the Meuse area as bases and had made themselves at home there. Of course, they admired the men at the front and the way they endured privations under fire in the mud, but they didn't let that dent their self-esteem. The further behind the lines you went, the more obviously the war metamorphosed into a system of administration and supply. A bunch of bureaucrats in uniform held absolute sway here. They didn't like to hear talk of later restitution. They requisitioned what they needed and paid with stamped paper, which France was supposed to redeem later. To them cleanliness, staunch service and the military for its own sake were the highest virtues. That they lived in primitive rustic stone cottages, without comforts such as warm water, tiled baths and leather armchairs, was to them a sacrifice for which the people and the Fatherland would one day have to compensate them; such was their war.

Damvillers, a modest village on the provincial railway line called Le Meusien, was one of hundreds with no influence on the fate of the wider area. That hobnailed German soldiers and distinguished officers in shiny boots now scraped across the paving stones and floorboards instead of farmers in blue jackets and clogs hadn't changed that one iota. Some were quartered permanently in Damvillers, some temporarily, while others went there for the day to relieve the tedium or get provisions for their units. Major Jansch was in the former category, Captain Niggl in the latter.

The tedium— the German state relied on officers: active soldiers and yeomen from the Landwehr, and behind the lines men from the military Reserve and reservists from the Landsturm, important gentlemen with dirks on their belts and helmets on their heads. The shiny spike on their helmets pretty much embodied the pinnacle of human existence for them. Neither Niggl, a retired civil servant from Weilheim, nor Psalter, a head teacher from Neuruppin, nor Jansch, Berlin-Steglitz, an editor, could imagine a higher peak, although Jansch was in a special position because he had played soldiers in civilian life too as editor of *Army and Fleet Weekly*. In peacetime, they'd drawn a monthly income of about 300 Marks. Now, for as long as the war lasted, the paymaster handed them three times that on the first of each month, besides which eating, drinking and smoking cost very little, and accommodation and letters home nothing at all. A man could certainly manage on that. And this was how it was for hundreds of gentlemen in Crépion, Vavrille, Romagne, Chaumont, in Jamez and Vitarville; everywhere that was occupied. As far as they were concerned, the war couldn't last long enough, even if they were often bored or required to do tedious, detailed work.

Where the lines of communication began with the field police sentries at the crossroads, a desolation descended on the men born of daily duty unrelieved by intellectual life or women and children, a struggle for existence with no science or art, gramophone music, cinema or theatre, and with almost no politics. The lines of communication were as indispensable to the front lines as a mother's bloodstream to her unborn child, feeding them, helping them to grow and continually supplying their every need. 'Supplies' was the magic word in the communications zone. Everything – from hay bales for the horses to ammunition, leave trains and bread rations – rested on its absolute reliability. Without it, the men at the front wouldn't have lasted a week. And so the staff in the communications zone bathed in the sunshine of their immeasurable importance. It radiated from every orderly and staff sergeant, but most especially from the officers. They did their duty, ate reasonably well, drank good local wine, conspired against each other and performed small reciprocal favours.

And so it was that Major Jansch, commander of the X/20 ASC battalion, came to clink his spurs on Lieutenant Psalter's steps. A major visiting a lieutenant. And not just any major, the Great Jansch. And not just any lieutenant – flat-nosed Lieutenant Psalter from the transport depot, with his close-cropped black hair, scarred face and myopic eyes. Was it the end of the world? Not at all. A lieutenant in the transport corps has access to vehicles. Ordinarily, an off-duty ASC major would take nothing to do with him, but if that major needed a favour, he had to ask nicely. The railway transport officer at Damvillers belonged to the Moirey park officers' drinking club, which was not on good terms with Major Jansch. The commander was in a position to question the whys and wherefores of every case of wine that Major Jansch sent home – if indeed it contained wine. This could potentially open up a great pit into which the major might quietly disappear. (The officers had agreed with

Herr Graßnick to shelve the unpleasant water tap incident simply in order to get one over on Major Jansch.) Major Jansch's goods therefore had to leave from other railway stations. And so even a newborn child could understand why Major Jansch was now affably pulling up a chair at his comrade Psalter's desk for a chat, or, as Herr Jansch put it, a chinwag.

Herr Jansch was a gaunt man of about 50 with a long, thin moustache, who in profile looked rather like a raven. On the other armchair in Lieutenant Psalter's rustic room sat a chubby-cheeked man with sly, watery eyes and a little beard that made him look quite friendly: Captain Niggl from the Bavarian labour company stationed on the other side of the Romagne ridge. He had come to Lieutenant Psalter with a concern of his own. As he was only passing through Damvillers, he wanted to make the most of his time and had asked to be dealt with quickly. His problem was one of the utmost importance to any soldier. It concerned beer, four barrels of Münchner Hornschuh-Bräu, which had been delivered into Captain Niggl's hands for his four companies by way of his brother-in-law, although they were actually meant for the infantry of the two Bavarian divisions at the front. However, the high-ups had eventually realised that the ASC men must have their turn too, and the four barrels had been lying at Dun train station since the previous day. If the infantry got wind of it, it would be farewell, amber nectar. A barrel of beer was worth a little thievery. Captain Niggl indicated that if Lieutenant Psalter's trusty lorry drivers successfully delivered the precious goods to battalion headquarters, there would be a drinking party and all the gentlemen from Damvillers would be most welcome. The beer could be watered down a tad for the ASC men. No harm in that.

Major Jansch eavesdropped on the Bavarian's love of the bottle with disgust. He had no taste for beer – nasty, bitter stuff – or for the sour red wine that the French conned fools into buying with names such as Bordeaux and Burgundy. He loved sweet things, a taste of port or vermouth, and even then in moderation, for his passion lay in other areas. But he hid his aversion, even going as far as to the invite the Bavarian for a breakfast tipple should his business in Damvillers be finished by 11. Herr Niggl said he had just one more tiny thing to attend to at brigade HQ. He wanted to have some files delivered to Judge Advocate Mertens at Montmédy Court Martial, and none of his own men could be freed up to do it. But Damvillers regularly sent orderlies up the line – he'd find someone to take them. In the meantime, Lieutenant Psalter had combined Jansch's and Niggl's business and sorted them both out by phone. One of his lorries was taking a sapper commando across the sector to Vilosnes at midday, as the bridge over the Meuse at Sivry needed strengthened. The driver could easily pick up Major Jansch's case beforehand, take it to Dun, and collect Captain Niggl's barrels there. The three officers went their separate ways more than happy.

At quarter past 11, Major Jansch entered the mess. Soon after Herr Niggl also wheezed in. The large room was completely empty; the communications zone commanders and Fifth Army generals had once again been pushing for official hours to be observed. There was in any case plenty to do, as the battle at the Somme called for more artillery, troops and transport on a daily basis. They were bombarded with demands from the Fourth Army, which was under fire. The Verdun sector was no longer unique. The blasted French weren't leaving all the work to the British and had even made more progress than them. It really would be a disaster if they got as far as Péronne. For the paradoxical game of war was about tracts of land as well as barrels of beer. It was a non-stop round of victories and defeats, just like Major Jansch's egg boxes, which he maintained held red wine that he'd paid for.

It was pleasantly quiet and cool in the stone house, where the first floor was reserved for officers. Major Jansch was served quickly. He was both a feared guest and a laughing stock on account of his meanness. That day he had a new victim to listen to his speeches – a Bavarian. They were busily drinking port, and the Bavarian was smoking a long cigar called 'Victor of Longwy' that cost 30 Pfennigs and was sold to the officers for 14. Major Jansch wasn't smoking.

The two men in grey Litevkas soon came to an understanding, a certain reserve on both sides notwithstanding. In his companion Niggl, Major Jansch saw someone whose political views he'd like to investigate. The war's second anniversary had been celebrated a few weeks previously, but the war couldn't end until the Germans were victorious across the board and could dictate the peace. Regrettably, a lot of people at home didn't understand that, said Jansch. They dreamt of a rapprochement, because that Red Indian hypocrite Wilson over in America had soft-soaped them. Yes, Niggl agreed, there were people like that in Munich too, but not many. Social democrats and pacifists. Long-haired types from the borough of Schwabing. Idiots. Carnival doughnuts. Right-thinking people just laughed at them.

Major Jansch frowned and took a swig of port. He had to disagree. People like that should be put in protective custody, and the sooner the better. Captain Niggl was prepared to accept this too. Very good. Protective custody, then. Or perhaps they should be drafted into a labour battalion. How about that, Major Jansch? And he blinked at his companion with his clever little eyes.

Major Jansch demonstrated his disagreement by saying nothing. Before his discharge, he had for many years been an upright Prussian garrison captain. Now he commanded 2,000 capable, hard-working men and had four averagely competent acting lieutenants as company commanders. He didn't want to hear of men in protective custody being put in the army. Even the very best commander wouldn't get an Iron Cross, first class out of their achievements. Unfortunately he didn't have that honour and the way things were going it didn't look like he'd ever get it. He was surrounded by too much envy and malice. But, then, didn't every officer sing the same tune?

Niggl agreed that they did but without much conviction. Deep down, he felt very pleased with himself. Things hadn't gone so well for him in ages. He'd settled a difficult matter, unpleasant for everyone concerned, and thereby confirmed his position as the father of the battalion with those involved. Unfortunately, his Third Company had suffered another lost in the preceding weeks, he told Jansch. A sergeant had died a hero's death, and it had been Niggl's painful duty to inform his relatives. Regrettably, the man had been entangled in some court martial proceedings in the past few months, but Niggl had been able to stall the investigation until the man was eventually killed. Coincidence, of course. Yes, the battalion had some dangerous advance positions. And a man who dirtied his own nest had to be kept away from the company. A man like that begrudged his comrades their bit of meat, rum and sugar. But the Frogs had done for Sergeant Kroysing in the end.

Major Jansch listened carefully as the Bavarian, who wasn't used to port, chattered on. Discipline had to be maintained. Subordination was of the utmost importance. A sergeant who denigrated his comrades could ruin the troops' morale. In any case, nothing was as dangerous in the army as the creeping discontent created by politicians' speeches and insolent enquiries. Those fellows were always criticising the German army; they didn't like the rations, or the leave arrangements, or the way complaints were handled. How was a commanding officer supposed to keep his troops under control, when they knew civilians could raise objections at any time? Yes, only the Pan-German Union knew how much the Reich owed its army, said Major Jansch, asking Niggl if he knew of this organisation.

Och, said Niggl dismissively, he had no time for unions and associations. His men in the Third went about their business quietly enough. News had got round quickly as to who it was who had met a hero's death at the hands of the Frogs. And the man had scarcely been in that position two months. It hadn't been possible to relieve him. During the battle of Verdun, things couldn't always be done by the book, and there weren't many volunteers to take his place. And as he wanted a commission and was going off on a course in the autumn, he had to get used life at the front, didn't he? Yes, a brother of his had come forward, a sapper lieutenant. He wanted his brother's effects, but he couldn't have them because they'd already been sent to the parents in Nuremberg – sometimes the Third Company was a little too diligent in performing its duties. The field post handled three million items a day, for goodness' sake – sometimes things went round the long way or got lost. So everything was resolved peacefully, and Judge Advocate Mertens could now put the files away.

Major Jansch sat there fingering his long moustache, watching the Bavarian in astonishment. This chap knew how to handle things, even if you couldn't tell it by looking at him. It was very clear that in an emergency the demands of duty required solutions that would never have occurred to an old veteran like himself. It was a lesson to Jansch. He'd always been too high-minded but he wasn't too proud to learn from a Bavarian beer drinker. He thanked his companion for a fascinating half hour in his genial company, for Niggl was wiping his mouth and getting ready to go. He had an appointment at quarter to 12 with the divisional chaplain, Father Lochner, who had offered him a lift. Naturally, he wouldn't have the same kind of conversation with the reverent gentleman, for earthly beings should not manipulate God's ways or use them for their own ends. And so the gentlemen said their goodbyes. The Bavarian trudged out, while the Prussian remained seated for a while. With a heavy heart, for he was very careful with money, he asked that the four glasses of port and the cigar – 114 Pfennigs – be charged to his account, consoling himself that what he had learnt from the Bavarian that day was worth 114 Pfennigs. Deep in thought, with his hands behind his back, he crept down the stairs and out into the glaring sunlight.

CHAPTER TWO

Oderint dum metuant

JUDGE ADVOCATE CARL Georg Mertens was the son of a famous German lawyer, a man whose *Commentary on Civilian Law* had provided clarifications of the utmost importance and formulations that were now standard. The book was known simply as *Mertens,* and its author had been received several times by the Kaiser. The son grew up in the shadow of his father's distinctions. He was an outstanding scholar and became professor of legal history fairly young. His passion was more for cultural history than for the law, but only an idiot would have spurned the advantages that the name Mertens brought in the German legal world. In the beginning, he had believed in the war and gone into the field with enthusiasm. Disillusionment ensued. He reconnected with his peaceful tendencies and accepted a transfer to a court martial, albeit somewhat hesitantly. He loved books and suffered greatly from the lack of good music. He appointed a Jewish lawyer with a gift for the piano as his assistant so he could play duets with him. When he discovered the small town of Montmédy's museum with its pastels and paintings by the Lorraine painter Bastien-Lepage he felt compensated for a great deal. He read a lot, improving his French through the novels of Stendhal. His days in Montmédy passed in a leisurely way. Into this quiet scholarly life, little touched by the scant legal duties in Montmédy, walked Sapper Lieutenant Eberhard Kroysing and he turned it upside down.

He appeared one morning shortly before 9am in his threadbare uniform, Iron Cross, first class and steel helmet, carrying incongruous new maroon leather gloves, and demanded to speak to the judge advocate himself. Because of the ambivalent attitude all those behind the lines have towards soldiers from the front, the clerks looked rather shamefaced as they said they were sorry but the judge advocate didn't start work until just before 10am and his deputy, Sergeant Porisch, had not yet returned from interrogating a French prisoner.

Kroysing laughed. 'Nice life you have here by the sounds of it. Mind the

Frogs don't get you in the neck sometime – the ones who aren't in prison, I mean.'

He hid his anger. If you wanted to get your way in the jungle behind the lines, you had to accept the habits and customs of the drones who worked there. And Eberhard Kroysing intended to get his way. He wanted to see his brother's file. At the same time, he was filled with deep mistrust towards each and every being in the area. They were all birds of a feather who flocked together unless someone forced them apart. These legal eagles would undoubtedly have more sympathy for the guilty parties in Christoph's company, the acting lieutenants and sergeant majors, than for Eberhard Kroysing, who had come to disturb their peaceful idyll.

The clerk, Corporal Sieck, who had taken a bullet in the chest and got the Iron Cross at Longwy at the end of August 1914, felt sorry for the tall, scrawny man. Sieck assured him that Judge Advocate Mertens would be there at 10am on the dot and asked if he'd like to have a look at the museum or the citadel in the meantime. Kroysing gave the rather talkative, bespectacled clerk a scornful look. 'Till 10am, then. Put a note on the judge advocate's desk: Lieutenant Kroysing asking for information. Hopefully your filing cabinet is in order.'

He saluted and left. It was a long time since he'd spent an hour wandering the streets of a town. He constantly wanted to shake his head. Nothing here was shot up. It was a peaceful provincial town: small shops, small cafés. The civilian life led by respectable citizens carried on, then. Kroysing went into the shops and spent money: handkerchiefs, chocolate, cigarettes, writing paper. The people who served him were reserved and taciturn. *Let them hate us as long as they fear us*, he thought in Latin, as at last he did climb the steep slope to the citadel to take another look at the undamaged countryside shimmering in the summer light. He marvelled at the Latin language, which could express this in three words where other languages needed many more.

Kroysing leant against the broad parapet and contemplated the hedge-lined meadows below, the streets, the railway line to Luxembourg and the local line he'd come up on that morning from Azannes. A sudden wild anger gripped him at the false peace in this fat, stinking world. God knew he wasn't the sort of man who begrudged others their pleasures just because things were less pleasant for him. But when he thought how he'd crawled out of Douaumont at 4am and then crossed an insane landscape of leprous craters only to spend an hour admiring the view like a lovesick schoolboy, he felt like peppering the place with grenades.

From a small door in the citadel's large keep a sergeant emerged with a folder under his arm and his cap perched casually on his cropped head. A local would have recognised him by the cigar at the corner of his mouth as the lawyer Porisch, traipsing back down to the town in his soldier's garb after interrogating a prisoner. When he saw the officer, Porisch took the cigar from his mouth, clasped the folder close and saluted with a sullen lift of his head. His round, bulging eyes sought the lieutenant's. Kroysing waved him aside contemptuously; he almost felt like snarling at him and sending him back.

In the meantime, Corporal Sieck had taken pity on the man from the front and sent an orderly to the judge advocate's quarters with the note, although Kroysing had only asked for it be put on his desk. Judge Advocate Mertens often didn't turn up at his unlovely office until 11am. There was no telephone connection to his quarters. He didn't want to be bothered when he was off duty. He'd discovered French painting and with the help of the musical Herr Porisch and various books of reproductions and art histories was feeling his way from Bastien-Lepage back to Corot and forward to Manet and the impressionists. The name Kroysing meant nothing to him. 'Came from the front. Hasn't much time,' the note also said. C.G. Mertens was a polite man who didn't like to keep people waiting. He hoped Porisch would be able to bring him up to speed quickly. As he ate his breakfast, it dawned on him that the Kroysing files related to a sergeant. *So it's a company commander wanting a nice day out in Montmédy,* he thought. It often took Professor Mertens a while to marshal his thoughts.

One minute after 10am, Eberhard Kroysing loped up the old-fashioned stairs two to three at a time. He'd expected a fat, comfort-loving military official and was initially thrown by the sensitive scholar in gold-rimmed spectacles with a head reminicent of Field Marshal Moltke's. Instead of marching into the room and aggressively confronting this bastard from behind the lines, he suddenly felt he had to be polite. It was clear from the quiet gaze in the man's blue eyes that no ill-will towards his brother or anyone else had emanated from this office. Eberhard Kroysing could be very charming, as plenty of girls could testify. He formulated his request in gentle words. With his head to one side, C.G. Mertens listened to the sapper lieutenant's deep voice, which seemed to resonate in his chest.

So this wasn't a company commander exploiting a pretext but a brother of Sergeant Kroysing against whom charges had been brought several months previously. Judge Advocate Mertens knew nothing more specific as the case had not got past the preliminary investigation stage. Mertens was from north Germany and separated 's' from 't' when he spoke in the typical Plattdeutsch manner, which struck Kroysing, who was from Franken in the south, as rather spinsterish.

'The state of affairs is being managed by my assistant, Herr Porisch, a former student of my father's as I've discovered. I tell you this, lieutenant, because Herr Porisch wears the uniform of a sergeant and any confusion would be most embarrassing.'

You clown, thought Eberhard Kroysing. *Who's your father and what's it got to do with me? Be better if you looked after your files.* Aloud he said, 'We were all something else before, Judge Advocate. I, for example, was a mechanical engineer at the Technical University in Berlin Charlottenburg, or "Schlorndorf" as we students called it. But now we have new skins and want to do the best we can.'

Herr Mertens didn't answer. He rang a bell and said, 'Please tell Herr Porisch to join this meeting' to the orderly standing to attention in the door.

Well, well, thought Eberhard Kroysing, as Porisch entered the room, round eyes protruding from his round face, a cigar in his left hand, his right playing an imaginary piano. *It's a good thing I didn't flatten him.* 'We've already met,' he said, as they were introduced.

'Fate did indeed provide a preview,' Porisch agreed.

'Sometimes a preview doesn't lead anywhere,' said Kroysing, 'but I'd now like some information about my brother's case.'

Franz Porisch showed what a good memory he had. The dossier against Christoph Kroysing, sergeant in the military Reserve, had been referred to his unit, a Bavarian labour battalion stationed near Mangiennes, several months previously, at the end of April. However, as the investigation of the accused and the accusations made couldn't possibly have taken so long, the battalion had twice been asked to return the files. Both times the battalion had replied that it couldn't comment on the whereabouts of the files as the Third Company had in due course passed them on to Kroysing's replacement unit at Ingolstadt.

'To his replacement unit in Ingolstadt?' repeated Eberhard Kroysing stiffly. He sat squarely on his chair with his hands on his thighs. *He looks like Ramses with his hooked nose, thin lips and those eyes that are about to scorch my little Porisch,* thought Professor Mertens, who was starting to find his tall guest rather captivating.

'*Relato refero*,' replied Porisch. 'I'm just repeating what we were told. About

10 days ago, the file came back to us through official channels along with other reports. It was marked "Accused killed in action" with the date and the company's official seal. Shortly thereafter the battalion called us to confirm the news and ask whether we intended to close the file. Naturally, we said yes, as a closed file is the sort of file everyone likes.' It then occurred to him that the man sat there was the brother of the accused, who had been killed in action and was therefore dead. Dropping his cigar in the ashtray in shock, he jumped up, bowed and stammered: 'My condolences, by the way. My sincere condolences.'

The judge advocate rose and reached his hand across the desk to express his condolences too. Eberhard Kroysing looked from one man to the other. He'd have liked to smash both their faces in, as he put it to himself. These men had effectively aided and abetted a murder with their sloppiness. Then he pulled himself together, half rose from his chair, accepted Mertens' limp, scholarly hand and asked without further explanation if he could see the file. Sergeant Porisch jumped out of the door, ready to be of service. And as Mertens watched Kroysing in silence so as not to upset his feelings, Kroysing froze and thought: *Christel wasn't imagining things, and the ASC man at the funeral wasn't lying. They murdered Christel; they let the Frogs sort it out for them. To Ingolstadt! That beautiful town full of bridges. While Christel was sitting in Chambrettes-Ferme waiting to be relieved, for a hearing. Cut off from God and the world. And I, bastard that I am, left him to deal with it all alone. A dozen villains conspiring against little Christel.*

Then he had in his hand the thinnest file that could ever have made it to a court martial: a couple of pages, beginning with a report from Field Censor's Office V and Christel's letter to Uncle Franz, written in his brother's fine, familiar hand, a couple of pages from a company report (exonerating the NCO corps), a statement from the replacement unit in Ingolstadt to the effect that Chr. Kroysing (currently in the field) had last been brought there in February and been assigned to Niggl's ASC battalion at the beginning of March. There was a long pause and then a note from mid-July from the field hospital at Billy: 'Brought in seriously injured'. And the next day: 'Buried Billy with two other NCOs, cross no. D 3321'.

It was very quiet in the room. Its pale grey sterility was enlivened only by a bookcase, an old engraving on one wall of Napoleon III, glazed and in a gilt frame, and a picture on the desk of the famous Professor Mertens, whom Eberhard Kroysing didn't know. From outside came the sound of fifes and drums, a company from the Montmédy recruitment depot marching on the practice ground. His heart thumping, Kroysing read his brother's letter, the clear, angry sentences, full of complaints about the injustice of the world; he couldn't sleep because of the wrongs visited on his men. *I mustn't get upset,* thought Kroysing. *Good that these strangers are watching, that I have to control myself. Would've made a good company commander, Christel, and a useful citizen later.* And, closing the folder, he asked the gentlemen if anything in it had struck them as odd.

Mertens leafed through the folder, then passed it to Porisch. Neither found anything unusual. It often took a long time to ascertain the whereabouts of a man who had been shifted about 'up front'. That was exactly why the courts were so slow. 'Exactly,' said the sapper lieutenant, his face very alert and his voice excessively polite. 'And you couldn't know about the slight catch in this whole thing: that my brother was killed at Chambrettes-Ferme less than one mile away from his company, and that it was the company itself that stuck him there at the beginning of May with no relief until the day he was so fortunately killed.'

The two lawyers looked at him in surprise. Then it would be hard to understand, noted the judge advocate softly, why the file was sent to Ingolstadt. Porisch was a quicker thinker. 'Time is always of the essence,' he said in his hearty voice. 'Stick in with the orderly room chaps.'

Lieutenant Kroysing waved his long hand. 'Bravo. And then along came death – as Wilhelm Busch says.' The three men all knew the spare poetry and drawings of the eccentric humorist Wilhelm Busch, which depicted life's cruelties with equanimity.

Judge Advocate Mertens would have preferred to concentrate on the French painter Corot, whose poetically transfigured landscapes greatly appealed to him. But something untoward had happened here in his sector with his help – an irregularity with apparently fatal consequences. His pale face flushed and he requested both gentlemen's attention: had he understood everything correctly? He repeated the facts just established. 'If that is the case,' he added quietly, 'we cannot consider the matter to be closed. We shall have to pursue our enquiries.'

'Forgive me,' said Porisch, 'but if that is so, then a new offence has been committed, which requires a new file. We must bring charges for the deliberate killing of Sergeant Kroysing by— yes, by whom?'

All three were silent, suddenly realising how murky the incident was. Who would be charged? Was there evidence against anyone? What had actually happened? At what point had a criminal intention come into play? The exigences of service meant Sergeant Kroysing had to stick it out at Chambrettes-Ferme, just as Lieutenant Kroysing was sticking it out at Douaumont and tens of thousands of German soldiers were sticking it out in the trenches at the front. The war was a tireless consumer of men, each of whom was bound to his place by orders. Who could prove that the order that fettered young Kroysing had the murderous ulterior motive of extinguishing his 'case'? A misdemeanour on the part of the Third Company could be proved. But they could probably talk themselves out of it by saying that an inexperienced clerk had sent the files to Ingolstadt in good faith, where they had been expecting Sergeant Kroysing to turn up at any moment on a transport, as he was clearly absent from his company. The three men went over it all, talking back and forth. Sergeant Porisch's head was cleared of Brahms' sonatas, and Professor Carl Mertens forgot about Corot. Their attention was taken by the emerging fuzzy outlines of a wrong, possibly a crime. The guilty parties were well protected, covered by the demands of duty. How could they get to them? Well, they had to and they would. In any case, Lieutenant Kroysing now saw that he could count on these two men and the legal machinery behind them. He suddenly felt very strong.

'Gentlemen,' he said, looking gratefully from one to the other with a warm glow, a release almost, in his grey eyes, 'thank you. We'll rock this baby until it falls out of its cradle. I can already smell the need for a confession. Without a confession from the perpetrators, we cannot rehabilitate my brother. And I want to do that. I owe it to my parents and Uncle Franz, if not to the poor lad himself, who won't really give a damn, however much it pained him to go to his grave. I still have a last letter from him, which I haven't yet been able to read for technical reasons. Perhaps that voice from the grave will tell us who our adversaries are. And then I'll take care of the confession. How, I don't yet know. There is also a witness still alive. My brother asked an ASC man for help the day before he died. Unfortunately, I've so far neglected to find out his name. But I can easily dig it out. It seems my men were working on the railway with those same ASC men. We're neighbours in a way – everything revolves around the old man of Douaumont, where I live.'

Sergeant Porisch's eyes widened. 'Are you stationed at Douaumont, Lieutenant?' He fell back into official parlance with the shock of it. 'Can a man survive there?'

'As you see,' Eberhard Kroysing replied.

'Isn't it under constant attack from the French?'

'Not always,' answered Kroysing in his deep voice.

'But there's a constant stream of wounded and dead there, isn't there?'

Kroysing laughed. 'You get used to it. Nothing's happened to me yet.'

'The likes of us can't imagine what it must be like there.'

'Not great from your point of view, wonderful from mine. A fabulous stretch of churned up wasteland and old Douaumont right in the middle like the battered carapace of a giant turtle. We sit underneath and crawl out the neck hole to play in the sand. Pretty much. Besides, you probably imagine it's much more uncomfortable than it actually is. It'll hold out a bit longer, old Douaumont.'

'Under high-angle fire,' said Porisch softly.

'That too,' answered Lieutenant Kroysing lightly. 'You get used to it. But if anything serious happens to me, I'll appoint a successor or substitute and give you his name and address. This matter certainly shouldn't suffer because of that. Thank you, gentlemen,' he repeated, standing up. 'Now I have a little private war to wage in the midst of this great war. But then all of us continue to pursue our hobbies if there's time and it doesn't affect our duties. In the final analysis, I've still got to pay the Frogs back for my brother. You might almost say,' and his long, thin lips curled in a sneer, 'that I'm ahead of the game on that one: some little exploding mines, you know, a bit of gas, a few canister bombs and finally the blockhouses in Herbesbois that we smoked out with flame throwers. They have a lot of respect for our uniform over there. But thus far I've just been doing my professional duty. Now it's a bit more personal between me and them.' He pulled on his left glove, put on his helmet, gave the judge advocate then the NCO his bony hand, pulled on his right glove and said: 'Don't be surprised if you don't hear from me for a while, gentlemen. If I don't peg it, I'll definitely be in touch.' He then wished them a pleasant lunch and left.

The two men left behind looked at each other. 'He's quite a man,' said Porisch, summarising both their thoughts. 'I wouldn't like to be in the shoes of the man who betrayed his little brother.'

Judge Advocate Mertens gave his soft, blonde, scholarly head a delicate shake. 'Goodness gracious me,' he said, frowning, 'how men abuse each other.'

CHAPTER THREE

The demands of duty

LIEUTENANT KROYSING MOVED differently now on the stairs. He no longer jumped but walked, and with each step a plan took shape within him. He needed to proceed in a strictly official way, and that's what he would do. If the demands of duty had allowed the ASC bigwigs to bring Sergeant Kroysing down, then they would allow Lieutenant Kroysing to force a confession. None of those fellows were men. They looked like men but they were hollow and made of tin. You only had to squeeze them a little and their guts came out. Lieutenant Kroysing looked very much at ease as he slammed the brown oak door shut and almost inaudibly – a sign of great contentment – hummed a tune under his breath.

A lorry carrying two leather-clad drivers braked immediately when a gaunt officer in a steel helmet raised his maroon-gloved hand. The lieutenant was in luck. The lorry was from Lieutenant Psalter's depot at Damvillers, had delivered express goods for transport to Germany by train and was returning practically empty. Two heavily laden men returning from leave sitting on their crates hardly counted. The only problem was that they couldn't really offer the lieutenant a seat.

'Would you care to sit next to me for two minutes, Lieutenant?' asked the driver, an NCO from Cologne, judging by his accent. 'We've still to pick up some post bags. Then we'll be able to offer you a nice easy chair, Lieutenant.'

'Easy chair, that's a good one,' laughed Lieutenant Kroysing. 'Be keeping mothers' letters warm, will I?'

The driver grinned. He seemed all right to Kroysing. He certainly wasn't stationed in Montmédy. When the post bags had been loaded, Kroysing said he preferred to stay up front. These lorry drivers went everywhere. They knew all the roads, everywhere of any importance, the approaches to the firing line. They were seasoned men, as they say at sea, and although guarded with officers they were still prepared to chat, express opinions and have a laugh and a joke, all the while keeping their eyes on the light strip of road. Eberhard Kroysing roared with laughter, sometimes grinned to himself, rubbed his hands in glee and ripped his eyes open in astonishment, saying 'already?' when the lorry pulled up at the farm where Captain Lauber and the division's sapper headquarters were installed.

'A great laugh, Sergeant,' said Lieutenant Kroysing. 'And now it's back to the serious business of life.'

People knew Lieutenant Kroysing here and were impressed by him. The branches of the armed services were small worlds of their own with their own languages and secrets, living side by side in combat units. A sapper lieutenant stood out among infantrymen like a goat in a flock of sheep, but within the structure of his own branch, which started with the broad base of the frontline companies, went through battalion, brigade and division staff, and culminated in the sapper general back at St Martin, he was as much at home and in his proper place as any animal in its herd. Kroysing was hungry. He'd already accepted a sausage and pork fat sandwich from the lorry driver, and he was very happy when Captain Lauber began by inviting him to lunch. Lauber ate with his staff and a few other officers from the area, who had set up a small mess in an empty apartment. They were purely technical troops, radio operators and anti-aircraft specialists, about a dozen men, all deeply preoccupied by their work, well trained and responsible. Captain Lauber, a swarthy man from Württenberg who had served longest of any of them, had established a few house rules. Talking shop at lunchtime was forbidden, as were politics. More than half a bottle of wine was forbidden. Everything else was allowed. Differences in rank didn't matter, good manners were taken as read, and even staff sergeants were included – even Jewish ones.

Everyone in the services knew that the sappers, artillery men and technical troops in the German army all suffered from neglect. Compared to the cavalry and the infantry they were largely left to their own devices. No princes or noblemen served with them. They always got a raw deal during manoeuvres, and in peacetime their training and upkeep were underfunded. It was only in the first two years of the war that people had started to talk about how valuable sappers were. Who threw bridges over the Meuse under enemy fire? The sappers. Who cut pathways through wire entanglements before an attack armed with nothing but pliers while enemy guns lay in wait? Who pushed the fire trenches forwards and dug out positions in impossible locations, in limestone or in swamps? Who threw hand grenades as big and round as babies' heads? Who humped the bloody gas canisters around? Who carried still-smoking flame throwers on their backs through enemy fire, risking being burnt alive if a bullet hit them? Always the sappers. Sapper lieutenants such as Kroysing had been involved in innumerable attacks and had survived uninjured only by the grace of God. And what about the telephonists, who mended essential cables again and again under heavy French fire or serviced the listening apparatus in the forward fire trenches where the gunners slaved – until very recently they'd all been the army's stepchildren. More recently than that in the feudal regiments, where they were still too refined to have backsides.

Lunch passed pleasantly. Many of the men retired for a nap. Others drank their coffee. Captain Lauber invited his guest to a game of chess, as work didn't begin again until half past two. Eberhard Kroysing was an excellent chess player. The coffee tasted good and so did his cigar. He'd soon begin a game of chess with an unknown adversary and he'd be back in his lair before the Frogs fired over their evening blessing. Life was worth living.

The hot and cloudy August day hung oppressively over the rolling hilltops. Jackets unbuttoned, Captain Lauber and his guest strolled through the long, narrow fruit garden where farmers who'd now been displaced had once grown cider apples. Squat, leafy trees stood in the middle of a grassy patch, groaning under the weight of their green fruits. The captain said the trees fruited like that back home in Göppingen too, except the Swabian apples ripened red, those here yellow. That was the only difference. And for that they were at war with each other.

Eberhard Kroysing was enjoying the company of this intelligent superior officer. He had to curb his stride beside the shorter man but was happy to do so. The captain said it was much better to discuss things in the open under the flitting shadow of the leaves than in the low-ceilinged farm house. No one could deny that, said Kroysing. The captain replied that he must have the initials O.C. for Sapper Officer Commanding after his name to talk like that. An ordinary lieutenant wouldn't dare. Even a lieutenant can think, said Kroysing. Even as a soldier he'd learnt that – especially as a soldier.

'Not many did,' snarled Captain Lauber. His short-cropped hair was greying at the temples and he was going on top. He waved away the persistent flies attacking his bald patch and asked how things were at the front. No beating about the bush. The short, sharp truth between men. He wanted to know that first before Lieutenant Kroysing unpacked his own troubles.

Eberhard Kroysing shrugged his shoulders. His own troubles? He didn't have any. It was precisely in order to tell the short, sharp truth that he'd come. The infantry needed help. Those poor dogs didn't have much to laugh about. Their so-called positions in shell holes and rifle pits extended across the valley, usually overlooked from right or left, and were the object of frantic fighting. The French had attacked 30 times, and the Germans had repulsed them 30 times or more, with the sappers always alongside. But they wouldn't get any further now. August was drawing to a close. They had six to eight weeks left at best. Then a new enemy would attack the men: rain.

They paced up and down, with Kroysing always on the captain's left, switching round at each turn. His relatively long hair was damp with sweat, and he dried it with his hand, wiping his hand on his jodhpurs before speaking again. Anyone who, like him, had been deployed here since the beginning of January and had seen the clayey ground transformed into a boundless morass knew the score. The fighting troops' morale was now being corroded by the savage bombardments, appalling losses and the ongoing stalemate in battle. They couldn't fetch food or move ammunition without men being killed or wounded. Attempts to relieve the troops or advance in larger groups left the men scattered, decimated or with shattered nerves. They didn't even have a decent shelter to sleep in. The only safe place in the whole area remained Old Uncle Douaumont. Even if the Frogs had a go at it, it was now 3km behind the actual front, and those 3km made all the difference. But what would happen when the rain came? How would they hold out?

Captain Lauber snorted. 'Hmm,' he said. 'I see.'

Kroysing's didactic tone and forceful manner sparked resistance in him. But he was a fair-minded man. Without detailed knowledge of every fold of the terrain and advice from the officers in the trenches, the high-ups had nothing on which to base their decisions. For they stayed at the rear: the higher up they were, the further back they stayed. In this respect, the approach of Hannibal and Caesar had been far superior to that taken in these glorious times.

'What do you suggest, young man? Tell me straight and don't sugar the pill.'

'Strengthening the garrison at Douaumont by an entire ASC battalion,' replied Kroysing indifferently. He was deep in thought, his eyes on the tip of his shoe, which played with a fallen apple full of worms. Douaumont was big and safe, and had plenty of room. Not a single crack in the casemate or the vaulting over the long passageways. Only the top parts had been demolished: the brickwork, supports, surrounds and earthworks. The concrete had held. It had taken at least 2,000 heavy shells, maybe even 3,000, since 21 February. Hats off to French civil engineering.

Captain Lauber puffed fiercely on his pipe. He'd have to look into it. It was his area. He himself was a civil engineer in uniform. He'd been in Douaumont three times but only ever in the yards and in the eastern armoured tower, never below. Had Lieutenant Kroysing ever measured the thickness of the vaulting? Kroysing shook his head. The weather had never been settled enough for that – too much metal in the air. But he reckoned the concrete ceiling was easily 3m thick. It would make a good impression if the captain came to inspect the depot administered by his sappers and took a few measurements while he was at it.

Captain Lauber's eyes flashed. It was a very good idea to stick another hundred sappers in Douaumont to relieve the fighting troops. With their own staff, company and battalion commanders, naturally. There were lots of gentlemen sitting about behind the lines, leading a nice life, who had no idea what a cushy number God had given them. At the same time, their men had long since turned into fully functioning front-line soldiers. They hauled barbed wire, trench props and ammunition like sappers, and dug trenches and came under fire almost like infantrymen.

Eberhard Kroysing listened with malicious enjoyment. He couldn't have put it better himself. Did Captain Lauber have a particular person in his sights? Whom did he want rid of? He surely wouldn't let on. The higher-up gentlemen liked to play their cards close to their chests.

(As it happened, Captain Lauber's discerning eye had lit on Herr Jansch, politician and braggart, whom he'd already removed from Lille – lit on him and moved on. Wouldn't work this time, more was the pity. The artillery – his friend Reinhard – needed the men. Shame.)

Kroysing was almost there. 'I'm thinking of a Bavarian battalion that my men are working with,' he said. 'Their headquarters is in Mangiennes, and the company is a little further forward – or perhaps I should say less far back.' He effortlessly plucked an apple from a fairly high branch, tossed it in the air and caught it again, before adding that some of them were in any case posted as reserve troops within range of the fort in the direction of Pepper ridge and could stay there. Most of them, however, would need to spend all of the coming weeks building dry dugouts with pumps and drains on the higher slopes. 'We'll get in touch with the infantry to tell them where the best spots are within eight days. In the meantime, you could put through a request for the Niggl battalion, Captain, and perhaps tempt the staff with the notion of medals and decorations.'

'That'll shut them up and make them obey,' said Captain Lauber. There was already bad blood between the battle-hardened soldiers at the front and the HQ behind the lines, which had expanded as if it were peacetime. What were men to think who'd spent four or five months being hustled back and forwards at the front, been withdrawn battle-weary and redeployed when refreshed, if they had a look round the communications zone and saw how they lived there? 'The likes of us would know how to lift the troops' morale. But it's better not to think about it too much.'

The two officers looked at each other. Of course it was better to keep quiet about such things. They thought about the Commander-in-Chief, the Kaiser's son and heir to the throne, who had on occasion turned up in tennis whites when fighting units where marching to the front and waved at them with his racket. Such scenes had been photographed and hawked to the newspapers, and a lot of officers found them perplexing.

Captain Lauber sighed. He was a good soldier, prepared to put everything he had on a German victory. Lieutenant Kroysing was taking his leave now, and that was right and proper. He should of course have the car, which would take him as close as it could to his foxhole. Large parts of the area were under long-range fire.

When Captain Niggl received his death sentence, written on an ordinary piece of paper, to the effect that he would be swapping his comfortable billet in Mangiennes for Douaumont, he thought at first he must have read it wrong. An ASC battalion has no adjutants or staff – just a sergeant major and a couple of clerks to handle its business. Furthermore, Herr Niggl was a Royal Bavarian official and so he liked to be the first to see the battalion's incoming mail. He sat there in his comfortable house jacket, which could hardly be called a uniform, at one with God, his namesake Saint Aloysius and himself, and stared at the half sheet of draft paper, which was signed by Captain Lauber in Damvillers on behalf of the Sappers GOC and sent him, Niggl, to his death. *What in buggery is this supposed to mean?* he thought, clasping his heart – his beer-fattened, Bavarian heart from Weilheim. It was bloody ridiculous. He was a captain in the Imperial Reserve and a father with two minor children to look after and a vivacious wife, Kreszenzia, née Hornschuh. There must be some mistake. That often happened in war. People were people and they could easily make mistakes. Nonetheless, he thought he'd better go to see Captain Lauber. He knew the Württemberg man. He'd sort it out with him. He folded the order up, put it in his worn, deerskin wallet and put the wallet in his trouser pocket. No need for anyone to see it just yet. It was easier to deflect danger if you hadn't talked about it.

He drove there in a state of forced calm. Above his fat cheeks, his shrewd eyes wore a rather assured look. He returned as a man who had seen the serious side of life. That Swabian bastard Lauber had gone puce with anger, the miserable noodle muncher. He'd asked him who he thought he was, if he was there to serve the state or to brighten the place up. Captain Niggl wasn't really handsome enough for that. And did he think he was the only father in the German army? He told him not bring shame on his men, to keep a stiff upper lip and set a good example to his honest ASC men. Soldiers fought quite differently when they saw that their superior officers, who were raking it in each month, at least put themselves in danger too. He would set out the day after next at 3am with his Third Company. The sapper depot at Douaumont would send him guides. From now on he was answerable to the depot. He'd be signed over to the 10th Army Corps and be part of the garrison at Douaumont. He would now have the opportunity to excel and experience life. Besides, the war wasn't about to end, and there was no life insurance policy for any German officer regardless of whether he was in Mangiennes, Damvillers or Douaumont. The Fourth Company would stay behind and take charge of the railway troops, but the First and Second Companies would follow when the works required. The works: dry dugouts for the infantry, which constituted the backbone of any defence and might earn him a medal.

Yes, there was nothing for it. He, Alois Niggl, from Weilheim in Upper Bavaria, was going to have to cave in and play the hero.

Pale moonlight. The crescent moon was in its second quarter and didn't rise until close to midnight. In deep silence, three columns of ASC men moved through Spincourt wood, heavily laden with haversacks, entrenching tools, packages and boxes. They knew the roads, having kept them in good repair. The wood, made up of beeches growing on damp soil, was amazingly dense, torn up in some places by shellfire and undamaged in others, depending on the twists and turns of the front and the artillery positions. The men looked pale. Some of their mouths were quivering so much they couldn't smoke. Many of the country boys said a rosary. Only a couple of urban big mouths talked like they didn't care. Hill 310 hadn't yet appeared on the horizon. They were to meet the guides beneath it at the junction with the road to Bezonvaux at 3am. Every man in that marching column wanted to drag out the time until then – to lengthen every minute and insert new units of time. No one was enjoying the change of scene or the damp, fresh air after the heat. They imagined Douaumont to be a kind of fire-spitting mountain and believed they would now disappear inside its bowels. There were also rumours about a gigantic explosion that had finished off over a thousand men, no one knew how. The sappers who'd been there before, with whom they'd now be dossing down, had told them about that. Many of them had pretended to know further details, including the fact that it could happen again any day. A whole battalion wiped out, the sappers said. It didn't encourage the men to put one foot in front of another.

By 3am their eyes had long since adjusted to the gloaming. They'd been sitting at the roadside for half an hour on boxes and bulging rucksacks each filled with two rolled-up mats, a coat and lace-up boots. They listened dully to the racket wafting over from the other side of Hill 310. On the top, dim white and red lights danced and flickered. Then three slim figures appeared, armed only with steel helmets and gas mask cylinders, carrying walking sticks made from branches. They eyed the ASC men's enormous packs with sympathy. An NCO reported to Captain Niggl, who'd already sent his horse back. The sappers took position at the heads of the three columns, and the men marched off in single file along well-trodden footpaths. The dark sky was reflected in the shell holes. The ASC men trudged on one step at a time, leaning on their spades. The sappers exuded calm. No need to worry, they said. There'd be nothing doing at this hour. The German infantry had had enough. The Frogs had got sick of it long ago. And the dead who lay decaying outside Souville, by the battlements at Thiaumont and around the ruins at Fleury weren't about to bite anyone. The path led downhill into a broad depression, where they briefly had a view of the horizon dimly lit by flares. Machine gun fire rattled away like the hammering of sewing machines. The men at the back were having to puff and stumble to keep up and avoid being overtaken by daylight. The night wind carried sweet and terrible smells. Formless patches of blackness intensified the darkness around them. Slanting moonlight filled the shell holes with light and shadow. Then a soaring peak loomed up, obscuring the view. The men climbed its flank, shivering in the first breath of morning air. That's Hill 388, the sappers said. The long, shell-pitted rampart, which was no longer a rampart, was still called Fort Douaumont. A tall figure with his cap pushed back on his head stood in the shadow of the great arched doorway, whose shattered masonry was patched up with sandbags. His avid eyes scrutinised the approaching column.

What smells did the men's reluctant noses pick up? Disintegrating masonry. Human excrement. Spent ammunition. Dried blood.

BOOK THREE

Inside the hollow mountain

CHAPTER ONE

Wild Boar gorge

THE MEUSE HILLS descended from left and right to the winding river like a herd of horses stretching their necks to drink in water. They began as outliers of the Argonne, rolling or tabletop hills running from west to east. The land was green. Green and crossed by streams, so that the valleys were full of marshy woodland. Between tall beeches, alder and ash, ducks nested and wild boar rooted about in the blossoming shrubs and briers of the undergrowth. Villages had grown up around the few tracks on the cleared uplands. There were mills by the streams, and the skilled and industrious Lorraine peasants grew fruit and corn, and raised cattle and horses. The land between the Moselle and the Meuse had been fecund and productive for a thousand years. Celts, Romans and Franks had cultivated it, and it was favourably situated beside the green and white lands of Champagne.

The city of Verdun had watched over the crossing where the Meuse forked and formed a natural fortress for 1,500 years. The citadel sat above old churches and monasteries with formal round windows and devout pointed arches. The streets bustled with the kind of life typically found in small French towns that work with the produce of a fertile landscape. Around 15,000 people lived from their handiwork and ingenuity, born of long-standing civilisation. They produced embroidery, sweets and linen goods, smelted metal, and built machines and furniture. They fished in the river, prayed at altars decked with flowers, drank aperitifs and coffee, dressed up for weddings, and let their blonde and dark-haired children play in the streets and courtyards.

The city was surrounded by a ring of several lines of entrenched forts, some modern, some older. The total width was more than 15km, the circumference over 50km. For across from the city, far off to the east and yet threateningly close, rose the colossus of the German Reich, which glorified war. The fortress of Verdun had known German guns and spiked helmets in 1792 and 1870. In 1914, the city was threatened with a third attack. It was averted by the French army's victory at the Marne, and by the help of the British and the Maid of

Orleans, who loved her home village of nearby Domrémy.

On 21 February 1916, after thorough preparation, shells fell howling into the city's streets, killing residents, splintering children's skulls and throwing old women down stairs. Fire. Smoke. Uproar. Havoc. Aircraft dropped whistling bombs on the areas the long-range guns couldn't reach. Over a thousand guns, among them 700 heavy guns including the heaviest available, spat cloudbursts of explosive steel on to the target area: a 30 km wide arc on the right bank the Meuse, the eastern bank, open to the south-west between Consenvoye and the Woevre plain. Then the German divisions burst out of holes and trenches full of icy mud for the attack. It was a surprise attack, and the Germans were counting on that, but the Posen grenadiers and the Thuringian reserves and the men from the Mark, Hesse, Westphalia and Lower Silesia met resistance wherever they went. Resistance from the earth, softened by snow, and from the water-logged shell holes. Resistance from the woods, which became silent clusters of auxiliaries, chained together like ancient warriors by creepers, brambles and briers that never tired. Resistance from entrenched field positions, blockhouses and barbed wire. Resistance from the French infantry, riflemen and gunners. After the first four days, the first week, the world knew that the surprise attack on Verdun had failed. Six army corps, nearly 200,000 Germans, had led the assault, and it had not been enough. The fall of Fort Douaumont made the world sit up and listen and gave the Germans a sense of victory, but victory was not theirs. The Fortress at Verdun was not to be taken by surprise attack.

The Germans refused to capitulate in the face of this outcome. Their troops had performed feats that surpassed the legends of centuries. They'd stormed woods, taken hill ridges, cleared blockhouses and driven the enemy out of the ravines. They'd stood up under the leaden hail of shrapnel and the steel knives of shell splinters, and then, angry and dogged and full of hate and a sense of self-sacrifice, they'd drilled their bayonets into French bodies and hurled their hand grenades. From the Souville ridge beyond Douaumont, their advance troops had glimpsed the roofs of the Verdun suburbs. One more push, the commanders said, and we'll have them. They said it in March, in April, in May and June and until the end of July, and then they didn't say it any more. The troops didn't know why they hadn't advanced. They were replaced then redeployed. Hordes and hordes of men were lost and replenished with ever younger men. It wasn't their fault that the fortress at Verdun held. They left their shattered lines at the ordained time. When ordered to do so, the sweating gunners, half deafened by their own detonations, fired. When ordered to do so, the infantry threw themselves at the French shell holes and trenches in the way they'd been taught and captured them. They raged amongst French flesh and blood, and gave of their own flesh and blood, their sweat and nerves, brains, courage and presence of mind. They'd all been told that they were defending their homeland and they believed it. They'd also been told that the French were exhausted and they'd believed that – just one last effort, one more push. They made that effort; they pushed forward once again. Orderlies fell bringing rations, lorry drivers were killed in their cabs, and the gunners worked under counter-fire. New troops were brought in to take up the charge: Bavarian divisions, Prussian guards, infantry from Württemberg, regiments from Baden and Upper Silesia. Then they finally realised that it wasn't working. Who had made mistakes? Who was to blame? More and more missiles had been hurled, and more and more men had been torn to pieces, killed, mutilated, taken prisoner or were missing. The defence of Verdun cost the French army a quarter of a million men, including nearly 7,000 officers. The Germans lost even more. The pretty villages were turned first to ruins, then piles of rubble and finally brickworks; the woods went from having gaps and tangles to being a battlefield full of white stumps, then a wasteland. And this wasteland stretched from Flabas and Moirey to beyond the village of Souville, over hills and through gorges on both banks of the Meuse. It was a white-flecked lunar landscape across its length and breadth, the colour of the dessert, full of round holes. But protected by its heavily damaged fort, the city of Verdun stood. There were attacks and counter-attacks, and the war rumbled on around it.

During August, ASC Private Bertin had come to feel quite at home in these ravaged spots that were still called Fosses wood, Chaume wood and Wavrille wood on the map. He had changed a lot since the beginning of July. He often looked unshaven, even bristly. His whole face was now deeply tanned and tighter. His mouth no longer fell open so easily, and behind his glasses his eyes had taken on a thoughtful, more mature look, for in the past two months he'd been plunged, much against his will, into a stampede of events. It bothered him, and the many thoughts he'd had about Kroysing's disappearance had altered him, as had the sight of the never-ending fields of felled trees, which he'd become so used to that his feet instinctively avoided the countless steel splinters. This best of worlds here revealed a flaw in the system, and the glorified necessities of existence on earth came to seem rather odd. He'd come under fire on various occasions and had run away from shells and shrapnel, and into them as well. He relied on luck. But now it had somehow been ordained that he should have an encounter with something much different – and much hairier – before he realised what was what in the world.

One day, in the middle of Fosses wood he heard his name being called from the far end of a valley. He was kneeling at the time, screwing a couple of rails on to a railway track that would allow ammunition to be transported to the 15cm siege guns. Startled, he shouted: 'Over here!'

A young lad, an NCO and sapper with a tattered Iron Cross ribbon in his buttonhole, strolled towards him with his hands in his pockets and gave him a questioning look. Above a childish nose, the lad's eyes twinkled in his long face like the piercing eyes of an animal. Yes, little Sergeant Süßmann resembled nothing more than a small knowing monkey that appears every couple of days, has a look around, then disappears again. His puttees had been put on carelessly, and he wasn't wearing a belt. With a cigarette in the corner of his mouth, he squatted down beside Bertin.

'It wasn't easy to find you,' he said.

'Well, you have,' said Bertin. 'I can't screw it any tighter.'

It was good that he'd learnt how to use all sorts of tools in his father's joinery workshop. As a result, he was considered not to be inept. Sergeant Süßmann gave it a try. The fishplate sat right across the two sleepers.

'All right,' he said in English. 'But I didn't come for that. I'm to take you to the lieutenant.'

'Which one?' asked Bertin.

'Mine, of course; Lieutenant Kroysing. It really wasn't easy to find you. You didn't give him your name.'

Bertin stood up. 'Are you one of his men?'

'But of course.'

They moved to the next section of track, taking the fishplates and nuts out of a sack. 'It doesn't do your hands much good,' Bertin said, looking at his fingers, 'but it's better than being stuck in an orderly room.' He knelt on the ground; Süßmann screwed down the other fishplate as if he weren't his 'superior'. Autumnal leaves drifted above their heads on a gust of wind. 'And what does he think about his brother now – in case you happen to know?'

'He's consumed with regret,' replied Süßmann. 'Apparently, he's quite certain of a few things otherwise his brother's company and battalion staff wouldn't be at Douaumont now.'

Bertin looked at him uncomprehendingly. 'Captain Niggl?'

'Now inhabits Douaumont. Coincidence. Douaumont is a large garrison. In my father's house there are many mansions. Now the lieutenant wants to know if you'd like to be there when that letter is read.'

'But what about my company?' Bertin asked uncertainly.

Sergeant Süßmann spat out his cigarette end. 'Lieutenant Kroysing is a big noise in these parts, and the further towards the front you go, the bigger a noise he becomes. Even the Panjes of this world know that. The only question is whether you have the guts. Douaumont and its approach routes are considered calm now, but our definition of calm is different from yours.'

'How do you know?' countered Bertin. 'Before I used to be keen to distinguish myself. But now after 15 months in the Prussian Army—' They both laughed. The 'old guard' with their caps pulled low and their easy stride preferred to throw themselves in the mud once too often than once too seldom. 'If need be, I'm sure I can manage in your area. But how do I get there?'

'We'll ask for you,' Süßmann replied simply, explaining what they had planned for Bertin. All the field railways in the area – and there were quite a few – were run by the sapper depot. Some of the workforce was billeted in dugouts, some in Nissen huts. They'd had nothing to laugh about throughout August, but things had calmed down now and as a result they were on holiday. A railway hut in Wild Boar gorge, which was east of Bezonvaux and not far from the Ornes heavy artillery batteries ('And it's always safe as houses where they are'), needed a temporary telephonist. They'd asked Bertin's company to supply one, and the man they'd sent – a deaf carpenter, who was scared to death of the switchboard with its measly eight plugs – had been sent back. Bertin bent over laughing. So he had; it was Karsch the carpenter. And it wasn't as if there weren't plenty of intelligent men in the company.

'But you won't get me,' Bertin said. 'They don't transfer Jews. That's against the laws of nature.'

'That's no laughing matter,' Sergeant Süßmann rebuked him. 'Every Jew should defend the equal rights of all Jews at every turn.'

'Defend them to Jansch and his gang,' said Bertin, frowning. 'There are 10 Jews in the company, and none of us is in the orderly room. Major Jansch is what's called a nationalist editor.'

'That won't do him any good,' said Süßmann contemptuously. 'Kroysing will ask for you. You and no one else. A fortnight in a little hut in the middle of the wood. On duty for eight hours, your own master for 16.'

'Done,' said Bertin.

'Take 15,' shouted Sergeant Böhne. ASC men appeared from all sides with canteens, drinking cups and swinging haversacks (only the gas masks in their little tin canisters were never taken off; gas shells were used a lot). Bertin walked over to his tunic, which was hanging from a shell splinter sticking out of a beech tree at the height of a man. Süßmann stuck by him. As they walked, Bertin asked him if the hut came under fire much. Süßmann shook his head. The hut itself never got shot at; that was why it had been put in that out-of-the-way spot. However, 60 paces to the left and 100m to the right you came into range of the French. They'd made the most of that, but since the Bavarians had captured the Fumin and Le Chapitre woods and the Alpine Corps had attacked Thiaumont, the French batteries had slipped back. From his haversack, Bertin took some of his bread ration, a knife and a tin of artificial honey, a yellowish spread made from sugar. He offered some to Süßmann, who shook his head.

'I prefer a hot breakfast,' he said, lighting another cigarette. 'No butter?' he asked. 'No lard substitute?' (Lard substitute was the name of a tasty conserve made from the fat and flesh of pigs' stomachs.)

'Not for us,' said Bertin.

'With us you'll get everything. Compared to what you're used to, Douaumont is luxury.'

'How far is it?' Bertin asked.

'If "they" don't shoot, three-quarters of an hour. If they start shooting, you'll have to lie down until they stop. And never forget your gas mask.'

'We've got used to eating some strange things, we Jews,' said Bertin, chewing away.

Süßmann smoked. 'Even before, I ate everything.'

'So did I,' said Bertin. 'But that didn't include lard substitute.'

'Pretty soon we'll be licking our fingers after eating it,' said Süßmann. 'Things are going to get serious this winter.'

'How old are you, Sergeant Süßmann, if I may ask?'

'Forced my way into the sappers as a volunteer at 16 and a half. Work it out.'

Bertin propped his open knife against his knee and stopped chewing. 'Good grief. I took you for 25.'

Süßmann grinned. 'I've seen a lot. I'll tell you about it later. So, you'll be asked for and you'll set off early tomorrow morning. Ring us about 6am. We have a direct connection to you, if it hasn't been shot to pieces. Kroysing will be pleased. He seems to think highly of you because you believed his brother straight away.'

Bertin shook his head. 'It wasn't hard to believe him. Only a brother could be so blind.'

'I'll split then,' said Süßmann in Berlinerisch, straightening his tunic.

Bertin was taken aback by his authentic Berlin dialect. 'Blimey. Sent you here from the Spree, did they?'

Süßman saluted. 'Yes, sir! Berlin W., Regentenstraße, Counsellor Süßmann. Tomorrow afternoon, then.' He nodded and strolled off, disappearing between the tree trunks. Bertin looked after him in amazement, then lay down on the warm trampled earth of the woodland floor, chewed his sweetened black bread, looked up into the blue sky and drew contentedly on a company cigar. And as he let the gold-tinged heavens seep into him with something like joy, he considered that up until now nothing had been imposed on him that he couldn't handle. He was still kidding himself; the war had not yet punched him in the face the way it had poor little Kroysing. You had to take your hat off to the older brother, who'd managed to manoeuvre those skilful gentlemen into his patch by their own methods. Life was a roller-coaster. The war had brought him ever closer to himself. Next stop Wild Boar gorge, then. After that Douaumont. That was fine by him. A writer shouldn't dodge fate's trawler nets. His eyes closed. He saw silver fish, their stupid mouths hanging open, swimming in the blue sea, all in the same direction. His hand holding the cigar fell to the ground. Nothing could happen to him. Nothing could happen to the fish either. He fell asleep.

The following day at 2pm, Private Bertin reported to his orderly room ready to march. It'd been thought important to smarten him up. He'd been given a belt, which held the lad together, and one of those grey oil-cloth caps with a badge and a brass cross that until then had been lying around in some Prussian warehouse or other.

It's hot in France at the end of August. Acting Sergeant Major Glinsky wanted to sleep, but he couldn't deny himself the pleasure of bestowing a parting blessing on Private Bertin. Open-collared and looking replete, Glinsky blinked as he circumambulated Bertin's rigid figure. Everything was in order: grey trousers tucked into blackened boots, infantry tunic, rucksack packed impeccably, one boot to the right and one to the left under the rolled-up coat and folded blankets. He sat down astride a chair, all friendliness. He knew and Bertin knew that if the order had taken him to a village behind the lines, the company would have tried to snatch him back even though he'd been requested by name. But it took him to the front, and life is ruled by chance. If the sappers wanted this particular man as a telephonist, they were most welcome to him. The company had no contact with the sappers and therefore didn't know who had made the request. Cooperation between the two units happened exclusively through the artillery depot – an arrangement that was jealously guarded – where nothing was known of what had happened to the Kroysing family.

'At ease,' said Acting Sergeant Major Glinsky. 'You're an educated man, so I need not waste words.' (*Oh no*, thought Bertin, *he's buttering me up. What's he planning?*) 'You have many mistakes to atone for, so we hope you'll make a good fist of things.'

Bertin adopted a military bearing and said: 'Yes, indeed, Acting Sergeant Major.' But even as he spoke these obedient words, he resolved to get a little dig in by mentioning the hospital leave to Billy that Glinsky had refused him.

'It's quite a nice little perk to spend 14 days at a switchboard,' Glinsky continued chummily. 'Just make sure you come back to us in one piece. Your post will be sent on. I assume we have your home address?'

Ah, though Bertin, almost amused, *he's scratching around now, poor soul.* Because what he meant by this last question was: who should receive the bad news should anything happen to him? Bertin acted daft and looked unconcerned. 'Yes, indeed, Sergeant Major,' he said cheerfully and waited for his moment.

'It must be a good friend of yours who got you this nice little posting,' Glinsky went on, winking confidentially. 'Sergeant Süßmann, wasn't it?'

This question had a sting to it as well – the insinuation was that a Jew always looks out for another Jew, at least that was the opinion men like Glinsky had of Jews.

But this was Bertin's cue. 'No,' he said, looking evenly into Glinsky's eyes – those sleepy, grey bulldog eyes. 'I assume it was Lieutenant Kroysing from the sapper depot at Douaumont who arranged it.'

That hit the mark. Still riding on the chair, his mouth fell open. 'What's the lieutenant's name?' he asked.

'Kroysing,' Bertin repeated readily. 'Eberhard Kroysing. He's the brother of a young NCO who met his maker in mid-July.'

'And he's in command at Douaumont?' Glinsky asked, still stunned.

'Certainly not, Sergeant Major,' Bertin answered. 'Only of the sapper unit attached to it.'

He didn't need to say more. Glinsky was quick on the uptake. There had been something funny about the transfer of the Bavarian ASC men to Douaumont (which, naturally enough, had got about), and this explained it, albeit in the most unsettling and unclear way. His expression darkened. 'Forward march!' he snarled suddenly. 'Dismissed! You'll have to work out how to get there yourself.'

Bertin about-turned and left the orderly room feeling very satisfied. He'd long since worked out how to get where he was going: with the drivers who brought the short, fat 21cm shells to the howitzer guns in the Ornes valley.

(Naturally, no one knew why the 1/X/20's rations improved so much after Bertin left: butter and Dutch cheese, big chunks of meat at lunch – magic! And this wonderful state of affairs lasted fully five days. On the sixth and seventh, it tailed off, and on the eighth the old menu took hold again as if nothing had happened: gristle in 'barbed wire', dried vegetables and the turnip jam known as Fat for Heroes.)

At 2.10pm, Bertin laid his rucksack down on the wooden floor of the telephone room at the artillery depot, so that his new duties could be explained to him. The telephonists from the Steinbergquell ammunitions depot were all very pleasant. They'd been worried for days that one of them would have to provide leave cover for the operator at Wild Boar gorge; they knew the score. That someone else now had to go out to that dreadful place where shells were always falling filled them with gratitude.

'Oh, it's child's play, comrade' they explained. 'You've got your eight switches for the stations in front and behind of you – for the sapper depot, the next exchange and the artillery group – and your new comrades will show you how to use the plugs in two minutes. And it's not dangerous at all because if the cable gets shot up, other men have to go out to mend it.' They kindly didn't tell him that as the newcomer he might have to run to the sapper depot and tell them that the cable had been shot up.

'And there are men from your part of the world nearby – Upper Silesians,' said the telephonist Otto Schneider.

Bertin wasn't particularly attached to men from his part of the world. He had more in common with Bavarians and men from Berlin and Hamburg. He only took an interest in one Silesian regiment: the 57th, which was on active service and where his little brother served. The day before yesterday, he'd received another letter from his mother. The fear that Fritz Bertin might be no more pulsated behind her faint handwriting. The lad had already been wounded once the previous autumn.

About 3pm, a message was sent up that the short 21cm shells had been loaded up. Bertin swung his rucksack on to one shoulder, took his knotty stick in his hand and ran downstairs, cheerfully parrying the curious, mocking shouts from his closer friends in the Third Company. Oddly enough, everyone was in clover that day; those who were staying behind were glad to be staying behind, and Bertin was glad he was going.

The Silesian gunners, bony men with strained faces, didn't stand on ceremony. 'Chuck your pack on top of the pots and let's get going, lad,' they said with their hard r's and high-pitched vowels. Bertin hid his disappointment. He hadn't bargained with having to help push the loaded trucks. But as he looked in some annoyance at the stubby, pointed shells lying there like chubby babies, he realised something: Glinsky had made no impression on him – he was neither confused nor worried. Something quite new and brilliant!

The track that formed the gunners' route forked off to the east in the middle of a desolate valley floor. Wild Boar gorge opened off the the right, they said. It was the third one along and quite narrow, easily recognisable by all its greenery. He'd find it. Despite his rucksack and tunic, Bertin walked very quickly. For the first time, he found himself alone under the open sky in the flashing sunlight. Death might crash down upon him at any moment from the summer air. He had to summon all his courage. He cursed his stupidity for following this order simply because he wanted Eberhard Kroysing to have a good opinion of him. Footprints everywhere between the shell holes. Who wouldn't get lost here? Sweat stuck to the lenses of his glasses, and his hands shook as he cleaned them. The deathly silence frightened him; every sound that wafted over the ridge frightened him; when a plane appeared up above, he felt like throwing himself to the ground – he was too short-sighted to make out if it was German or French. He scurried on, teeth clenched on his pipe, pursued by his humpbacked shadow, just as one of his forebears might have dragged his wares from farm to farm in the mountains of Austrian Silesia in the time of the empress Maria Theresa. He counted the openings in the land ahead: one was already behind him, there was one opposite and two shimmered in the sunlight ahead. He looked at his watch as if that might help him. His heart thumped wildly on account of his load and from loneliness. If he hadn't been thoroughly used to crushing his internal demons, he would've turned round and not carried out his orders. He rested briefly at the edge of the next shell hole, drank a couple of slugs of lukewarm coffee from his canteen, relit his pipe and forced himself to breathe calmly. At last he was steeped in solitude – as he'd longed to be. He cursed himself and called himself an ass. He was like a peasant from the countryside blundering about in the bustle of city traffic for the first time. The peasant is frightened of the cars, trams and hurrying people and doesn't dare to ask his way. He feels like he's fallen to earth from the moon and when he finally does open his mouth, he finds he's already at his destination. Bertin narrowed his eyes and shaded them with his hands. That there, diagonally to the right, could be the opening of Wild Boar gorge. He set off at a trot, bounding up the hillside then slowing down on the valley floor. A tangle of green beckoned to him. The chopped and scattered remains of felled trees with terrible butchered trunks covered the slope to his right. Pale, yellowed leaves covered the branches and bisected crowns. A profusion of young shoots, dried rose hips and beech saplings that soared like flag poles pushed through them above shell holes as white as bones. A German bombardment must have caused this. The slope was open to the north. The southern side had been similarly ravaged by the French. There the mown down trees had larger, greener leaves and were piled up horizontally.

Suddenly a sign with an arrow rose up in front of him: 'Wild Boar gorge! Lower reaches may be subject to enemy observation'. Bloody hell, he thought and feeling relieved and worried at the same time, he set off at a trot through the fallen trees and found a footpath. A few minutes later, something screamed past. He was down before he knew it, pressed against a beech tree with his rucksack thumping into the nape of his neck. A dull thud on the hillside behind him, then a second. He waited. No explosion. Duds, he thought with relief. The French were using new American ammunition, and it was useless. The howling of the shells alone, that desolate, ripping sound, had got to him this time, and he hurried on, his hands filthy from the swampy ground. The dead trees struck him as unearthly. How would this destruction of nature ever be made good? A minute later, the valley took a turn: pristine wood, primaeval.

He was surrounded by green and shadows. Birds called in the beech tops. Bundles of young shoots as thin as fingers or children's arms rose up beside the sun-dappled tree trunks high enough to open their leaves to the light. Bramble bushes spread out their tendrils, heaving with late flowers and pink and reddish black fruits. The steep slope shone green with the sword-shaped leaves of the lily of the valley. Hawthorn and barberry bushes intertwined, and the feathery bracken fluttered above the moss and stones. It was amazing— like a mountain wood on a holiday walk at home. It was wonderful to sit there with his rucksack propped against a stone and his stick between his knees, free from thought, relaxed. The air among the tree trunks was cool and refreshing.

Five minutes later, Bertin again came across the light railway track, a branch line, and a blockhouse with a corrugated iron roof. At last! He reported military style to a corporal, a bearded man, who was sitting by the door cutting a stick.

'Ah, here you are,' the corporal said equably.

He had a Baden accent, as did his colleague, who came over, barefoot and in shirt-sleeves, pleased that the new third man had actually arrived. Bertin was asked if he could play skat – he could – and if he'd brought a lot of lice with him. They said he'd be able to keep clean there. Thank God, said Bertin.

At a push, the two reservists from the Landsturm could've managed alone. They only had one fear: being recalled. The telephone box, which was looked after by the railway service, did indeed only have eight switches, but someone had to stay awake day and night in case one of the switches dropped. Bertin checked over his new bed, hung his rucksack on the post, unrolled his blankets and unpacked his smaller items: washing things, writing things, smoking things and a picture of his wife in a small, round frame. This would be his home for the next fortnight.

Just before 6pm, he put a call through to the sapper depot at Douaumont at the suggestion of the corporal. He was called Friedrich Strumpf and he was a park-keeper in Schwetzingen, not far from Heidelberg. When Bertin spoke into the black mouthpiece and asked to report to Lieutenant Kroysing, the man from Baden looked at him suspiciously. The new boy seemed to have fancy friends. After a while, Sergeant Süßmann answered: the lieutenant sent his best wishes and he, Süßmann, would pick Bertin up at a convenient time the following afternoon. Happy working until then. 'Fine,' said Bertin. He then set about reassuring his new colleagues that he was an all right sort.

He offered the men from Baden a cigar, chatting away about how he'd swum in the river Neckar in 1914, and describing the castle grounds at Schwetzingen. They contained a mosque, didn't they, built by the prince-elector Karl Theodor? And beautiful birds kept in an aviary. There was also a Chinese pavilion and a little marble bath. After five minutes of this, he had won Strumpf the park-keeper's heart. Strumpf beamed. Soon he was showing Bertin a picture of his two children – a boy with a satchel and a 10-year-old girl holding a cat in her arms – and enlightening him about to the character of the third man, a freckled, sandy-haired tobacco worker from Heidelberg called Kilian. Kilian was quick-tempered and argumentative and didn't like to be contradicted but he was a good comrade when you knew how to take him.

That afternoon, Bertin learnt what his duties would be, which batteries were firing nearby, when the French shot and what their targets were, how the land lay. Douaumont was to the south-west, and to the north-east, behind them beyond the great depression, was the Ornes valley, and Bezonvaux, or what was called Bezonvaux, was practically due east. To their left, the French were attacking an artillery position, and three-quarters of an hour to the front were the field howitzers. They sometimes got post from them; they brought it past with their ammunition. If they didn't show up for a couple of days, you had to remind them. They were a dour lot, Poles from the Russian border, and when they spoke, the words clattered from their mouths like bricks, but their lieutenant was nice and bored to death over there. Schanz was his name.

Later when they were at their evening meal – tea with rum and toast with rashers of bacon – and Bertin was holding his sandwich skewered on a twig over the fire, a clamour sounded above the roof. Outside it began to boom, sing, roar, gurgle and rattle, fading away then returning again and again. The two men from Baden didn't even look up. It was just the 15cm guns' evening blessing on its way to Thiaumont and beyond. It was a repulsive, unnatural sound, whose deeply evil nature was instantly apparent. Private Bertin sat there deeply affected by it. What he heard wasn't the drone of a man-made implement whose purpose and use were determined by men. To him, it was as if an ancient force, a bit like an avalanche, roared out there, for which the laws of nature, not man, were responsible. The war, an operation instituted by men, still felt to him like a storm decreed by fate, an unleashing of powerful elements, unaccountable and beyond criticism.

CHAPTER TWO

A voice from the grave

SUDDENLY, THE FOLLOWING day at noon, Erich Süßmann was there, looking around with his piercing eyes and promising the men from Baden to send the newcomer back in time. Their route took them past the field howitzers. Great. They strode off like a couple of ramblers, crossed the light railway tracks and the stream on some planks, climbed up the slope through branches and bushes dappled with light and shade, turned into a gorge on the right, which was currently a mass of pulverised woodland, and followed a sort of cattle path halfway down the slope that led to the railway tracks in the valley. Sergeant Süßmann knew all these woods by name: they were in Moyemont, Vauche wood was further back, Hassoule with its ravines further on. Each one had literally cost streams of blood, German and French. They turned on to a narrow path, and Bertin grabbed Süßmann's shoulder. 'Look! A Frenchman!' A few feet from them was a blue-grey figure with his back to them. His steel helmet hung round the nape of his neck and he was pressed against a bush as though about to walk on.

Süßmann gave a short laugh. 'God, yes, the Frog. He signposts the way to the field howitzers. No need to be scared of him. He's deader than dead.'

'And no one has buried him?' asked Bertin in disgust.

'Where have you been living, dear chap? In the Bible probably and with Antigone. They needed a signpost here and took what came their way.' Bertin looked away as they walked past the murdered man, who was nailed to the truncated tree with a shell splinter like a sword. 'Heavy mortar,' said Süßmann.

Bertin felt ashamed in the presence of the dead man. He had an irrepressible urge to scatter earth on his helmet and shoulders, to atone for his death, to give him back to Mother Earth. His gaze sought out the ravaged face and desiccated hands. Good God, he thought, he might have been a young father. He might have carried his little son on those shoulders the last time he was home on leave. He trotted along silently beside Süßmann. Unexpectedly, they came upon piles of ammunition covered by greenish tarpaulins. To the left, the railway reappeared beneath their path. Shortly thereafter, the heavy barrel of a gun, whose mounting was wedged into the earth, reared up among the ruined trees. Only then did Bertin notice the overturned tree trunks bound together with wire cables, sandbagged and covered with canvas camouflage. A heap of useless iron in the form of spent cartridges rusted nearby. Someone called to them. Süßmann spoke to the guard, who was strolling around without a rifle, and learnt there was no post that day. Next day perhaps. The hard Upper Silesian dialect was unrecognisable on the lean soldier's stubbly lips.

At last the hillside to the fort towered above them like a mountain that had had part of it blown off. The earth: it was beyond Bertin's worst dreams. It bared its scabs and pus like a piece of leprous skin under the microscope. It was scorched and crumbling, and the remains of roots wormed through it like veins. A bundle of spoiled hand grenades lay in a shell hole. Of course, thought Bertin, the place had once been full of water. Scraps of cloth fluttered on a jumble of barbed wire – a sleeve with buttons, cartridge cases, the remains of a machine gun belt – and there were human excrement and tin boxes everywhere. But no bodies. In his relief he mentioned this to Süßmann, who waved a dismissive hand.

'There were plenty of dead bodies here at the beginning of April. Naturally, we couldn't let them stink away to their heart's content. We buried them in the big shell holes back there.'

'How long have you been here?' asked Bertin in astonishment.

'Forever,' laughed Süßmann. 'First we captured it, then came the rumpus inside the bowels of the place, then I was away for a few weeks and then I came back.'

'What do you mean by the "rumpus"?'

'The explosion,' answered Süßmann. 'I tell you, it's a strange world. I was practically dead, and that wasn't half as bad as being tormented by the question: why? Who are we doing all this for?' Bertin stopped to catch his breath. All the answers that drifted into his head seemed impossible. In this place, every word smacked of rank pathos. 'Yes, my young friend,' joked his little guide, 'even you don't know what to say to that. It always feels to me as if people like you have fallen out of a balloon by chance and need some information about the planet they find themselves stumbling across.'

'Gratefully received,' said Bertin, not offended in the least. 'If the Frogs give us time—'

'Why wouldn't they?' Süßmann sniffed. 'They're as deep in hot water as we are. They won't lift a finger.'

The approach turned into a mountain climb, and Bertin's stick came in handy. Süßmann laughed as they stepped over the drawbridge and passed the barbed wire defences – the spikes of iron gratings bent by direct hits stared up from the moat – and Bertin sniffed the musty smell of rubble and other strange substances. 'That's the Douaumont smell. So we don't forget the place.'

The sentry hadn't challenged them. 'Salute when you see an officer here, oh stranger,' Süßmann instructed him. 'You're never off duty.'

'I actually can't see a thing,' Bertin answered, his voice echoing in the dark tunnel. Vaults opened off to the right and left, and there were small electric lamps in the ceiling.

'We're in the north-west wing,' said Süßmann. 'At the end of March, the Frogs were practically dancing on our heads, but they didn't pull it off.' ASC men ran past them with bundles of tools on their shoulders. A couple of sappers covered in dirt nodded to Süßmann. 'They'll be able to sleep today,' he said, 'but otherwise we're trained to be night owls. Funny how you get used to things. It seems there are no limits to what human nature can take.'

'And what do you do?' Bertin asked.

'You know what I do: build field railways. That's our way of recovering. And today I've been for a stroll. Later, I'll take you back, and tomorrow morning I'll visit your colleagues in Fosses wood.'

'Give them my best wishes,' Bertin laughed.

The sapper depot occupied half a wing of the mighty pentagon. Nobody smoked; it wasn't just rolls of barbed wire, trench props and iron spikes that were stored here. Bertin glanced in passing at the two-handled wicker baskets shaped like giant arrow quivers. The tops of heavy mortar mines bored downwards into them. Crates of tracer ammunition reminded him of the crates of powder at his own artillery depot. They were brand new. An unshaven NCO was handing flares out to a couple of infantrymen. He carefully counted out the cartridges on a plank of wood laid across two kegs. Behind him was an open door to a white-washed cellar with zinc containers for liquid.

'Oil for the flame throwers,' said Süßmann.

'You've got everything here,' marvelled Bertin.

'Resurrection stores,' replied Süßmann. 'We take up a fair bit of room in this old colliery, don't we?' Right at the back in the uncertain light from the lamps the Bavarian ASC men were handing in their tools. 'They'll get 12 hours' rest now,' said Süßmann. 'The lieutenant takes damn good care no work gets sent their way in their free time. Captain Niggl finds it all rather surprising.'

'And how deep into the earth does the place go?'

'Deep enough for Sunday and Monday,' answered Süßmann. 'There's 3m of concrete above our heads and an entire barracks, armoured towers, machine gun emplacements – in short, every possible comfort. Our lieutenant lives here.'

Bertin entered a vault and stood to attention. Lieutenant Kroysing was sitting by a window, an embrasure facing a wall split by two direct hits. 'Nice open view,' he laughed, welcoming Bertin. 'I can even see a bit of sky from here.'

Bertin thanked him for getting him a nice job. The lieutenant nodded; he hadn't acted out of kindness but so that there would be at least one person left who could explain the whole business to Judge Advocate Mertens in Montmédy. For it was down to him to clear Sergeant Kroysing's name. 'My father will get over Christoph's death and mine if I kick the bucket. The rank and file march with death now. No exceptions, you understand, no special fuss. But if it gets around in Bavaria – and it will get around – that a Kroysing only escaped sanction from a court martial because he died, he'll feel like a discredited outcast, and I'd like to spare him that.'

Bertin looked into his sallow face with compassion. It seemed even more gaunt than last time. It was terrible, he said in an undertone, to have to deal with such nastiness in a private capacity as well. Kroysing dismissed this. It wasn't terrible at all. It was a game and it was revenge, and in that moment his face looked as pitiless to Bertin as the cratered earth outside.

The room was lit by pale daylight. Sergeant Süßmann brought in a dish of warm water. Lieutenant Kroysing took a couple of sheets of blotting paper from a drawer; it had taken more than a fortnight to get hold of them. Then with his long, slender fingers he unwrapped his brother's letter, now gone stiff, from a white handkerchief and immersed it in the water. Three heads, two brown-haired and one blonde, pressed close together and watched as a pink then dark red colouring pervaded the water and settled on the bottom of the dish.

'Careful now,' said Süßmann. 'Leave the preparation to me.'

'Preparation. That's a good one,' muttered Kroysing.

It was a delicate businesss to make it possible to unfold the letter without destroying the paper or washing the ink away. The timing had to be exact. The dead man had used an army postal service letter card. You could write on both sides and on the inside of the envelope, and it was all held together with glue. Warily, Süßmann swayed the paper back and forwards. Soon the water was entirely brown.

'May I pour it away?' he asked.

'Shame,' answered Kroysing. 'Now I won't be able to make anyone drink it.'

Süßmann silently emptied the dish into a bucket and poured new water on the letter, whose gummed sides were already starting to loosen. The letter softened, and a third lot of water remained clear. The pages were laid between blotting paper. The writing was only slightly blurred.

'Good ink,' said Kroysing flatly. 'The lad loved clear, black writing on the page. Do you want to hear what it says?'

This is it, thought Bertin, his breath catching. Who would have thought it possible?

'Dearest Mother,' Eberhard Kroysing read, 'forgive me for writing to bother you with my troubles this time. Up until now, I've made my situation sound rosier than it is. We were brought up to tell the truth and never to shrink from pursuing what is right; fear God more than people, you used to say. And although I no longer believe in God, as you well know, that doesn't mean that I've forgotten everything that was ingrained in us as children. In April, I wrote a letter to Uncle Franz describing to him how our NCOs misuse the men's rations and live it up at their expense. Uncle Franz knows how important an unblemished sense of justice is to the men's morale. Things are what he would call a bloody scandal. My letter was opened by our censor. Papa will explain to you why a court martial investigation was then started, and not of the NCOs but of me, and why our battalion doesn't want this investigation to go ahead. As a result, I've been shifted on a permanent basis to the most dangerous place there is. If you only knew, dear mother, how much it pains me to write this. Now you'll be sick with worry and sleep badly, imagining me already in the ground. Don't believe it is so, dear mother. I appeal to your clever heart. I've been living here for two months in the cellar of a big farmhouse, and nothing has happened to me yet. You can tell from that how little chance there is that something will happen. But it can't last forever or I might come a cropper after all. Please therefore wire Uncle Franz immediately. He must get me brought before the court martial in Montmédy as a matter of urgency. He must give the court martial my exact address, because I suspect Captain Niggl has had me declared "whereabouts unknown" or some funny business like that.' ('Well spotted, lad,' muttered the older brother as he turned the page.) 'He mustn't allow himself to be fobbed off. He must phone the court martial immediately and support me to the hilt. He doesn't have to worry. I'm exactly the same as I was two years ago when I volunteered. My sense of responsibility simply wouldn't allow me to look on in silence. I've tried to rope Eberhard in, but he's extremely busy – you know where he is and what he's doing – and as an officer he shouldn't be getting involved in my business. I haven't heard from him for a couple of weeks. And I'm not sending this letter to you directly but through the good offices of an ASC private and scholar whom I got to know today. Act quickly and prudently, dear Mama, guiding light of our family, as you always do. You've had a hard time with us. But when we're back and there's peace, we'll understand what life is worth, how good it is to be home, and what we have in each other. Because a great deal has turned out to be lies, much more than you realise, much more than ought to be. We'll all have to start again to spare the world a repeat of what we've seen here with our own eyes, done with our own hands and suffered with our own bodies. But the mutual love between parents and children – that has proved durable and dependable, and that's where I'll finish. Always your loving son, Christoph. PS: Give Papa a big kiss and tell him he can write to me himself.'

The audience of two was silent. The faint rumble from the daily artillery fire rattled the closed windows. 'If you think about it,' said Eberhard Kroysing, 'if you really think about it, we are no closer to the earth's surface than the author of this letter – with one small difference that Captain Niggl is soon going to know all about.'

Suddenly, Bertin ducked. A brief, wild howl. Then a shattering crash nearby that echoed dully against the walls. Then a second. 'This all helps,' smiled Kroysing.

CHAPTER THREE

Captain Niggl

CAPTAIN NIGGL— AFTER the march-in he'd lain down to sleep with a mixture of elation and disgust on an iron bed, which, to his eternal relief was tucked under a white-washed vaulting of reassuring thickness. 'Safe wee billet, Douaumont, isn't it?' he kept saying to the garrison commander's adjutant in his outmoded Bavarian accent. At least there was a good cart load of cement above his head. If he managed to sleep here for two weeks he'd definitely get the Iron Cross, first class and become a great man in Weilheim for the rest of time – and not just in Weilheim. Such were his thoughts. He'd convinced himself that the men of the Third Company, who were billeted in an enormous vaulted casemate in the same wing and had received hot coffee, bread and tinned dripping after their night march, would sleep reasonably well on their three-high wire bunks and sacks of wood shavings and that their first duty the following morning would be to scour out their new quarters.

But first thing in the morning, the French sent him and his men a warning not to confuse this place with the previous one. While searching for a latrine, Privates Michael Baß and Adam Wimmerl ended up in a large courtyard open to the south that it was better not to enter at certain times. While they were still looking for somewhere to squat, a long-range battery, with which the garrison was very familiar, fired its first shell of the morning and blew them to bits. This caused a great deal of alarm, and struck the captain as an omen. It weighed heavily on him. Much weighed heavily on him. The air was bad, and the tunnels in this wing, unlike those in the other wings, were jet black with soot. The electric wiring had been newly laid. A side tunnel was completely sealed by a wall, which, though fairly new, consisted partly of old debris and boulders. The echoing vaults really were no fun, and the duties the company had been assigned were unpleasant: blasting operations while the French and German artillery exchanged fire; night-time spadework during which talking and smoking were forbidden, although the French front lay nearly 3km to the other side the fort. The commandant, a polite and taciturn Prussian captain from the Münster area, wasn't a promising drinking buddy, much less the infantry officers, stationed here with a relief battalion, the radio operators and telephonists. The artillery lieutenant in charge of the armoured turrets was somewhat more affable. But when Niggl appeared in the towers, he pulled his head in nervously like a turtle, and the artillery officer hated that. Niggl hadn't yet spoken to the sapper officer under whose command the Third Company was working. The sergeant majors had been in touch, and the lieutenant had inspected the men. But Captain Niggl had the right to expect the lieutenant to visit him first.

This happened. One morning between 10am and 11am, while the captain was writing an overblown letter to his wife, there was a knock on his door and the sapper lieutenant entered. Captain Niggl's room was exactly the same as the lieutenant's own, except that, as already mentioned, it faced one of the other sides of the moat, the north-west. This meant the entire length of the fort, some 300m, separated them. The lieutenant almost had to duck as he entered, and he rose tall and thin in the light from the window. Captain Niggl had turned his left side to it so that his writing hand didn't cast a shadow on the paper. The captain was delighted to see the lieutenant and stood up to greet his visitor. But the visitor's first words took his breath away. The sapper lieutenant asked that he kindly be allowed to introduce himself: his name was Kroysing, Eberhard Kroysing, and he hoped that he and the captain would work well together. As he uttered these harmless-sounding, official words, his eyes searched Herr Niggl's face. A career in the civil service engenders self-control. Herr Niggl politely offered his visitor a seat, but his inner eye was scanning the threatening outlines of some shadowy connections.

'Kroysing?' he repeated in a questioning tone.

The tall lieutenant bowed in confirmation. 'Exactly so. You know the name.'

'We had an NCO in the Third Company—'

'That was my brother,' the lieutenant broke in.

Sadly, sadly, death always takes the best ones, said Captain Niggl sympathetically. Sergeant Kroysing had been a model of conscientiousness who would have been a credit to the officer corps. He'd only have had to hold out for another couple of months, and the worst would have been over. He would have got home leave and then gone to officer training and everything would have turned out well. Wasn't it just like the thing that the Frogs had got him just before?

The lieutenant bowed in thanks. Yes, war didn't pick and choose, and his parents would slowly get over it. His brother had implied something about a court martial procedure the last time they spoke. But that had been at the end of April or beginning of May, if memory served, soon after the dreadful explosion at any rate and during the heavy fighting towards Thiaumont-Fleury, and he really hadn't had time to deal with it. He'd only spoken to his brother for about 20 minutes. What had the whole thing been about?

Captain Niggl began by asking how the lieutenant had come to serve in a Prussian unit when the Kroysings were a good Bavarian family, Franconian if he wasn't mistaken, from Nuremberg. The lieutenant explained that he had been drafted into the Mark sappers as a staff sergeant in the military Reserve immediately after the end of term at the Technical University in Charlottenburg and had remained there as a lieutenant. This was a reflection of the unity of the German Reich that their grandfathers had talked so much about and that their fathers had fought for in 1870. But to get back to the court martial procedure: what was it really about?

Nothing, said Herr Niggl. Or as good as nothing. The army postal censor was overly nervous, and honest young Sergeant Kroysing had unfortunately written a couple of injudicious phrases to a high-ranking military official. He really couldn't remember anything more specific at the moment. He'd been terribly annoyed to have to investigate such a good soldier for something like that. But it wasn't up to him, and besides young Kroysing would definitely have emerged from the investigation untarnished. Alas, everyone underestimated the dangers the ASC men faced. Had the lieutenant heard that two of his men had been blown to bits only yesterday morning, just as Christoph had been a couple of months before?

The lieutenant made a mental note that Niggl had said 'Christoph'. His expression remained unchanged. He too was sure that the court martial would have rehabilitated his brother, he said. But where were the files? Whom should he approach to get the process underway? Herr Niggl said he didn't know. The files had gone through official channels, the way of all flesh. Perhaps the Third Company's Sergeant Major Feicht could provide some information. Sergeant Major Feicht, the lieutenant repeated, noting the name down. And what about his brother's effects? There were all sorts of valuable items, some from the time of their great-grandfather, Judge Kroysing in the Royal Bavarian Court, and personal things that might console their mother. And papers, maybe sketches or poems. Christoph had written some now and then. Their mother would probably want to pull together a small memorial booklet for relatives and friends. In short, where were these things?

Captain Niggl was taken aback and said that they had remained at the military hospital, which had sent them home as it was obliged to do. No, said Lieutenant Kroysing, that was not the case. On the day of the funeral, the military hospital had told him that the company had claimed the effects straight away in order to send them home itself. Ah yes, said the captain, it just showed how faithfully the Third Company's orderly room looked after its men. The items must have been sent to Nuremberg immediately. Hmm, said Lieutenant Kroysing, then all that remained was for him to express his thanks. With the captain's permission he would ask at home if the effects had arrived in the meantime and report back. But now he wouldn't encroach on his time any longer. He'd interrupted him about a purely private matter when he was in the middle of writing a letter. Just one more question, this time of an official nature, and with this he stood up: in order to encourage his men, might the captain occasionally like to accompany the early-morning bomb disposal units or the night-time construction parties? It would definitely make a good impression and help the captain with the commanding officers. Danger lurked both inside and out. With that, he bowed and took leave of the higher-ranked, senior officer with the prescribed salute: heels together, finger to his cap. He didn't give him his hand.

Niggl the retired civil servant from Weilheim sat there gazing after him as he wiped the sweat from his brow. He suddenly realised that he was being held prisoner here in this vault, that it was like a trap, perhaps even a grave. Why had that idiot Sergeant Kroysing not looked more like his brother – as dangerous as him? Why had he had such a harmless, boyish face and behaved like a fool? God help the man who came under the scrutiny of the brother's eyes, into his hands. Only a bonehead could believe it was a coincidence that he and his Third Company – they and no other – had ended up here. That man knew something – what remained to be seen. Now he even wanted to send him, Niggl, out on official business into that bloody awful shell-cratered world, where a man could so easily be taken out by a shell splinter or a bullet. He would have to write to Captain Lauber immediately, or better still telephone him – immediately. Someone had deceived Captain Lauber: this was private revenge through official means. He and his ASC men were out of place here; he'd surely see that. Or should he first inform Simmdering and Feicht? What had happened to Kroysing's effects? Were they still lying about in company storage because no one had found the time to read through the lad's scribbles?

Had the foxes been at them? No, there was no rush. He'd be able to take advice long before Kroysing had an answer from home. The most urgent matter was to discover the enemy's intentions and find out what he knew.

Most urgent of all was that he keep his head. That he'd lost his nerve so suddenly was simply down to this dung heap, Douaumont. He'd allowed himself to be too impressed by the word. It looked almost exactly the same here as in the cellars of Ettal Abbey or Starnberg Castle. If he were sitting there he wouldn't feel like giving up just because a man with whom he had to work was the brother of another man with whom he'd worked before. He sat there eyeing the white-washed wall in front of him. When he examined the whole discussion, it really hadn't been so suspicious after all. He alone had ascribed a vengeful role to his visitor; he alone, persuaded by the fact that this stupid pile of bricks wasn't called Ettal Abbey or Starnberg Castle but Douaumont, had given the situation sinister connotations. If you looked at it soberly, nothing could be proved. The question about the files was as natural as the one about the effects. The fact that a Lieutenant Kroysing was in charge of the sapper depot was as harmless as his brother being an NCO in the ASC. The lieutenant hadn't really looked after his younger brother. And now he was meant to have had his brother's company and battalion commander transferred in order to exact revenge. Rubbish! Preposterous nonsense! Young Kroysing was dead and couldn't say anything. There were always ASC companies pottering around in Douaumont. If this wasn't a coincidence, then there was no such thing as coincidences, and the Holy Father was right to believe in a jealous God sitting above the world observing wrong-doers and protecting the innocent. And it wasn't hard to deal with the Lord God. You went to confession and did what the priest told you. Then you put one over on the devil – and his envoy, this lanky bloody Prussian, who wasn't even a real Prussian but a Nuremberg imitation. Nothing's up, Niggl. Write your letter home and don't let on to the wife and kids.

Captain Niggl's day passed tolerably well. The midday bombardment startled him. He was to go out with the men that night and he'd requested and studied maps and was reassured by the several kilometres that lay between him and the French. About 5pm, his company commander, Acting Lieutenant Simmerding, pushed into his room looking horrified. He closed the door and stuttered out a question: did the captain know what the fort's sapper commander was called? In his cocksure way, Niggl tried to calm him down. Of course he knew; he'd known for ages. An affable chap, Lieutenant Kroysing.

They'd be able to work well with him. Then why, hissed Simmerding, hadn't he told Feicht and him anything about it? They were in hot water now. And he handed Niggl an official telegram, white and blue, as they always were when the telephonists transcribed a message over the wire: 'Christoph's effects not received, Kroysing,' it read.

Niggl looked at the piece of paper for a long time, then asked flatly where Simmerding had got it from. He said the little Yid Süßmann had brought it over for his attention, requesting that it be returned. Niggl nodded several times. His pathetic attempts at self-deception were useless. You didn't mess with a man who smiled politely and fired off telegrams like electric shocks.

'You were right, old pal,' he said amiably, 'and I've been an ass. Herr Kroysing is a dangerous man. We'll have to get a grip on ourselves and use our nous. To begin with we'll blame it all on the army postal service.' But his hand was shaking as he relit his cigar, and when Simmerding huffed, 'Fat lot of good that'll do,' he didn't know what to say.

Three days later, Captain Niggl was to be seen running down the echoing corridors, head bent. In that short time, the company had recorded two more dead and 31 wounded. French shells had twice exploded in the column, and although that word designated loose groups of men rather than a marching line, the ASC men and their officers nonetheless had the impression that they were helplessly exposed and must be prepared for anything when outside the stone pile. Captain Niggl now ran, hands pressed to his ears, for piercing shrieks were coming from the side corridor where the dressing station had been installed. The same shrieks had rung out across the field when the two dead men and nine of the wounded were shot down 50m in front of him. The lovely morning mist had been suddenly torn apart – the rest could be imagined. Herr Niggl wasn't used to running. His belly shuddered, and his sleeves rode up. They looked much too short. But he ran. Under the dull light from the electric bulbs, he fled the unrestrained howling of tormented flesh.

CHAPTER FOUR

Dress rehearsal

WHEN EBERHARD KROYSING thought about Captain Niggl, his soul danced and sang, and the fort's murderous grey air seemed to twinkle secretly. He was biding his time. There would be a lot to do in the coming days, for rain had suddenly set in overnight, and many were looking on it as the start of the autumn downpours. A fine, persistent drizzle fell from leaden clouds; when they woke in the morning, the land was already glistening with countless puddles and pools. The war had gone silent in astonishment.

'Süßmann,' said Kroysing, smoking his pipe in his cell and sprawled lazily on his bed, 'we'll finish my painting this morning.' The plan for the construction of six new mine throwers drawn in crayon lay unfinished on the table. 'But in the afternoon, we'll have a look at the damage. If this doesn't stop, we've seriously miscalculated and started our preparations too late.'

Süßmann confidently asserted that it would stop. 'It's just a shower, as we say in Berlin,' he predicted. 'And a benevolent one. Hurry up, she's saying. Where are the First and Second Companies, she's saying.'

'And she's quite right,' said Kroysing cheerfully, 'and deserves a schnapps or even a brandy. Pass me the bottle, Süßmann. We'll allow ourselves one as her proxy.'

Süßmann grinned happily and fetched the tall bottle, still half full, from the lieutenant's cabinet, along with two of the kind of small tumblers found in every French café. He poured two shots and put them on the iron stool by the head of Kroysing's bed. The lieutenant told him to dig in, inhaled the scent from the golden liquid that filled the room and took a slow swig with unconfined pleasure, lost in the drink, man's great comforter.

'Listen, my friend,' he said, speaking to the ceiling, 'around midday when the captain has caught up on his sleep, wander over to his orderly room and nonchalantly ask where the two companies are. And then as an afterthought ask if you could please see the post book. The Third Company must have kept some kind of record when it entrusted my brother's belongings to the choppy seas of the army postal service. Because, dear Süßmann, the parcel is lost. A certain percentage of packages and letters must get lost just by the laws of probability. And that Christoph's few things were among them – coincidence naturally. We Kroysings are an unlucky lot.' Süßmann would have preferred to go straight away, but Kroysing didn't want to be alone. 'If our friend Bertin is a hardened soldier then he'll hoof it over here this morning and show his rather crooked nose,' yawned Kroysing. 'Do you think he'll dare come?'

Süßmann said that if he stayed where he was it would only be out of shyness. In order to propel him over, he'd telephoned that morning – but lo and behold the bird had already flown. He was on night duty and was free during the day, and according to Strumpf from the Landsturm he'd gone to see a friend from school whom he'd discovered among the field howitzers. Then he planned to continue to Douaumont. 'Would've been a miracle if there wasn't someone he knew among all those Upper Silesians, poor lad,' concluded Süßmann.

'Why are you making fun of him?' asked Kroysing.

'Well, apart from the fact that everything strikes me as funny, I've never known anyone to have so many doubts about everything and anything.

Kroysing looked up. 'Do you think he's a coward? I don't fancy that.'

Süßmann shook his long head. 'Absolutely not,' he retorted. 'Did I say cowardly? I said he has doubts. The lad is more of a naïve daredevil, motivated by a mad desire for novelty – the devil only knows what drives him. One thing's for sure, though, he's scared of his superiors. Of the military, you know. Shells are no problem, but show him an orderly room or an epaulette and the poor dog shits his pants,' he added thoughtfully.

Kroysing rolled on to his stomach and propped himself up on his elbows. 'You don't understand a thing about it. It's got to be like that. The common man, according to Frederick the Great's theory, must fear his superiors much more than the enemy, otherwise, he'd never attack. Furthermore, I imagine Bertin's tendency to panic would disappear with a good military education. What are men like him doing in the ASC? Do me a favour, Süßmann, watch him for me. If he looks like he could do something better, I'll be happy to help him. He's intelligent and educated, he's been out here long enough and he's a decent lad. It just depends whether he has guts – cold-blooded guts. You know what I mean. If he does we'll put him on the usual road to a stripe and later a commission – like you.'

Süßmann banged on the table with a red pencil he'd been using to doodle on an army postcard. 'Then he'd first of all have to request a transfer from his unit.

'That he would.'

'He never will,' asserted Süßmann. 'His scruples will get in the way. We had a chat on the way back last time. He's had his fingers burnt. He volunteered for the west, but was assigned to a convoy for the east. That blunder landed him in Jansch's battalion. Regret about that gnaws away at his soul. Never volunteer: that's his motto now. And not a bad one, I'm sure you'll admit.'

Kroysing shook his fist. 'Scoundrel! Up with volunteers! They're in the best Prussian tradition and a matter of honour for sappers. Didn't you ever learn about Sapper Klinke and the Dybbøl trenches at school? "My name's Klinke, and I open the gate," wrote your countryman Fontane, and he should know.'

They both laughed, as Süßmann added: 'Poets can do anything.'

'Nothing against poets,' warned Kroysing. 'Here's ours.'

Sure enough, there was a shy knock and Bertin entered, rather wet and with filthy boots. They commended him on his timely arrival. Kroysing offered the visitor a glass of brandy so he wouldn't catch cold, got up to greet him and gave him something to smoke: Dutch pipe tobacco. Kroysing wandered across the narrow room in his padded waistcoat of slightly worn black silk to wash his face, and as he was drying it, he told Bertin about his delicate conversation with Captain Niggl. Bertin cleaned his rain-splattered glasses. In the pipe smoke, his myopic eyes could barely pick out Kroysing's face and the flapping towel. He told them he hadn't been able to sleep after the letter opening. Its contents had stayed inside him, spoken in the voice of the – he swallowed – dead man, which, curiously, he remembered extremely well. What kind of a man was Niggl that he could simply disregard an exceptional young lad such as Christoph?

Kroysing pulled on his tunic and slid past the visitors and furnishings into his seat by the table at the window. 'A very ordinary man,' he said in his deep voice. 'One of x millions, a workaday scoundrel, so to speak.'

'And what do you plan to do with him?'

'I'll tell you,' replied Kroysing. 'First, I'll put him under pressure. The surroundings, this atmospheric mole heap of a fort and the Frogs will help me there. Next step: I get him to sign a paper confessing that he kept my brother at Chambrettes-Ferme until he was killed – in order to forestall the court martial investigation.'

'He'll never sign,' said Süßmann.

'Oh yes, he will,' replied Kroysing, looking up. 'I'm curious myself as to how it will happen, but it will happen. I feel like an adolescent boy again, full of drive and vengeance. That's the only time you can really hate properly and persecute people for months. Perhaps the war has uncovered the ancient hunter in us, who drinks evening tea from his enemy's skull. After two years of it, it's no wonder.'

'Do you call that a good thing?' asked Bertin, shocked.

'I call anything good that extends my life and finishes the enemy off,' said Kroysing brusquely, carefully marking the locations of the new mine throwers with a green pencil; he'd already used blue for the German positions, red for the French and brown for the area's contours. 'This isn't a girl's school,' he continued. 'The lie about the spirit of the front and the comradeship of war may be fine, and it may be necessary to keep the show on the road for those behind the lines and our enemy over there. Supreme self-sacrifice, you know. Very inspiring for war correspondents, politicians and readers. In reality we're all fighting to have as much as possible in our own domain. It's a battle of all against all. That's the right formula.'

'I've often felt that,' said little Sergeant Süßmann drily.

'Exactly.' Kroysing blinked at him. 'We all have, if not as keenly as you. And anyone who hasn't felt it, hasn't been to war.'

'Do you really believe,' said Bertin with a secret sense of superiority and the trace of a smile, 'that the drive for honours, for a career—'

'Rubbish,' said Kroysing. 'Our own domain, I said, and our own domain is what I meant. Domain can mean different things to different people – every man has his own thumbprint. Some collect medals and give their hearts to metalsmiths. Others want to carve out a career and swoon with delight when they get ahead. But the great mass of people just want dosh. They loot French houses or share out dead men's effects. Our friend Niggl just wanted a quiet life.'

'And what does the lieutenant want deep down inside?' asked Süßmann, pulling a funny monkey face.

'Not telling, you cheeky monkey,' laughed Kroysing. 'You may assume that I want to be feared among my clansmen.' And he added more seriously: 'Never before has anyone spat in my soup the way that man has.'

They were silent for a moment, then Bertin said diffidently: 'I must be abnormal then. I want nothing more than to perform my duties as an ASC private to the best of my abilities and for there to be an honourable peace soon so I can go back to my wife and my work.'

'Wife,' mocked Kroysing. 'Work. Honourable peace. You're in for a shock, and anyway you can find someone else to believe that— what was that?'

All three of them sat up straight as pokers and listened. A lacerating howl descended on them from the clouds, a dreadful sound; then a primordial crashing and rolling smashed through the rooms – not as near as they'd feared. 'Up and have a look,' called Süßmann.

'Stay put,' commanded Kroysing. There was running in the corridor outside the door. He picked up the telephone. 'Ring me immediately you get news.' The telephonist's voice was still shaking with fear. Kroysing surveyed his guest with satisfaction. Bertin was surprised at himself: he felt the same wild delight he had when he chased across the shelled area with Böhne and Schultz. Sergeant Süßmann's hands shook as he said that it could only have been a long-range 38cm or a 42cm, a German one that had fallen short. The telephone rattled; highest calibre, direct strike to the western trenches, reported the exchange. Extensive damage to the outer walls. Kroysing thanked them. Out of the question that the 42cm was so far out. Three thousand metres too short – no way. Even with the dunderheads back there.

'Watch out,' he warned. 'Number two.' This time all three of them ducked. Süßmann slid under the table. No one breathed. The splintered air screamed behind the lump of steel, getting closer, close, there. Red and yellow flash at the window. Thunder blast in the room. Plaster and paintwork on the table. The electric lamp went out. The men's chairs shook beneath them. 'Strike,' said Kroysing calmly. The crash above their heads had been brighter and wilder than before, and had boomed louder too.

'No harm done,' said Süßmann, jumping up entirely without shame as if he were the only one who'd responded proportionately. Kroysing stated that unless he was very much mistaken the strike had taken down the armoured turret in the north-west wing. He asked to be connected to the turret. The other two watched expectantly as his face broke into a satisfied smile. 'Damnable nation, the French. They can shoot but they can fortify too. The turret took a direct hit and withstood it. A new calibre, according to the NCO, a mortar heavier than the 38cm from Fort Marre. A new type, then, probably ordered in for the Somme.'

'And they're rehearsing it on us,' said Süßmann, while Kroysing tried to speak to the turret again. This time the exchange reported that the turret had been temporarily evacuated on account of the gases from the explosion. It hadn't been entirely spared. It could no longer be turned. 'As long as that's it,' said Kroysing, hanging up. And then he sent Süßmann and Bertin off with emergency lights to see how the ASC men were coping with the incident.

They didn't have to go far. The tunnel in front of the Bavarians' casemate was filled with the ASC men's cursing, wailing and crying, as they crouched down or struggled to get away. Their NCOs, brandishing torches, only just managed to stop them rushing out into the courtyard. At the entrance to the intersecting corridor, faintly illuminated by the daylight, stood Captain Niggl, his bottom lip between his teeth, bare-headed and in slippers, with his Litevka unbuttoned. Acting Lieutenant Simmerding pushed through to him, while Sergeant Major Feicht tried to calm down the men at the back of the corridor in his hoarse voice. The men were hopping mad, panted Simmerding. They didn't want to stay in this place. They were unarmed reservists, not frontline soldiers. They'd no business here.

'Not that mad,' said Niggl under his breath, his eyes staring and becoming angry when Süßmann appeared with his black miner's lamp. Unfortunately, the sapper's strict military bearing gave him no way in. Niggl told him to inform the lieutenant that the men's sleep had been interrupted, some of them had been thrown from their beds, there had been instances of grazed skin and a sprained wrist, and their nerves had of course taken a jolt. The bloody thing must have come down right above the casemate. Süßmann uttered soothing words, mainly to the men: the shots had been meant for the B-tower, which had also been hit, and the fact that the concrete had withstood such a heavy strike was the best proof there was of the vaults' strength. For it had been a new type of gun, also a 42cm – he had no idea how close this improvisation was to the truth. And so the men should not let their rest be disturbed, for goodness' sake, and should take consolation from that and go back to the casemate and to bed. The depot would issue an extra ration of rum with evening tea because of the shock.

Wanting consolation, the ASC men pushed into the light and listened eagerly. They knew this little man who was rumoured to have died and come back to life. They'd also heard that the lieutenant's name was Kroysing. In many of their dull minds Süßmann was therefore accorded some of the trust they'd had in Sergeant Kroysing, who had also been quite short and brown-haired. As a result, his encouragement worked. All those patient men really wanted was reassurance, something to soothe their souls and help them come to terms with the situation. Süßmann stood in the midst of his three enemies and glanced fleetingly at their faces. Behind those faces, they were shaking. Oh, he felt exactly how much. Should he ask for the post book now? No, too potent a moment. They could have refused him with good reason. First they needed a chance to have other thoughts. After lunch then. He clicked his heels together, swung round at attention and vanished with Bertin into the endless, dark tunnel. The electric cable had been cut somewhere.

CHAPTER FIVE

Between neighbours

LATE IN THE afternoon, Captain Niggl asked Sergeant Major Feicht to come to his room. It was dark inside; the electricians were still working on the lighting cable. The captain cast a formless shadow on the wall in the dim light from the stearin candle on the table. He was sitting on his bedstead and had been asleep. He planned to spend some time in the open with the entrenching commando that night, but for now he was wearing breeches and grey woollen stockings that his wife had knitted and slippers – black slippers from Weilheim, each with a white Edelweiß embroidered on it. The sergeant major stood to attention in the doorway. In a tired voice, the captain asked him to close the door, come in and sit down on the stool. Sergeant Major Feicht obeyed, giving his superior officer a look of deepest sympathy. He too felt dreadful.

Feicht and Niggl came from the same area. Before the war, Ludwig Feicht, who was a native of Tutzing and married to a local woman, had worked contentedly as a purser on the handsome steamers that plied Lake Starnberg, or Lake Würm as it was also called. When the visitors from north Germany were standing in groups on the deck admiring the beautiful old coppices of trees, the clear water, the silver gulls circling above, Purser Feicht stepped forward in his blue reefer jacket with gold braid and his marvellous peaked cap and explained to the summer holiday-makers in broad but not impenetrable Bavarian that this was the up-and-coming spa resort of Tutzing and that was Bernried, with its little church that was much older than even the most impressive churches in Berlin. He was flattered when the clueless Berliners and Saxons addressed him as 'Captain' and asked indescribably stupid questions: was Rose Island over there by Tutzing artificial and had King Ludwig by any chance had a castle on it?

Ludwig Feicht loved his summer life on the long lake, and his broad, red face radiated goodwill. He had two small children in Tutzing, and while he was away his wife Theresa single-handedly ran a grocery shop and delicatessen for the many spa guests who packed the place out. Even now – especially now –

the starving Prussians descended on the place to fill their bellies with Bavarian milk, dumplings and smoked meats, leaving their money behind, the new brown or blue 20 Mark notes. And Ludwig Feicht had been very happy with his life. He'd even faced the transfer to Douaumont with a certain composure, believing himself immune to the vicissitudes of fate. But as of that day, as of the two instances of shellfire, that feeling had been abruptly overturned. That the French had fired those two shells at the fort, that they were so bloody expert that they only needed those two: this took his breath away when the gunners from turret B explained it to him. His goal had been to return home in one piece with some tidy savings. Now he wasn't sure what to think.

'Feicht,' the captain said in his new, depressed voice, employing the thick Bavarian dialect of their lakeside homeland, 'answer me one question – not in your official, military capacity, but as a neighbour who's in, you know, the same tight spot as me, as a Tutzinger to a Weilheimer, who has a dispute with someone from Nuremberg. Imagine the two of us are in a shooting hut above the Benediktenwand ridge and a nasty Nuremberger is due to turn up early in the morning wanting something from us – a Franconian, a right bastard.'

Feicht sat there squarely on the stool, bent forward, elbows on his knees. This was it. This was why he'd been brought to this evil vaulted place. He'd always made fun of clergymen and churches and pilfered from the steamship company without a second thought. Money was his second favourite thing in the world. But he should have kept his hands off dead men's belongings. There was something wrong with that. 'Captain,' he said hoarsely, 'I know what this is about.'

Niggl nodded. An intelligent man such as his neighbour would of course understand the ways of the world. Who would have thought that meek little mouse Sergeant Kroysing would have the devil incarnate for a brother. The brother had claws and he dug them in. He pursued his goal with tenacity, and his goal was to destroy.

Yes, exclaimed Feicht, waving his right hand about, which, being a sergeant major who understood what was proper, he'd never have done in a different mood or under other circumstances. Lieutenant Kroysing struck him as a crab that might skewer a pencil someone had put between its claws as a joke. There was only one solution: wave goodbye to the pencil or chuck the crab in boiling water.

'You see, Feicht, that's just it. We can't chuck the crab in boiling water, but perhaps the lanky bastard will fall in by himself when he's floating about with his mine throwers at the front line. Perhaps we could help him, shine a torch on him when he has us all up at the front and we're under cover and he's on the top. Until then, we'll have to give him the pencil. Have you got the list?' Feicht said that he had. 'Do you know where the various things are?' Without so much as a blush, Feicht considered for a moment, then said, yes, he knew where the things were.

'What writings there were are still among my paperwork,' said Niggl. 'I'll pull them together for you and leave them packed up here on my bed. Package everything up nicely while we're gone – everything, old chum! Work out his pay up until the day of his death, not a Pfennig short. Can we produce the paper that the company commander signed when the belongings arrived?' Feicht nodded. 'By tonight the package is to be on the table in Lieutenant Kroysing's room. I'll answer any questions he may have. We mustn't leave him any openings, Feicht,' he said, eyeing his portly subordinate pensively. 'For the time being, we have the weaker hand. For the time being. Now, be off with you, old chum. Tell Dimpflinger to get me a decent bit of meat, even if it's from a tin. I want to see this game through. We'll see who laughs last.'

Feicht looked with deepest sympathy at the gentleman perched on the bedstead in his slippers and blue knitted waistcoat with deer antler buttons. Here was a proper compatriot who wouldn't turn his men over to that insane, scrawny Nuremberger, that rag and bone merchant. 'It'll be all right, old boy, even if it *is* a bit of a headache,' said Feicht. 'Whoever puts his trust in this retired civil servant from Weilheim will always have family. And when we're all happily back home, Feicht will know whom to thank.'

'Off you go, Feicht.'

The sergeant major walked to the door, turned the key and clicked his heels together, every bit the soldier. They'd understood each other without speaking plainly.

When there were spoils to share out, the sergeant major kept the lion's share and gave something to the clerk who was working on the case, as well as the postal orderly and one or two of the NCOs to whom he was well disposed. It was very painful to have to cough up gifts already received, but a wise man does not questions orders from on high and he would no doubt get his reward in due course.

All alone in the small, square room that had been assigned to him and Simmerding the company commander as a billet and office, Ludwig Emmeran

Feicht busied himself with the objects that the now almost forgotten sergeant had left behind in July. The company's list lay on the table, and the cheerful electric light was working again. The door was closed, and a tumblerful of red wine and a filled pipe sweetened the unpleasant task. A coup had failed – never mind, they hadn't meant any harm. Now in slippers himself, the portly man moved about putting everything in order, then sat astride the stool to take stock. Every time he found something he made a cross on the list with a freshly sharpened pencil.

First a leather waistcoat, worn but still usable, and (secondly) this fountain pen with the gold lever: they had formed the clerk Dillinger's share. He'd been wide-eyed when he handed them back but he'd understood. Funny how the whole company had grasped that something to do with dead Sergeant Kroysing was in the air when that lanky fencepost of a brother appeared. Oh, they'd gloated a bit at the beginning, the little ASC men. But not any more. They visited their comrades in the sickbay and thought bitterly about how they had Lieutenant Kroysing to thank. Perhaps one or two workers from Munich thought about it more deeply and held the orderly room responsible for the disaster. But that way of thinking had no momentum, because the French shells had so much more momentum; he who dies, dies. Nowt for it. And so the Frogs helped keep discipline, and one army supported the other.

Pipe, tobacco pouch and pocket knife; Sergeant Pangerl had obediently brought them back. The knife had a deer antler handle and was stuck in its sheath like a dirk. The lad Kroysing had hardly used the pipe, which was of the best Nuremberg workmanship, and had kept it in a leather pouch. Now it would atrophy in a drawer – what a shame. Sergeant Major Feicht looked tenderly on the broad ebonite mouthpiece, the gleaming briar wood bowl and the wide tobacco chamber fitted with an aluminium tube. He put the parts back together again, wrapped the pipe in its pouch and crossed it off the list. A wallet full of slips of paper, a notebook, a leather-bound booklet with the calendar for 1915, a narrow moleskin notebook with writing – with poems! The kinds of verses that rhymed at the end. Ludwig Feicht's lips curled in contempt. Typical. People who wrote verses should steer clear of other activities. If things went wrong for them, they only had themselves to blame. But now the most important items: the purse, watch and ring. Shame about the ring. He'd intended to give it to his wife Theresa as a souvenir, a holiday surprise. It was set with a beautiful green stone, an emerald, and the ring itself was in the shape of snake biting its tail and was patterned with scales. He,

Feicht, had wanted to wear the watch, either on his wrist or strung on a long, thin gold chain across his waistcoat. It had all gone sour.

He hadn't done too badly in this unit, but it was nothing compared to the infantry and cavalry, who'd marched into wealthy Belgium at the beginning of the war, into Luxembourg and northern France. They had seen some loot and no mistake. The clocks of Liège, the gold of Namur, and even the small provincial towns. Of course those dirty north German rogues hadn't let the Bavarians at it. It was the Rhinelanders and Saxons who got stuck in, by Jove it was. Had it not always been considered right and proper that soldiers who were risking their life for the Fatherland should pocket something? Did the bigwigs behave any differently when they swallowed up whole provinces – Belgium, Poland, Serbia and the beautiful stretch of countryside here that they called the Briey-Longwy iron ore basin. If you didn't get rich at war, you'd never get rich. And what a waste it would've been to melt down the beautiful watches, chains, bangles, necklaces, rings and brooches when the small towns were razed to the ground because they were full of god-damned *franctireurs* resistance fighters. Where had he met that clever man with the travelling military field library, which had a false bottom with drawers you could pull out – nothing but Belgian watches in them? Had it been in Alsace? Yes, that man had known what was what. But the war wasn't over yet. A lot could still happen. All of France might be up for grabs if the Germans won. And they would win and must win – or all was lost. Feicht wasn't the only one who knew that. So he could restore this Swiss watch with its beautifully engraved gold back cover to the lucky heirs with confidence. It kept good time, he could vouch for that. The money – he counted the folded notes. Seventy-six Marks and eighty Pfennigs – ah well! He could've got the children new clothes with it, pleated taffeta skirts, green silk pinafores and tops. But it didn't matter. Theresa was doing very nicely out of the starving north Germans. He'd get over it. He'd kept it safe, and there you were – he'd been right. The last item on the list was underwear. Ludwig Feicht dipped a pen in ink and wrote an asterisked note on the list, placing it so that the company commander's signature hovered protectively below it: 'Distributed to comrades in need, as the deceased would have wished.' Full stop.

The pile of goods lay on the grey-painted table carefully wrapped in the leather waistcoat. Dependable Feicht now took from a box a large piece of orange-coloured oil paper reinforced with woven-in threads and wrapped the whole lot up so that the affixed address label adorned the middle. He tied it with string, took sealing wax and the company seal and sealed Sergeant Kroysing's effects with two big red stamps. He left the address intact. It was addressed to the Third Company orderly room, and the sender was given as the Fifth Echelon Army Postal Depot. A whole stack of letters had arrived from there after the battalion had been on the move for a week, battering over from Poland to Verdun. That now proved rather handy. Ludwig Feicht filled out a small yellow slip of paper in narrow, spiky handwriting: 'Return to sender. Address incomplete. No duplicate enclosed.' He checked the postmark – delightfully illegible.

He would suggest to the captain that he enclose a judiciously worded covering letter, saying that the package had been correctly addressed to Councillor Kroysing, but that due to an oversight on the part of the clerk Dillinger the army postal address of the company had been given instead of the Kroysings' address in Nuremberg: Ebensee, Schilfstraße 28. What a silly mix-up! Dillinger had been severely reprimanded and would have spent three days in prison, but they had decided to put mercy before justice as his wife had just had a baby and his thoughts were back home. If the company hadn't been suddenly 'transferred', the package would have been in Nuremberg long ago. That's how it was, Lieutenant. Did the lieutenant have any further questions? Ludwig Feicht the purser grinned quietly to himself, dipped a small brush in the glue jar, stuck the return slip on the right-hand corner of the address label and rubbed it a bit with the sole of his slipper to make it look as though it had gone through the post. He then stamped it with the company stamp in such a way that only two of the curved lines and an asterisk were visible; ink doesn't take very well on oil paper and he'd been careful not to press the stamp in the ink pad. With his hands behind his back, he contemplated his handiwork. Excellent job. The captain would be pleased.

As the men marched out that night in the deepest gloaming, Herr Simmerding and Herr Niggl met at the back of the column. Although Captain Niggl was a half bottle of Bordeaux to the good, he found the reek of alcohol off his company commander discomfiting. It wasn't that he disapproved of Dutch courage. He drank himself and so did everyone in the army. They tramped along beside each other in virtual silence. Eventually, Niggl began to feel sorry for the other man with his hunched shoulders and pinched neck. They too were close compatriots. The Simmerding family lived all along the north shore of the lake. And so, in an undertone, he asked how he was doing after the shock earlier at midday. Fine, grunted Simmerding. Niggl said that was good, because he had every reason to feel fine. Sergeant Major Feicht had now sorted out the unpleasantness to do with young Kroysing's effects.

'Really,' said Simmerding, with a wild, fleeting glance at the man on his right. 'Sorted it out, has he? Ha, ha! Has Feicht brought young Kroysing back to life then? Got him out of his coffin, blown new air into him and put him back in the ranks? Because that man in there will be satisfied with nothing less.'

'Simmerding,' said Niggl soothingly, not allowing Feicht's anxious tone get to him, 'pull yourself together. All is by no means lost.'

Simmdering came to a halt. His clenched fists stuck out from the wide arms of his coat. 'All is not lost! All has long since been lost! I'm sick of this whole business with Christoph Kroysing, if you really want to know! Sick to here—' he raised his hand to his mouth. 'I could kick myself for having got caught up in sending him to Chambrettes and that game with the files – your game.'

'No one forced you, Acting Lieutenant Simmerding,' said Niggl coolly. 'Make sure you don't fall too far behind your company. And say a couple of Ave Marias during the night.'

What a lily-livered specimen, he thought contemptuously.

Passed down from the front, the same warning resounded over and over again: 'Watch out, wire below. Watch out, wire above.'

CHAPTER SIX

Snatched booty

WHEN LIEUTENANT KROYSING came home that night and turned on the light, his whistling abruptly stopped. He was always happy to get back to the welcoming vaults of the fort – welcoming vaults! He laughed to himself at the expression. He appreciated its irony, which came from the extent to which the world was distorted. The hours spent on the winding uphill route from the infantry positions, the rude presence of mind, born of repeated experience, needed to evade the French shells – it all meant he felt positively happy as soon as he heard his steps echoing off the stone walls. That's why Lieutenant Kroysing was whistling. He broke off in the middle of the most beautiful part of the *Meistersinger* overture. Kroysing looked in astonishment at the surprising postal gift on his table and the folded note between the oil paper and the string. *Uh-huh*, he thought scornfully, *who goes there?*

He swung his steel helmet on to the coat stand, carefully hung his cape and gas mask under it, threw his belt with his dirk and heavy pistol and his torch on to the bed and sat down beside them to take off his puttees and mud-caked shoes. In other circumstances, he'd have rung and woken his batman, sleepy Sapper Dickmann, who only had one virtue: he could fry schnitzel and make coffee like no one else. But he wanted to be alone with this package. While he was bent over undoing his laces and putting on his house shoes, he didn't let it out his sight for a second, as if it might disappear just as suddenly and magically as it had wafted in. *Yes*, he thought, this was a victory. *Victory number two, won by fearlessly advancing, constantly upping the ante and exploiting the enemy's weakness – precise knowledge of the terrain. The tactical instructions applied to Lieutenant Kroysing's private war with Captain Niggl were bearing fruit. Funny, he pondered, I never for one moment thought that this could be one of the welcome packages from home that sporadically reach us. I've got my teeth some way into Captain Niggl.*

He read the accompanying bumph signed 'Feicht, Sergeant Major' and written in Feicht's best handwriting, examined the wrapping paper suspiciously and nodded knowingly. There was nothing to prove that the package had really been sent back by the army postal service. Asterisks and curved lines might convince a schoolboy. However, nothing proved the contrary either. The conspiracy against the young lad had been carried out by shrewd and experienced soldiers. They weren't so easily unsettled. They'd parried his strike splendidly and hung the clerk Dillinger out to dry in the customary manner. If he fell for it and demanded that Dillinger be punished, the clerk would definitely be sent to prison, but as recompense for his silence he'd be off on leave in the next round. A wolf like Kroysing wasn't about to be seduced by such tricks. His steady grey eyes looked through the wall at his target, the captain. He wasn't finished with him. He pulled out his knife, slit the string with an audible rip and opened the package. Enclosed in the soft brown leather waistcoat he knew so well lay all that remained of Christoph on earth. It had without a doubt been shared among his enemies as booty: watch, fountain pen, purse, the little snake ring, a wallet, a notebook, his smoking things.

Breathing heavily with his balled fists pressed into the table, Eberhard Kroysing looked at his younger brother's effects. He hadn't been a good brother to him – definitely not easy to put up with. We don't love our younger siblings. We want our parents' love all to ourselves. We don't want to share our domain. We want to be the sole object of their affection. As we can't push aside siblings that are born later, we subjugate them. Hell mend them if they don't obey. The nursery can be a mini hell. It can. Boys are very inventive and instinctively know how to wage war inconspicuously. That's how it is – and not just in the Kroysing household. If the parents intervene, it just makes it worse for the weaker ones. In his case, it carried on until the bonds of home loosened and the brothers began to move in different circles. A cool indifference had then crept into the older brother's attitude towards the younger. Only much later in the university holidays did he suddenly realise that his little brother was growing into a man with a good heart – a potential friend. Then the war started and he'd been turned into a savage again, and just when he was hoping that they'd both get leave by Christmas at the latest and be able to enjoy the festivities with their parents, it was too late. A couple of scoundrels had let the French finish the young lad off to spare themselves a bit of unpleasantness. He'd get his own back on the Frogs, but here and now written on the walls of this monk's cell were the words: 'too late'. 'Too late' on the ceiling and the window, 'too late' on the floor. 'Too late' hung in the air. Nothing was more natural for men at war than to believe in kingdom come, life after death, a reunion on the other side. The fighting man's simple, forward-driven mind couldn't grasp that those who were carried off had disappeared forever; his imagination couldn't deal with it. The enemy had to live on, so that victory was eternal. And a brother had to live on so you could make up for all the bad and evil things you'd done in your youth.

Kroysing grabbed the little watch, wound it and set it. It was half eleven. From the distance came rumbling and crashing. It must be from the Fort Vaux area, where fighting was constantly flaring up and the French were improving their positions. Nonetheless, the tick of the watch was audible in the quiet room. The young lad's heart couldn't be made to tick again. But at least he had already made an offering to the dead boy. And he would pursue Niggl until he confessed. Then Judge Advocate Mertens would take up the case and deal with Niggl, and his machinations would all have been in vain. He'd thought about it and made up his mind. He could cheerfully have spat on the retired civil servant before witnesses, slapped his face or wrung his neck. But duelling was forbidden in wartime, and however satisfying it might have been to haul that fat, trembling lump in front of his gun, the legal route was the only possible one and actually the more effective. He would totally and utterly destroy Herr Niggl. Even if Niggl survived, he'd take no pleasure in his life. He'd be a social outcast, dishonoured by his years in jail. He'd be dismissed from his post and, as the bureaucrat's life was all he knew, he and his family would starve. Perhaps he'd open a little stationery business in Buenos Aires or Constantinople. But wherever the German officer corps had connections he'd be a dead man, despised by his wife and hated by his children.

Will that satisfy you, Christoph? he wondered. You're soft. Your enemy's scalp means nothing to you, but it means something to me. It won't be tonight or the day after tomorrow, but we'll get it. And then we'll make Bertin a lieutenant in your place. He resisted the temptation to look through his brother's notebook, wrapped his effects up in the leather waistcoat, undressed, got into bed and turned out the light.

BOOK FOUR

On the fringes of humanity

CHAPTER ONE

Profound effects

DURING THE NIGHT and towards morning, when the captive balloons' eyes were shut, the field kitchen staff tried to creep up on the infantry positions. They'd find some cover and distribute from there the warm food the men had long done without: thick bean soup with scraps of meat, bluish barley stew, yellow peas and ham – all packed in heat-retaining tin containers, which the food carriers lugged down the final stretches to the trenches. The operation had its dangers. A soldier with warm soup in his belly fights better, and causing privations that might break the men's morale was part of the civilised nations' machinery of war. Advance batteries lay in wait for the field kitchen staff. Sometimes they miscalculated but usually they didn't, and their actions were always disastrous.

In the early morning around 6.30am, when the ground mist, which had long since turned into autumnal morning fog, parted for a moment, the French at Belleville caught sight of Captain Niggl's ASC men at work. They had known for a long time that the Germans were expanding their positions behind the lines and had marked the presumed locations of these bases on their maps. For weeks, the Germans had been planning the push that would reclaim Douaumont village and Fort Vaux. They'd been saving up ammunition, improving their approach roads and preparing their field batteries for the advance. The construction of the German front had many advantages, but flexibility wasn't one of them. Communication between the artillery and the observers in the infantry, especially those in the forts, was handled much better, more quickly and more intelligently by the French. A couple of minutes after the suspected field kitchen was discovered, shrapnel burst over the area in the gathering fog, whipping down on the ASC men, who scattered in panic. Only eight men were injured in all because the French made the mistake of rapidly moving their fire further forward on to the huge depression that opened out to the south from Douaumont, and through which the food carriers should indeed have run. Nonetheless, the company returned at 9.30am instead of

8am, and that hour and a half was nerve-racking for Niggl.

He'd been so happy, so pleased with Feicht, who really had turned things round in a most satisfactory manner with his idea about the army postal depot, the accompanying letter and all the rest of it. He could now calmly wait for the lieutenant to make his next move. He'd even metabolised the increase in work, worry and to and fro caused by the arrival of his first two companies. Douaumont was now rammed with men, and so his Bavarians could no longer complain, since more and more ASC battalions shared their fate. The Somme battle hadn't just ripped half the batteries out of the Meuse east bank sector like eye teeth from a jaw (whether one believed this or not); it had also stolen away entire infantry squads – how many, no one knew – which were to be replaced with ASC men and Landwehr. It all sounded preposterous, for what were the ASC men to do there? Niggl knew full well what: they were to relieve the infantry regiments of the heavy lifting and reinforcing of the supply lines in the rear positions. It was a fine mess that meant his men were chased across the field like hares and his casualty list had trebled. They'd got off lightly this time. Sergeant Pangerl had taken a bullet in the backside, five men had been more or less badly injured and were looking forward to being sent home, and two others looked as if they might be finished with their grey uniforms for good – joy unconfined. This all ran through the captain's mind, as he tossed and turned in his bed trying to catch up on his morning's sleep. He had lice and missed the warm bath he'd always been used to as an officer in a foreign country. At home in Weilheim he seldom bathed. Now the dreadful suckers were tormenting him as if he were a common soldier. It was already 10.30am when he eventually fell asleep. His cell, as he called it, was pretty dark even during the day. He had a host of unclear, largely unpleasant dreams, and any refreshment his slumbers might have brought vanished thanks to the way he was woken up.

If a shell hits the roof you're sleeping under, the noise of the impact wakes you – or you never wake again. If it falls near you, however, 50m to your right or left, the dreadful howl of its approach bores into your soul first. You spend five faltering heartbeats still dazed but wide awake waiting for the blast, and that fraction of a minute saps your vitality. At exactly the same time as the recent attack, a second 40cm mortar battery fired at Douaumont, but this time on to the opposite corner of the pentagon. The first shot landed some 30m to the right of the fort on the disintegrating slope. Herr Niggl slept through its approach, though his subconscious was on high alert. This was the first sign of attrition and exactly what the attacker wanted. He was awoken by the burst and thunder of the explosion, which shook the fort's foundations from the side. *Train crash*, he thought still half asleep. *I'm on the Augsburg to Berlin sleeper on my way to an official meeting about awarding Hindenburg the freedom of Weilheim.* Then he woke up. He wasn't on the sleeper train; he was in the most accursed place in Europe. That had been a heavy-calibre weapon, a repeat of recent events. The French really were gunning for them. There wouldn't be a minute's peace from now on. It was all kicking off now. This was the final hour.

'Oh, most holy Saint Aloysius, pray for me now and in the hour of my death,' he cried. 'I shall go to Hell impenitent. My soul will burn forever. Bring a priest. I must confess!'

And then, oh yes, oh Jesus, down it howled, dragging a trail of hellish screaming in its wake. It was the devil, whinnying and hissing. Where, oh where would it strike? He dove under the bedclothes. A blaring and crashing, an echo rolling through the fort's corridors and tunnels, signalled relief. It had landed further off this time, in the northeast wing by the sound of it, the sapper depot where his enemy lived. Limbs aquiver and sweating from every pore, Niggl huddled in his bed, listening to the men's shouts and the clatter of their boots running past his door.

'Don't let your imagination run away with you, Alois Niggl,' he told himself. 'It's too much to hope that the French will have carried off the second brother too. No one gets that lucky.'

His hair fell in his eyes. An irksome fly drank his sweat. At last, the clerk Dillinger rushed in to report a direct hit on the sapper depot: nuffink damaged. Smoothing his hair over his forehead, the captain calmly asked if Lieutenant Kroysing had been informed of the company's recent losses – if he was in fact in the fort.

Dillinger answered both questions in the affirmative. The lieutenant had just been called into a meeting with the airfield commander when the first one struck. Although everyone knew there must be a second, the lieutenant nonetheless set off and what was more took a short cut across the inner courtyard, which was littered with great fat shell splinters. There could so easily have been an accident.

'We'd never have got over that,' said the captain, adding that the orderly room should try to find a Catholic chaplain to bestow spiritual consolation on the men in their time of need. Dillinger's face lit up; the orderly room would get on it straight away. The division currently holding the sector was admittedly from Saxony and Protestant, but such difficulties could be overcome with a bit of ingenuity.

'Very good, Dillinger,' said the captain. 'Let me know when you've sorted it out.'

When Private Bertin heard about the Bavarian dead and wounded, he went slowly pale under his tan both from the shock and on Lieutenant Kroysing's account.

It was now September, and this part of the front had never been so quiet. There were good reasons for the Germans not to attack, but the French weren't budging either, and that gave pause. It was a magical September. In the unspoilt ancient woodland, some 60m wide, small yellow leaves flickered in the burnished light. The longer nights were perfect for a game of skat. The two genial Badeners and Bertin took turns on the switchboard. Friedrich Strumpf, park keeper at Schwetzingen, was convinced he'd seen grey feral cats, and so he often took his infantry rifle out at noon, hoping to get a catskin for his rheumatism. He always came back grumbling, down two cartridges and with no catskin. The little minxes just wouldn't stand still, he said. Meanwhile, the rear part of the valley was being filled with wood stacks of various sizes. The rainy season was approaching, and the construction troops and sappers were getting ready to raise the narrow-gauge railway platforms.

Almost every morning or afternoon, Bertin wandered over to the field howitzer emplacement to get the post, choosing a time when the light was bad. 'You have the youngest legs, lad,' the Badeners said. 'You still enjoy running about.'

Bertin did enjoy it, for as well as sating his thirst for adventure, he had found a genuine countryman and passing acquaintance in the lieutenant and battery commander there. Lieutenant Paul Schanz had taken his school leaving examination as an outside student with Bertin's class at school some years previously. He was from Russian Poland, where his father worked as head foreman in a coal mine. The lieutenant had initially taken a bored tone with Bertin but had softened when he recognised him. By the end of Bertin's second visit this tall, blonde man with blue eyes was inviting him to linger for a game of chess. The lieutenant was delightful company when he opened up. He and Bertin sat in the entrance to the dugout with a box between them shuffling the black and white pieces around. They talked to each other about the past and the present. They spoke about peace, which must surely come at the beginning of 1917. Bertin got the inside track on the light field howitzer – its mechanism and range, and how best to use it. Lieutenant Schanz, smart and clean-shaven, with smooth skin and a boyish laugh, told him how his men were getting into all kinds of careless ways, partly because they were so used to what they did and partly because they were sick of it. They were fed up with the whole bloody business. They no longer used a charge of salt to dampen the gleam from their shots because they didn't want to have to clean the dirty barrels. They'd left their carabines at the rest camp so the locks wouldn't get rusty – there were a lot of water trickles among the rocks – and anyway he didn't even have the prescribed number of canister shells for close combat.

'Who needs canister shells here?' he said. 'We'll see to it that the Frogs don't break through, and we'll never have enough shrapnel.' Thus, at the back, under a green tarpaulin, was a store of what were called canister shells, but in fact it was a dump of another 300 shrapnel.

The battery hardly fired now. Strict orders to save ammunition and keep it hidden from the French observers. On all the hills, sound-ranging troops lay in wait in the trenches on both sides, intelligent men with good eyes able to calculate a gun position's distance from the interval between firing and impact. Using this information and with the help of the captive balloons, both sides were able to mark the enemy's gun positions on their maps. The day would come when this information would be needed. Bertin also got the chance to look through the periscopic binoculars in Lieutenant Schanz's observation post. They had been cleverly installed under a jutting rock behind the guns with a decoy barrel in a treetop 80m to the side to deceive the French aeroplanes. Through that curious apparatus, he saw inclines, scarred hillsides, tiny beings moving about, sharply alive, walls of earth and small hollows. Sometimes clouds appeared and drifted away. Those were the Belleville ridges, Schanz explained. Behind the horizon was a French battery, probably 400m to the rear, 5,500m from barrel to barrel.

'I'd like to know if there's another Schanz lying in wait in a dugout over there with his eye on our battery,' he said.

Bertin didn't want to let the amazing instrument go. 'All in aid of destruction,' he said, shaking his head and looking again into the grey-rimmed lenses. 'When will we use this magic for something constructive?'

'When indeed? After the peace, of course. When those chaps over there have realised they don't have us by the throat.'

They were united in their desire for peace and they strolled back through the light, sunny air to have a smoke and think about how their lives might turn out. Paul Schanz hoped for a career in the administration of the Upper Silesian coal mines, where his father now worked. There was a lot of work to be done there. His father had written that the mines were being ruined. Nothing could be replaced properly, and the workings were threatened by gas and water. German coal was one of the most important tools of war: neutral and allied countries couldn't get enough of it. Transport trains left Upper Silesian railway stations bound for Constantinople, Aleppo, Haifa.

Bertin's visits often lasted only half an hour. He needed to be on the move again. One time, he didn't meet his friends. They were further forwards installing new mine throwers. There was to be a local operation in mid-October to improve the infantry positions. But the next time, he'd arranged to meet Süßmann and as they walked along, chatting amiably, Süßmann told him about the casualties that had so put the wind up Captain Niggl.

'Our author is horrified by the burden on your conscience, Lieutenant,' joked Süßmann shortly after they arrived at Kroysing's billet, taking a deep drag of his cigarette.

Bertin, who was enjoying the first puffs of a freshly filled pipe, met Kroysing's astonished grey eyes calmly. He knew he'd have to choose his words carefully in order not to cause offence. 'Four dead,' he said, 'and so much suffering. I'm sure you're not indifferent to that either.'

'Why not?' asked Kroysing.

'Does that require an answer?' countered Bertin, whereupon the lieutenant told him not to sit there feeling pleased with himself but to think logically.

'Is the war my responsibility? Obviously not. I'm not even liable for the transfer of Niggl's battalion; that was some area commander or other. And in the final analysis it was a signature from the crown prince that put his men under my command. So, what do you want from me?'

Bertin asked him to leave this nice big picture aside and concentrate on one, perhaps incidental detail: who had had the men flung into Douaumont and why?

'Because duty required it!' Kroysing roared.

Bertin stepped back, blushed and was silent. He didn't tell Kroysing that people roar when they are in the wrong. Instead, he resolved to leave again as soon as possible.

Kroysing frowned darkly, annoyed by his outburst. He bit his lip, glowered straight ahead, and then at his shocked visitors. 'I'm sorry,' he said at last. 'But you're so naïve it can really get on people's nerves.'

'That's a shame,' Bertin answered. 'I was really enjoying your tobacco, and now my naïvety has spoilt my enjoyment.'

Kroysing considered. The man was sensitive. That was the good side of the self-pity that had provoked his own outburst, and it made up for it. 'Sir,' he said jokingly, 'you're a sensitive soul. I obviously need to bone up on the correct treatment of ASC men. How about a conciliatory drink?' He opened the cabinet behind him – he was so tall he only needed to stretch out his arm – pulled out a familiar bottle and filled some glasses. 'Well, Prost,' he said. 'Here's to getting along.' Bertin took small sips, Süßmann knocked back half his glass and Kroysing downed his in one with a satisfied look in his eyes. 'Ah,' he said. 'That's the stuff. You can wage war without women, ammunition or even trenches, but not without tobacco and definitely not without alcohol.

In an effort to beat down his hurt feelings, Bertin expounded on Serbian plum brandy, which was nearly as good as this cognac. Kroysing pretended to be very interested and said that if he ever got tired of the western front, he might be tempted to go to Macedonia on account of the slivovitz – in other words, there was an uncomfortable atmosphere.

Little Süßmann looked wisely from one man to the other. 'No,' he said, 'you gentlemen aren't going to sort things out like this. You need to take your dispute seriously. It was really me who caused this problem so I need to resolve it. Our author thinks that you brought the ASC men to Douaumont and are responsible for what befell them, because you have a private matter to settle with their captain. Isn't that right, my dear author?' Bertin nodded. 'To you, the Bavarian ASC men were just an appendage of the captain, unimportant statistics,' continued Süßmann, 'but our author's moral searchlight is now trained on them. Look, he says: dead and wounded. Mortal beings. Your move, Lieutenant,' he finished, stubbing out his cigarette. The ashtray on the table was made from a flattened brass cartridge case from a large howitzer shell. They were often used in this way in sapper depots.

Kroysing thought for a moment. 'Sergeant Süßmann gets an honourable mention for setting out the characters before us correctly. Let's consider these men. Did any of them lift a finger to stand by my brother? Not at all. And on whose account had my brother incurred Niggl & Co's disfavour? For those men. In a certain general sense, they therefore share responsibility for his death. In the same general sense, I tossed them into a slightly more dangerous frying pan than the one they were in before. I'll take responsibility for that.

Duty demanded that some labour company or other did it. I chose that one.'

Deep in thought, Bertin took another sip of cognac. 'I'm afraid there's something not quite right there. The dead and wounded far outweigh the degree of guilt that can be attributed to an individual ASC man, because the company's guilt is collective, and you must take account of the fact that the common soldier has few rights.'

'Those affected will have to settle up with those who have so far been spared,' said Kroysing shortly. 'It's nothing to do with me. I'm not playing God. And how do you explain your part in it?' Bertin looked amazed. 'Look at that innocent angel,' laughed Kroysing. 'Yes, someone always has to hit us over the head with our own part in things. Who set the whole thing in motion, eh? Shook me out of my lamentable indifference? From whom did I first learn that my brother had been set up? It's enough to astonish a layman and surprise an expert,' he finished triumphantly, using an expression current at the time.

Bertin looked at Süßmann in shock, then at Kroysing's triumphant face, then pensively up at the vaulted ceiling, which formed an impenetrable barrier between him and the sky. 'I hadn't thought of that,' he conceded honestly. 'There's certainly something in what you say. It's hard to unravel the tangle of cause and effect. But I didn't want that.'

'Exactly. Neither did I. But answer me this, dear sir: would you have kept quiet if someone had told you about my dangerous character? Weren't you rather keen for me to right the wrong, as I was the victim's brother and the best man for the job?'

'Yes,' said Bertin, sunk in thought, analysing his own motives, 'that was more or less what I wanted. In a vague way, you know. Something terrible had happened. The world had gone awry, but things have come to a pretty pass when it's sent further awry by our attempts to put it right.'

'Yes,' laughed Krosying amiably, 'the world's construction is a bit faulty, at least from the point of view of us humans. It short circuits and backfires all the time. If we built an engine along those lines we'd probably be in heaven quicker than it takes to get from here to our new mine throwers.'

'But where's the fault?' asked Bertin passionately. 'It must be mended if our world view isn't to collapse.'

'Why shouldn't our precious world view collapse?' asked Sergeant Süßmann in astonishment. 'Hasn't yours collapsed?' he asked pointing a crooked index finger at Kroysing. 'Hasn't mine collapsed,' and he turned the finger on himself. 'It's just too bad about yours, isn't that right, my writerly and prophetic friend? Four dead and about 40 wounded,' he continued, 'and here in Douaumont. If it weren't so boring for the lieutenant, I'd tell the gentleman here the story of this hollow mountain as I experienced it. I promised him I would, in any case.'

'Oh yes, that's not to be missed,' said Kroysing. 'He ought to hear it, and I'll be fascinated to watch our author's face. On you go, Süßmann.'

'A couple of thousand years after the Deluge had dried up, when God had turned his countenance away from the world and people had multiplied like ants, on the 21st of February of the year 1916, men rose up out of their trenches, sappers to the front.' Süßmann blinked and continued in the same tone: 'In those four days as the attack advanced, legion upon legion of grey and grey-blue martyrs died as they'd been ordered. Their bodies were strewn between Caures wood and the hills, and their souls multiplied the heavenly host by an army corps.'

CHAPTER TWO

Little Süßmann

'WE LAY FLAT on the ground at the edge of the glacis and looked over at Douaumont, which was covered in snow and giving nothing away – a detachment of sappers attached to men from a platoon of the 24th. The ground was frozen, but we were hot. We'd all been drinking and besides we were scared. Not a shot came from over there, do you follow? It was so threatening. Who would have thought that Douaumont, the cornerstone of Verdun, would be undefended with no garrison? French shells were dropping on the wood behind us but they came from somewhere else. Our own artillery was bombarding the village of Douaumont and the barbed wire outside it, and there was a French machine gun rattling over there. But the block of rock itself was silent. We had our coats on but we were soaked through underneath. Crawling through frozen mud is no fun. We wanted to feel something dry under our feet, to undress, light a stove and sleep. Our artillery kept battering the bare escarpment of the casemate, but there wasn't a whisper of a reply. Eventually, we threw ourselves forwards, the first lieutenant at the front, headed downhill to the barbed wire – which thankfully wasn't electrified – clambered on to the monster's roof and to hell with it. Then we were on top and wanted to get down because our goal was inside. And as we were talking and staring apprehensively into the depths below us, we suddenly saw a detachment of men nosing their way very carefully out of a tunnel, and before we could shoot them or they us, we realised they were our neighbouring platoon. The two officers glared at each other, and if I'm not mistaken they still argue today about who the genuine conqueror of Douaumont was. Inside, we took the garrison prisoners: about 20 gunners in an armoured turret. They'd been firing for four days and four nights and now they were asleep – bit rude, no? Just when we arrived. But we kindly excused them. That's how Douaumont was captured by the heroic first battalion of the 29th regiment, and anyone who doesn't believe it can pay me one thaler.'

Kroysing watched Private Bertin's baffled face with amusement. Bertin sat there in his uniform, hair shorn like a real soldier, but seemed to have believed all the Supreme Army Command's pompous self-congratulation and to want to live in a world of heroic deeds like a child in a book of fairytales. 'So that was the famous storming of Douaumont? Before his Majesty's eyes...'

Raucous laughter. 'Oh boy,' cried Kroysing, 'spare us!' And Süßmann, giggling like a little imp, gasped: 'Where was Douaumont, and where was the Kaiser?'

'Gentlemen,' said Bertin, not at all offended, 'that's what it said in the report. We read it out to each other from the bulletin board at brigade headquarters in Vranje, a small mountain town north of Kumanovo in Macedonia – a crowd of field greys in the spring sunshine – and I can still hear a young hussar lieutenant next to me shouting: "Brilliant, now there'll be an end to this shit." How am I supposed to know what really happened?'

'Oh boy,' cried Kroysing again and his eyes shone in the light from his third glass of cognac, 'haven't you worked out yet that it's all a lie? Lies to the rear and at the front, lies on our side and over there. We're bluffing, and they're bluffing. The only ones who aren't bluffing are the dead – the only decent ones in the whole show...'

'Nothing is true,' said Sergeant Süßmann, 'and everything's permitted. Are you familiar with that expression? The Assassins' motto.' Bertin confirmed that he was indeed educated and knew about the Assassins – an oriental murder sect from the Middle Ages, whose sheikh was called 'The Old Man of the Mountain'.

'You're educated,' said Kroysing, calming down. 'Thank God. Now we just need to understand how a world works where young men such as yourself are knocking about like Parsifal in squaddy's boots. That motto rules here, my dear boy. Nothing that's printed is true, including the Bible. Everything men want to do is permitted, and that includes you and me if we have the guts. I don't want to hold up the youngster here, because he'll paint you a picture of how things really are here, but if you believe what the reports say, that we captured Fort Vaux in May and then magnanimously left "the ruins of the armoured fortress" to the French the next day, you deserve the Iron Cross. We laughed ourselves silly, my boy. But the infantry were furious because they were still under fire from that concrete monstrosity, which the French were defending like mad, but now they were also being pelted with questions and threats, and being dressed down by telephone, just because some idiot from headquarters had probably looked through his periscopic binoculars, from God knows how many kilometres to the rear, and had mistaken the backs of German prisoners being led into the fort by the French for those of our heroic conquerors taking their prize. Fort Vaux fell in June, and that's all there is to it, and the way it held out amazed the world. War only runs smoothly on paper. A plague on all writing jackals.' And he tipped out his fourth cognac, smaller this time, and drank. 'And now it's your turn, young Süßmann, and I'll become a Trappist monk.'

'We'll believe it when we see it,' joked Sergeant Süßmann. 'At least we had Douaumont and we stayed there, but the French advance positions weren't far below. Now the show really began: counter attack! At the end of April, the French were actually tramping about above our heads. They'd retaken the upper works as far as the northwest corner, but the machine guns in the embrasures and the flanking positions stopped them coming down. Then our reinforcements arrived, and they had to leave with their tails between their legs. That's when we learnt from the French prisoners that our success in February had been due to a bit of standard military confusion. Two fresh divisions had taken over the sector, one to the left and and one to the right of Douaumont. Each one was convinced that the other had occupied the fort, and the relieved division had withdrawn so bloody quickly to Belleville ridge that no one knew how things stood. If we'd had fresh reserves back then, our victor's luck might have taken us forward to Fleury and Souville, and who knows if Verdun would still be in French hands today. It would still have been tough, but it would have bucked us up and the reports would have been glorious. But the miserable French weren't giving us anything for free. We had to attack Thiaumont and Fleury, and that's what we were doing when the great explosion happened that gave me a glimpse of the Hereafter. Prost to that!'

He drained his glass and Kroysing refilled it. Staring intently into a corner of the small room, Süßmann continued with his story in his even, boyish voice. At that time, the beginning of May, Douaumont had been the strongest support point on the front. It was packed with soldiers, supplies, ammunition and sapper equipment, and it had a large dressing station. It was like a huge communications tunnel leading to the front and back. The Bavarians storming Fleury slept there before attacking or collapsed exhausted on the paving stones afterwards. The great attack of 5 May failed after a massive bombardment, but down below the fort still teemed with life.

'Back then, our depot was over where the ASC men sleep now underneath the armoured turret, which the French had used as an ammunition store. A few dozen shells were still left over. Our mines and flamethrower oil reserve tanks were stored there. More harmless stuff, such as flares, was lined up against the corridor wall, with crates of hand grenades on the other side. On the right of the corridor were steps leading down to the hospital rooms, where the doctors were busy day and night. Orderlies dashed back and forth, hauling in the serious cases, while those with minor injuries or who were just shell-shocked or had been buried crouched by the walls, sleeping or dozing, until they got soup, which they spooned down as if it were heaven-sent. But as we know, heaven is right beside hell, and there must have been a couple of nut cases among them, because, using the boxes of flares as cover, two or three of those Bavarian morons went over to heat up their chow with a hand grenade – it was too cold for them, do you see? In order to make it taste better, they invited the devil in.

'Now, anyone can unscrew an infantry hand grenade and use the head, which contains the charge of powder, to warm up his food if he has a couple of stones to stand a pot on and everything nearby is harmless. But as bad luck would have it, my Bavarians picked up a hand grenade that had already been filed off or was defective, and it blew up in their faces. That might have just been their private misfortune. Screams. Three or four more dead. A few wounded. That didn't count for much in the battle for Fleury. But Satan decreed that the splinters should fly through the open door into the ammunition dump and stick into one of our harmless flame throwers, which are filled with a blend of heavy and light oils. The stuff flowed out, evaporated, and contact with air turned it into an explosive. I saw it with my own eyes; naturally, I don't know where the bit of burning wood came from that set it alight – a smouldering cigarette would've done it. "Fire!" screamed those around the hand grenade cooks. At the same time, heavy fragments were hurled against the roof and the burning oil tipped on to the rocket crates made of nice, dry pinewood.

'In that moment, we were already running. We ran forwards, the clever ones in silence, some screaming with terror. You know the long tunnel where I met the captain just now? It's 80m long, I believe. Men ran into it from all the side passages. We were fighting for our lives with our friends and comrades. Woe betide anyone who stumbled or turned round. We men from the depot were pretty much the furthest back. In front of us were the minor casualties and the Bavarians who'd just been relieved. The ASC men were in the side passages and the infantrymen were up front – a seething knot of anxious grey backs, necks, heads and fists. Then a crash came from behind. There was thick smoke and heat, a dreadful stench as the signal rockets exploded like some colossal fireworks. The flames were bound to reach the shells and they did, but first they reached our hand grenades. There was a rumble from behind, and a jolt with the force of an earthquake flung us all against the walls, me included. I was 40m into the tunnel when I fell over. Actually, I didn't fall over; I passed out. I lost consciousness propped against the curved wall and hung for I don't know how long wedged in the throng. I assume I gradually sank to the floor with them. That must have been when the explosion came that wiped out all life in the tunnel, the side corridors, the casemates, the hospital – everywhere. I choked on the poisonous gases. I was actually dead, subjectively speaking. If you can feel fear, it's terrible, because your lungs struggle for fresh air and inhale ever more poison and muck, your throat burns, your ears roar – but for me expiry was a relief. Let's drink to that.'

He took a small mouthful, and Bertin, who was listening intently, finally drained his glass. For a moment, Süßmann seemed sunk in the distant past. Then he resurfaced, lit a cigarette and continued: 'I came to in the rain. I was lying under the open sky on the rubble-strew paving stones of the inner courtyard. I gazed up at the grey clouds, at first uncomprehendingly. Everything inside me felt raw and burning, but I was alive. It was probably a while before I gave any sign of life. I watched men in smoke masks dragging soldiers' bodies out of the opening to the blackened tunnel, where a plume of black smoke curled. I wanted to check the time, but my watch was gone. I always used to wear a small ring I inherited from my grandmother on my left hand – a lucky turquoise. It was gone too. I searched for my cigarette case. Also gone for good. My tunic had been unbuttoned and my shirt ripped open. My chest was bare, which was probably what woke me up and rescued me. But there had been quite a bit of wages in my neck pouch, and it had also vanished. I sat up then – the damp paving stones felt good on my hands – and saw that all around me were stone-dead men: blue, suffocated, blackened faces. A column of 400 men takes up a fair bit of room, but there were many more than that lying in the courtyard and the orderlies kept bringing out more. They'd cleaned me out, but I didn't begrudge them it because I was breathing air again. I don't ever want to be hanged or choked. I never turn on the gas tap and when I hear about our gas attacks I feel sick. I'd prefer a shell splinter in the head or a bullet in the heart.

'I buttoned up my tunic, even turning the collar up, and staggered to my feet. I felt dizzy, it hurt when I coughed and I had a dreadful headache, but that was all. The medical NCO who saw me first was amazed. "Well, you're a lucky devil," were his first words to me. I was already a sergeant by then but I'd forgotten that. I was still a bit dazed and so I saluted and said, 'Private Süßmann, sir,' and I'm told I grinned stupidly, though I consider that slanderous. I was given something to drink, Aspirin for my headache, a couple of whiffs of oxygen, and then I told them what had happened. I didn't know much at that point, but it was enough to make them decide not to clear out the extinguished crater. Our captain had the dead all carried back in again, but I was already asleep in the new hospital section on a nice, comfy bed by then – still wood wool, of course – and when I woke up the second time I was really fine. I wasn't coughing any more. My head was throbbing and there was a ring of raw flesh on the inside of my throat, but that was about it. Later on, I saw our construction squad walling up the passages. They're still there now, the dead residents of Douaumont, a whole battalion of them, can't be much fewer than 1,000 men, all the occupants of the far end of that wing: Bavarians, sappers, ASC men, the entire dressing station.

'That was the explosion in Douaumont. It wasn't reported, and if you like I'll take you to the spot later and you can pray for the souls of the fallen. Since then, I've thought about things more carefully and I no longer find them all that agreeable. And now you should be heading back.'

Bertin said he should and thanked Süßmann for telling him his story. But something still troubled him. 'Did you go straight back on duty after that as if nothing had happened?' he asked, stretching himself.

'What do you think? Sergeant Süßmann retorted. 'I got some sick leave, naturally. Fourteen glorious days in May at home, where I didn't breathe a word about any of it. Civilians don't like their picture of the war to be spoiled by the real war. And, anyway, we'd been told to keep our traps shut.'

'It's always like that,' said Lieutenant Kroysing. 'He who knows too much dies young. And how did Captain Niggl respond to my kind enquiry after his health? Will he be able to turn out tonight?'

Sergeant Süßmann pulled a grave face and said the captain still felt ill. The doctor had prescribed – or at least authorised – bed rest, particularly as there were now three acting lieutenants present who could take his place.

Kroysing's tone was also grave: 'Shame. I do regret causing an old officer nothing but trouble. And I'm not very congenial company. When you come back, my friend,' he said, standing up and offering Bertin his hand, 'Niggl's health will have got a lot worse.'

Sergeant Süßmann arranged his cap in such a way that both cockades hung over the bridge of his nose. He planned to accompany Bertin some of the way. Then he asked whether the lieutenant wasn't perhaps being too optimistic about the captain's health. The telephone exchange had received instructions from the captain's orderly room to find a Catholic field chaplain. He'd be arriving in the next few days if the Frogs continued to behave themselves.

A thin smile played on Kroysing's lips. 'He wants to confess,' he said. 'Does no harm if a man's going soft on the inside. Mulch is the name given to that condition in apples and pears. Thanks, Süßmann. After that news, I think I may turn out tonight myself.'

CHAPTER THREE

Father Lochner

'IT'S GOING TO be a hard winter,' observed Strumpf the park-keeper a morning or two later as he stepped out of his hut, which had once been a French blockhouse.

Blue sky and sunlight flashed through the clouds of mist. Beechnuts hung heavily from gilded beech branches, and red berries shone among the rowan leaves, barberry sprigs and bramble bushes. Unperturbed by the approaching thunder, a pair of squirrels worked in the treetops, driving out a squawking magpie.

'A hard winter's all we need,' countered his comrade Kilian in Baden dialect.

Bertin was at the switchboard communicating with the Cape camp. Through the open window, he heard Friedrich Strumpf expanding on how nature alleviated bad cold snaps for birds and wild animals by providing a surfeit of fruit, almost as if someone were looking out for the innocent creatures. Kilian the tobacco worker laughed at that: he was a free thinker, a Darwinist, as he proudly explained, saw the struggle for existence everywhere confirmed and would have preferred harsh winters to be alleviated for the women and children at home first of all. As he spoke, he sat happily in the early autumn sunshine darning a grey woollen sock. He had time for that kind of thing now, while his wife, who had taken his place in the factory and was bringing up two children, couldn't possibly be expected to mend his winter things as well. Bertin, earphones on his head, nodded. Every individual man in the army, himself included, was attached to threads that travelled far back behind the lines. Then the switchboard buzzed again, and he received instructions from the sapper depot in Fosses wood about changing the points, with enquiries about construction troops and the number of wagons on the siding. He liked the little railway operation. This tiny cog in a giant wheel helped him to grasp the human ingenuity required to power the front line, how everything had to be done exactly right, so that when the crucial moment came a smooth and decisive blow could be struck. The two Badeners were happy with him. They just shook their heads at his enterprising spirit when he headed off past the field howitzers to Douaumont. Karl Kilian understood him better than his older colleague; it was right and proper for a newspaper reporter to do that, he said, so that he could relate the truth later.

Bertin knew full well that the good times were coming to an end. In a couple of days the man on leave would return. Bertin would then have to pack his things and go back to the stuffy, noisy barracks, his company and the poisonous fug around Graßnick and Glinsky, where all finer feelings were steamrollered like grass beneath a rolling donkey. Group living seemed to drain people of energy. He'd recovered here in the sunshine. He slept better in the clear air, he had time off and he enjoyed his food more because Friedrich Strumpf knew how to liven up the rations with all kinds of flavourings. Night hours spent awake at the silent switchboard reading under the electric light gave him the peace and solitude to be himself. He often saw beyond the printed pages to young Kroysing, who'd already been swept so far along by the river of life, and his wild brother who was wading through its centre, knee-deep today, waist-high tomorrow... If ever a man had needed this war it was Eberhard Kroysing – to find himself, express his nature, test his range, as he put it. It was the urge for such experience that had made an entire generation of German youth flee the strictures of the pre-war period for unbridled war – Kroysing, Süßmann, Bertin, all of them. In 1914, they'd all felt that real life – a life of danger and hardship – was just about to begin. Now here they sat sunk in the disgusting realities of it and expected to come to terms with them. If anyone could have predicted to the schoolboy Süßmann how he would feel two years after the start of the war or what he would have gone through... boy, oh boy!

Then Süßmann's cheerful voice crackled in Bertin's ear. He said he was to say hello to Bertin from his company, or at least from the Fosses wood unit. He'd worked long and hard with them the day before. In particular, two Berliners had been asking for him: a funny chap with fat cheeks, freckles and very clever eyes (Bertin nodded to himself: Lebehde) and a bad-tempered hunchback (aha, Pahl). They'd said to tell him there was plenty of company news and that he should come back soon if only to see the arrival of a new sergeant major – something he would no doubt welcome.

What rubbish, thought Bertin listlessly. *And from next week that will be my world again, day in, day out. Yes*, he quoted the poet Schiller, *the great days of Aranjuez would soon be over.*

'You're leaving us,' said the lad. 'Kroysing still has a lot to discuss with you.

He said to ask you to stay the night with us tomorrow.'

'That's easily arranged,' said Bertin, somewhat taken aback. He'd make sure to arrive before the evening bombardment so the gunfire didn't spoil his journey.

In the entrance tunnel to the fort, Bertin got caught up in an eddy of departing infantry – a battalion waiting for nightfall to move up to the front and send the current trench crew for a so-called rest. A great deal of food had been handed out, and the men's cooking pots were steaming, possibly for the last time in weeks. In one corner of the yard, sergeants were bent over postal bags calling out the names of their squads: 'Wädchen!' – 'Here.' 'Sauerbier! – 'Here.' 'Klotsche!' – 'Here.' 'Frauenfeind!' – 'Here.' As Bertin pushed through them, he got a whiff of them and saw their thin faces, skin stretched over bones, and exhausted expressions. Few of them were more than medium height; none of them was fresh. He almost felt guilty in their presence, because he looked upright, reasonably well fed and refreshed. Their sing-song Saxon speech helped to neutralise the bitterness that saturated their exchanges. In their caps (they wouldn't change into steel helmets until they were at the front) and shabby uniforms they looked half-grown, more like 17-year-old schoolboys on a class outing than the living wall, which, according to the cant in the newspapers, was protecting the homeland on French soil.

It was nearly 4.30pm. The September sun bathed the pentagon's massive inner chamber and the deep cut leading to the casemate in rich, golden light. Bertin wove his way patiently through the throngs of men, who had laid down their bundles of hand grenades, assault equipment and gas masks. Muzzle covers gleamed on their rifles, and the locks were wrapped in rags to protect them from the dust in the narrow approach trenches and shelled zones. A group who'd already eaten stopped him and asked him for a light for their cigarettes and pipes. Bertin spent a few minutes with them. They were curious because of his grey oil-cloth cap and yellow brass cross, and his glasses gave them the idea he might know when peace would come. Weariness was etched on their brows, and they made no secret of it, but Bertin knew that wouldn't stop them giving their last. As usual, their rest days had not been restorative. They'd improved rear positions, brought up materials and been subjected to all kinds of roll calls designed to maintain discipline. The only difference compared with the front line was hot food, undisturbed sleep and plenty of water to wash in. It was something but it wasn't much. As they swarmed around in the fort, they seemed to Bertin to be like animated fragments of the wrecked upper works, which looked as though they had long ago lost all powers of resistance. Shell holes bordered shell holes. Scraps of yellowed turf still clung on in the shadow of the ramparts, but the brickwork had collapsed, falling into the trenches outside and blocking tunnel entrances inside. The ramparts were like mounds of earth dotted with steel splinters, which was particularly astonishing when you considered the unshakable fastness of the underground fortress. The infantrymen were like that too. They looked like drifting herds of death, workers in the factory of destruction, and displayed all the indifference that industry and machines force on men. But inside they were unbroken. They went to the front without enthusiasm or illusions, buoyed only by the hope of returning in one piece in 10 days. Forward again and back again until released by a wound that hospitalised them – or death. But they didn't like to think about that. They wanted to live. They hoped to go home. And now they wanted to sleep a couple of hours longer.

Still brooding on their fate, Bertin climbed down over some sandbags and disappeared into the bowels of the fort. With no guide, he initially got completely lost in the passages. Eventually, he ended up in the telephone exchange where a man who like himself wore glasses told him the way. With the Saxons' lilt still in his ear, he found the telephonist's clean Hanoverian tones almost disconcerting. He himself was a Silesian. He was visiting a Franconian and a Berliner by birth. The Germans had become thoroughly integrated and had learnt to respect one another.

'Come in!' Kroysing called out curtly. A visitor sat in his room, a gentleman. On the bed lay a kind of riding hat with one upturned brim. The visitor had violet lapels, a plump, brown, clean-shaven oval of a face with an exceptionally small mouth and very clear, bright eyes: a priest! A field chaplain in Douaumont with a silver cross round his neck! Bertin knew you were supposed to salute these men like officers and that they set a lot of store by that. He'd have preferred to make an immediate getaway, but Lieutenant Kroysing, behind his desk as usual, was emphatically warm: 'At last, my friend. May I introduce you gentlemen? My friend Bertin, a trainee lawyer currently in the garb of an ASC private. Father Benedikt Lochner, currently in cavalry trooper's garb.'

The priest laughed heartily. His hand in Bertin's felt fat but strong. 'You shouldn't speak about cavalry troopers, Lieutenant. I came here riding pillion on a motorbike – what Berliners call the bridemobile and Viennese the dolly stool. So take your pick: I'm either a bride or a dolly bird.' He ran a smoothing hand through his thin blonde hair, dabbed his head with a handkerchief, said he found it rather hot down below and took a sip of cognac. His jovial, urban Rhineland dialect sounded odd on his delicate lips.

'It's absolutely fine for my friend Bertin to hear what we have to discuss,' said Kroysing, resuming their conversation. 'In fact, no one is more qualified to listen in and comment than him. He spoke to my poor brother the day before he died, heard about his troubles and offered him help – the only man to do so in a desert, or should I say a vale of tears – and I'll remember that until the day I die. You won't mind that he's a Jew. Compared to Protestant heretics, they're chips off the old block.'

Bertin sat glumly on Kroysing's bed. He'd have preferred to be alone with him. The priest assessed Bertin, the shape of his skull, the beginnings of a bald patch on his crown. *True enough,* he thought. *This young man looks like a monk in some famous painting. I can't remember which one, but it's bound to be Italian. He may make my job easier or harder. In any case, he clearly labours and is heavy laden.* Aloud, he said that he didn't know how Captain Niggl would feel about this three-way discussion.

Bertin made to stand up, but Kroysing stretched out a hand to stop him. 'Nothing doing,' he said. 'You're staying. Shall we postpone our discussion, Father Lochner? That would be fine by me. Bertin's here today for the last time. He has to go back to his lousy company, and I'm planning to give him a goodbye present, a special memento. I'm going to the front tonight. Our mine throwers are in position, and the section officers want to talk to me. I assume you're prepared to risk it, Bertin? Everyone ought to see the show.'

Bertin blushed and confirmed that he would of course come. 'I was expecting a booze-up from what Süßmann said but I prefer it this way.'

'Huh,' said the priest, adding that such chances didn't come along very often and that he'd like to join them if they didn't mind.

Kroysing raised his eyebrows and contemplated the priest's long, fine tunic, wide-cut riding trousers and almost elegant lace-up shoes: 'Won't it damage your robes?' The priest emphatically denied that it would, and Kroysing said: 'You'll meet a lot of Christian men, Lutherans in fact, but such distinctions evaporate out there. Machine guns welcome Jews and atheists just as warmly as Catholics and Protestants. The position we'll be visiting was relieved yesterday. The lads here in the fort are being sent somewhere worse, I believe, further to the west. Do you want to postpone our business, Father? I don't mind, though I'd prefer it if you said your piece now.'

Glad of an excuse, Bertin got up. 'If we won't be getting any sleep tonight,

I think it's best if I ask Süßmann for a bed now and lie down for an hour. A man needs his rest.'

'Not an easy life for an educated man,' the priest mused, when the door had closed behind Bertin. 'I'm constantly surprised by how well our Jews adapt to military life.'

'Why wouldn't they?' asked Kroysing. 'They do what everyone else does and often a lot better. They want to prove themselves to us. And, anyway, I know of no more war-like book than the Old Testament with all its fire and brimstone.'

The priest skilfully parried the mildly antagonistic subtext he discerned in this remark with a general observation: trench warfare had dispelled many prejudices, not just those against Jews. Had there not at one time been doubts about the value of soldiers from industrial areas? And now? And now, agreed Kroysing, townsmen, especially from the cities, were the backbone of the defence. They were less afraid of machines than country lads. The latter had perhaps provided the best human material in the first year of the war, but the trench war required more adaptable men of nimbler intelligence.

'And on the topic of country areas, Lieutenant,' interjected Father Lochner abruptly, 'what's gone wrong between you and Captain Niggl?'

Kroysing leant back. 'Surely he must have told you, when he asked you to mediate,' he growled.

'We had a chat,' the priest replied, kneading one of his hands with the other. 'He gave the impression of being a man deep in struggle. He said you two disagreed about your poor brother, that you thought the captain had maltreated or abused him.'

'Is that all he told you?' Kroysing asked, his expression unchanging.

'Yes. Or at least, I took no more from what he said. Those Bavarians are all from farming stock. They speak in such a way that you can read a great deal or very little into what they say, depending on how familiar you are with their customs.'

Kroysing lit a cigarette and threw the match into the squashed shell case: 'Let's suppose he was fibbing. How does that square with the respect he has for you as a clergyman and the eternal punishment he may be lining up for himself?'

Father Lochner gave a frank laugh. 'I was a curate for two years at Kochl at the foot of the mountains. I didn't get to know the people there very well. That would've taken a lifetime. But I did learn a few things. No one lied to me in holy confession, especially as they only had to speak in generalities, but they thought it was extremely clever to lie to me day-to-day whilst still availing themselves of my spiritual office.'

'Excellent,' said Kroysing. 'So, you're not biased, as I feared.'

'Oh no,' said Father Lochner expansively, lapsing into Rhenish. 'That'd be nuts – mad, I mean. Man is a frail creature. Catholics simply have the advantage over you of knowing about original sin and being able to compensate for their fragility through our sacraments and the Church.'

Kroysing listened to the gentleman's clever chatter with a grim delight that he concealed. Had Niggl really represented their dispute to the priest in such a harmless way? It was possible. Field chaplains got bored, and the cleverer they were, the more bored they got surrounded by the ossified commanders and clowns at headquarters behind the lines. Father Lochner might very well have ventured over to Douaumont on a motorbike for a bit of a change, without asking for a compelling reason. Perhaps sorting out a quarrel between two officers was an interesting opportunity for a former theology student. Well, he might find things surprisingly intense at Douaumont.

'What do you think about the story of King David and his field captain Uriah, Father Lochner? Excuse me asking so directly.'

The priest started. 'It was murder,' he said. 'Shameless, premeditated murder over a woman. A mortal sin, and the House of David had to atone for it. Even the grandson from that union lost the majority of his realm, despite David's remorse and the deeds of Solomon.'

'I see,' said Kroysing casually. 'So what temporal and eternal punishments will be visited upon the Niggl dynasty? For I'm pursuing the captain for that same sin. The only difference is that the woman is not called Bathsheba but "The Third Company's Reputation".'

Father Lochner sat stiffly on his chair. 'You must make yourself very clear, Lieutenant, if you want to make accusations of that kind.'

Kroysing was glad to have sickened the other man's happiness. 'Wanna do and can do,' he said in Berlin dialect, opening a drawer and taking out two pieces of paper. He gave the larger piece of paper to the field chaplain and asked him to read it.

Father Lochner slowly pulled on his horn-rimmed spectacles. Then he read Christoph Kroysing's last letter. His lips moved as he read, and his eyes scanned each word conscientiously, which Kroysing noted appreciatively.

'You don't seem troubled by the state of the paper and the writing, Chaplain. The letter was a little stuck together when we received it. You can see the traces in the corner.'

'Blood?' asked Father Lochner with a shudder. 'Terrible,' he said. 'But Lieutenant, not wishing to upset you, have you any proof? Captain Niggl – does seem very pleasant. Although one is used to things not being as they seem...' He let his voice float off.

'My dear man,' laughed his companion, 'surely you don't still attach any importance to appearances? Haven't you noticed that power doesn't agree with a lot of men in the two years you've been at this? That your average man needs an average amount of pressure to function normally? Being a member of the officer class places such average men in too rarefied an atmosphere, and the likes of Niggl and his cronies get carried away. Then a travelling wine salesman – or, let's say, a retired civil servant with a bit of wit – starts to act like King David, except that he cowers behind a stranger's back when he feels the avenger's fist on the scruff of his neck.' And he raised his right hand, curling his fingers into a claw.

'Tell me what happened,' said Father Lochner in a haunted voice.

CHAPTER FOUR

Two subordinates

MEANWHILE, TWO TIRED soldiers, Süßmann and Bertin, were lying on iron bunks, one on top of the other, in a former guardroom that accommodated 15 men – Kroysing's sappers in charge of routine work in and around the depot. They were smoking a cigar and talking. Bertin, on the lower bunk, felt quite excited about the forthcoming excursion.

'Do clergymen give you the willies like they do me?' he asked. 'All of them, I mean – even ours.'

'Seldom clap eyes on them,' muttered Süßmann.

'We sometimes do,' said Bertin. 'Our company held a Whitsun service about half a year ago before Verdun, and we were all ordered to attend. There was the priest preaching about the Outpouring of the Holy Spirit in our cartridge tent and all around were baskets with yellow and green crosses on the labels.'

'Brilliant,' said Süßmann. Bertin didn't need to tell him that yellow and green crosses denoted two of the three poisonous gases used in shells.

'In his defence, I believe he was short-sighted,' said Bertin, not joking.

'Why?' retorted Süßmann. 'Surely the Prussians believe anything that serves the Fatherland pleases God. And we Jews should keep quiet,' he added in a more serious tone. 'Our Old God fits right in with this war.'

'Yes,' quipped Bertin. 'I depart in my wrath, and my shadow falleth towards midnight upon Assur, so that the people crawl into caves and Rezin, King of Syria, laments in his palace of Damascus, and I strike the first born of Mizraim in the south, and shake my spear and lance, and like the hooves of the wild ass I trample down the seed of Ammon and the walls of Moab, saith the Lord.'

'Nice sort of God,' said Süßmann. 'Where's that from?'

'From my heart,' answered Bertin. 'But I could just as easily have made it up.'

'This is what happens when you hang about with poets,' said Süßmann absently. He was watching a spider, a large, black female, who'd spun her web across a ventilator in the corner and was now dashing back and forth, irritated by the cigar smoke.

'Poets...' Bertin continued, thinking aloud. 'No, not poets. Witnesses, writers. The hallmark of a poet is that he uses the full palette of his imagination – inventiveness and artistry. No scrimping on gods and goddesses, and a plausible fiction is better than the truth. But what is needed today in our situation is truth, not plausibility. Think about it, Süßmann. Our company toiled away at Steinbergquell depot for four months and nothing really happened. Then I was sent up to the front, I met young Kroysing on my first day there and he asked for my help. Is that plausible? Could I put that in a fictional story? No. But it's true. And the truth goes on in that vein. The very next day, no sooner, no later, the lad is killed. The day after that, I go to look for him again so I can take his letter and help him out of the mess he's in. He's already dead, and his battalion has got what it wanted. But my eyes have been ripped open, and I've been galvanised into action. No, it's not about poets – for now. As long as the effects of this war continue to shake the world, the survivors will need true accounts. Those who don't survive will already have given everything humanly possible.'

'What about me?' a voice boomed from above, echoing off the ceiling. 'I've already given everything humanly possible. I was actually dead. Shell splinters from our own hand grenades were whistling past my ears. It's a miracle I survived. Shouldn't I be able to call it a day?'

'My dear Süßmann,' said Bertin soothingly, 'no-one expects any more of you.'

'Thanks for the get-out,' the thin, boyish voice snapped in the gloom. 'That's not what I was asking. I was asking if the whole business makes any sense. Is it worth it? That's what I want to know. Will we at least get a decent new society out of all this appalling fumbling and fidgeting – a cosier home than the old Prussian one? A boy starts to think a bit when he reaches 16. By 17 he begins to imagine he knows how his future might turn out. I keep asking myself what the point of it is. How did it start, where will it lead and who's benefiting from it?'

Bertin lay there, shocked. Shouldn't he be the one asking these questions? But he'd given himself over entirely to the present now. He took what came, lived with it, abandoned himself to it. The devil only knows why I was naïve enough to confuse what is with what should be, he thought. I never used to do that; now I do. Perhaps I'll understand later.

'If my thoughts were all as harmless as that, things would be fine,' Süßmann continued. 'But there are a couple of things I haven't been able to get out of my mind since I told you my story about the explosion. I picked your Sergeant Schulz's brains about it yesterday. He maintains that secured shells, even French ones, only explode in certain special circumstances. But that explosion was a really big deal. Floors split down to the drains. Windows ripped out. That impact that threw us all against the walls. If it wasn't the shells in the empty gun position, what was it?' He became introspective for a moment, like someone who is turning a debatable point over and over in his head and therefore can't converse. 'Don't think I'm just wallowing in my exciting past. Perhaps the vigilant French concealed a stack of mines so they could blow their own fort to bits if need be? And then our doughty Bavarians touched one off with flame thrower oil, flares and hand grenades. Brr,' he shuddered and got down suddenly from his bed, appearing pale-faced at Bertin's side. 'I wouldn't want to go through that again. What if we're walking on a loaded mine and any idiot could accidentally make the contact and blow us to bits?'

Bertin sat up and looked into the desperate eyes of this 19-year-old with a man's strength of judgement and suddenly shivered. 'Sit down, Süßmann,' he said soothingly. 'Assuming that's true, then you're just as much at risk when you're asleep as when you're awake. You and your comrades at the front whom we'll be crawling over to later. Does it really change your situation? I don't see that it does. It makes it a shade worse, but what does that matter to a man like you?'

'Hmm,' said Süßmann, eyes to the ground, searching for caches of explosives under the layers of concrete. 'Nicely put, but you're just a visitor here.'

'That's not the point,' countered Bertin, 'I get the feeling I'm meant to record something of your sufferings and great deeds for the coming generation. It's not just by chance that we met, you with your story to tell and the Kroysings with theirs. There'll be more lies told about this war than about any other international conflict. It'll be up to the survivors to tell the truth, and some of those who've something to say will survive. Why not you? Why not me? Why not Kroysing? Whether there's a stack of explosives or not, Süßmann, you've already been through enough. Death never calls twice.'

Süßmann stuck his lip out defiantly. Then he laughed and clapped Bertin on the shoulder. 'And I thought we didn't have any decent field rabbis. You're wearing the wrong gear, Bertin.'

Bertin laughed too. 'My parents would gladly have made a rabbi out of me, but I read too much and had too many doubts. A clergyman must believe the way that priest in there with the lieutenant believes in his cross. And I don't believe.'

Süßmann breathed more easily. 'And yet you talk about destiny and being in good hands. You're not much of a sceptic, Reverend Bertin,' he said almost tenderly. 'It's amazing what words can do. Now I almost believe too, by which I mean believe it's worth battling on here and that the men we're going to visit at the front aren't completely mad.'

'...will sign.'

ENTHRONED ON HIS hard, low-backed wooden stool, Father Lochner no longer looked as happy and confident as he had. 'Tell me what you want, Lieutenant,' he said quietly, 'and I'll do my best to get Captain Niggl to agree to it.'

Lieutenant Kroysing took a second piece of paper from the table, a small square sheet, and read: 'The undersigned confesses that, in order to protect the reputation of the Third Company of his battalion and avoid court martial proceedings, he did, in conjunction with the heads of the company, intentionally and systematically precipitate the death of Sergeant Christoph Kroysing. Douaumont, 1916— the date, month and signature to be added.'

Father Lochner stretched his folded hands out in front of him. 'Merciful Jesus, no man can sign that. It's suicide.'

Kroysing shrugged his shoulders. 'It's recompense,' he blinked. 'When this paper, duly signed, has been passed to Judge Advocate Mertens in Montmédy, who is working on the files against my brother, then certain wheels will be set in motion, as God sees fit, and Herr Niggl and his men may look for quieter quarters, if service interests permit. But if he does not sign he'll be staying here in my harmless little molehill, even if his soul turns to buttermilk.'

'Blackmail,' cried the priest. 'Coercion, duress!'

Kroysing smiled genially, a wolfish glint in his eyes. 'Do as you're done by, Father,' he said in a deeply satisfied voice.

Father Lochner thought for a moment, almost as if he were alone. 'I accept everything,' he sighed at last. 'It wasn't you, Lieutenant, who involved me in this matter. Neither is it your fault that I came here as a harmless field chaplain and now find myself gazing into the most ghastly depths of the human soul. And I cannot just stand there and gaze. I must intervene, take sides, concede that a son of my Church behaved like a common murderer towards your brother, which would have been bad enough if your brother had been your average, common man. However, his letter demonstrates that the Creator had housed within his body a most noble and loveable soul. There can be no recompense for such a loss either for the parents or the brother or the nation. Measured against it, earthly vengeance seems grotesque. I imagine that's clear to you, though it doesn't of course diminish your loss. What then do you hope to achieve?'

Eberhard Kroysing wrinkled his tan-lined brow. 'If we take the impotence of punishment as our starting point, the fact that we cannot recreate that which has been destroyed, we'll get nowhere. Let's make things easy for ourselves. I want to cleanse the Kroysings' reputation, which Captain Niggl besmirched. Why don't we leave everything else out of the equation.'

Father Lochner exhaled. He didn't understand himself why he'd sided so firmly with a miserable type like Niggl. *I didn't side with him* although *he is miserable,* he thought quickly, remembering his training, *but* because *his lowly soul needs so much compassion, warped as it clearly is.* 'I knew it,' he said in relief. 'It's always words that stop two reasonable men reaching agreement. Allow me to draft a text that will give your family full satisfaction without destroying Captain Niggl.' He made to grab a piece of paper and began unscrewing his fountain pen.

But a look from Lieutenant Kroysing stilled his hand. 'Excuse me, Reverend,' he growled amiably enough, 'but I'm with Pontius Pilate on this one when he said, "What I have written I have written".' And as the priest pulled his hand back, he continued: 'I'm a physicist and an engineer. Captain Niggl unleashed a rotary movement against my brother that ended up hurling him tangentially into the void. But that didn't stop the movement. Now it will seize Niggl himself and hurl him tangentially into the void. Or if you prefer, the balance of things has been disturbed. My brother tipped the scales a little in the direction of good. To compensate for his loss, I'm going to stamp out an adverse element, maybe even three. I hope it may earn me a civic crown,' he finished, and Father Lochner shuddered at the young man's savage mastery and sparkling intelligence.

The priest sat up straight and his eyes, small in his plump face, took on the implacable expression of the confessor. He thrust his lower jaw out, and under the electric light his mouth became a moving line. 'Lieutenant,' he said, 'we are both quite alone here. Our conversation crossed the normal boundaries of a negotiation between two uniformed officers long ago. What I'm about to say puts me in your hands. None of my Church superiors would defend me if you wrote a letter to HQ saying that Field Chaplain Lochner from the Order of St Francis told you what I'm about to tell you. But whit mus be, mus be,' he added in plattdeutsch.

'The sickness of our people, the moral sickness, can no longer be affected by the existence or otherwise of Captain Niggl. I was in Belgium with our Rhinelanders when force was used against neutrality and justice. What I saw, what our men proudly carried out in the name of service and duty, was murder, robbery, rape, arson, desecration of churches, every vice of the human soul. They did it because they were ordered to and they were delighted to obey, because their souls – even German souls – were in the possession of the devil's joy of destruction. I saw the corpses of old men, women and children. I was there when small towns were burnt to the ground in order to terrify a people weaker than us so that they wouldn't impede us as we marched through. As a German, I was shaken with horror; as a Christian, I wept bitter tears.'

'The *franctireurs* resistance fighters shouldn't have kicked off then,' said Kroysing darkly.

'Who can prove that they did?' Father Lochner stood up and paced from one corner of the room to other. 'We maintained that they did, and the Belgians denied it. We are accuser, accused and judge in one person. We didn't allow a neutral investigation – so much the worse for us. But there is a man in Belgium with an indomitable conscience, and as a Catholic and a member of a religious order I'm proud to call him a prince of our Most Holy Church. His name is Cardinal Mercier, and he repudiated the *franctireurs* story in the strongest terms. And the soldier in you must agree with me when I say that even if Belgian civilians did join the fight, which no one has admitted, our actions in Belgium were the vilest heathenism. That was no war between Christian nations, but a barbaric assault on a Catholic country. My esteemed friend, do you really believe that this can end without permanent damage being done to our German soul? The murder of thousands of innocent people. Thousands of houses burnt down. Residents driven into the flames with kicks and rifle butts. Priests hung in bell towers. Villagers herded together and massacred with machine guns and bayonets. And the stream of lies we unleash to cover it up. The iron face we show to the better informed world so that our own poor people may cling to the delusion that the Belgian atrocities are a fairytale. My dear mannie,' he said in Rhenish, 'we have besmirched our souls like nae ither civilised folk. How do you propose to rebalance that with your Niggl? We shall be very sick men when this war ends. We shall need a cure such as cannot yet be foreseen. Of course, the other nations can't talk. The Americans with their Negroes. The British with their Boer War. The Belgians in the Congo, and the

French in Tongking and Morocco. Even the honest Russians. But that doesn't give us carte blanche, and so I say to you: assign this matter to the Lord, safe in the assurance that Herr Niggl...'

'...will sign,' the Lieutenant broke in, unmoved. 'You see,' he began, filling the deep brown bowl of his full-bent pipe for a long smoke, 'you see, Father Lochner, you've risked saying what you have because you understand me. Your courage is to your credit, I like your openness and I'm impressed by your knowledge. But overall I feel sorry for you. Why? Because you are trying to maintain a fiction – an important fiction, I concede. But here's a nasty truth about the Christian nations and Christian codes of behaviour for you. I don't know if we had any reason to call our Reich Christian in peacetime. As a future engineer, I serve commercial enterprise and am entirely dependent on people who have money to build machines and pay workers' wages, and it's not up to me to decide whether capitalism and Christianity can march side by side. But what is clear is that they do march side by side all over the world and no priest has yet taken his own life over it. Your expedients of poverty, chastity and obedience change nothing. That's just shirking – or worse. Let's leave peace to one side, then. But I find it disturbing that you maintain that this war here, this little project that we unleashed two years ago, has anything to do with Christianity. I know what you're going to say' – and he waved the priest's objection aside – 'you keep alive such remnants of Christianity as our people are able to digest in your soul so you can give them comfort in their despair, which is more than anyone else can give them – the same comfort in the same despair that poor Private Bertin gave to my brother when no Christian soul was moved by his fate, to get back to the topic in hand. We live in nice, clean heathen times. We kill with every means at our disposal. We don't scrimp, sir. We use the elements. We exploit the laws of physics and chemistry. We calculate elaborate parabolas for shell-fire. We conduct scientific investigations of wind direction the better to discharge our poisonous gases. We've subjugated the air so that we can rain down bombs, and as surely as my soul lives, I would hate to die such a dirty, cowardly death. In half an hour when we go to eat, each of us will put a steel pot on his baldy skull' – and he leant his long head forward with a smile and pointed to his thinning hair – 'and then we'll proceed into the joyful world of unvarnished reality and European civilisation. What was that quote we heard the other day from our educated schoolboy Süßmann who's already been dead once? "Nothing is true, and everything is permitted." Where we're going that phrase applies, and there's no quarter for the phrase:

"Love your enemies, bless them that curse you!" That tells you all you need to know. For just as water always seeks the lowest point, the human soul will sink as far as it can go as a group with impunity. That's heathenism, sir. And I'm an honest adherent. And if I survive, which isn't in the stars, I'll make sure that my entire family are equally honest heathens. In the conflict between truthfulness and Christianity, in 1916, I choose truthfulness.'

Father Lochner regarded him fearfully. He said nothing, lifted the piece of paper from the desk, folded it and went to the door, where he turned. 'I wish, Lieutenant, that I might one day be allowed to relieve your soul of its bitterness.'

'See you in half an hour,' said the heathen Kroysing.

CHAPTER SIX

The slip of paper is returned

AS THE EVENING'S last red flashes paled to smoky brown in the west, three men and a boy in steel helmets stood by Douaumont's southern exit, called the "throat", and eyed the pitted landscape bending away from them in troughs and mounds. They looked bold in their metal headgear, like mediaeval warriors, which was exactly how young Bertin felt. He held his head high and was filled with mettle; the coming hours would transcend all others in his life. To their left below Hardaumont, some sort of pond gleamed like a glowing log. Otherwise, the landscape was a world of churned earth floating in the violet evening haze. The three men and the boy inspected the sky. To the east, rose a large, wide crescent moon the colour of brass, enveloped in a halo. It was waxing. The boy – Sergeant Süßmann, the most experienced of them all – pointed to it with his thumb. 'There'll be a new moon in three days, and that'll be the end of the good weather.'

Father Lochner, the heftiest of them in his cloak, asked if the dark nights presaged attacks.

'Something much worse, Reverend,' answered Süßmann. 'Rain.'

'It could cheerfully hold off for another month,' muttered Kroysing behind them. 'We're nowhere near ready.'

'It could but it won't,' said the youngster. 'The land is very unobliging towards its conqueror,' and he laughed at his own joke.

The four men, so unalike in rank and experience, made their way slowly down the slope. Their eyes had adjusted to the gloaming, and they easily picked out the well-trodden paths. Each had a stick. The two officers were wrapped in their cloaks, and the two men had hooked their coat tails back. A damp chill hung over the field, and it would get colder as the night wore on. Süßmann knew the area like his way to school in Berlin and led the party. An excited Bertin followed him, and Lieutenant Kroysing took up the rear behind the priest.

'That was once a trench,' said Süßmann, as they changed direction and headed for the patch of ground where the village of Douaumont had once stood with its imposing houses and a church. Now it was indistinguishable from the jagged earth all around. And that earth was beginning to smell; it breathed a sweetish, putrid odour on the four men that became scorched, sulphurous and sick. In his even, boyish voice, Süßmann warned that they'd have to duck under the barbed wire that covered the hillside all the way to the fort. He also read the smells. They came from shallow graves, stale faeces not properly dug in, the poisoned gas shells that had soaked the soil here, incendiary shells and piles of rotting tins in which leftovers had been lazily dumped. He explained to Bertin that the smell was much worse when it was sunny and windy. Then it got mixed up with the dust and the stench of this whole pulverised, putrefying area that stretched 2.5km to the French lines and the same distance again to the girdle of forts at Verdun. Their route, he continued, cut diagonally across the switch position known as the Adalbert line, where things became more dangerous. The former road between the villages of Douaumont and Fleury ran dead straight to the front and was a huge temptation both to the French field artillery and their targets – relief troops, stretcher bearers, orderlies, anyone on two legs.

The eerie quiet was broken only by the sound of rats scattering. On the barbed wire that they now walked alongside fluttered scraps of material and paper blown over by the wind. At one point shortly before they left the trenches behind and turned in a different direction, a formless black mass hung from the barbed wire. Shortly thereafter, the four men met a couple of panting soldiers and exchanged a few words with them. They were guides running at a trot up to Douaumont to bring down the relief battalion. The regiment had thought the deathly quiet so suspicious it had brought the normal departure time forward by one and a half hours. The trenches, Bertin suddenly realised, were occupied. Those little things sticking up must be steel helmets. After 30 paces, they jumped behind a steep wall, a switch position. To their right stood a figure peering to the south. He radiated tension, and the new arrivals felt the pressure. They breathed more heavily and were tempted to stay put with their backs leaning against the cool earth instead of descending into the flat, mist-wreathed field. Süßmann and Bertin were half a minute ahead of the other two. Mists came in from the Meuse, Süßmann explained, and sometimes caused gas alarms. Better one too many than one too few. Over to the left was Thiaumont farm and further forward lay the Thiaumont line, a dark ridge etched on the night sky. This trench was thinly populated. Bertin suddenly realised how nerve-racking it must be to be responsible for what could happen and how that responsibility must weigh on the couple of officers and staff sergeants in the battalion command. They obviously wouldn't have that sense of security that still coated daily business at Douaumont. His cheerful mood evaporated; for the first time since he was a boy he felt hostility in the air.

He'd seen all kinds of things. He'd got used to handling military equipment on a daily basis. Dead men were no longer a novelty, neither were exploding shells or aerial bombs. Furthermore, he'd been listening to the war reports for two years. The idea that war exists was as familiar to him as his uniform. But as he himself had no enemies, felt no desire to destroy and was not filled with racial hatred when he thought of the French, the struggle and intensity of war was missing from his world view. Only now did he feel it physically, and it constricted his chest. Hordes of men were lying in wait, peering at one another through the night in order to kill one another. Way over there, a French soldier with a flat steel helmet on his head was pressed against a trench wall looking northwards with a view to shooting at and perhaps killing him, Bertin, as he advanced. Over there in the dark, just the same as here, the issue of an order could turn a knot of men into assault troops, throwing themselves against the lines, always ready to strike the first blow. They weren't glad to go or keen to die, but when ordered to do so they mounted an attack upon the bodies of their enemies. *We've come far,* he thought bitterly, *we Europeans of the year nineteen hundred and sixteen. In the spring of 1914, we met these same French, Belgian and British people at peaceful sporting gatherings and academic symposia. We were delighted when German fire engines rushed to France to help with a mining disaster or French rescue parties appeared in Germany. And now we're organising murder parties. Why aren't we ashamed of this trick?*

Eberhard Kroysing and the priest, now rather pale, came round the corner. 'Move on,' said Kroysing nervously. 'I'm think there's going to be a bit of a to-do tonight.'

Young Süßmann sniffed the air like a hunting dog. 'Not here,' he said confidently. He scaled the trench parapet, walked upright alongside the barbed wire entanglement and led Bertin through the narrow alleyways that zigzagged across the steel network. The barbed wire entanglement was very wide and very new. 'ASC job,' Süßmann said, as a kind of compliment to Bertin. To their left was a ridge of high ground. They kept to the valley and hurried across the shelled areas, avoiding the broad road, which shimmered palely in the dark despite its parlous state. Their path then turned once again. In front of them, white in the distance, flares rose in the haze, shooting straight up or hovering in milky cascades. Telephone lines sometimes ran near them, but their well-trodden path constantly changed direction, though always heading downhill and to the south. They kept alongside earthen walls, trench walls, sometimes waist-high, sometimes neck-high. Then with the suddenness of an electric discharge, shots cracked at the front, wild as whiplash, and machine gun fire rattled. For a moment, Bertin stood watching the chains of red flashes as they traversed the valley, then a fist pressed his helmet against a mound of earth. Something whistled over their heads like scuttling rats and clattered down out of sight spraying them with loose earth.

'A dud,' said Süßmann beside him.

'A dud can still take you out,' a voice grumbled in a neighbouring shell-hole. Then the two men heard excited whispering nearby, but couldn't follow it, for the gruesome churning of the machine guns had started up again, German guns this time.

'Lieutenant, I'll stay here,' Father Lochner groaned in Kroysing's ear.

'Bad idea,' was Kroysing's emphatic reply. 'You're right in the middle of the shrapnel zone.'

'But I can't manage it,' moaned the priest. 'My legs won't go any further.'

'Nonsense, Reverend,' said Kroysing. 'Just a little attack of nerves. A wee nip will cure that,' and he offered him his canteen. The aroma of cognac wafted out as he uncorked it. 'Have a drink,' he added in a calm, maternal voice tinged with mockery. 'Only healthy men have nipped from that bottle.' With shaking hands, the chaplain grasped the canteen by its felt cover, put it to his lips and took two sips, then a third. The liquor felt hot in his stomach. 'Watch out. It works,' said Kroysing, hooking the canteen back on to his belt. 'You should've taken your quota before.' Then he noticed that under his wrap the chaplain was worrying a silver cross with one hand and handing him something white and folded with the other.

'You'd better take this slip of paper,' he said. 'It could be dangerous for you if your enemy got hold of it.'

Kroysing jerked round to face him, wild-eyed under his steel helmet. 'Good Lord,' he said, taking the paper and stuffing it inside his leather puttee. 'Thank you. That could easily have looked like blackmail. But you'll pass my message on verbally, won't you, Reverend?'

'If we get back in one piece,' answered Lochner, already more composed. 'Schnapps is one of God's gifts.'

153

Three things were required to wage war, Kroysing muttered in reply, still disconcerted by his own carelessness: schnapps, tobacco and men. And then he leant his long frame over the earthen slope; it really had been a dud. *Gratitude is a great virtue,* he thought. *That was a colossal act of stupidity. With that scrap of paper in his hand, Niggl could easily have proven that I had him moved to Douaumont purely out of private revenge and that I put him under pressure to sign a declaration that was a pack of lies. I was skating on thin ice there* – and he wiped the sweat away from under his helmet. 'Are you okay now?' he asked the priest.

'I'm okay.'

'Let's go then.'

They crawled down the last 1,000m, stooping for cover the whole way. When white flares shot up over the way, they halted unless they were in a particularly deep section of trench. Their narrow path, pitted with holes and buried in places from the gunfire, wound forwards through traverse trenches, giant mole heaps and smashed tunnels where black holes marked the entrances to the dugouts. Eventually, drenched in sweat, they caught sight of the backs of soldiers, boys really, and the curve of German steel helmets among the ridges of upturned earth. Suddenly, machine gun fire rattled near them. In a corner, smoking a pipe, sat a bearded sapper NCO, who'd been waiting for them.

'Bang on time, Lieutenant,' he grinned. 'Everything's fine here. The battalion is virtually set up. The officers are waiting for you in the big dugout.' He spoke in an undertone and with a certain familiarity that didn't seem to faze Kroysing. Then he frowned anxiously. 'There seems to be a lot going on across the way. The Frogs are so bloody quiet. I think they're listening to the racket of the relief troops arriving, and the new lot aren't even in yet.'

'Then we'll have to blow some smoke in their eyes,' answered Kroysing. 'Father, why don't you have a lie down? There'll be a space in the next medical dugout. I'll pick you up from the medical men later.' He disappeared with the guide, and Lochner left with another man.

Bertin followed Süßmann through the deep, narrow cutting, above which the Milky Way hung like two balls of white smoke. Infantry men pushed past them, crawling out of dugouts and disappearing into others. In one place, some of them were using spades to widen a passage that incorporated a large shell hole further on. Everything was done wordlessly and as far as possible without a sound. In the former shell hole, a short, thick pipe such as Bertin had never seen before sat on a mount, and right beside it a newly dug tunnel slanted downwards. They sat down on two-handled wicker baskets filled with large shells: the lightweight mines.

'If those are lightweight, I wouldn't like to see the heavy ones,' said Bertin.

A screen of wire and branches covered in earth protected the mine throwers from aerial view. Hot coffee was brought to them from the dugout. Süßmann suggested going down. Bertin asked to stay up. The cold, damp earth and the smell that escaped from it disgusted him. He watched the small, thin Saxon men at their posts in horror. There were so few of them, and their faces were wretched. This was the front – the grey Wall of Heroes that protected Germany's conquests. They were already worn down and overextended. Gingerly sipping his hot coffee, Bertin asked Süßmann if the surrounding dugouts would withstand a bombardment.

Süßmann just laughed and said they were safe against shrapnel, nothing more. In an emergency, they might withstand one 7.5cm shell, but not 10. If the rain came, it would get inside. He pointed to the pale, hazy ball of the moon, which cast a faint glow, and said that rain was on its way as surely as their wages. The newly replenished battalion of over 700 men had 12 light and six heavy machine guns at its disposal, and with that it was expected to hold an area twice as wide as the previous month. And the French were always putting fresh divisions in the front line, and they withdrew their men after a short stint for a proper rest and a good feed. They didn't undermine their nerves with inadequate rations of fat, poor quality jam and stale bread made with leftovers. The four mine throwers were to replace two batteries taken out of the line. Everyone was ready for peace, that much was clear, but it didn't much look like peace. Men in helmets and caps kept rushing past them, stumbling and swearing under their breath. Like a dark cloud, danger, palpable to all, seemed to roll in across the upturned earth from the other side of the trenches. Two hundred metres of land is a broad stretch but for a bullet it's nothing. Advancing infantrymen cover it in five minutes, a shell in a second. So this is the war at last, thought Bertin. Now you have it. You're stuck on its outermost edge like a fly in glue. Your heart and lungs are pounding, and the enemy isn't even doing anything. Pale light poured down from above, casting black shadows in the trench. Had they missed the sound of the rockets going up? There'd definitely be more action tonight. Bertin noticed that his knees and hands were trembling with suppressed tension. He made to leave his cover and climb up the recess cut into the trench wall.

'Have you gone mad?' Süßmann hissed in his hear. 'They'll be able to pick out your pale face against the black earth quite easily from over there with their night glasses.'

Nothing would happen in their sector, but if the French were paying attention the battalion that was being relieved might get some grief as the troops were being exchanged. Suddenly – and Bertin's heart seemed to stop – the machine gun they had passed earlier spat out a furious volley. It thrust maliciously up into the night, though he didn't see its fire. Three or four of the same weapons continued the noise. Nearby, rockets whistled up and released their signal lights, bathing the huddled soldiers' faces in a strange red glow. Soon, a wild gurgling roared over their heads and there was a crash far in front of them.

'Barrage fire,' said Süßmann in Bertin's ear. 'It's just for show to fool the Frogs.'

From the way the two Saxons had pressed themselves into the ground, Bertin could tell that they were frightened too – the guns often shot too short. What if the diversion worked and the French replied? It did work. Flashing and roaring ahead, with blinding light from the sides. Men in artillery caps appeared from the dugout with an aiming circle. Under the protection of the mine throwers' screen, they sighted the flashes from the French guns and shouted figures to one another. Bertin wondered how long this terrible din would last, the explosions, flames, flickers, howling and droning in the starlit night. He couldn't stand it. There was a thunderous ringing his ears, and the once repellent dugout now seemed like a refuge. He stumbled down the stairs, pushed aside a tarpaulin and saw brightness and men sitting and lying on wire grating, their weapons to hand beside them. A stearin cartridge on a box cast a thin glow, and the air underground was thick and smoky. The faces of the sappers, gunners and Saxon riflemen made him feel almost sick. Until now he had garlanded them with splendid delusions, draped them in noble titles. But no illusion could hold out here. The men in this boarded clay grave were just lost battalions, the sacrificed herds of world markets, which were currently experiencing a glut in human material. Crouched on a plank under the earth 200m from the enemy and yawning suddenly from exhaustion, he saw that even here the men were just doing their duty – nothing more than that.

The earth rumbled above him, chunks fell from the walls, dust rained down from the timbers and as the infantrymen calmly carried on smoking their cigarettes, he wondered hesitantly how he had come to see this truth. It hurt! It robbed you of the strength to endure life. Surely it couldn't be the same everywhere else as in his own company. He must tell Kroysing about it.

Was that Kroysing coming through the door? Yes, there was young Kroysing in his sergeant's cap, smiling engagingly. Things were pretty jolly in the cellars at Chambrettes-Ferme. The sausage machines were rattling away and guts were being stretched for sausage skins, and on the door hung the new regulation about using human flesh, grey human flesh...

Sergeant Süßmann looked at Private Bertin's face both in amusement and complete sympathy. He'd fallen abruptly asleep and his steel helmet had fallen from his head. Süßmann took Bertin's hand and moved it to and fro, establishing that the boy had come through it all fine.

'The relief of the battalion took place one and a half hours ahead of schedule. Nothing to report.'

CHAPTER SEVEN

The gift

AROUND 11PM, SÜSSMANN woke Bertin in darkness; the candle had burnt down and gone out. He'd been dreaming about an incredibly violent storm on Lake Ammer. Lightning seemed to whip up the expanse of water, and thunder echoed off the mountain walls against underwater banks.

'Up you get,' said Süßmann. 'Big fireworks display. It's worth a look.'

Bertin knew immediately where he was. His head hurt, but it would clear in the open air. Outside, the trench was full of men, all looking behind them. A roar like an organ playing filled the night with thunderous tones. Flames sprang up over the neighbouring sector. Fiery discharges rained down, methodically spread out across the approach routes and familiar hills and valleys. As the shells hit, they hurled up fiery gasses and earth in cloud-like columns. The howl as they approached, the pounding tide of vicious hissing, the ringing, rattling and manic cracking, made Bertin's heart tremble, but he also pressed Süßmann's arm in fascination as the full force of the human drive to destroy was unleashed – rejoicing in evil's omnipotence.

A thin, bespectacled Saxon sergeant standing next to Bertin surprised him by calmly observing: 'That's what we can do, bastards that we may be.'

As Bertin looked at the man's stubbly face under his helmet, his narrow cheekbones and shrewd eyes, and the two ribbons, black and white and green and white, in his top buttonhole, he felt a surge of pride and admiration for his comrades, these German soldiers with their sense of duty, their hopelessness, their grim courage. They'd seen it all.

Luckily, the first battalion was to get off lightly this time. It would all be over in 10 minutes, Süßmann shouted in his ear. Then, Bertin knew, the German artillery would take its turn, and this squaring of accounts would create more destruction – a new day of anti-creation.

In the meantime, the young Saxon calmly lit his pipe, and a couple of others shared his lighter. The wild noise gradually petered out. They could hear one another again. It was only above the Adalbert line that shrapnel was still exploding. That's where the long 10cm guns were, said the Saxon. They'd obviously received a big batch of ammunition and were now getting rid of it. Of course, his neighbour confirmed. Otherwise, they'd have to take it back home if peace broke out that day. The young sergeant pooh-poohed this. Peace wouldn't break out that quickly. Plenty of time to pour a few more pots of coffee before that happened. There were many more medals to be pocketed and bestowed before peace could be allowed to break out.

'Of course, it's not just medals,' said the neighbour. Bertin listened up. These men were talking like Pahl, like the inn-keeper Lebehde, Halezinsky the gas worker and little Vehse from Hamburg. In the pallid darkness that had once more descended, their faces shimmered like masks under the sharp edges of their helmets.

The men who were still on duty looked ahead again, while the others began to vanish into the dugouts. The bespectacled Saxon had just expressed his amazement at Bertin's cap and was asking what kinds of folks Süßmann and his lieutenant had brought to the front, when Father Lochner's substantial shoulders came into view, topped by Kroysing's tall form. Süßmann quickly kicked the Saxon in the shin, and he got the message equally quickly. 'I'm a theology student too and I've never been out of Halle in my life,' he said.

'A colleague?' asked the chaplain innocently.

'Yes, Pastor, sir!' replied the sergeant, standing to attention. Bertin bit back a grin. 'Sir' and 'pastor' didn't go together.

Father Lochner didn't notice. He wanted to be kind to the young man. 'The hand of our Lord God will continue to protect you,' he said and made to move on.

But in his polite voice and as if agreeing with the priest, the young theologian replied, 'I almost believe that myself. Nothing will happen to us for the time being. The likes of us get killed on the morning of the armistice.'

Lochner twitched, said nothing and tried to move on. The Saxons nudged one another. As they moved on, Kroysing spoke into his companion's ear, asking him if this sample of sentiment at the front was enough for him and if he'd like to head for home.

'Ten minutes and a schnapps,' the priest requested.

Kroysing was happy to oblige. 'When will you speak to Herr Niggl?' he asked casually as he unhooked his canteen.

Lochner's face took on an imploring look. 'Tomorrow afternoon,' he promised. 'As soon as I get back.'

Kroysing's head revolved on his long neck like a lighthouse. He was looking for Bertin. 'I want to gather in my chicks,' he explained.

Sergeant Süßmann cocked his thumb Bertin's direction. 'He's studying no man's land.'

Bertin had forced his head into a gap in the screen above the mine throwers. Hands cupping his eyes, he peered into the night at the glinting barbed wire entanglements. The reflection from the explosions no longer blinded him. Far back to the right, German shells were now bursting. Something formless menaced in the distance, something dark, strange and fascinating. And he remembered a school excursion he'd gone on one morning as a 13-year-old to Three Emperors' Corner, where the German Kaiser's Reich met those of the Austrians and the Tsars behind the town of Myslowitz. The greenish waters of a stream called the Przemsa snaked between them. Nothing distinguished one bank of the stream from the other: flat green land, a railway bridge, a sandy path, and in the distance a wood. Only the uniform of the border Cossack was different from that of the German customs guard. But the young schoolboy had nonetheless sensed the foreign on the other side of the stream, another country both threatening and fascinating, where the language was unintelligible, the customs different and the people uneducated, perhaps even dangerous. Borders, thought Bertin. Borders! What tales we've been told! What had that clever Saxon said when the French were shooting? 'Bastards that we may be.' We: that's what it was all about. Who had held his canteen to a Frenchman's thirsty lips? And now this...? There was no hope of getting to the truth.

Kroysing watched his charge approvingly. He'd brought him here partly to study his behaviour at the edge of the abyss. No doubt about it: he'd done well. Let him go back to his stuffy old company, he thought, and then my suggestion will seem to him like a message from heaven.

'Why are you shaking your head, Bertin?' he asked behind his back.

'I can't see anything,' Bertin answered, climbing down carefully.

'Reason should have told you that would be the case.'

'Sometimes we believe appearances more than reason.'

'All right,' said Kroysing. 'Now we can get some sleep.'

On the way back, the moon and stars lit the pitted area. Refreshed from his sleep, Bertin gladly breathed in the air, which cooled as they pushed on. The burnt smoke from the explosives hadn't blown this way; the night wind had driven it to the river. After half an hour of walking in silence, Kroysing tapped

Bertin on the shoulder and pulled him back a little.

'I don't know if we'll get a chance to speak tomorrow, as you're sleeping in Süßmann's billet and clearing off early,' he said. 'You've seen what kinds of nice surprises the Frogs have in store for us. We got off lightly today; tomorrow could be a different story. For that reason, I'd like to prevail on you again in relation to our small family matter. There are a couple of objects in my desk drawer that belonged to my brother and a couple of papers that Judge Advocate Mertens must receive as soon as someone has signed a certain harmless slip of paper. If I'm not able to do it, I'll rely on you. Will that be okay?' he asked urgently.

And after a moment's thought Bertin said, 'That'll be okay.'

'Excellent,' said Kroysing. 'Then all that remains is for me to carry out a commission on behalf of my brother, who sends you his fountain pen through me.' Kroysing's big hand held out a black rod.

Bertin was taken aback. His eyes under the rim of his helmet timidly sought those of Kroysing, whose war-like face was dusky in the gloaming. 'Please, don't,' he said quietly. 'This belongs to your parents.'

'It belongs to you,' retorted Kroysing. 'I'm executing his will.' Bertin hesitantly took the gift from Kroysing's fingers and looked at it, concealing his superstitious feelings. 'I hope it will serve you longer than it did the youngster and remind you of the Kroysings' gratitude every time you put it to paper. A writer and a pen like that go together.'

Bertin thanked him uncertainly. The pressure of the long, hard object in the breast pocket of his tunic felt new and strange: the Kroysings held him fast.

BOOK FIVE

In the fog

CHAPTER ONE

October

THE EARTH WAS a rusty disc, capped by a pewter sky from which rain had been falling for a month.

On 20 October, four tired ASC men trudged up morosely from Moirey station. They and Sergeant Knappe, the ammunitions expert, had been engaged in the tedious task of loading powder charges on to a goods lorry and now they were done. All of them longed for a cigarette or a smoke of a pipe, but it was out of the question. Their wages weren't due until the day after next, when they would all get their tobacco ration for the next 10 days. Until then, they helped each another out. Private Bertin, for example, had promised to give one of his remaining cigarettes to each of the other three, as the paper irritated his sensitive throat. Shivering and fed up, the four men tramped back along the main road to the depot. The road was covered in a layer of whitish mush as thick as a thumb unsuited to their lace-up shoes. The men wore tarpaulins wrapped round them like short hooded coats to protect them from the rain, but as they'd already done a day's shift in Fosses wood, the stiff canvas material was soaked through. The canvas jackets they wore underneath were damp too. Only their tunics were still dry, and if it got any colder they could put their coats on for another layer. These four very different men had all volunteered to help the ammunitions expert; Lebehde the shrewd inn-keeper had offered because he hoped to bum a smoke from the railwaymen, Przygulla the farm labourer because he did everything Lebehde did, good-natured Otto Reinhold because he didn't want to leave his fellow skat players in the lurch and Bertin for reasons connected with his visit to the front-line trenches.

Sergeant Knappe, a thin, hollow-cheeked men with a straggly, blonde beard, was extremely conscientious and reliable, the sort who usually makes it to 80 although he looks like a consumptive. Lebehde the inn-keeper was a well-known figure. Until his death by a Reichswehr bullet in the desperate workers' uprising of 1919 in the Holzmarktstraße-Jannowitzbrücke area of Berlin, he would use his energy and powers of persuasion to pursue what he thought was right, a benevolent smile always crinkling the corners of his eyes. Przygulla the farm labourer, a neglected child from a family of nine or 10, might have turned out differently and had a livelier intelligence if the growths behind his nose had been removed when they should have been. As it was, his thick lips hung open because he had trouble breathing, which made him look stupid. Otto Reinhold, finally, was pleasantness itself. His friendly face, toothless smile and bluish eyes might have lent him a spinsterish air, but a carefully trimmed moustache asserted his virility. He was also a respected master plumber from Turmstraße in Berlin-Moabit.

Private Bertin had changed a lot since he'd been 'up front'. Everyone said so. He couldn't forget the Saxons' haggard faces, their worn skin and sleepless eyes – couldn't forget that it had now been raining in those trenches for a month, that the men 'up front' scarcely saw hot food and were surrounded by a layer of sludge, which covered their hands, clothes and boots. Their dugouts were irretrievably swamped, and their every step took them through slippery, squishing mud. All the shell holes were now flooded pools, and the roads, pathways and traverses had been impassable for ages. It was inhuman, which was why Bertin had volunteered to do overtime that day. He'd explained this to his comrade Pahl, but Pahl was having none of it – he said it was for those at the front to think about the causes and consequences of their situation.

The four men were tired and hungry. They wished they had something to smoke and longed to remove their wet things by a warm stove. It was between 4pm and 5pm, and the damp air made the early dusk even darker. It happened not to be raining at that moment, but just wait until evening.

At the end of the road, along which those French prisoners had once marched, a car appeared. It approached quickly with its lights off as regulations required. Karl Lebehde studied the approaching vehicle, his hand under the peak of his cap. 'Blimey,' he said to Przygulla the farm labourer, 'take a look at that. Looks like that chap's hung a cloth over his headlights.'

Meanwhile, the 'chap' had drawn considerably closer, and the cloth was revealed to be a square black and white pennant with a red border. The large dun-coloured saloon with two officers in the back was hurtling towards them. 'Lads,' shouted Przygulla the farm labourer. 'Line up! The crown prince!'

The regulation salute for members of the imperial family was for the men to stand stock still at the side of the road and follow the passing vehicle with their eyes. The four weary men now did this. They stood in the clabber, pressed their hands to their sides and awaited the inevitable muddy spray from the vehicle. The driver, who was probably a common soldier like them, would not be allowed to slow down just to save four ASC privates in grey oil-cloth caps an hour cleaning their uniforms. Splat! The vehicle sped past. But then something remarkable happened. As a slim man with his chin wrapped in a fur collar lifted his glove in the direction of his cap, the other man in the back of the car lent out of the window and threw something. It landed some way back due to the speed at which the vehicle was travelling. The speeding car disappeared into the distance, and it was all over.

Well, not quite all. Some small, square packages lay on the muddy road – four paper packets, undoubtedly cigarettes, which the lofty gentleman must have brought to distribute to the men and which his adjutant had thrown at these ones. The four men stood on the road digesting what had just happened, still taken aback, looking after the car then at the surprising gift. What was the crown prince doing here? What business had he at the front? People said he looked after his troops. But the army just shrugged its shoulders over him, because people knew only too well how little the fact of the battle of Verdun had disturbed his princely way of life. While the German tribes had been spilling their blood for him at the front for seven months, he'd been playing around with his greyhounds, with pretty French girls, nurses and tennis partners. But now he'd been here bestowing cigarettes, and if they didn't pick them up soon they'd be soaked and spoilt. Otto Reinhold was already bending over, grunting happily, prepared to get his fingers dirty for all of them.

Someone grabbed his wrist. 'Leave them,' Lebehde the inn-keeper commanded in an undertone. 'There's nowt for us there. Anyone wants to give us a present, they can give it to us properly.'

Reinhold, shocked and ashamed, looked into Karl Lebehde's fleshy, freckled inn-keeper's face, at his compressed lips and angry eyes. Lebehde ground the nearest packet of cigarettes to a pulp with his boot, then he carried on up the stairs that led past the water troughs to the barracks. Bertin and Przygulla the farm labourer followed him wordlessly, and so, with a murmur of regret, did good-natured little Otto Reinhold. Three pale, abandoned packets were left shining on the muddy road: 30 cigarettes.

Bloody hell, thought Bertin, *that was something else. That Lebehde can handle himself. No one complained; we all obeyed.* Maybe Przygulla the farm labourer or Reinhold the master plumber would creep back out of the barracks quickly later – but that would be it. As they climbed the steps, Bertin caught himself wondering what he would have done if Karl Lebehde hadn't been there. He'd laughed in a superior, philosophical way when the gifts came flying out of the car. And besides he wasn't bothered about cigarettes. But he was honest enough to admit to himself that he would definitely have picked them up so as not to waste them. The crown prince had driven past – a strange experience. He'd probably been distributing a load of Iron Crosses and was now hurrying back to Charleville, little suspecting that Lebehde the inn-keeper had condemned his behaviour.

The crown prince travelled through the dusk, his lips pinched. He was deeply dissatisfied with circumstances, which were stronger than him, and with himself, who was weaker than circumstances. He had not in fact been distributing decorations. He had travelled to the front to ascertain that he had once again been right, though he had not prevailed, that he had been overruled and had once again not had the guts to stand up to the All Highest, stop the truck and get out. It was a seductively commodious truck, splendidly upholstered with every comfort. But what good did that do him if incorrect military decisions were being taken in his name that would ultimately be attributed to him by history? Two days previously in Pierrepont, on the railway line from Longuyon to Metz, the Kaiser had chaired a meeting of the generals together with representatives of the Supreme Army Command, which had inveigled its way into the whole business since the end of August. The alarming situation outside Verdun and what to do about it was the topic. The day was marked by a refreshing openness, and he, Friedrich Wilhelm, crown prince of Germany and Supreme General of the Prussian army, heard his most secret convictions vindicated – all his complaints and grievances. First, the attack was on too narrow a front, and secondly, reinforcements had been promised but not sent when the first thrust proved inadequate. Many a mother's son had died a hero's death for nothing because the attack had not from the beginning been launched on both banks of the Meuse simultaneously with double the troops. The strength of the French resistance had also been underestimated. The French did yield but they always fought back again, so that the exhausted Reserves could advance no further than Douaumont. Then, all of a sudden, enough troops were deployed to conquer tiny strips of land at a terrible cost of lives – advances that did nothing to prevent the French from preparing and launching their attack on the Somme. And so now a decision had to be faced: admit bankruptcy outside Verdun and preserve the lives and health of tens of thousands of young German men, or maintain the façade, keep up appearances, prolong their suffering and fill the hospitals with casualties.

The prince lent back and closed his eyes. In his mind, the grizzled heads of the generals from the day before yesterday and the young faces of the infantrymen from earlier were strangely intermingled. First one group then the other pushed forward in time with his heartbeat. It had only been raining for a month, but the casualty figures for the rifles had already reached 30 per cent, sometimes more. Men caught cold, were feverish and had to be sent to the rear for treatment. It was because of the position of the front line. The front line had resulted from the furious fighting in July. It had not been selected or prepared for winter conditions. It was no use either as a base for future attacks or as a defensive position should the French ever decide to attack between Tavanne and Pepper ridge, since it was overlooked, badly damaged and drowned in mud. The artillery was in a hopeless situation except where it was served by the narrow-gauge railways. That was the only way of bringing materials and ammunition up to the front line. He had agreed wholeheartedly when a couple of officers said that the line should be moved further back, relinquishing the gains of recent months, that positions should be prepared on the hills of Hardaumont, Fort Douaumont and Pepper ridge, and that the front should be 'shortened' one night and the whole quagmire chucked back to the French, and good luck to them.

The prince shivered. He pulled his fur rug tighter round his legs and rubbed his shoulders inside his fur jacket nervously against the upholstery. The twin lines that ran from his nostrils to the corners of his mouth gave him, in profile, a certain resemblance to his ancestor, Old Fritz. Unfortunately, such half measures wouldn't fix the problem. The East Meuse Group Command had sent in its most capable officers, and they had established that moving the line would do nothing to alleviate the main problems of long approach routes, lack of accommodation for reserves, and inadequate supplies and ammunition. Neither would it be possible to use the position on the hills for further sorties, as the French were much too clever to allow themselves to be lured into the sludge. It was tough, but what was required was to evacuate the ground so arduously conquered and pull back roughly to where they'd been before the February attack. That would mean moving to near the railway line to Azannes; they couldn't even hold Hill 344 and Fosses wood. It was very sensible – and completely impossible. Given how the year 1916 had turned out, the House of Hohenzollern's reputation could not tolerate such a retreat. The battle of the Somme had turned out badly, and the eastern front, thanks to the Brusilov offensive, very badly. The Austrians were taking a pasting as usual. They were stuck in the Adige valley, and entire regiments had deserted in Bukovina – the Czechs had simply had enough of the Habsburgs. And you only had to think back to the year 1908 and the annexation of Bosnia by Aerenthal to realise that the entire war had started with Habsburgian home affairs. Now the Romanians were intervening with 15 army corps, which was hardly small beer. It looked bad for Germany. And added to that, a retreat on the western front? Impossible! The German soldiers would start to have doubts, and the officer class, which they still trusted blindly, would be seen in an unfavourable light, with potentially unpredictable consequences within Germany. Germany was facing its hardest winter yet. It had been necessary to reduce the bread ration to half a pound, and even the soldiers faced months of hardship. It was morale alone that kept the people going, belief in the imperial house, the unvanquished army and the certainty of eventual victory. To admit that the battle of Verdun was hopelessly lost was to elevate Karl Liebknecht to the status of prophet, invite attack from the parliamentary majority in the Reichstag, and make the imperial house and army command look like fools, which would lead to demands that all the 'senselessly spilt blood' be accounted for. Should that be allowed to happen? It should not. Was it avoidable? It was avoidable if they did nothing, left everything as it was and, with a heavy heart, burdened the German soldiers with yet more sacrifices. The German soldiers would bear it. They'd be glad to die for the glory of the Fatherland, would stand all winter uncomplaining in the sludge, keeping guard against the ancestral enemy. Signs of weakness and false humanity must be avoided at all costs. The Germans liked to be led, loved a strong hand. Then they'd fetch the stars down from the sky.

The crown prince visualised the wrinkled face of the old Junker who spoke those words with such conviction, his small eyes and rasping voice, and smiled to himself. Others had contradicted him, for example von Lychow, who had been in command on the left bank of the Meuse for some time. But their arguments didn't hold water. They were very sensible, but you didn't get the stars down from the sky through good sense alone. He, the prince, had watched his father, the supreme warlord, while the generals were arguing. Ah yes, Papa understood how to give the right sort of appearance, how to play the royal chieftain of the council of war, imposing as an eagle. But he didn't fool his son. His face sagged, his eyes were wreathed in wrinkles, and it was a struggle for him to maintain his confident imperial mien. His son knew what only sons can guess: that dear Papa had imagined the war would turn out quite differently when he unleashed it with such panache. More like his manoeuvres no doubt. But that wasn't how the barrow was rolling, your majesty; it was rolling quite differently. At the beginning of the war, the old man had thought he'd be his own chief of staff; that had been a lovely dream in the idle hours of peacetime. Then he'd had to send brave old Moltke out into the desert, followed by the unctuous Falkenhayn, and summon two new gods whom he couldn't stand. Half-measures, nothing but half-measures! The war would be over in six months if they would stop worrying about neutral countries and order the U-boats to sink whatever passed in front of them, knocking out Great Britain's provisions and the American shells supplied to France. The American gentlemen and their Wilson could protest as much as they wanted. They could even send their miserable army over. They'd be very welcome. Fodder for the field howitzers, nothing more.

The car ran well. Perfect engine, springs made of outstanding German steel. When the Romanian business was sorted out, Papa wanted to risk a bid for peace in order to shut the pope up. It couldn't hurt because Belgium would certainly stay in German hands, as would the Briey-Longwy iron ore basin. If you thought about it properly and took a look at the map, the whole Verdun offensive was really just about strategically safeguarding those conquests ahead of the coming peace agreement. Naturally, they didn't say that to anyone, not even to their esteemed members of parliament, who liked to honour General Headquarters with their annexation memoranda. Military decisions, naturally, were taken for purely military reasons. That was why poor Falkenhayn had invented the famous 'battle of attrition' after the first strike on the fort failed and the Verdun adventure lost its shine. From a military point of view, Verdun was just another fort behind which the French, supported from Châlons, had prepared another line of defence. But politically speaking, Verdun was unique and irreplaceable for Germany's future and for her industry. And for that reason, the old front line would have to remain, the heir to the throne saw with a sigh, and the men would have to get through the winter there.

It was now completely dark. The car's wide headlamps swept the road as it sped towards the gleam of light on the horizon called Charleville, where well-heated, comfortable rooms and a decent dinner awaited. The prince's musings had warmed him up; he felt cheerful now and was in a good mood. He turned to his adjutant, who had evidently been dozing: 'We should have taken a detour, old chap, and had coffee with Sister Kläre at Dannevoux field hospital,' he said jokingly. 'That would've been an idea, eh?'

That would indeed have been much more pleasant than hurtling around in the wind and dark like some latter-day version of Goethe's Erlking, agreed his companion, whose duty it was always to have an answer ready. 'We could just as well have stayed at home, Imperial Highness. Retreat or not – what difference does it make? "It's a long way to Tipperary," as the Tommies sing – and our field greys sing: "For this campaign, Is no express train, Wipe your tears away, With sandpaper." Nations have broad backs.'

What was to happen over the next four days had been settled long ago. Four French citizens, all experienced soldiers, had decided it between them. Up until the morning of 24 October, the French guns fired as usual. Then 600 guns unleashed a barrage of heavy fire. An annihilating wall of exploding steel hurtled towards the German line. Then suddenly the guns were silent, as though the infantry attack were at last about to begin, and 800 German guns, over 200 batteries, let rip in order to throttle that supposed attack. Which was what the French wanted. The German emplacements had long ago been marked on the French artillery maps. Now the French laid into them. Shells tore into the gun emplacements, demolishing the guns, ripping the gunners' arms and heads off and exploding the shell stacks in volleys of wild crashing. The dugout ceilings fell in, and the dugouts themselves filled with thick smoke as their supports collapsed. Observers fell out of the treetops or were smeared against the walls of their hideouts. Death strangled the stranglers that day between Pepper ride and Damloup, and steel hatchets smashed the shell factories. When the real attack began at midday on the 24th, there were no more than 90 German batteries across the entire area to respond to the enemy bombardment.

The enemy bombardment. What the Germans had withstood up until then was unimaginable, those seven weakened divisions, some 7,000 men in total, scattered and lost across the ravaged terrain. They'd gone hungry, crouched in watery sludge up to their waists, dug themselves into the mud because it was their only cover, gone without sleep, fought fever with Aspirin and held on. Now they began to crack. The air turned to thunder, crashing down on them in the shape of steel cylinders filled with Ecrasite explosive. Impossible to leave the trenches, which now hardly were trenches. Impossible to stay in them, because they were moving, squirting, undulating, spurting up towards the sky and pouring themselves into the chasms that kept opening up all around. The dugouts in which the men sought refuge subsided. The occupants of the deep tunnels, which had been stopped up by the heaviest shells, were buried by them, gasping, shivering, mentally decimated, even if physically unhurt. Behind the trenches lay the spitting, knife-sharp steel barrier of the field guns. The fire of steel from the heavy calibre guns and trench mortars struck the trenches themselves. The machine guns were swept aside, the nice new mine throwers got covered in mud or broken to pieces, and even the rifles were damaged by the flood of clay and steel splinters. The Germans had created the battle of materials in February but had unfortunately neglected to patent it. The French had taken it over some time ago and now mastered it. Their artillery, tightly bound to the infantry, worked systematically, exactly according to the map and timetable, even when there was no visibility. It covered the advancing infantry with a double volley of fire, creating one death zone of shrapnel 160m in front of the infantry and another of shells 70-80m in front of it. The speed of the advance was stipulated exactly: 100m of impassable sludge to be crossed in four minutes.

At 11.40am the French front started to move, in thick fog. It hadn't lifted that day and formed an impenetrable, milky white layer over the earth as it does high in the mountains or at sea. No need for thick smoke to wrap the battle zone in impenetrable mist. Visibility was less than 4m; no one saw the 24 October sun. The German dead lay staring upwards at the gods and their unfathomable decree with glazed and fractured eyes; the living, numb and too weak to resist, awaited their fate. Twenty-two German battalions were swept away before the attack had begun in earnest; the survivors screamed for barrage fire, a German barrage to stop the advancing troops and fend off their bayonets and hand grenades, so that it at least made a whisper of sense to fight back against the better-fed Frenchmen, who had enjoyed proper relief and were less worn out because their positions were more favourable. Trembling hands fired red rockets into the air. Barrage! But they disappeared in the white haze. The men who had fired them gazed after them into the milky blanket that lay over the whole area. Those artillerymen who were still alive, their officers, sergeants and gun pointers, waited by their guns, seeing nothing. The firing in front had stopped. Now the French would advance. Now was the moment to pepper their legs with contact shells, but where were they? No red light flashed in the fog, no telephone call came along the shot-up lines, no arrangements had been made for sound signals or direct contact with the infantry; only the group commands had the right to issue orders.

The minutes passed. The men in the trenches stared ahead, eyes popping.

Surely they'd advance from over there, there in front. Could they hear them now? See them? Was there any point in waiting to be slaughtered with no artillery and the heavy weapons beyond use? The Fatherland couldn't expect any more of them than what they'd already withstood. Singly and in groups they threw their rifles away and waded out into the sludge and fog, into the shredded, blown-down barbed wire entanglements, slithering and stumbling in the shell holes, hands as far as possible raised above their heads. 'Kamerad,' they shouted into the fog. 'Kamerad!'

Kamerad – that word would be understood. He who shouts 'Kamerad' and raises his hands is surrendering and will be spared. He who abuses the word consigns himself and many of his fellows to death. Kamerad – now they appeared from the fog in their sky blue coats, slithering and stumbling, with assault packs and bayonets. Under their steel helmets, their faces were black, coffee-coloured, light brown: France's colonial regiments from Senegal, the Somali coast and Morocco. And elsewhere were the Bretons, the southern French, the Parisians from the boulevards, the farmers from Touraine. France was mother to them all. They all knew they would be defending basic freedoms if they liberated French soil from the invaders. In no sense did they play the part of dashing warriors as they climbed out of their storm positions cursing and laughing, teeth darkly clenched, pale with determination. But they were fully engaged in the task ahead, these intelligent soldiers of France. They too had been told: just one more push and that'll be it. They let the German prisoners through in silence and pushed them back towards the reserves at the rear, and then they crossed the German line and advanced on their objectives, with Fort Douaumont and Fort Vaux at the centre. They pushed into all the valleys and overran the wooded slopes from Lauffée to Chapître wood, from the Thiaumont line to Ravin de la Dame, from Nawe wood to the stone quarries of Haudraumont. On the German's left wing, the trench systems named after Generals Klausewitz, Seidlitz, Steinmetz and Kluck were lost, in the centre the Adalbert line and everything that had once been called Thiaumont, and on the right wing the ravines, positions and remnants of woodland between the village of Douaumont and Pepper ridge. The three French divisions pushed deep into the land, stormed the German military Reserve's dugouts and positions, lashed out at the batteries with bare steel, finally exacting revenge for months of shell raids and shrapnel rain. The question was: would they succeed in breaking right through the German defences?

The front held at several places in the sector. On the escarpment north of the village of Douaumant, in Caillette wood, east of Fumin and in the Vaux hills the German clung to their ground and threw themselves at the French with hand grenades and such machine guns as were undamaged. The fighting lasted all day, then night fell. The German's resistance boosted their prestige, but it made no sense. The next morning the French artillery restarted their terrible games, and the Germans had nothing to set against them. Two days previously the French had been fewer in number than the German artillery; now they dominated the field, placed their long-range guns on Douaumont's eastern slope and decimated the casemates of Vaux with wild salvoes. They combed Caillette wood with fire, clearing gateways for their infantry, and smashed the fortifying outworks of Vaux. The field batteries advanced on the German flank, obtaining a foothold on Douaumont's steep eastern slope and cutting all rearward communications in much the same way that a doctor amputates a smashed arm hanging by strands of muscle and skin. *Go back, German soldiers, you've done enough.* In some places it took the French just two hours to conquer what they'd planned to take in four, in others it took four days. They took 7,000 German soldiers prisoner and killed and wounded three times that many. *You have done enough for your 53 Pfennigs a day, German soldiers, and for the Briey-Longway iron ore basin. In the impenetrable fog, you gave the last of your strength to fulfil orders, not questioning whether they made sense or not. Men from Poznan, Lower Silesia, the Mark, Westphalia, Pomerania or Saxony: peace is all you need and now you have it – the peace of the dead. Protestants, free thinkers, Catholics, Jews: your bloated corpses will surface in the clay and fog of Verdun and then disappear again into our national pasts. You'll be ungratefully forgotten, and the memories of those who were once your comrades will hardly be disturbed by even the palest reflection of your suffering.* But what was to become of Douaumont?

Since the 23rd a column of smoke from the shell explosions had been hanging over Douaumont like a large black flag.

CHAPTER TWO

Breakthrough

IN THE DAYS before the decisive move, the Fosses wood detachment marched out in the morning and back in the afternoon with the regularity of a pendulum. To stop the mud getting into their boots, the men tied their bootlegs closed with string and so managed to march with confidence. Relaying railway sleepers higher up isn't the most pleasant work in the world but it isn't the dirtiest either, not by a long shot. And the lack of visibility took the danger out of it. Now that the air had turned to milky soup, the Frogs sensibly refrained from peppering it with shrapnel. A certain someone had predicted what a hard blow the transfer from Wild Boar gorge back to Steinbergquell depot would be for Bertin. You could see how disgruntled the men were by their puckered brows and tightly drawn lips, and by the way they stared straight ahead while their legs wrestled through the thick mush on the roads. It squelched and sucked, crackled and gurgled, and squirted up past the ASC men's knees if they were too lost in thought to test the ground with their sticks and carelessly stepped into a sludge-covered hole. For days the pendulum swung undisturbed. But that day... They were already at Ville height when a dull rumble wafted over to them. Far behind, out of sight, a really heavy gun had bellowed after weeks of deceptive silence. While they were still listening and looking at one another, something started up behind, battering down like rain on a wooden roof, faraway and frightful: a barrage from Verdun just like in the worst months of summer – the French! They set off apprehensively on the march home. The air seethed and clamoured behind the horizon as they entered the barracks. The noise followed them into the kitchen, and they listened to it as they washed their canteens and hours later at their evening meal. At bedtime, Private Bertin thought about Kroysing, Süßmann, that poor, pitiable scoundrel Niggl, and the Saxons in their water-logged trenches, and he sighed heavily and turned over.

The noise swelled during the night rather than slackening off, and a wild clanging cascade was hammering down behind the hills by the following morning. The men heard it as they marched out and the German reply: a shot every two minutes. There were no shells. They shook their heads as they went about their work in the morning but found themselves back in the barracks before lunchtime. There was almost a sigh of relief in the ranks when the order came in the early afternoon: all working parties suspended, all men to stand by to unload ammunition. Naturally, the company had to wait a good two hours to be assigned its task. The men chatted and exchanged thoughts, and then finally two engines shunted a line of wagons up the track, maybe 40, maybe 50 – the ASC men lost count. The men spat into their hands as they were split into groups and set to it. Men who knew the ropes climbed into the open wagons and with a practised grip lifted on to their shoulders a wicker basket from which either a long or a squat 15cm shell stuck out like a bundle of spears in a quiver. Carefully balancing the unaccustomed weight, the men from the working parties trudged along the slippery boarded walkways. They groaned as they heaved the shells down from their shoulders and stacked them between grassy hillocks – the heaviest of them weighed 85 pounds. They recovered on the way back, rubbing their joints in preparation for the next steel load. Even before night fell, miners' lamps were hung in the wagons, and their dim glow illuminated from below the faces of the three men between the sliding doors. And as they bent and lifted, while a constant stream of men passed them, presenting their shoulders to receive their loaded baskets, carrying on and then disappearing into the gathering twilight, they looked to Bertin like the labourers of destiny doling out to mortal men their allotted burdens. Men were just a number here, a shoulder and two legs. The tramp of hobnailed boots banished any thoughts coursing through their minds. When the last wagon had been emptied at almost 11pm, sturdy Karl Lebehde had carried exactly the same as Bertin who was much less strong and Pahl who was almost a hunchback.

The following morning, the milky dawn air breathed cold and damp across the barracks and ammunition dumps of the depot; the sun would not show itself there that day. From a few metres away, the cooks dispensing morning coffee looked like pale and shadowy demons in the steam from their kettles, bestowing a ladleful of the River Lethe on the souls of the dead. Then the working parties disappeared: the Orne valley commando, the commando for hill 310, the Chaume wood commando, the Fosses wood commando. But in barely two hours they were all back. All hell had been let loose in front. No one could get where they were going. The immobile wall of fog, thick as cotton wool, that hung over the camp dampened all sound, turning the depot into an island. The ASC men were delighted to be ordered to stay in their barracks and rest. The depot commander, First Lieutenant Benndorf, knew what had been required of them the night before and would be required of them again that night. Suddenly, around midnight, the rumour spread that the French had broken through, Douaumont had fallen, there was a gap in the front line. Within quarter of an hour, most of the men were in the grip of a vague anxiety. The NCOs were called out; they and the other trained men returned pale and silent. They had received ammunition, live cartridges and carbines, and in half an hour shooting would begin. This was no laughing matter for the ASC men. If things had got to the point where their peaceable NCOs were being called upon to fight, then they and the recruits from the depots in Crépion and Flabas would be thrown into the gap the French were meant to have torn in the front line too, wielding picks and shovels. Everyone agreed with Halezinsky the gas worker when he said: 'Wow, if they haven't got anyone better than the likes of us, they should sue for peace.'

But after lunch, the atmosphere lightened again, and this, oddly enough, was partly due to the men being completely cut off from the world, which gave them a deceptive sense of security. At 2.30pm they were assigned duties as usual; before that everyone who knew their way around at the front had been ordered to report to the field gun depot. Bertin joined them, though he didn't know if he was supposed to, as he'd never had anything to do with field guns. But he knew his way around at the front, no doubt about that, and information was probably what was wanted.

Guides were required. NCOs and field artillery officers crowded round the map in chief ammunitions officer Schulz's hut, while some ammunition was packed into the gun carts and some stowed in the small dump cars dotted around the depot. Fresh batteries were being brought in, some from the practice grounds at the rear, some from the other side of the Meuse. A carrier pigeon and a couple of runners had brought news; this was a black day. Sergeant Schulz assigned Bertin to the gunners who were to take ammunition up ahead on the narrow-gauge railway – the very line that led to the telephone hut in Wild Boar gorge. At the words 'Wild Boar gorge' something sparked in Bertin's soul: Kroysing! Süßmann! If they had escaped, they would have gone there. He hurried back to the barracks to get his coat, gas mask, tarpaulin and haversack, and his gloves – it would be easier to push and brake the trucks with those on. Before leaving, he was also told to call the depot from the switchboard at the halt station to check if the line was working. The station wasn't currently answering.

The gunners, strangers to Bertin with braid on their collars, said they were attached to the Guard Reserve Division. Big men from Pomerania, they spoke to each other in rapid Plattdeutsch. In the trucks lay the field shells in their long cases like cartridges for an enormous gun. Creaking and bumping, the long, low-slung ammunitions train pushed off into the void. Bertin had never had such a strong sense of confronting the unknown as he did then, clinging on to the front wagon as he left the familiar area behind in the half-light. Nothing to his right, nothing to his left, in front of him 1.5m of track, behind him two clearly visible wagons and one he couldn't make out, two gunners beside him, further back noise and confusion. Otherwise all was quiet. The fog was so dense their heads seemed to touch the clouds. Their feet, the feet of seasoned soldiers, jumped automatically from sleeper to sleeper and over the boards laid by the track as a walkway. Not a shot was heard. The Germans didn't know where the remnants of their infantry had assembled or where the French were gathering. All that was certain was that Douaumont was lost and that the corps would, if possible, mount a counter-attack to support the artillery. Bertin had heard this when he was in the ammunitions expert's hut. But he had also heard – and this filled him with hope – that Douaumont had been voluntarily evacuated during the night. Voluntarily – that could cover a multitude of sins. At the same time, a thought that had flickered within him earlier resurfaced: a man like Kroysing wouldn't go further from his post than was absolutely necessary. Was it 3pm or 5pm? Time was dissolving in clouds just as space was dissolving in the yellowish mist.

Wild Boar gorge... could this really be it? Calls, cries, curses, questions: 'Fourth Company!' 'Where in God's name is my platoon?' 'Paramedic, paramedic!' 'Second battalion – what's left of it.' 'Sergeants, sergeants stand by for orders!'

The lovely autumn quiet of the valley, that paradise of beech and rowan trees, was getting its fair share this time. The ravaged wood teemed with a confused throng of grey tunics. The little stream was blocked by fallen tree trunks and had overflowed. The tatters of tree stumps, lopped beech trees and far-flung treetops emerged as Bertin left the main line to climb the familiar path. Men stood in the water trying to clear the stream, free twisted rails and make a bridge out of planks. Sappers, ASC men and Saxon infantrymen worked at it together, and among them, issuing instructions, Bertin thought he heard a familiar voice. On the steep side of the valley, a number of undamaged trees still offered cover. There exhausted, grey-faced men, thick bandages round their heads or arms, sat, crouched or slept. Ripped tunics; ragged trousers; men who looked like they'd been pulled from the mud; big dark patches of blood. The small man directing the work, his left hand in a sling made of haversack straps, really was Sergeant Süßmann. He was having a siding cleared, which the blocked stream had covered in mud and slush. 'Good heavens,' he said when Bertin called to him, 'it's like being on Savignyplatz in Berlin.' His eyes were no longer restless – to the contrary, they were very clear – but his hair was singed and his face was black from smoke.

Without asking what had happened to him, Bertin said: 'Where's the lieutenant?'

'Inside,' answered Süßmann, nodding in the direction of the railway hut. 'Telephoning.'

'I'm supposed to call my depot to check the line.' Bertin was still looking at Süßmann, his mouth half open in shock.

'When the egg is laid, the hen clucks. Go on in. We fixed it a few minutes ago.'

Half a beech tree, its crown still covered in yellow leaves, was propped against the hut's corrugated iron roof. In a tangle of similar felled treetops next to the hut, three figures lay on a tarpaulin, covered in mud from head to foot, an encrusted layer of clay on their coats. Something about the cut of their clothes said they were officers. They were resting on the natural spring mattress created by the branches. Because their eyes were closed, their haggard faces – one of them a boy's face – looked oddly like dirty plaster casts of death masks. But these death masks were talking to each other languidly in Saxon dialect, their faces expressionless.

'If that mad sapper in there—'

'Do you think he's mad?'

'Of course. Those eyes. And the way he bares his teeth. Recapture Douaumont...'

'Straight out of a padded cell,' giggled the one with the boy's face.

The one in the middle chipped in again: 'If that madman in there gets orders to recapture Douaumont, will you go along with it?'

The oldest one, whose chin was covered in brown stubble, didn't reply for a while. On the gorge floor, the blocked stream had been cleared and was gushing along its old course. Finally, he said: 'Of course he's mad. Of course it would be pointless. But would you want to take responsibility for it all going wrong because you refused to take part? Because a surprise attack could miraculously succeed in this bloody fog.'

'Three to 100 it'll fail.'

'Three to 100, of course. One to 50 even. Different matter if the ground were firm underfoot, but in these conditions...'

'And as all three of us think it's mad, all three of us will go along with it and drag our men into the shambles with us, because we're worried about responsibility.'

'Stop stirring, Seidewitz. That's the way of the world. A madman can get a lot done.'

As Bertin opened the door, he knew full well that his trusty Baden Landstürmers would have slipped off to the rear as soon as the shooting started in the gorge. A tall figure was crouched by the switchboard, headphones over his ears, angrily ramming the plugs in and shouting futile hellos. Bertin closed the door softly and moved closer. And despite the horror of the situation, he couldn't keep a note of humour out of his voice as he announced himself by clicking his heels: 'Would you permit me to try, Lieutenant?'

Kroysing started, glared at him and gave a silent laugh, showing his wolfish teeth. 'Ah yes. Good timing. It's in your line of work,' and he slid the headphones on to the narrow table.

Bertin threw his cap on Strumpf the park-keeper's bed and checked the connections that could be made on that stupid switchboard with its couple of plugs: to the central exchange – in order; forward to Douaumont – broken; rearwards via the Cape camp – also in order. The telephonist there answered in some amazement; he tried to make the connection to Steinbergquell depot. Now there was a bit of trouble. Schneider, the on-duty telephonist, was a busybody who advised Bertin to return immediately and stop shirking his share of the unloading. They must all have been feeling a little weird over at the depot, for when Bertin tersely told him not to talk rubbish and put him through to Damvillers immediately, he received a testy reply. What did he want to talk to Damvillers for anyway? Instead of answering, Bertin turned to Kroysing, who bent over the mouthpiece with ominous calm: 'Listen, you little swine, sort it out right this second or I'll hang a charge of military treason round your neck. Connect us to Damvillers, understand?'

In the depot's smoky telephone exchange, Private Schneider nearly fell off his stool. That was not the voice of the insignificant Private Bertin; this man sounded like a beast of prey, who might pose a threat to stronger men than a primary school teacher such as himself. 'Certainly, Major! Right away, sir,' he stuttered into the instrument and made the connection.

'Officer Commanding Sappers, Captain Lauber,' a voice said. Kroysing sat in front of the instrument again, gave his name and was understood. Bertin stood beside him, filling his pipe. When he realised the conversation was going to last a while, he spread a newspaper at the foot of the palliasse and lay down for a few minutes, following the example of the Saxons outside. The way those men had looked, covered in a crust of dried sludge, flattened by exhaustion. They should be put on display in the officers' mess at Damvillers or in a Dresden concert hall, so that people could see what war was really like. But what good would that do?

It was a strange conversation. Captain Lauber greeted Lieutenant Kroysing with overwhelming relief, delighted that he was still alive and able to report, and asked where he was speaking from. Lieutenant Kroysing told him he was speaking from a railway siding, a blockhouse in Wild Boar gorge. It was the nearest rearwards telephone station to Douaumont, and he had immediately thought that if anything had survived that bloody bombardment, it would be this. He asked if he might keep his report brief. Douaumont had taken a pasting. The French had never thrown over so much heavy stuff before. Some of the new 40cm mortars must have been in the mix. The outer works had been battered in five places. Fire had broken out in the sapper depot – those bloody flares had caught fire again and filled the place with smoke. The dressing station had been hit again with heavy losses. There was no water to put the fires out as the pipes were burst. His men had tried – and he wasn't joking – to bring the fires under control with sparkling mineral water, which the sick no longer needed, but the carbon dioxide content was too low. The detachments in the fort had suffered substantial losses, including the ASC. This had all happened during the course of the previous afternoon and evening. Then, however – and he begged permission to express the view that this was incomprehensible – orders had been given to evacuate Douaumont.

His voice had taken on its usual deep, calm tone, but there was an undercurrent of barely suppressed anger. Captain Lauber must have asked something that betrayed his astonishment. No, Kroysing answered, he would not have issued such orders had he been in command of the fort. Only the upper casemates had been damaged by the 40cms, along with the masonry and brickwork. The concrete cellars were undamaged. The men would have been as safe in them as in bank vaults. Certainly, there was gas, smoke, nothing to drink, discomforts of every sort. But that was no reason to give up Douaumont, which had been bought and held since 25 February at the cost of 50,000 lives. Was there a risk of explosion? Yes, there was. There might be concealed mines, but that was a risk that had to be run – the Fatherland was owed that much. He had opposed the evacuation with all his might. Even when most of the garrison units were outside, he had raged and argued. It was mad to leave only Captain P and his handful of artillery observers inside. He'd always been a fan of logic. Either Douaumont was not suitable for occupation by German soldiers, including gunners, because of the explosion risk, or it was needed for strategic reasons – and then it had to be defended, for goodness' sake! He'd talked through the night, until he was blue in the face, and finally this afternoon had succeeded in having these crazy orders withdrawn, machine guns brought up and men assembled. As soon as the French stopped shooting at 11.30am he went round to the rear with a few reliable men to bring back those who'd skedaddled, but before he'd managed to round up more than 30 or 40 men above the village, the Moroccans had slipped through the blasted fog into the fort. They'd captured that precious position without firing a single shot. (He was practically weeping with anger. Bertin watched him in shock and amazement.) He could not accept that the evacuation was meant to be final. Headquarters had reached a premature decision on the basis of inadequate information and a bit of smoke. If he might be permitted to make a request, the captain should mobilise everything he could for an immediate counter-attack. The French were not established in the fort. They'd pushed through deep into the area behind, but based on what could be heard through the fog, they had met with heavy resistance southeast of Douaumont. The artillery fire there had not abated, and machine guns could still be heard. If it hadn't been for the fog, the barrage would not have started half an hour too late. Surely something could still be done. For his part, he intended, unless he received orders to the contrary, to take some infantrymen and sappers from the gorge here to sound out the approach to Douaumont.

His voice, so emphatic under the sounding board of the low roof, was silent for a moment. He seemed to hold his breath as he listened to the other man. 'Thank God,' he said in relief, and then twice in succession, 'Thank God.' He said he would pass this explanation on to the Saxon officers. There would definitely be pockets of resistance above the village of Douaumont, and so they should assemble to the east and to the rear. Could he pull in any ASC men he might meet? All hands would be needed to prepare the roads, clear the rubble and rebuild the dugouts. Then, in a concluding tone, he promised the captain that he would do his best and would report from somewhere should he get through. In the meantime, he thanked Captain Lauber for his help and bid him farewell. He sat motionless for a moment, then slipped the headphones off and turned in his stool to face Bertin, shoulders hunched, arms hanging between his long legs. 'Have you got any tobacco, Bertin?' he asked and filled his big, round pipe.

The blockhouse had small windows, and it was dark inside. But Kroysing's bright eyes still flashed in his mud-splattered face. Bertin knew that he was about to receive a private report. 'What about Captain Niggl?' he asked quietly.

'Escaped,' said Kroysing. 'Temporarily escaped. Without signing. Imagine that.' The flame from his lighter momentarily lit up his steely face. 'I'm telling you, he was as small and used up as cigar ash after that last month and especially the last four days. We had a little private chat. Everything was looking good, and it seemed my family's reputation would be restored. The blighter told me he was going grey. Gave me some sob story about his children and begged for mercy. I offered to set him free with his men as soon as the French stopped firing in return for his signature. Then came the order to evacuate, and he skedaddled. He escaped from me just as I was about to finish the business off. I don't understand it,' he said, shaking his head. 'Did those bastard French really have to help that swine out as well as giving those numbskulls at the rear such a fright that they evacuated Douaumont? But—' and he drew himself up to his full height, fists clenched— 'he won't get away from me. I'm not dropping out of the race yet. He can't have gone far. Even if I have to grab him by the scruff of the neck, I'll get him back. But first I have to settle some scores with those gentlemen over there who smoked me out of my own private little hell. Why did they have to fling their blasted regiments upon my domain? Well, they'll be sorry,' he finished, straightening the heavy pistol on his belt, 'I've got a crate of hand grenades waiting for them somewhere. I've always wanted to get them back for killing Christoph, though obviously I'd have preferred to do it after I had the signature. Now I'll have to change the order. Why don't you walk towards the front with me for a bit, Bertin? Don't you have a childhood friend there?'

Bertin stood up and scratched behind his ear. A knock at the door stopped him from answering. Two soldiers in steel helmets walked in, followed by young

Süßmann, whose boots were dripping water. 'This is the man, Lieutenant,' he said.

'Bit dark,' said a young voice, which Bertin thought he'd heard before. He fetched Friedrich Strumpf's candle and lit it: two field artillerymen, a lieutenant and a staff sergeant whom he'd seen at the depot.

'Got it nice and comfy here, lad,' the lieutenant said to Kroysing before realising his error. The officers then introduced themselves as if the blockhouse were a railway compartment, which one of the them had just entered. The young gunner with guard's stripes on his uniform was looking for his guide. Kroysing laughed and said he must mean his friend Bertin who'd arrived with the artillery ammunition half an hour earlier.

'That's right,' said Lieutenant von Roggstroh. 'It's you I'm looking for. The sergeant said you'd show us the quickest way up to a battery position: 10.5cm field howitzers. Can you do that?'

Bertin replied that he'd just been discussing it with Lieutenant Kroysing and was ready to go with them but had just received an order from his company to head back at once. He said he'd put the lieutenant through to the depot so that he could quickly explain. He plugged in and tried to get through: the equipment depot was engaged.

'Never mind,' said the gunner. 'We'll write you some bumph to take back. Is there a pen and paper here?'

The men from Baden hadn't had much time to pack, and an unfinished letter ('Dear Fanny') lay in the drawer. Von Roggstroh pulled his glove off and in clear, German handwriting wrote: 'I requisitioned the carrier as a guide.' He signed his name and rank, and folded the 'bumph' up. Bertin stuck it in his cuff.

Kroysing searched Bertin's face as he squeezed into his wet coat, fastened his buckle and got ready to go. 'Take a look at this ASC private. We've been knocking around together for the past month, but I don't seem to have rubbed off on him, do I?'

Von Roggstroh looked from one of the two entirely different men to the other. Men said a lot of things the night after a battle, even in front of strangers. 'It takes time to rub off on someone,' he said soothingly.

Kroysing examined his torch. 'Too long,' he muttered. 'In due course, he should be taking the kind of orders my brother took.'

'That's just a whim of yours,' countered Bertin.

'Ah.' Roggstroh looked up. 'Do you mean your friend should register for further training?'

'Exactly.' Kroysing stared absently past Erich Süßmann's reproachful face to the corrugated iron roof.

Bertin had a creepy feeling. Was he to stand in for Christoph Kroysing, then? 'Are you serious?' he asked.

Kroysing stared at him and shrugged. Then on the threshold, he turned. 'What I mean is that you owe it to the Prussian state,' and he pushed open the door, which creaked on its hinges.

They all stepped out into the cold, damp air of the gorge where a fire burned on the left bank. Bertin saw indistinct shadows pass and the outlines of men crouching and warming themselves. The three Saxon officers were no longer lying on the ground; they sat on the broken branches smoking and shivering. Kroysing, hand on his helmet, went over and negotiated with them. Then whistle blasts rang out and soldiers ran over and gathered in groups on the right bank of the stream. Kroysing returned relieved and with renewed drive. 'The officers have decided to reconnoitre towards Douaumont with my sappers, clear things up in the great hollow if necessary and try to make contact with the ridge,' he told Roggstroh. 'They have over 100 rifles. We can get somewhere with that. I have one request for you, comrade: if you find a gun intact, let it loose on Douaumont. It doesn't matter if the range is 1,500m, 1,700m or 2,000m – whatever's possible. Imagine if we could get the old shack back!'

'Do you think that's possible?' asked Roggstroh.

'Anything is possible,' said Kroysing, 'with a bit of courage and a lot of luck. On you go, Süßmann,' and he turned to the wee lad. 'You know the lay of the land. You lead – taking all due care, of course.'

Süßmann made as if to click his heels. 'Cheerio, Bertin,' he a said, extending his hand. 'I wonder where we'll meet again. I'm going to bestow this pot on you as a parting gift,' and he took off his helmet, held in the tips of his fingers, placed it on Bertin's head and shoved Bertin's oil-cloth cap under his arm. 'I'll have plenty of helmets to choose from up front – and you need to preserve that brain of yours.' And off he walked, looking very boyish with his short hair.

'Our ways part here,' said Kroysing, sniffing the air with his wide nostrils. 'It smells of winter. We're going to have a wonderful Christmas. Did you hear that?'

Dull thuds, as though wrapped in cotton wool, could be heard coming from the dense fog that began a few paces away.

'The bastard French are starting up again. We thought we could pull the stars down out of the sky and had victory in the bag. That's never good. Once again, Bertin, cheerio. Chin up, my young friend,' he added with a wave of his right hand. 'Cheers. Happy New Year to one and all. Vive la guerre!' He saluted, turned round and headed off, becoming more ghostly with every menacing step he took. The three men watched him until he dissolved into the fog.

'Right, let's go,' said Lieutenant von Roggstroh. 'It can't get much darker.'

They crossed the valley on the newly erected plank bridges. Roggstroh said the bridges showed what a blessing it was to have sappers and ASC men to make sure the artillery didn't get their legs wet before they had to. The feverish wounded shivered and groaned by the fires. As they passed them, a tall man rose and, eyes tightly closed, said: 'Buried, Doctor. Volunteer Lobedanz, University of Heidelberg, currently in the field.' Then he sat down again and pushed his hands against the rock behind his head as though it might collapse.

They climbed the disintegrating path that led to the battery. From time to time, the lieutenant flashed his torch. That's how they picked out the 'signpost' – the dead Frenchman still standing against the beech tree, nailed in place by a shell splinter. Not for the first time, Bertin thought that he should be underground. The lieutenant said: 'They pull some tricks round here.'

German shells swooped and groaned overhead like giant birds of the night. No one knew where they came from or where they were going. His heart thumping, Bertin thought that Lieutenant Schanz must be dead or they would have heard his howitzers firing – what he liked to call 'giving a concert'. The howl of battle, rising every quarter of an hour, thundered across from somewhere further forward, somewhat to the left. Then a sudden burst of rifle fire: Kroysing's men.

'We're holding Caillette wood,' said the lieutenant. 'And we're holding Fort Vaux and Damloup, or at least we were two hours ago. Do you know what the field of fire is like? How does it lie in relation to Douaumont?'

'Unfavourably,' answered Bertin. 'Douaumont dominates the whole area.'

As they came on to the top, walking in goose step and feeling a few paces in front of them with their sticks, they could hear the gun battle more clearly, though they couldn't see anything. A figure appeared from the fog, a man, a corporal, panting and shaking with fear. A lost infantryman from one of the battalions that had lain in reserve and been called out that afternoon to clear the area leading to Douaumont of French shock troops. With him was a small group that had been on the far left wing and had got separated from the company. Lost in a wilderness of mist, craters and sodden earth, they battled the terrain, expecting to drown in a sludge-filled shell hole at any moment. Lieutenant Roggstroh decided they should take the men with them. They were from the Mark, Brandenburgers from the fifth division of the military Reserve. When they reached the advance guard a minute later, the four remaining men were waiting motionless and panic-stricken. They'd been afraid the path they were on would lead them straight into the vengeful arms of the French. Now they trotted behind the officer in relief, like children who attach themselves to someone else's mother because they've lost their own in the woods. They had thought there couldn't be a soul left alive in that wilderness. The French had taken them by surprise, suddenly appearing after the wild bombardment, but had been beaten back.

'They're sick to death of it too,' said one of the four, who was exhausted and caked in sludge. 'If you fall down wounded here you'll drown in the sludge whether you're French or German,' and he made an all-embracing arc with his arms. Now the artillery sergeant, who until then had been listening and watching attentively, prodding the sodden earth with his stick, opened his mouth. 'How are we going to get our guns forward?' he sighed. 'The poor old nags.'

The lieutenant didn't answer and shrugged his shoulders. You could tell from his frown that he too loved his battery's horses. A sudden crash and howl signalled the start of the French shrapnel fire. They heard the shells burst but saw nothing. The main valley was clearly under fire. *Kroysing's down there,* thought Bertin dull. *It doesn't matter any more.* Finally, a splintered tree loomed up before them and what looked like a wall of earth or a rock. Breathing heavily, Bertin said: 'It's downhill a bit on the right. There were no canisters or carbines here.' He pushed forwards and disappeared from view. 'Schanz,' the others heard him calling. 'Lieutenant Schanz!'

A groan seemed to answer from the void – or was it an echo? The remaining seven men entered the former battery with bated breath. They flashed their torches around, and the white beams of light pierced the fog ahead. The stone and earthworks of the shelters had been blown sky-high. Strands of barbed wire hung across the pathway from what had once been trees. The twisted corpses of dead men lay all around. A direct hit had toppled heavy gun number four and its mounting. The gunners' dugout, which had fallen in or been torn apart, gaped like a dripstone cave. A blood-drenched swamp had formed by the entrance. The next gun seemed undamaged, though its breech mechanism was missing. The ammunition dump behind it had exploded and flattened a second dugout. The other two guns must have been engulfed in a rain of shells. Number one with its barrel lowered looked like an animal broken at the knees.

'The French have been here,' said the infantry corporal, flashing his torch around and lifting up a flat steel helmet.

'So it would seem,' said Lieutenant von Roggstroh tightly. They found gunners lying on the floor, two armed with shovels, one clutching a ramrod in his fists. 'Where's our guide?'

'Here,' called the sergeant, flashing his torch on Bertin, who was kneeling on the floor. Beside him lay an outstretched corpse, stabbed in the chest and apparently shot too, clutching a pistol in his right hand by the barrel like a club. Bertin kept feeling the man's pulse. His soft, blonde hair still felt alive, but Lieutenant Schanz's eyes were sightless now. Bertin peered myopically at his face. 'Take the lamp away,' he said. 'I can see him without it.'

'Not every man gets to see such a clear picture of his future,' said Lieutenant Roggstroh.

Bertin said nothing. He closed the dead man's eyes carefully with his fingertips, as if he might hurt him. His heart was full, but he was speechless and numb. 'Does this make any sense?' he wondered out loud. And inside he thought: *didn't we all believe in a father in heaven, and then when we grew up in some kind of rational conception of life? And now this? What's the point?* 'Why did things have to turn out like this?' he said. 'He enjoyed life so much.'

Piercing groans came from all sides. There was a stifled scream from one of the dugouts and whimpering from the shattered gun. 'My leg!' someone screamed in a Silesian voice. 'You lot are crushing my bones, goddammit.'

A man they'd taken for dead, propped against a timber near where the screams had come from, clasped his head in his hands and stuttered out a little of what had happened. He'd been hit on the head with a gun butt. Brown devils had suddenly broken in. They must have dragged their dead and wounded back with them. Even before that – the air was full of shells. The medics in their dugout had been the first to get it. The lieutenant had fought on until the end. Then the gunner had got hit on the head and that was all he remembered.

'He's lying there now,' said Lieutenant von Roggstroh. 'What a lovely night it's going to be.' Then he ordered his men to gather up the dead and help the wounded as far as possible. 'We'd better set up here,' he said.

Bertin was suddenly freezing. 'I think,' he said hesitantly, 'that I'd best get back now.'

The lieutenant looked at him. 'What do you actually do in the ASC? That sapper was right. You should apply for a transfer. You could make something of yourself with us.'

'I don't think I'll ever voluntarily apply for anything again,' said Bertin. 'You shouldn't kick against the pricks.'

'So, you're a Bible reader,' said the lieutenant with a hint of contempt. 'Well, make sure you get home safely. You certainly shouldn't get lost.' Bertin hesitated. He wanted this young man's approval, and so he said that an ASC man's lot was not an easy one. 'I know,' said the lieutenant, 'but men like you need to take responsibility rather than disappearing into the masses.'

Bertin wanted to say that he had taken on a great responsibility, but it was impossible to explain this to the lieutenant in the short time available. He went to have a final look at his neighbour Schanz. His chest was riddled with black holes, but his blonde head lay upon the earth like that of a man asleep. 'I'll remember your face, Paul Schanz,' he whispered to him. He remained by his side for a few silent moments, arms hanging. Then he pulled himself away, told the lieutenant he was ready to leave, was dismissed, about turned, climbed carefully over the dead and pushed off into the fog. In 20 minutes, the engulfing fog had wiped out the world, isolating any human figure. Bertin shuddered. He was cut off from where he'd been and where he was going. As he trudged on, bent over like an old man, using his torch sparingly, he felt exhausted, near the end of his strength. He'd had enough. He must put in for leave. He could claim 10 days. He'd taken four days in June, and so the battalion owed him six. Tomorrow, or the day after at the latest, he'd put in a request. From time to time, he stopped, cupped his hand round his ear and listened to the dull thuds from the area around the Vaux ridge, Hardaumont and the Hassoule ravine.

There is a natural human tendency to drift to the left when finding their way in the dark or blindfold. The detachment of 100 rifles quickly succumbed to this law as it made its way out of Wild Boar gorge on to open ground, marching in single file in a long column, sappers at the front. Those with the longest legs inevitably ended up at the head of the column. And in the impetuous heart of one of those tall men burnt the desire to lay his hands on his goal – whether that was the fort or the man who'd escaped from it, he didn't yet know. It wasn't long before Lieutenant Kroysing was all alone. He hadn't noticed that the column of men behind him had lost its way and drifted to the left; and to the left of Wild Boar gorge lay not Douaumont but the rear.

He, Eberhard Kroysing had an internal guide and one in front of him too: the schoolboy Süßmann, who, having travelled back and forth between the fort and the construction squad, knew the hollow and the surrounding area like his way to school. Kroysing could barely see him but he constantly heard him rattling his equipment or shouting out: 'Shell hole on the left!', 'Watch out, railway lines!', 'Dud on the right!', 'Look out, stakes!', 'Shell hole on the right!', 'Firm ground half right!' The wee man splashed on, and Kroysing waded after him, his eyes boring into the impenetrable yellow-grey fog that grew darker with each passing moment. His hand was clenched round the butt of his pistol. His senses ran ahead of him, ripping aside the accursed blanket of fog, and his heart thumped as he imagined tearing it to shreds and sinking his clenched teeth into that which eluded him: all the forces of resistance. This mad world had conspired against him. The phrase 'we thought we could pull the stars down out of the sky' came back to him. He didn't know what had first made him think of it, but it was true – or perhaps more correctly false. They should have pulled the stars down out of the sky, along with all its ghosts of superstition and residual spirituality. This blanket of cloud, which had left them high and dry at the crucial moment, proved it. To the devil with you, he thought, as he listened out for Süßmann and at the same time turned to catch the clatter of the Saxons behind. They'd achieved nothing. It was all a pile of shit. If you couldn't command the weather, couldn't devise some instrument to blow away this kind of spray and achieve visibility, then you were nothing and you shouldn't start a war. Certainly, people knew how to create fog, but clearing it was another matter. Could he hear the Saxons or couldn't he? Was this silence an hallucination? Would the bloody French batteries over there in Caillette wood defeat this final desperate attempt as well?

Sweat poured over his eyes and down to the corners of this mouth. 'Süßmann,' he called imperiously. 'Süßmann.' He was up to his knees in a muddy hole. He had to push his stick deep into the soggy ground, hold his pistol up high with his left hand and wrestle himself upright in order not to fall over. 'Süßmann!' Nothing. He groaned in anger, wiped the splatters of mud from his mouth with the back of his hand and listened. Was that a clattering he could hear far behind him? Was that someone calling way over there to the right? He realised that his undertaking had already failed. It had been madness to start it. The Saxons had been right. Now he was going to pay the price and come to a miserable end in a shell hole somewhere. And, bang, there was a crash above and a whistling cacophony descended: shrapnel. He couldn't see it, thank God. It's hailing, he thought with malicious enjoyment. Turn your collar up, Herr Kroysing! Yes, it was hailing. Thankfully, not in his immediate vicinity. Who could tell whether the French were firing too long or too short. Who indeed? An airman, of course. Airmen could tell. Airmen can do anything. They're superior to their enemies, set above them, beings of a higher order, a step forward in the sluggish development of the vertebrate known as man. And as he stood there, literally rooted to the spot – for where should he go to escape the lead balls, as he couldn't see them and could only hear their hissing and howling, their snapping and bursting – as his ankles were sucked deeper into the earth's grip, the point of his walking stick became ever more embedded in the ground, water filled his shoes but didn't quite penetrate his puttees, as he stood there like that, bent and tense like a pine marten about to jump, enlightenment filled his heart; the heavens weren't the problem, it was the ground, the earth, this muck we're born on and condemned to roam upon until we die and are reabsorbed by it. *No, my love,* he thought as he struggled to free his feet at all costs and trudge on. *Do you know the only thing you're good for? As a springboard, nothing else. We should kick you in the face and fly away. What a bit of luck that we invented the internal combustion engine, we masters of fire and explosions!* And in that moment he reached a firm decision: he'd become an airman. Just wait until this mess was over and everything was cleared up, until an iron fist had knocked the French flat for daring to stick their nose into German territory, and a certain someone would throw in this sapper business and join the air force. Crawling around in the dirt was good enough for the likes of Süßmann and Bertin, men with no fighting instinct, no fire in their punches, old men. He, however, would metamorphose into a stone dragon with claws, a tail and fiery breath, which smoked little critters out of their hideaways – all the Niggls and other such creatures. He'd have a fragile box beneath him, two broad wings and a whirling propeller, and hey ho, up above the clouds he'd soar like a Sunday lark – admittedly not to sing songs but to drop bombs on the people crawling around below, to splatter them with gas and bullets as part of a duel from which only one person returns. He stretched up to his full height, grabbed his pistol in his fist and shook it at the air from which the shrapnel was hissing down.

BOOK SIX

Attrition

CHAPTER ONE

The imaginings of a Jew

THE WAR HAD reached its zenith. All the omens, which thus far had favoured the Germans, turned imperceptibly. For a people who had only recently formed into a nation state, the Germans had performed miracles. With his left arm, the Teutonic giant had held off the Russians, already bleeding from multiple wounds, while attacking the two finest fighting nations of the nineteenth century with his right: the British, who had defeated Napoleon, and the French, who under that same Napoleon had been the bane of the old armies. The giant's right foot had kicked the warlike Serbs into seemingly irreversible submission, while his left had felled the Romanians with a blow to the kneecap. He had terrorised the Romans at the battle of Teutoburg forest, and now he thought the future belonged to him and he wanted to drag it into the present. Only a handful of people on the planet knew that the giant was soft in the head under his steel helmet, quite unable to grasp contemporary realities, and that, just like in a fairy tale, he would forgo that which was within reach out of greed for some other unquantifiable treasure.

That poor feeble head... The Saxon counter-attack the night after the disaster was as ineffective as that mounted by the Silesians and Brandenburgers, because every available rifle had already been thrown into the breaches. The men didn't show their dejection. That would have been defeatism and would have poisoned the atmosphere. And the French attack was accorded only secondary importance in the highest quarters. The staff studied their mistakes, learnt from the French that the front zone could be moved and that a closer alliance between the infantry and the batteries had advantages, and perhaps regretted the decision taken at Pierrepont. But no one suspected that the French would not be satisfied with their success. The German staff were much too proud and self-important to suspect that. And yet the French sector commander was already preparing his next attack, and this attack was also destined to succeed because it was based on clear thinking and a proper assessment of the realities. They were going to storm the Meuse heights.

But things had not yet got to that point. In a hub like Damvillers, the officers' messes still filled with bustling gentlemen every lunchtime. Many a new face appeared among them, for example that of Captain Niggl. Captain Niggl went about his business in an unassuming manner – his battalion's headquarters and Third Company were now stationed in Damvillers – but he was in fact labouring under the burden of fame. Captain Niggl was a hero. He had loyally held out at Douaumont until the last moment at the head of his brave Bavarian ASC men. He was sure to be awarded the Iron Cross, first class. If his king's military cabinet consented, he might also get an early promotion to major and receive a high Bavarian honour on King Ludwig's birthday. Bets were being laid in the officers' mess as to whether he'd receive his Iron Cross on 18 January, the order's anniversary, or on 27 January, the Kaiser's birthday. Portly little Niggl wandered among his comrades with an expression of reluctant sociability on his rather sunken face, but his shrewd eyes shone in triumph. His temples had turned grey, white even, but victory had been his. He had not signed, he had not allowed himself to be cowed by a big-mouthed lieutenant, that criminal who had now disappeared. He had bent but he had not broken. His wife and children and he himself would come through this business unscathed – the same was true of Feicht and the others. He ought to reward himself with a nice holiday: Christmas at home with the children, setting up the crib with the Baby Jesus, the shepherds, the ox and the donkey, retouching the gild on the star of Bethlehem. Of course certain papers remained in that shithole of Douaumont. Well, the Frogs could wipe their arses with them. He'd been tested and had passed the test. He padded through Damvillers, which he liked enormously, even in the rain, with a friendly, somewhat battle-weary air. Those he visited felt honoured. Major Jansch felt very honoured, as he visited him quite often.

Today, Jansch sat as usual in his living room at a big desk strewn with newspapers, files and large-format maps. It was very agreeable for Major Jansch to be admired by the hero of Douaumont, and Niggl's eyes shone with admiration for the Prussian officer.

Editor Jansch was not much liked in Damvillers on account of his being a political know-all. But retired civil servant Niggl found his views fresh and astonishingly broad. Jansch asked him if had he ever heard about the Free Masons' conspiracy against Germany. He certainly had not. And yet the Grand Orient de France lodge had incited the world against the Reich; otherwise Romania would not have been so stupid as to start a quarrel with world war victors. And what about the role of the Jewish press in spreading enemy propaganda, eh? Jewish journalists spent every day penning poison about the German Michael, especially that Jewish press baron Lord Northcliffe whose newspapers had inundated the world with made-up stories about atrocities, particularly those supposedly committed in Belgium. The British had known what they were doing when they made that bastard a peer, and the Americans also had half a dozen such Jewish journalists, of whom Hearst was the most prominent. They were everywhere, those ink-spilling swine. He even had one in his company. He'd got himself the name of Bertin; no one knew how. He probably came from Lviv and was called IsaASCon a few years or decades ago. This Yid had now had the nerve to claim six additional days of leave that he supposedly hadn't got in the summer. In the summer, he had in fact got married to some Sarah or other. He'd persuaded her to marry him, in that typical Jewish way, so he could exploit the regulations. He'd got his leave, but the minimum four days of course. And now he'd had the audacity to demand the missing six days under the pretext that he'd been in the field since the beginning of August. Phenomenal! Where should he have been? Instead of being grateful to the Prussian state for allowing him to wear its uniform, he pulls this trick of wanting leave twice in the same year thereby denying some comrade who hadn't yet been home the same pleasure. Fortunately he'd come to the right man. The First Company had duly passed his request on, but with a note explaining how things stood. The little jumped-up egghead was hoping to receive his leave papers and travel pass today in the orderly room with the other men due to go on leave. No one had told him he was going to have to turn tail and march back disappointed, then go straight back on guard duty. That would give him time to ponder his insolence, because the Jews were insolent – unimaginably so. As long as those sorts of people enjoyed equal rights with their racial superiors and proper Germans, things would never improve in Germany for all her heroic deeds. This was Jansch's confidential view, whether Comrade Niggl agreed with it or not.

Niggl had nothing against Jews. He didn't know many, but those who lived in his area gave no cause for complaint, and the Bavarian army had never had any problems with its Jewish officers. He knew that some Prussians had a bit of a thing about them, as did the Austrians. In Bavaria, it was really only the journalist Dr Sigl who went on about the Jews, and he was actually much more vehement against the Prussians. Personally, Niggl had had much worse experiences with Protestants, but he didn't mention that to his friend Jansch out of politeness. But what difference did it make to him if a squaddy had to march back disappointed and go back on guard duty instead of getting on the leave train? It wouldn't do the man any harm. After all, things hadn't been particularly pleasant for Niggl in Douaumont.

A bleak November afternoon hung over the roofs of the village of Damvillers, and drizzle fell in front of the windows of the battalion headquarters. The lamps had been on for a while in the ground floor orderly room. The personnel were eagerly awaiting the 10 men from the First Company due to go on leave, who were to be led in by Herr Bertin. But instead of Bertin, in came Corporal Niklas, who also belonged to the first. He sat down by the stove in his spruce tunic looking quietly pleased. Things had been arranged like this so that the men in Moirey, especially Bertin himself, didn't suspect anything, because only 10 men ever went on leave, never 11. This way the joke was bound to come off. The men going on leave would definitely be there by 4pm. They would all be champing at the bit as they had to get the train in Damvillers then catch their connection to Frankfurt in Montmédy. Well, it wouldn't hurt them to dash about a bit. They'd have 10 days to relax at home with mother afterwards, and the Prussian mindset did require that every blessing be paid for with a little hardship.

Captain Niggl started when he peered through a crack in the door and caught sight of Private Bertin, the only man who wouldn't be going on leave but would be returning to his company. He'd seen that face before. It hadn't been as pale as it was now in the lamplight with the weight of disappointment; it had been browner and fresher and it had been at Douaumont. This man, standing there rigid while the sergeant major drily informed him that the battalion had not authorised his request, belonged to his oppressor Kroysing's gang. Back then, he'd run around with that little sergeant, Sußmann or Süßmann – another Jew. Perhaps there was something to this business about the Jews. Perhaps clever Herr Jansch was right about that too, and he, Niggl, the retired civil servant, had been too trusting. He'd have to think about it. In any case, this man had to go. He might know a lot, a little or nothing, but he couldn't be allowed to wander about talking. That was the law of self-preservation, which was in fact a necessity that knew no law. Niggl would keep his eye on this man, make a note of his name. First, however, he must find out where the scoundrel in chief was. If he was still missing, as Captain Lauber had told him he was, to his genuine distress, then it was time to start clearing up and get rid of the rest of those in the know. It was quite right that this man wasn't going on leave, and he shouldn't go until it was his proper turn. That could be spring or it could be summer, and a lot could have happened by then. Captain Niggl, with his reluctantly sociable expression and his shrewd little eyes, had got a lot out of the spectacle that Herr Jansch had supplied; thank you, my friend. Did you notice perchance how the man swayed a little as stood there, my friend? Won't do a stuck-up, four-eyed sort like him any harm – what was he called again? Bertin. Bertin? Was that right? Unpleasant looking chap, Herr Bertin, with his sticky-out ears. The sort you see in police mugshots. Retired civil servant Niggl had seen some criminals in his time, but he didn't want to say anything against his friend Herr Jansch's First Company. Perhaps the Jews really were the ones to watch. He'd mull it over before their next meeting and perhaps join the Pan-German Union, because it really had become necessary to stand up to the Free Masons and campaign for all-out U-boat warfare.

Private Bertin set off on the main road to Moirey. The dark grey around him matched how he felt inside. To his right and left stretched sodden land; inside him beat a desolate, sodden heart. The rain speckled his face, and cold water trickled down between his chin and upturned collar, soaking his neckband. It wasn't physical exertion that had left him so tired that he thumped down on the puddle edges. He'd completed his allotted day's work of railway construction in a swamp between Gremilly and Ornes, where new field railways were required because of the new position of the front. Warm at heart and gaily anticipating his leave, he had happily helped to bind brushwood bundles and lay a causeway through the alder wood, along which the rails would run. They'd worked up to their ankles in mud, but it hadn't bothered him; he was going on leave and would be with Lenore the following evening and have six days of being human again in her beloved presence. He'd eaten quickly, almost without appetite, hurriedly cleaned his equipment, rolled up his blankets and buckled them on to his rucksack, which he'd packed the night before, and presented himself in the orderly room neat and clean-shaven. They'd sent him to Damvillers with the other nine men without a word of warning, although they knew what was going on. They'd even made him leader of the little detachment, responsible for answering any questions about where they were going and why from any field police conducting checks or curious officers. And then they had dropped him into the abyss. Diehl, a long-faced clerk with black eyes, had tried to warn him at battalion headquarters with much shaking of his head and closing of his eyes, but it had been in vain. They'd played this trick on him out of sheer nastiness – whoever was behind it. The decision must in any case have come from the major, Herr Jansch, that measly editor of *Army and Fleet Weekly*. From him had come the decree that there were to be no exceptions in the Prussian army and no one was to go on leave twice in one year. It sounded good, harsh but fair, but it was just a pretext. Anyone who knew how things worked here knew how many favoured laddies got sent home two or three times a year. It wasn't always called leave. Usually it was called travelling on duty, helping to ensure the safe transport of boxes and cases whose contents were well-known. If only a certain Metzler, who'd helped him secure his wedding leave in the summer, had been in the orderly room. But he'd long since been drafted into the infantry. Goethe said we shouldn't complain about villainy because the Almighty's hand was still at work in it. And it had to be suffered through to the end. The orderly room wouldn't bother to suppress a grin when they saw someone back from leave so soon. And one or other of his chums in the barracks would be sure to throw in a crack. He couldn't even go to sleep and get over his grief that way; he had to go on guard duty, which meant long, hard hours walking back and forth in the night rain with lots of time to think. He was filled with grief as he trudged along the main road – the same one where the crown prince's car had sped so elegantly past a few weeks previously— it was an impersonal kind of grief, grief at a system that had revealed its true colours to him, lonely Private Bertin, in the same way that those cigarettes chucked out of a window had shown the system's true colours. All the suffering, privations and sacrifices that the common solder constantly had to endure were amplified by these petty slights and unnecessary humiliations. He had performed his duty faultlessly for its own sake; nothing could be said against him. Furthermore, he'd volunteered time and again for difficult duties, and, as was fitting, had kept that to himself. And if the company had refused his request point-blank, he would have been disappointed but would have accepted it in the light of the general need. But those men had staged a nasty little scene and humiliated him for their own satisfaction. He'd seen that the door leading from anteroom into the orderly room was ajar and had noticed the gap widening a little and eyes and part of a nose appearing. And that was intolerable. That was below the belt.

The wind whistled through the branches of the trees and shrubs. The road dipped and ran along the edge of a steep slope. Below was the sparsely lit train station at Moirey, and those must be the barracks to its right, black against the dark sky. He'd better pull himself together now and present an indifferent face to the world, drink the bitter dregs. What an idiot he had been back in June when he left his young wife on the nice, clean platform at Charlottenburg and got into the train that would bring him back to this camp. Back then he'd sat down in the compartment with the feeling that he was going home, back to where he belonged. Well, he'd seen through that now. Lieutenant Kroysing and Lieutenant Roggstroh had been right! He didn't belong here, didn't fit in with this sleazy lot. Well, he only had to apply for a transfer and new horizons would open up. But that wouldn't do either. Even in this moment of anger and bitterness he admitted that to himself. Thick glasses are still thick glasses, and no one should throw himself into danger on a whim unless he's prepared to die. He was and remained condemned to be in the ASC. And like a condemned man he had to cling to the railing as he climbed the slippery wooden steps that led to the orderly room. He was sweating beneath his heavy rucksack, and his neck was freezing from the rain.

The next morning he reported sick. He'd felt strange during the night, gone hot and cold and been plagued by weird thoughts. He definitely had a fever; his temperature when he was examined was 37.4 degrees. Not all that high, said the young doctor, but as Bertin was an educated man he decided he should spend a night in the infirmary, as the sickbay was called. *Ah,* thought Bertin, as he stood to attention, *so if I were a waiter or a typesetter I'd be thrown out on my ear and sent back to work despite my disappointing temperature, and have to catch my death of cold before I'd be counted sick.* Were health and sickness also class-dependent? Comrade Pahl certainly thought so.

During the whole day, which he spent relaxing, sleeping and writing – he had to explain to his wife that his request had been denied – during that whole day in the clean and peaceful domain of Schneevoigt, the hospital sergeant, it didn't occur to him that he'd never had a thought like that before. Something had started to shift inside him – though unfortunately not quickly enough to save him from further harm. For little predatory creatures possess a good sense of smell, even in the jungle of human society, and always like to pick on wounded prey.

CHAPTER TWO

Rallying cries

THE INEXORABLE, WRETCHED grind outwardly continued over the next weeks. Each day, the work parties set off before dawn, damp and stiff, to build the crucial field railways in the rain: sometimes in the swampy woodland around Ornes, sometimes in the undulating country of Fosses wood. They were subject to continual harassing fire, and a smattering of shells would explode dusky red at sunrise, and it didn't matter if there were four or eight of them, the splinters were enough to take out Private Przygulla one morning at Gremilly, slashing open his stomach not 30m from where Bertin lay flat in the mud. Then in Fosses wood a while later they witnessed a German plane above their heads roaring down in a forced landing. After a panting 10-minute run, the ASC men lifted the dying pilot, whose back was riddled with bullet holes, from his seat. Scarcely had they hidden him behind the nearest furrow along with his assistant and the most important pieces of equipment when a shell set the great rickety bird alight – exciting moments in those grey and gruesome weeks. The nights drew relentlessly in, and the bleak dark, cold and wet gripped the men, undermining their spirits – they seemed to hang like feeble flies in a powerful spiders' web, grey on grey. When they pulled their blankets over their heads at night, because the wind whistled through the barracks and the little smoking stove, fuelled by wet wood, created more coughing than warmth, Bertin lay among them, almost indistinguishable from them, and Lebehde the inn-keeper and Pahl the typesetter no longer needed to complain that he was a stuck-up prig because he chose to shove a thing made out of meerschaum in his gob when he smoked a pipe. No, Private Bertin hadn't smoked a meerschaum pipe for a while – metaphorically speaking. They realised that when Sergeant Kropp saw an opportunity to play the big man with him.

Since the beginning of October, the depot command had ordered the NCOs to give the men from the outside working parties a day off in rotation so that they could attend to themselves and their things and didn't become entirely squalid. Lieutenant Benndorf had brought the measure in and enforced it strictly, much to the annoyance of the units working within the depot and their NCOs. So, when Sergeant Kropp, a bad-tempered farm boy from the Uckermark, found Private Bertin sleeping in the barracks one afternoon when everyone else was on duty, the colour rose in his sallow face and he said he was going to report him for evading duty. Bertin, knowing he was innocent, laughed and turned on to his other side as the clod Kropp marched off.

That day, 12 December, didn't just stick in Bertin's mind but in that of the entire world. When the army communiqué was pinned to the black tarboard wall in the orderly room after the washing-up was done, a growing group of men immediately gathered in front of it and read the badly printed text out in excited undertones: it contained the word 'peace'. Germany was suing for peace! She had staunchly held her enemies at bay for two and a half years, and a week to 10 days previously her infantry had occupied the Romanian capital of Bucharest after bitter exchanges: no need to fear, therefore, that this salutary step would be misunderstood. Canteen in hand, Bertin peered at it myopically, listened, asked questions and just stood. This was... this was the most important day of his life. His chest heaved in a sigh of relief that was for the world. Sadly, it only lasted until he had fully understood the wording of the imperial communication. The statement lacked the key phrase by which practically any halfway grown-up person could tell whether the proposed steps were serious or not: the return of Belgium and compensation for the devastation inflicted. With a bit of goodwill, such details could be dealt with in due course. The main thing was to get the enemy to the negotiating table. Private Bertin certainly couldn't be accused of lacking goodwill. Nonetheless, the wings of his hope shrivelled like wilted leaves and folded back in... He kept rereading the communication but no matter how hard he tried he couldn't find a single phrase which the enemy powers could respond to without humiliating themselves. After the odd enthusiastic shout of 'Listen to that!' or a more disgruntled 'Hold on, Otto!', the ASC men had nearly all slouched off, talking in undertones. A bandy-legged Bavarian gunner from the depot staff with a cigarette behind his right ear and a brimless cap tilted over his left, turned to Bertin before leaving: 'None too keen on it, are you, comrade? Me neither.' Then he checked there were no NCOs or clerks in the vicinity and finished by asking if anyone had any idea what kind of fresh shit those fatheads in Berlin imagined they were going to drum up with this peace initiative.

Bertin left too, feeling pensive, almost sorrowful. The white sheet of paper flashing on the orderly room wall looked stranded in the pale afternoon light. And after nightfall when his comrades from the Fosses wood party had erupted into the barracks and there had been a fierce debate about the news, they too eventually arrived at a not dissimilar position of disgust and scepticism. And Bertin, struck by this consensus among Bavarians, Berliners and Hamburgers, wondered at his initial surge of joy. He felt Pahl's eyes on him and Karl Lebehde's questioning looks. Hiding a certain embarrassment, he told them about Herr Kropp's oafish behaviour and said Kropp was sure to get the brush-off from his superiors. Pahl and Lebehde exchanged a glance. It was on the tips of their tongues to tell him to deal with the report immediately and inform the depot orderly room about it, but neither of them did so. Their friend Bertin was the sort of man who only learns from experience. After all, he'd fallen for the peace initiative.

When Bertin had gone off to write another letter home, the two squaddies were left sitting opposite one another at the narrow end of their table near the window, now darkening in the early December dusk. The barracks were full of the muffled sounds of a large group of men, their tobacco smoke and murmured chat. Tunics and canvas jackets had been hung out to dry between the beds, and tarpaulins were stretched across the ventilators. A load of freshly washed handkerchiefs was drying on the long, black stove pipes that followed the angles of the walls to the windows, where, carefully sealed, they opened to the outside. Lebehde had on a brown wool tanktop and green-striped slippers, and Paul wore his grey lace-up shoes and a grey cardigan. They looked like family men determined to finish a task before home time: darning socks in Lebehde's case and answering a letter in Pahl's.

But Lebehde wanted to ask Pahl for advice, and as always Pahl was happy to give it. Pahl had a lot on his mind too... Lebehde said that the Böhne working party had started a new track that day, which was to lead to the ruins of Chambrettes-Ferme. (Pahl and a couple of other men had for weeks been in Corporal Näglein's auxiliary squad in another, less exposed area among the many ravines of Fosses wood.) The idea was to hide two 15cm howitzers among the ruins and then build the crucial narrow-gauge railway. And guess who had appeared while they were working? Little Sergeant Süßmann. Today of all days, he'd come sauntering out from the emplacement behind Pepper ridge with his little monkey's face and restless eyes. How many times had Bertin asked the sappers from Ville about him and his lieutenant, and got no information? Well, there he was, and now the game had taken a new turn;

now he was asking questions and sending greetings, and telling everyone how they had survived the Douaumont debacle relatively unscathed, but had been pretty much stuck on the far right wing of Pepper ridge not far from the Meuse since then. They were cheek by jowl with the French and were pelting them with heavy mines, and all their communications to the rear had been shifted westwards and they couldn't even get their post from Montmédy as they'd done before. Lieutenant Kroysing therefore had a favour to ask of Bertin: to forward a letter to the court martial in Montmédy and a parcel to a post office within the Reich.

'Do you understand what that means, my son?' said Lebehde. 'Apparently, Herr Kroysing doesn't want to hand over any items with the name Kroysing on them to our field post and censors. People get suspicious when they have time on their hands.'

Süßmann said that Lieutenant Kroysing would express his gratitude to Bertin in due course. 'He may be an old devil but my lieutenant is the most decent man in the world. He wouldn't even take a pipeful of tobacco from you without giving you something in return,' he said, adding that he, Süßmann, would be getting his staff sergeant's sword knot on the Kaiser's birthday and probably some ribbons in his buttonhole too – all thanks to Kroysing. And at that he pulled two largish packages out of his haversack, a flat one and a soft, round one, and said they contained Christoph Kroysing's last effects.

'I don't mind saying that made me feel a bit funny,' said Karl Lebehde. 'A bit horrible. Wee Sergeant Kroysing spent every day and every night of his last months at Chambrettes-Ferme. It was down on the valley floor, if you remember, over to the right where those two long goose-neck guns were dragged away – French guns or something like that – that Bertin promised to forward his letter. And now up pops Süßmann, waving Kroysing's old gear around and wanting to bother Bertin again, although it's perfectly clear that it's an ill wind that blows nobody any good. But I'm a polite man and so of course I didn't say no and I took the things...'

'Where are they?' asked Pahl.

'Don't get carried away and break a leg, Wilhelm. No sooner had the boy left than I started to ask myself what you would have done.'

'Kept my hands off it.'

'Why?'

Wilhelm Pahl pressed his chin to his chest and looked his friend in the eye. 'Because Bertin shouldn't be messing around with lieutenants the whole time.

Because he takes every chance he gets to do something stupid.'

'Well, here's what I finally realised: every sausage must come to an end, and this sausage has gone on long enough. What good would the stuff in those packages do anyone? It won't help the parents. It'll only set their waterworks off. I can still hear the howls of an old woman I witnessed in a similar situation back in 1914. And the good people of Nuremberg won't be any the poorer either if the stuff disappears. Army postal package gone astray – that's that. Is it right to bolster people's prejudices by letting them think that all they have to do is ask someone to do something, and they'll suspend their judgement and become their postman? So I crawled down into the dugout in the old cellar at Chambrettes-Ferme. The rain had seeped in and soaked all the muck in there. It stank, Wilhelm – I take my hat off to the gunners who had to crawl about under there. And as I picked my way through the muck, I saw two eyes. Of course, I thought of young Kroysing, but only in a joking way, because I was at the back of the queue when superstitious natures were being given out. As surely as I've ever propped up a bar, there was a cat sitting on the upper bunk glaring at me. I checked with my torch and I was right. A great grey-striped she-cat was living there and she was either fat on rats or pregnant. Listen, kid, I said to her, just don't make a fuss and look after this little lot for me, okay, and I shoved the soft package between the palliasse and the wall. When I was above ground again, I gulped the air down. So, now tell me: did I do the right thing?'

'You did,' said Wilhelm Pahl.

'But what about the papers? Shouldn't our post orderly perhaps...?'

Wilhelm Pahl bit his lower lip. 'No, we'll sort it out another way, Karl. The day after tomorrow 10 family men are going on Christmas leave.'

'Goodness me. Is it that time already? Maybe peace will break out while they're at home, and they won't be able to get back and they'll die from missing you and me.'

Wilhelm Pahl ignored this joke. 'Among them is Comrade Naumann Bruno. He's conscientious and he'll stick the letter in the postbox at Montmédy train station. Then he'll go on his way, and no one will know where it came from.'

Karl Lebehde reached his freckled hand out to his friend in solemn silence. 'Done,' he said. 'But let's do it straight away.'

In Naumann Bruno's barbershop (everyone put the barber's first name after his last to distinguish him from Naumann Ignaz, the company idiot), it was quiet, warm and light, and smelt of almond soap. On a chair sat Sergeant Karde, who'd just had his hair cut. This Leipzig bookseller, whose small publishing house currently lay idle, and who was no doubt worried about his wife and children just as the workers did, enjoyed considerable respect among discerning members of the rank and file because of his sincere, humane attitude, although politically he was closer to their opponents, the 'German Nationals' as they were called. As the two men walked in, Karl Lebehde cracked a couple of jokes, and Karde laughed while admiring his haircut in two mirrors. Lebehde sat down for a shave, and Karde put his belt back on, counted out 20 Pfennigs, saluted and left.

'Close the door, Bruno,' said Lebehde as if that were a normal thing to do. 'I'd like to give you some concrete proof of my faith in you, and I want you to put it in the postbox at Montmédy station the day after tomorrow. I'm going to put it here in your drawer. And now show Comrade Pahl the letter from your old lady and the bit of newspaper she wrapped the badger hair brush in that she sent you. Because, in case you hadn't noticed, Wilhelm,' he said to the astonished Pahl, 'surprises, like trams, always come in twos, and I've been holding on to this one for a day or two.'

The barber's round, ruddy face twitched though he didn't for one moment doubt Pahl's reliability. He wasn't nicknamed Liebknecht for nothing. 'The old girl takes too many chances. I go to burn this scrap of paper every evening, and every morning I tell myself it would be a shame.' He opened a decrepit cardboard box and took out a carefully folded letter and read from the middle of it in an undertone: 'There's a lot going on but not with me...'

Pahl had sat there listening carefully and wondering why this harmless letter was being read out to him. He took it from Naumann's hand. The barber silently bent over him and drew arcs with his shaving knife connecting two pairs of words to create the words that now formed on Pahl's lips: 'Zimmerwald' and 'Kiental'. Pahl looked up with a start. 'Bloody hell!' he said.

Educated workers knew that the leaders of minority socialist groups from different countries had met that year and the previous year in the Swiss towns of Zimmerwald and Kiental – individuals and representatives of small groups who rejected their parties' majority view in support of the war. Among their number had been the German member of parliament Georg Ledebour, an elderly man respected even by his political foes. The new passports had been introduced by then, and the two most dangerous malcontents, the MP Liebknecht and the writer Rosa Luxemburg, either weren't allowed a visa or were already in prison. The meeting had already sent out an appeal to the workers of the world in 1915, saying that for them this world war was the brutal consequence of the economic tensions and conquering greed that were the very essence of the capitalist world order. German newspapers of all hues had mocked the Zimmerwalders' obstinate refusal to face reality; all around Europe men battled for victory, something even the stupidest farm boy could understand, while these café intellectuals wafted through the storm giving lectures on why the difference between war and peace didn't mean much to the workers. If the workers' position vis-à-vis business was contemptible in peacetime, they said, the war only made it worse, because the fathers and sons of the working classes suffered each and every day, and so first and foremost, down with the war. 'Tell that to the French!' proclaimed the German papers. 'Preach to the Germans!' said the French. And soon the minor event to which Frau Naumann had bravely alluded was engulfed in silence. Fingers quivering, Naumann the barber now opened the drawer in the table where he kept his razors. It was lined with old newspapers. He took out a small sheet. It was slightly yellowed, highly inconspicuous and had been screwed up and flattened out again. Pahl read it:

'Where is the prosperity you were promised at the start of the war? The real consequences of this war are already all too apparent: misery and deprivation, unemployment and death, malnourishment and disease. For years, for decades, the costs of this war will sap nations' strength and destroy the hard-won achievements that have given your lives greater dignity. Spiritual and moral desolation, economic catastrophe and reactionary politics – those are the blessings brought by this disgusting international wrestling match, as with all those that went before...'

Pahl's face went grey. His ugly features shone with emotion and he felt for his heart. Somewhere in the world, in free Switzerland, it was possible to think, say and print these things. Mankind was not entirely sunk in darkness. A tiny glimmer of truth still shone somewhere... Naumann, fascinated against his better judgement, had read the lines too over Pahl's shoulder. 'Hey, hurry up,' he said, starting suddenly, 'someone could come by at any minute.'

Lebehde silently tucked a towel into the neck of his jumper and wet his face. 'Let him read it by himself, razor hands,' he said. 'We know what it says.'

Naumann went over to him, soaped him up and said to Pahl: 'We must be mad. Close the drawer. Open the door and read it to yourself. Put it in the army newspaper.'

Pahl did so. The dangerous piece of paper covered the journalist Edmund Goldwasser's report about the crown princess's gracious visit to the Cecilia

Hospital at Potsdam. He read: 'In this intolerable position...' He saw them sitting round the table, these representatives of the suffering nations, their brows furrowed, their faces clouded in thought, as they discussed the declaration of war for which they were prepared to go to prison. They declared war on hatred among nations, on all forms of national madness, on all those trying to prolong the war, and called for an alliance across borders, for mutual assistance among the oppressed classes. They pledged to take up the fight for peace – a peace that renounced any violation of the people's rights and freedoms. The unshakeable foundation of their demand was the right to national self-determination, and they called on the subject classes to rescue civilisation and fight for the sacred goals of socialism in the implacable class struggle – their true purpose – with the same total fearlessness they had displayed since the outbreak of war in fighting each other.

Outside, someone was meticulously cleaning his boots, having evidently stepped off the boardwalk that made it possible to negotiate the camp into the reddish brown clabber underneath. Pahl calmly folded up the piece of newspaper and clamped it under his arm. 'Let me take it,' he said to Naumann. 'I'll look after it.'

'You're welcome to it,' he replied. 'I'll be glad to see the back of it.'

The door opened and in came Sergeant Kropp, disgruntled to see two men ahead of him in the queue. But Pahl the typesetter kindly offered to come back later, saying that he had more time than the sergeant and tomorrow was another day. 'You'll find your own way back, Karl,' he said and left. Outside he stopped, closed his eyes and breathed. He had heard a call and understood it. The stars might be covered in cloud but they were still up there. And as sure as there were stars in the sky, the triumph of reason advanced behind the struggling working classes, and the welfare of nations, understood properly, was inextricably linked to that struggle. Yes, it was time to act. If by any chance the orderly room had been telling the truth when it had reported that industrial companies at home could no longer claim men fit for service, then he would have to offer a little sacrifice and make himself unfit for service. A couple of toes or a finger – carried out with the utmost care of course on account of military prison... The laws of the ruling classes had a thousand eyes, but intelligence had more – and it had wings. Warmth flooded into him from the newspaper clipping, which he had pressed against his heart. He would have liked to dance, shout, sing: 'So Comrades, come rally...'

When Karl Lebehde returned to the barracks a little later, smoothly shaved, he grinned and said that ass Kropp had only wanted his hair cut so he could make a good impression on the company commander the following afternoon when he brought Bertin in for punishment. Man's stupidity was bottomless and its subtle variations were a constant source of amazement.

CHAPTER THREE

'Write!'

THINGS NOW TOOK on the hyper-reality of a fantasy, the solid outlines and soft, fluid forms. Unrest was in the air when two small groups of sinners were lined up outside Acting Lieutenant Graßnick's hut after lunch. On the left was Sergeant Kropp with his closely cropped hair and Private Bertin, whose platoon leader, Sergeant Schwerdtlein, was planted next to him in case a character witness should be required. On the right was Sergeant Böhne, whose friend Näglein had pulled the prank of reporting two shirkers from his platoon. The deaf carpenter Karsch and little Vehse the upholsterer had sloped off into a dugout when fetching ammunition to avoid exploding shells and hadn't rejoined their comrades until the march back. It was the second time Karsch had done this. He had an incurable fear of those wild iron birds that ripped into men's bowels with a deafening crash. Böhne moved restlessly from one foot to the other, twirled his moustache and fumed inwardly at Näglein, who had thrown his weight around by making a report rather than letting him, Böhne, deal with the matter.

There were rumblings on the horizon all around the camp. But the disturbances were no longer coming from German guns – enemy explosions had taken their place. Something was up – nobody suspected what. It would have been a wise moment to remember the old proverb that eating stimulates the appetite. The French were thinking of replying to the Kaiser's peace offer with the spears of their bayonets. As they were much better off in terms of ammunition and relative troop numbers than eight weeks previously, they fully expected to reach their goal – a line running from Pepper ridge through Chambrettes-Ferme to Bezonaux, that short front right across the Meuse heights, whose advantages certain gentlemen in Pierrepont belonging to the German General Staff would learn to appreciate. The attack rolled forward slowly; when it peaked the men in the barracks and among the ammunition dumps might notice something. Until then, profound peace reigned.

It must have been 2.30pm when Lieutenant Graßnick appeared in the door of his well-appointed hut, which was protected by a grey waterproof tarpaulin. Bertin studied him calmly, the warm fur waistcoat under his open tunic, which the deft company tailor Krawietz had turned out for him for next to nothing, the fashionably cut britches, the high-peaked cap, the monocle set in his fat, red face. A sideways glance and a little contented smirk revealed that 'Panje of Vranje' was pleased to hear that Bertin was in trouble. In the doorway the broad chest and massive legs of the company commander's bulldog also appeared, a solemn, tan-coloured beast with a white bib, which was hated because it consumed as much meat as two men, and which for that reason was never allowed to take a walk by itself in case it disappeared into a cooking pot. The acting lieutenant was in a sunny moody. Everyone knew that he was going on leave the day after next and staying away over New Year. And for that reason he gave the two truants a dressing-down in his rasping voice, accused them of betraying their comrades and only sentenced them to a hour's punishment drill in full equipment instead of sending them straight to the cells. Böhne radiated relief. Bertin thought: *now I'm curious*. As Kropp stuttered out his report, Bertin opened his mouth to explain the circumstances, but with even more of a sideways smile Graßnick lifted his hand: 'I know what you're going to say. You're not guilty of course. Three days' solitary confinement. Dismissed!'

Bertin swung round. After the officer had disappeared, Sergeant Schwerdtlein came up to him and said in a low voice, 'You can complain, but only afterwards.'

Bertin thanked him for his advice and said he would think about it. As he had to serve his time anyway, he needn't decide whether to complain for a couple of days. Schwerdtlein walked off, shaking his head, unable to fathom either the unjust punishment or Bertin's equanimity.

In May or June, who knew when it had been, Bertin had done something stupid that he definitely wouldn't do now. The acting lieutenant had deigned to play a game of chess with him, and Private Bertin had been unable to resist the temptation to put him in checkmate on his third move. He fully realised that this was against the world order but he couldn't stop himself. This latest trick of the acting lieutenant's had settled the account. Perhaps Graßnick thought it would be a hard blow but he was wrong. Bertin ranked the places he could be as follows: he'd rather be among the charred, wet trees of Fosses wood than in the throng of the company, and he'd rather be within the four walls of a cell than in Fosses wood.

Having poured out of the depot, the ASC men from the loading parties were gathering, tired and damp, on the ridge around the camp. The Frogs had unleashed a terrifying bombardment on the right wing from Pepper ridge to Louvemont. Now their shells were exploding on the road to Ville, on Caures wood and on the ruins of Flabas. From the camp perimeter, ghostly clouds of earth could be seen rising up as columns of smoke formed above the exploding shells. The ASC men watched unperturbed. The guns couldn't fire any further than they were doing at the moment. They'd never reach the depot and its 40,000 assorted shells.

A guard locked Private Bertin in a cell with his coat and blankets, and he slept for 12 hours that evening almost without stirring. His nose stuck out sharply in his thin face, his lips were pressed in a bitter line and his small chin disappeared under his grey blanket; he had been freezing all night without noticing it; he had withdrawn into his inner life. When he awoke, his joints were stiff, but he was refreshed and in the mood for thinking. It was better to stay lying down for a bit, to freeze and think, reflect on who he was and where he was, than to get up, get washed and get involved in discussions. He was stuck here like a scrap of muck and any boot could tread on him. But if that boot belonged to the lowest of the low, then it was better to be a scrap of muck swarming with maggots in the shape of thoughts. We invite you, Herr Bertin, to turn your attention to yourself, said the cell walls, the locked lock, the hard plank bed, the pale morning light in the open sash window. The window had no glass, instead tarpaper was nailed to its frame. He would have had to get up and stand on the plank bed to prolong the welcome darkness and he didn't feel like doing that. He didn't intend to get up until he heard the clatter of coffee being fetched. He intended to use this spell in prison – this gift from the shabby gods who watched over white men at the end of 1916, this kind offering of injustice, revenge, cold and loneliness – to clear his head. He'd been blundering around like a carefree puppy up until now, sometimes endangering himself inadvertently, sometimes irritating others. It was time to wake up, time to keep a weather eye on the machinations of fate. Kroysing and Roggstroh had been right. This wasn't the place for him. He'd have to change – how remained to be seen.

The tall men in the guard squad, the first squad of the first platoon, were sitting at breakfast. They invited Bertin to help himself. They looked worried. Bertin listened. The guns had not roared like this since the heavy fighting in May and June. The wild barking of enemy fire could be picked out clearly in the frantic bombardment. But fat Sergeant Büttner exuded unshakeable calm. 'Your squad has delivered various things for you about which I know nothing,' he said.

Under a bench stood the lid of Bertin's canteen neatly packed with his evening rations from the day before, some butter and cheese, his writing case and black oilcloth notebook, and five cigars in a screw of paper. *Ah*, thought Bertin with a surge of warmth, *they're looking out for me, they're backing me up.* Sergeant Büttner said that if Bertin wanted something to read or his pipe he would turn a blind eye. Hot coffee did a person good when he'd been freezing all the night. But what did a bit of freezing matter? Thousands of men would have given years of their lives to have frozen as tranquilly as he had done in the last 12 hours. Now the heating was on, and a pleasant warmth circulated through the whole ramshackle structure of planks and pasteboard. No one made any distinction between the prisoner eating his breakfast and his jailers.

Back in his cell, he decided to smoke a cigar, and the blue smoke wafted out of the window – it was rotten weed, company weed, but still it was a cigar. There was uproar outside – people running back and forth – no one would pay any attention to the cell window. He stretched out on the plank bed, closed his eyes and took the time to breathe again as if he were alone in the world. The cause of his incarceration slipped into the shadows. Perhaps a man had to be put in solitary confinement and robbed of his freedom in this fairly mild way to find himself.

As he blinked idly into the space in front of him, a figure appeared behind his eyelids: tanned face under a peaked cap, imperious look in his dark brown eyes, shoulders bent. The figure hid his left arm; the ribbon of the Iron Cross glowed in his buttonhole as if caught in a sunbeam. The figure's dark grey outline remained in place although the gaps in the boarding showed through it as Bertin blinked. Kroysing, Bertin said in an undertone to the spectre, which was looking at him, I did everything I could for you. I'm just a louse, as you know, a humble ASC private, and I've been under close observation since the incident with the water tap. I found your brother and gave him your legacy. We read your letter, and Eberhard set off at full tilt in pursuit of justice but he hasn't got anywhere yet. You've got to leave me in peace now. I'm a helpless soldier if ever there was one. I can't write to your mother, can I? That's up to your brother, and I can't write to your uncle either. 'Write!' echoed the figure silently. *Tanned face*, thought Bertin, *somewhat drawn, narrow cheeks, a rounded forehead, straight eyebrows, long eyelashes, kind brown eyes.* They'd gone after him and brought him down, and he'd been rotting in that sodden grave in the swampy wood at Billy for quite some time now – hardly a peaceful resting place. It was understandable that he should reappear. Write? Why not? He had the time. Before he'd always fashioned his torments into shapes, sculptures made with the ivory of words; there were 12 of them out there now for people to read. This ghost within him couldn't be laid to rest until he'd captured it in words. He had a pad of writing paper with a heavy cardboard cover and a fountain pen – of thought-provoking origins – which one of his comrades, probably Strauß the shopkeeper, had wrapped in with the cigars. *So that's what I'm supposed to do with it,* he thought in shock.

Bertin the writer pulled on his coat, wrapped one blanket round his body and legs and another round his shoulders, leant his back on the barracks wall, rested his feet on the plank bed and made his thighs into a desk. The cold daylight fell over his cap on to the square of his writing paper. His left hand, which was holding the paper, reached for a glove, which he put on. He began to write the story of the Kroysings. He wrote from morning until midday. His squad sent him lunch, and he hid his work. He ate his soup, washed out his canteen, was locked up again, climbed on to his bed, wrapped himself up and wrote. The glorious mercy of inspiration was upon him. Sentence after sentence slipped from his unconscious into his pen. He was warmed by that wonderful creative fever that allows individuals to expand, to leave themselves behind and become a tool of the urgent forces the spirit has laid within them. He cursed the gathering dusk; he had to write! He put his work away, his Kroysing story, which didn't yet have a title, and knocked to be let out.

The tall blacksmith Hildebrandt came to let him out. Bertin had had some good chats in the past with the Swabian from Stuttgart, who'd been a comrade since Küstrin days. 'Boy,' he said, 'there's something going on out there and no mistake.'

Bertin didn't say that he hadn't heard anything until just then. Until a few minutes before he'd been sunk in months gone past, beneath Chambrettes-Ferme, on the valley floor with the gun emplacement. There was much agitated talk in the guard room. It was a lucky thing that Sergeant Büttner's large frame filled the doorway, radiating calm. The battery fire had not let up, and neither had the seething, rattling shellfire. The French were definitely going to attack, perhaps that night, perhaps not until the morning. Rumours were rife; batteries rang constantly to check the lines were still intact; some of them that had still had a connection that morning hadn't rung since midday.

Two field artillery limbers had made their way over earlier through Ville with heavy losses – two horses and three drivers – and were now loading up in the field gun depot, the deepest and most sheltered position in the whole area. Hildebrandt the Swabian had spoken to them; they were dreading the thought of taking the carts back through but they had to get through or their batteries would crumble. It was effectively a death sentence for some of them. No matter: the limbers were being loaded and were going back. The loading parties were moving out of the park in grey and reddish brown columns; it was drizzling, and they had their tarpaulins round them. Bertin was lucky to be under arrest. Escorted by Hildebrandt, he visited the latrines; you always met people there. Wild rumours about French attacks from Douaumont, the whole area under heavy fire. They were going to get a nice strip of land for themselves that day – how much, no one knew. (A lot. The whole right bank of the Meuse captured between March and September at the price of mountains of corpses, all the trashed woods and gullies: Chauffour wood, Hassoule wood, Vauche wood, the Hermitage, Caurrière wood, Hardoumont wood – everything, absolutely everything.)

Little Vehse came in as Bertin was about to leave. 'There's your answer to the peace initiative,' he said dejectedly in his Hamburg accent, and his eyes revealed how strong his hope had been. He had married young and was due to go on leave in February, or perhaps the beginning of March, when he intended to wallpaper his bedroom. A few days previously he'd been asking Bertin's advice on colours. He preferred green, but green wallpaper was often poisonous and his wife was sensitive, so it might affect her lungs.

Bertin had negotiated with Hildebrandt for a candle. He was locked up again and again he listened to the surging ocean of fire behind Caures wood, not blocking out the seething misery of the world that came from there. Then he pushed the window frame over the ventilation flap and set to work. The candle gave enough light. It would make his eyes worse, but that didn't matter. This war was an unhealthy enterprise, and being a fraction more short-sighted could come in handy for future medical examinations. At first he faltered but then things loosened up and he found his thread. Bertin brought Kroysing, his friend of one day, back to life at least to himself in that moment. It would be painful to relive his destruction, but he wanted to get to that point that day. The next day he'd describe how delighted the sergeant, the company commander and the battalion leader had been at Kroysing's accident. One man's owl is another man's nightingale, as they said in Hamburg. He'd have to invent other names for Feicht, Simmerding and Niggl, not forgetting the wonderful Glinsky. That was enough for one day. His eyes hurt, and he was starting to freeze sitting there in the damp night air. He had his dinner, smoked a cigar and lay in the dark, limbs trembling. His excitement receded, and he tried to warm himself up by taking deep breaths; and so Bertin fell asleep without noticing that the crash of the explosions was moving ever closer.

'They're shooting in Thil wood! 'They're shooting at Flabas!' 'They're bombarbing Chaumont!' 'Soon it will be our turn!'

The guard room was full of excited voices. Bertin walked in from his cell, refreshed but freezing. He'd slept exceptionally well, dreaming of the sandpits of his youth. It was 15 December, and the rain had stopped. The sky was cloudy, presaging harder frosts in the coming days. Bertin felt the frost that day had been hard enough.

The company felt under threat, that much was clear. Because of where it lay it would make sense for the company commander to postpone his leave for a few days. He was responsible for the lives of 400 men, living without dugouts among mountains of shells and house-high piles of explosives. Unfortunately, there hadn't yet been time to build them. For how would the carpenters and bricklayers have found time to prepare elegant billets for the orderly room gods if they'd had to install underground shelters at the depot for the men? Querfurth the bearded clerk ran past, terror in his eyes: Sergeant Büttner and his squad would have to go on guard duty again that day. They make a show of grumbling about it but were of course delighted not to have to haul shells around for another 24 hours.

'I suggest you clear off to your cell,' said Sergeant Büttner casually to Bertin in his boyish voice. Bertin was curious about the ordeal his company was about to face and even a little amused by it. 'But we won't lock you in. Who knows what's going to happen?'

Bertin gave him a grateful, trusting glance and obeyed. As he was nodding off to sleep the night before, he'd began to wonder if the work suddenly taking shape in his head was really any good. He now flicked through the manuscript, shaking his head uneasily. He couldn't judge something he'd created so recently, but his increasingly cramped handwriting at least showed that it had flowed. It had certainly surged up fully formed, and as he read it over he again felt the excitement of the previous day's writing. *A writer is lucky,* he thought. *He can set up shop anywhere in the world, put his feet under the table and write.* His raw material is his own life: everything that hurts and makes him happy, his dissatisfaction with the world and himself, the restless feeling that there is a better, more meaningful way of life. Admittedly, he had to learn his trade and art.

Bertin stuck the work in progress in his coat pocket. He was powerfully attracted to the world outside that day. He climbed on to his plank bed and looked out of the small window, enjoying the spectacle outside as if he were watching from a theatre box with a restricted view. Fresh ammunition trucks seemed to have arrived, and the whole company was clattering up the wooden stairs to the depot, which extended as far as the road to Flabas. The orderly room was to his right; a little later some men came out of the open door engaged in debate, but unfortunately he couldn't hear them. However, he understood what was happening. The company commander appeared first in his coat and cap, booted and spurred, followed by his batman, Herr Mikoleit, who was wearing a peaked cap as if he were an NCO and hauling a two-handled crate. Bertin banged his head against the window surround in astonishment: Graßnick was going on leave after all! The company commander was pursued by Staff Sergeant Susemihl, agitated and sweating. So, Susemihl asked, was he supposed to take over the company then? He was just an honest policeman from Thorn. He'd stuck it out there for 12 years to provide for his wife and child. And what was this? Was dapper Staff Sergeant Pohl also planning a trip? Wasn't it Pohl, a teacher in civilian life, who had given them lectures in Serbia about a soldier's responsibilities and pursuing duty to the utmost? And now he was doing a bunk? Bertin smelt a rat. Panje of Vranje, his monocle screwed firmly into his face, was waving his arms in the direction of Chaumont and Flabas, no doubt presenting Herr Susemihl and his few sergeants with a reassuring picture of the situation and telling them how safe the depot was. It was a clear case of rats fleeing a sinking ship.

Then Sergeant Major Pfund came out – an old regular. He'd buckled on his sabre and waxed his moustache, but in his hand he held an iron box: the cash tin containing the company's canteen money. For nine months, the men had all been forced to contribute a couple of pennies every pay day towards supplies for the company canteen; excess profits were supposed to be paid back to the men after a certain amount of time. Sergeant Major Pfund set about distributing this money. His ruse was to go to Metz, where he was well know, buy cheap trinkets (duff knives, red-patterned hankies and ordinary lighters, as it later transpired) and pocket the rest. 'What a fiddle,' said Bertin to himself. 'He'll have got a fair bit, and no one will dare say anything, me included, although we could all do with a couple of extra Marks.' Bertin resolved to work out later how much the orderly must've had in that iron box; for now he wanted to watch what was going on. (If all the men paid in just 10 Pfennigs every 10 days it came to 1,269 Marks.)

It was clearing up. Suddenly, a shaft of weak sunlight glinted off the brass sabre scabbard and Herr Graßnick's eye glass. Herr Graßnick then made a dignified exit, for the train, small but clearly visible in the distance, was being coupled together at Moirey station from empty goods wagons and passenger cars, some with white in their windows. Bertin couldn't discern any more details with his short-sighted eyes, which was just as well, as the white was bandages; the cars had come from Azannes and were full of wounded men. The company was to be left alone then. A thick brown cloud hung over Chaumont, which was on fire. The officers were tramping down the steps now. In a moment they'd appear on the road and pass in front of him. There they were: Acting Lieutenant Graßnick with his brown dog on a lead, Staff Sergeant Pohl with his blonde beard, Sergeant Major Pfund with his cash-box, his sabre over his coat, and Mikoleit the batman with his crate. They were joined by 20 happy ASC privates going on legitimate leave who seemed to have been waiting for them on the road. Bertin's cell suddenly felt too small. He needed to get out, breathe the fresh air and stand in the sun for a moment. The men on guard had now calmed down. It wasn't yet 1pm, but because men were going on leave lunch had already been served to the entire company – a festive meal of beef and haricot beans – proving that the kitchen staff could sometimes get things done on time. After lunch the guards sat in the sun with their prisoners, enjoying the faint warmth on their faces and hands. A captive balloon had gone up to the southwest – the Frogs checking the area out. The wind was blowing in from the east that day, bringing the dull clang of exploding shells and the thunder of defensive fire. Bertin decided to use the daylight to write some more. He'd been thinking and had drafted a couple of short chapters, one of which took place in the home of Kroysing's parents, possibly in Bamberg. The home of a well-to-do official. The news arrives that the younger son has died a hero's death. What he had to convey was their genuine pain, clouded by the inflated ideas of the time, so starkly at odds with reality. What name should he give poor Kroysing? Artistic distance and licence required that he transform his subject just as an artist would in a painting.

Back in his cell, he was puffing on a cigar, imagining he felt the warmth of the sun through the black roof, when he heard a familiar howl up above. It hurtled closer, roaring, shrieking, and shattered with a desolate crash. Bertin jumped up; it had landed in the depot. 'How come?' he thought. They couldn't... a second crash, a third, then the dull roar of an explosion. One of the explosives dumps had been hit! Although Bertin could only see the street and the hollow of the valley from his window, he jumped on to the plank bed: crowds of men from the company thundered across the steps and paths. They were off. *Quite right,* thought Bertin. *Their leaders have left, and now they're leaving too.* A fourth and fifth strike hit the depot. Now people were screaming. An unspeakably shrill howl drove him from the bed and out into the guard room. Büttner, an industrialist in civilian life, stood in the middle of the room, pale and calm. His men were yanking on their boots and screaming: 'They've got us!'

The next strike crashed even nearer. 'You'd better take your things,' said Büttner, opening the locker. Bertin stuffed into his pockets the belongings he'd handed over two day before. While he put on his watch, the depot was emptying. Streams of grey-clad soldiers dashed into the barracks – on a cold night like that you needed a blanket. With a nod towards the open door, Büttner set his prisoner free to join the stream of fleeing men. But Bertin thanked him and declined, saying they would all be safer from shell splinters where they were. Just then Schneevoigt the medical orderly and his men, three pale Berliners and a native of Hamburg, ran out into the strike zone. It was their duty to do that – that was why they wore armbands with a red cross – but amidst the general chaos and flight it was encouraging to see men not copping out.

Huge clouds of black and white smoke billowed up from the depot; the explosives dumps were on fire. A gently sloping 12m high earthen ridge still stood between the barracks and the exploded shells. But the swathes of smoke would tell the French gunners where to aim. Standing in the doorway, Bertin was suddenly aware of two contrasting movements. Lieutenant Benndorf, the depot adjutant, was hirpling up to the orderly room with his walking stick, while Sergeant Schneevoigt, dirty and pale, was trotting down the earthen ridge followed by two of his men carrying a bulging tarpaulin between them.

'Who've you got there?' Büttner's boyish voice soared past Bertin's cap. Old Schneevoigt, a barber by trade, didn't answer. He was swallowing hard, and his face was almost the same colour and as his moustache. He just shook his fist at the columns of smoke.

'It was once little Vehse,' said one of the stretcher bearers for him. 'He's gone.'

Hildebrandt the tall blacksmith had come running over in the meantime. He'd collected a few bandages from the sick room and said there were three more dead among the explosives dumps: Hein Foth, the dirtiest man in the company, and the illiterate farm labourer Wilhelm Schmidt. They'd both run right into an exploding shell. Another man by the name of Reinhold had been killed by a direct hit. Bertin started – good-natured little Otto Reinhold. 'One of the original ones from Küstrin, if that's who you mean,' confirmed Hildebrandt.

A man from his own squad. And Wilhelm Schmidt and the lice-infested Foth were near neighbours of his too. No doubt he'd have been ordered out into the depot too if he hadn't been 'inside'. But there was no time for these deliberations now. Old Schneevoigt had found his tongue again and walked a few steps towards them. 'Get out of here!' he shouted. 'There are a dozen wounded lying in the ditches by the road. Do you want to join them?' and he trotted back into the sick bay, while another two of his men dragged over a tarpaulin, a brown one this time.

Sergeant Büttner gathered his pale lads around him. All of them were tall, but he was taller. He explained to them that the company had left, and so they were dismissed from guard duty and could leave too if they wanted. They buckled on their belts and rolled up their blankets. Bertin disappeared into his cell. While he hastily parcelled up his rations and blankets, pulled on his coat and felt in his pockets, he said his goodbyes to the slatted walls, the plank bed and the window. They'd brought him refreshment and allowed him to plunge back into an earlier existence, and he would never forget that. Now the Frogs had brought it to a premature end. In the guardroom, heavily laden men pushed towards the door. Just then another tarpaulin was carried past. Schneevoigt could be seen in the open doorway of the sick room, kneeling beside something unrecognisable and half in shadow. With an immense howl another shell crashed into the depot. Everyone ducked and pulled their heads in. Smoke billowed outside the window. Shell splinters or lumps of earth drummed against the wall. Then from the orderly room a clear voice shouted: 'Everybody out! Firemen, fall in. Forward march to the depot. Put out those explosive dumps!'

Lieutenant Benndorf stood there, fighting with his coat. His right arm was already in the sleeve, and he pointed with his walking stick to the soaring columns of thick smoke. The men in the guardroom shrunk back the tiniest bit. They weren't firemen, but they'd have to obey the order. Bertin in particular felt compelled to obey, though he wasn't sure why. He was overcome by a sense of responsibility for things that had nothing to do with him, and felt an impulse to throw away his bundle of blankets and follow his officer, who would shortly disappear past the barracks into the field of fire. But what happened? The lieutenant was indeed moving, but he turned his back on the orderly room, hobbled frantically towards the road, turned at the top of the stairs and again shouted: 'Put out the explosive dumps!' then clattered down the steps to the road on his gammy leg. There – Bertin could hardly believe his eyes – a grey car pulled up. Colonel Stein, his red face unrecognisable against the wide back seat, was waving both his arms about like a madman, his mouth a round, shouting hole. Eventually the lieutenant flung himself on to the other seat, and before he had even slammed the door shut the car sped of towards Damvillers. Bertin stared in blank astonishment, then he slapped his thigh, burst out laughing and turned to Büttner who'd followed him outside.

'Might as well scarper,' he said with contempt.

'Company to report at Gibercy!' shouted a passing telephonist who'd just run out of the switchboard room. The next minute there was a fresh crash, this time on the earthen ridge, and shell splinters whistled over the guardroom hut. A stream of tall ASC men thundered down the steps. The remaining heroes from 1/X/20 were evacuating their depot.

CHAPTER FOUR

A telephone call

'COMPANY TO REPORT at Gibercy.' Private Bertin, in his overcoat and field cap, with his bundle under his arm, stopped halfway down the steps to the street and deliberated. He was now almost alone. There would soon be another crash behind him. He knew exactly what he was going to do. His thinking was crystal clear – he was no longer an oppressed soldier led by others. He was an educated man of 28 evaluating the situation. The village of Gibercy lay among large empty camps beyond the hills. But the road leading there crossed a broad flat hollow vulnerable to shells and to observation from the captive balloon. Where was the most secure place in the camp complex? Definitely the former mill, once a bathing station and now the field gun depot. Field gun ammunition is the most dangerous of all because it comprises cartridges and shells, and men who knew what they were doing had chosen to store it in that depot... Bertin ran. Down the stairway, along the slope of the road and the duck boards, between the grass mounds that separated the various ammunition dumps. The ammunitions expert Sergeant Schulz lived in a hut on the bank of a stream called the Theinte with two subordinates: little Strauß and stiff-legged Fannrich – just as Sergeant Knappe lived beside the siege gun ammunition in the upper park, though being a more solitary type than the lively Schulz he lived alone. The hut was empty; its occupants had fled. *Never mind*, thought Bertin. *I'm here now: j'y suis, j'y reste.* A warm stove, a camp bed and blankets, dry wood, a canteen, stores of coffee, sugar and cigars. The coffee was good enough for a family; you just had to grind it on a bit of newspaper with an empty bottle. Bertin listened uneasily to what was going on outside: dull crashing. It seemed to be following the little troop that had hurried up the hill earlier. Much better to roam round someone else's billet with the kettle boiling. On the right was Fannrich and Strauß's room, on the left Herr Schulz's sanctuary, demarcated by a tarpaulin, and in the middle a little hall where a telephone sat on a small table. You could live the high life here. Nice view of the tumbling burn, afternoon sun on the windows, no men from the company, no depot commanders, nothing... *They fairly skedaddled,* Bertin thought, as a hiss told him the water was ready. And as he tipped the roughly ground beans into the boiling water and stirred the thick mixture with a shard of wood: *they really did scarper!* Be fair, he told himself, as he hung his tunic up beside his overcoat and a pleasant coffee smell mixed with the smoke from the cigar he'd pinched: be fair, man. Officer's stripes don't protect you from shell-fire. And Benndorf had been hit long ago, which was why he limped, and fat Stein as well, back in the days when high ups such as colonels got wounded in the field. Even Panje of Vranje had once sat bravely on his nag until the last man in the column had swung into cover. How long ago was that? Nine months? That was life behind the lines for you.

The sky had darkened in the meantime, and rain began to drum on the roof. *Well,* thought Bertin, *that'll put the explosives dumps out without any help from me, and then everyone will be happy.* You can never have too much rain in wartime. *Four dead,* he thought, *more than a dozen wounded, and the administrative heads are on leave and the officers have buggered off in a car – funny old world, and it certainly does make you think, though my name isn't Pahl. They can all go to hell, as far as I'm concerned.* Strauß had books, some of which Bertin had lent to him. He decided to celebrate by reading for an hour or so. He examined the bookshelf by a pile of old newspapers. He could've looked over his own manuscript but he wanted to steer clear of the present, and so eventually he chose *The Golden Pot,* magicked up by E.T.A. Hoffmann 100 years previously. It was raining outside. He savoured every mouthful of his black coffee, steeped in a timeless world of gnomes and salamanders, ghostly advisers and charming maidens, and the city of Dresden as it had never been... Then the telephone shrilled. Bertin started, torn from the waking dream Hoffmann had created. It really didn't concern him. The three men in charge of that phone would be playing skat in a dugout somewhere on the Flabas road – God alone knew which one. But Private Bertin was at the table about to lift the receiver when the phone shrilled again.

'No one there,' Bertin heard the voice on the line say.

'Hello, hello,' he said quickly. 'Steinbergquell field gun depot.'

'They're there now, Lieutenant,' the voice said.

'Hello, you've not been flattened then? We heard you were on fire.'

'We're fine,' Bertin replied. 'There was quite a bit of smoke, but we're still here.'

'Can we stock up with you, then?'

'Depends on the calibre,' Bertin replied.

'For goodness' sake,' came the angry reply. 'Have you just fallen from the moon? Which bore do you think a German field gun has?'

So the telephonists had faithfully plugged the connection before clearing off. This really was a field gun battery on the line. Now he could hear someone else chipping in, an officer. *Where do I know that voice from?* he wondered. *Have I done something stupid?* Then he gave the required information. The bombardment had caused severe damage to the heavy ammunition. The company had departed and the depot commanders had withdrawn, presumably to Damvillers.

'Withdrawn – hmm. And how come you're answering the telephone?'

'Coincidence, Lieutenant,' Bertin replied in embarrassment, unable to think of anything better on the spur of the moment. How could he have known he was speaking to the field guns? He couldn't have. *But where do I know that voice from,* he wondered again.

'A happy coincidence,' said the other man. 'In any case, you obviously haven't "departed". That shouldn't be forgotten. We'll be there about five, five thirty – as soon as we can. We're going to hold on here,' Bertin heard him shouting to his men. 'God preserve me but one of the lads has kept his head. Tell me,' he said, reverting to Bertin, 'haven't we spoken before? Aren't you that lad with the glasses from Wild Boar gorge, who in October... what's your name again?'

Bertin had a flash of illumination. 'Am I speaking to Lieutenant von Roggstroh?' he asked.

'Ah, you see,' said the lieutenant with satisfaction, 'you haven't forgotten me. But now you must tell me your name.' Bertin told him and asked to be excused if he had done anything wrong, explaining that he really was in the field gun depot by chance and didn't know how it operated. 'That doesn't matter,' said the lieutenant. 'You're the last of the Mohicans, and I'm going to put you in for an Iron Cross just as surely as we were together in that dreadful howitzer emplacement on the Mort Homme. I always knew you weren't really cut out for the ASC.' Bertin flushed and protested nervously that the field gun depot had simply struck him as the safest place and he didn't deserve a medal for being there. 'Of course,' said the lieutenant. 'Exactly. Have you ever heard of anyone getting an Iron Cross because he deserved it? Goodbye, my young hero. See you at five or half past.' Thinking he might now venture a question of his own, Bertin asked if the French had advanced very far. 'They got what they needed,' said the lieutenant evenly. 'We'll take a look at the damage tomorrow. See you later.' And he hung up.

Bertin sat there for a moment, dazed, then he replaced the receiver. Had the black coffee agitated his system or was he trembling with joy? He had thought the mean spiritedness that pervaded the battalion had extinguished any spark in him. But it must simply have hidden it, for he was alight now. What would the battery have done if he had fled too? Four guns with no ammunition were about as much use as four sewing machines. They'd have had to be hauled out of their emplacements and sent back, assuming the horses could manage it, and would've been no use that night, the next day or perhaps forever. He had prevented that, and it hadn't just been chance and because he wanted a comfortable billet; it was also down to clear thinking on his part. Bertin strutted round the room in grim elation. He was master of an entire ammunitions depot, of all the shrapnel, cartridges and shells, of the telephone, grassy mounds and burn, and he'd just helped hold the front. Everyone did things their own way. They're welcome to give me the Iron Cross, he thought. The war won't be over tomorrow. What had poor Vehse said just 24 hours before he was hauled away in that blood-soaked tarpaulin? 'That's your answer to the peace initiative...' Yes, it seemed the French didn't go a bundle on imperial pronouncements... But happily there were lieutenants who held firm, and their words carried weight. No sense hiding your light under a bushel. On 27 January, the Kaiser's birthday, Herr Graßnick would have to call Private Bertin out of the line again, but this time he'd be rasping out a congratulatory speech. Pretty good going for a skilled craftsman from Kreuzberg to have two sons in the newspapers because they'd got the Iron Cross.

At nightfall, Sergeant Schultz opened the hut door and walked in with Privates Strauß and Fannrich to find Private Bertin cosied up by the stove, puffing on his pipe.

'You've certainly made yourself at home,' marvelled Strauß.

'What the hell are you doing in my den?' asked Schulz in amazement.

'I thought it was the safest place,' said Bertin confidently. 'They can't drop shells here.'

Schulz took off his coat. 'Oh, can't they,' he joked. 'My dear man, if they had raised that damned long-range gun over there, which gave us such an untimely pounding today, just a fraction higher, you and the whole kit and kaboodle would have been blown to kingdom come.'

Bertin sat down on a bunk, nonplussed. 'Really?' he said.

Fannrich nodded, pouring fresh water on the coffee grounds. 'You can depend on it,' he said.

Crestfallen, Bertin tried to defend himself by saying he'd made himself useful.

'By making coffee,' said Strauß.

'By negotiating with field gunners,' countered Bertin.

Schulz swung round to interrogate him about what had happened. 'Thank God you kept your head,' he said, relieved. 'Who knows what would have happened to me. But you'll have to report at Gibercy now. If Susemihl gives you any trouble, put him on to me.'

Bertin gave the moustachioed technician a disappointed look. He would've liked to stay. 'Herr Susemihl won't give me any trouble,' Bertin snapped. 'Lieutenant von Roggstroh from the Royal Guard Artillery will see to that. By the way, if he asks for me, please explain why I left.'

'Why would he do that?' said Schulz impatiently. 'Did you find some rum or something?'

'I'm afraid not,' said Bertin, standing up. 'Why, have you got some?'

'Get a move on, man, or it'll be dark before you're back with your company.'

Despite Bertin's confidence, it soon became clear that the ammunitions expert with the little twirly moustache knew the world better than he did. When he finally pitched up at Gibercy, Susemihl, who was in charge, gave him a bit of a ticking off. Bertin defended himself calmly, and his composure and the lieutenant's name did make some impression. But the elation he'd felt as he made his way back home in the dark to the massive troop tents of the camp evaporated. Nothing in particular happened, but his elation shrivelled up to be replaced by a terrible exhaustion. Perhaps he'd expected too much, and that was why he was disappointed. Or perhaps the constant confusion within the company – the familiar traffic of countermanded orders and revoked decisions – weighed on his soul.

They buried the dead at Gibercy, with a fifth coffin added to the previous four – the salesman Dagener had died of his wounds. In the murk of the shortest day, battered by wind and rain, the column trudged over to Damvillers, received orders from the battalion issued by a sallow and angry Major Jansch, and marched back to Moirey to dismantle the Steinbergquell depot. At the depot, the men piled ammunition, planks, trench props, barbed wire and tarpaulins, all dripping with icy sludge, on to lorries and took them

227

back to Damvillers. They stayed there for a day in draughty huts, before driving the same heavily laden lorries back to Moirey to carry out orders to set the depot back up on exactly the same spot as before. Out of the muck, into the muck, muttered the ASC men bitterly. And so it was that they spent Christmas and New Year in the same barracks they'd been chased out of with so many casualties. At Christmas, Herr Susemihl gave a speech under a tree covered in lights, stuttering on about the peace the enemy didn't want. And then Herr Pfund distributed the Christmas presents he'd procured in Metz – blunt pocket knives, hankies with red borders, apples, nuts and a little tobacco – and the deceit radiating from his shining eyes and from the gifts themselves gave the more discerning men the creeps. And if the crown prince hadn't given each of his brave Verdun campaigners a curved steel case filled with cigarettes or cigars, which fitted comfortably into the pocket and was enamelled in black and adorned with the donor's portrait, it might have been a pretty miserable Christmas. But that all paled into insignificance when they returned to the half-empty barracks where the second half of the company including Bertin's squad was now billeted. A couple of candles burned in canteen lids, and the men lay around in silence or talking quietly. Quite a number of comrades were missing, and unlike the ones who'd left before because they were reassessed for active service or had been claimed for work at home, these ones wouldn't be heard from again. They'd been part of the men's lives. They'd argued with them and made up again, and now little Vehse, poor Przygulla and that kindly soul Otto Reinhold lay buried in French soil and would be replaced in the New Year, this time from Metz. But they couldn't be replaced, and their ghosts slid invisibly among their comrades and fellow skat players, evaporating only very slowly. And yet no one spoke of them, just as no one spoke of the daily routine unless something irksome or funny happened. Everything the men had experienced, and that the world had experienced during this war, slid beneath the layers of their consciousness into the deeper chambers of the mind, where sooner or later it would spit and rage. But the men needed to concentrate in order to deal with the demands placed on them each day and on the surface they showed only the usual permitted feelings and emotions, above all affection for their families. If they felt sorry for themselves or mourned their dead comrades, they did so obliquely in the general gloom. It was with such nuances of feeling that Halezinsky the gas worker looked at a picture of his wife and children with tears rolling down his Slavic face from his brown eyes. Only Lebehde the inn keeper carried on making punch cheerfully on his own from rum, tea and sugar, and its spicy aroma soon filled the room.

'It's all very sad,' he said to Bertin, 'but what can you do? We were obviously meant to smoke Willy the Eldest's cigarettes.' And he sat down on the bunk next to where Bertin was lying, pulled out the iron box inscribed on the back with 'Fifth Army, Christmas 1916', awarded himself a cigarette and adeptly removed the portrait of the crown prince from its embossed setting with his new pocket knife. It was easily done. 'It looks better without it,' he said. 'Where all is love, Don Carlos cannot hate,' he added. He didn't know where the lines were from, but Bertin recognised them as Schiller's *Don Carlos*. 'Listen to the peace and goodwill outside,' he supplied.

Outside the guns were thundering. It was Christmas night, an emotional time for the Germans, but they thought they'd best dilute such indulgent emotions with a dose of virile brutality. The German guns distributed steel Christmas presents, and the French replied in kind. Peace on Earth, sang the gospel. War on Earth, thundered reality. And so it went on as the year lurched to a close. Under beetle-brow heavens the wind blew ever colder, and weather pundits predicted frosts from the east, heavy cloud and starless nights. When Private Bertin took his evening stroll before bedtime and looked up at the sky with his myopic eyes, he could find no hope of an early peace reflected there no matter how hard he tried. In a couple of days they'd be writing 1917. The war was approaching its fourth year. He'd heard nothing further from Kroysing or about his Iron Cross from Lieutenant von Roggstroh – only depressing news from his wife and parents. There was no pleasure in living any more or in being a soldier. It was just a question of getting through, of curling up into a small, ugly ball in the hope of going unnoticed. Shoulders bent, he made his way back to the refuge of his comrades. Human warmth still came free.

CHAPTER FIVE

Professor Mertens resigns

A SNOWLESS NEW YEAR'S EVE afternoon, short and bleak, weighed on the streets of Montmédy. The French prepared for the celebrations and did their shopping furtively and without pleasure, making the bustle in the officers' messes and soldiers' billets seem all the more cheerful. Candles would burn once more on the Christmas trees from the Argonne, a great deal of diluted alcohol would be served and men would sit round tables singing stirring, sentimental songs. The year 1916 must be brought to a close befitting the heroic status it was sure to enjoy in the annals of the German nation.

That's what was going through Sergeant Porisch's mind, as he stood in his braided Litevka looking down with almost maternal concern on the gaunt, lined face of his superior. The judge advocate lay on the sofa with a blanket pulled up round his chin, and as Porisch took his leave of him with a file of papers under his arm, he said: 'Can I help you with anything else, Judge?'

'Yes, Porisch, you can. Please give my excuses for tonight to the officers' mess. I'd just be in the way. And I'd be grateful if the doctor, Herr Koschmieder, would look in on me again tomorrow about noon after everyone has slept it off.'

Porisch nodded, satisfied. He almost congratulated his superior on his sensible behaviour. Instead he tapped the orange folder on the table. 'Should I take this away with me?'

'Leave it there, Porisch. I may have another look. Will there be much gunfire at midnight?'

Porisch blew out his cheeks. 'The inspector general has expressly forbidden it, because it's a waste of ammunition, but if I know the Bavarians they'll fire a few blank cartridges. After all, it's their custom, and you can't change people with an order.'

Mertens closed his eyes in silent agreement, then he looked up at his subordinate, pulled his arm out from under the blanket and gave him his hand. 'Quite right, Porisch. People don't change or if they do it's so slow the likes of us can't wait that long. In any case, thank you for your help and I wish you as good a New Year as possible under the circumstances.'

Porisch thanked him, feeling almost moved, returned his good wishes and left. Afterwards, he'd maintain he could still feel Mertens' small-boned scholarly hand in his great mitt years later.

As the door clicked shut behind Porisch, Mertens breathed a sigh of relief and his dark-ringed eyes lit up for a moment. Porisch was a decent man who meant well, but he was a human being, and Professor Mertens had had enough of that species. That particular animal's flat, flesh-coloured face with its holes leading behind the mask to the inside gave him the creeps: the mouth cavity, the nose vents, the wedge-shaped depths from which the eyes stared – to say nothing of the ears, receivers of noise but never of understanding. It was a wretched thing when a man had so completely lost respect for his own species that he no longer saw any point in life – his own or other people's. What was he to do then?

A new year was beginning – what a gruesome prospect. He'd seen in 1914 and 1915 in an orderly manner with his Landwehr company in northern Poland, surrounded by sparkling snow, full of hope for an early peace, believing in a vastly improved post-war Europe. The following year he'd been home on leave, and there had been much solemn debate over punch and pancakes in the quiet, candlelit home of Herr Stahr, a king's counsel and his father's last surviving boyhood friend. The house had already experienced death, as the youngest son had just been killed. And the composure with which the family bore their pain, the dignity they drew from their terrible loss, afforded a glimpse of the enormous obligation the heroic deaths of this generation of young men would place on those left behind. 'So many noble dead dug into the foundations of this new Reich,' said the tipsy, white-haired old man as the New Year bells rang out from the cathedral, the Memorial church, St Matthew's and St Ludwig's – all the churches of western Berlin. 'They'll have a job proving themselves worthy of it.' And they drank to the freer, less prejudiced Germany they were sure would be the reward for the terrible sacrifices the nation had made. And Professor Mertens had believed it all.

He shivered and pulled his father's long-fringed travel rug back up under his chin. The deep green hues of the soft Scottish wool merged with the sleepy cosiness of the twilit room. He no longer had beliefs or hopes. During the past year, all his illusions had been shattered; the whole beautiful sham, so wonderfully embellished by poets and so pitilessly blasted by the philosopher Schopenhauer, to reveal the agonised world underneath, was gone. If

Schopenhauer himself, son of a Danzig salesman, hadn't been such a nagging old woman, filled with unbridled hate of everything he was not, he could have been a great source of comfort. As it was, he was no use to anyone; his gifts sparkled and faded into the night like the fireworks the Bavarians lit on New Year's Eve, and his wonderful phrases left nothing behind but emptiness and the desolate night.

Mertens sat up. His eyes, seeking the light switch, glided over the orange folder, a splash of light on the black table. His eyelids twitched, and there was an unpleasant taste in his mouth. He sank back. It was that business there that had started it all. The pathetic little case of Sergeant Kroysing had been the catalyst, a minor catalyst but enough for someone like Mertens, who perhaps already harboured concerns. But now it wasn't about individual cases. Man's whole dubious existence stood ready to be sentenced before the spiritual jury of a man who, guided by his father, had spent his first four decades searching for truth and justice. Things had become so bad that he couldn't hear certain words without coughing and feeling sick, above all the German word for nation: *Volk*. If you said the word *Volk* over and over to yourself – *Volk, Volk, follow, follow, follow* – you ended up with nothing but herds following. You should follow, you must follow, and never mind whom. Aristotle had known that, and Plato had known it even better. People were *zoon politikon*, political animals: what else could that definition mean but that they were condemned forever to wretched dependency? Except that for the two Greeks and their scholars in Europe this fact of nature laid a great moral imperative upon individuals and intellectuals to improve this deplorable state of affairs, to create balance through wisdom and insight, to convert and reform humanity through moral duty and kindness, patience and self-control. Churches and intellectuals worldwide had ceaselessly tried to fulfil this duty since the renaissance of reason in the Italy of Lorenzo the Magnificent, triggering religions, reformations, revolutions – with the result that in this war the pinnacle of our development had become blindingly clear. The spirit of Europe was prancing about in uniforms, and there were only nations, peoples, *Völker*, standing there in the scarlet, black and white of their sacred egomanias, and civilisation served at best as a technology for killing, a means of whitewashing, as a phrase to justify the conquering zeal that had rendered the world too small for Alexander the Great. At least the Romans had paid for their conquests with a paltry 500 years of peace and a world civilisation. How would they pay? With goods and lies.

Carl Georg Mertens' heart felt like a soft clump hanging in his chest. He threw the blanket back and, shivering slightly, walked through his rooms, which had been put at his disposal by headquarters after expelling the owner. How long had this house been here? More than 100 years for sure. When it was new the names of Goethe, Beethoven and Hegel had shone over Germany, and Europe stood in the shadow of Napoleon I, who had at least atoned for the devastation caused by his campaigns through comprehensive political and legal reforms. Now, 100 years later, conquests brought nothing but moral disintegration, obliteration of all individual values, an ardent wearing down of the moral culture that had revived since the Thirty Years' War. He wondered what his father would have made of this war, of its unanimous glorification by Germany's intellectuals – a war they knew nothing about but that they were all resolved to whitewash and falsify, to distort until it fitted with their view of the world. Lawyers and theologians, philosophers and doctors, economists and history teachers, and above all poets, thinkers and writers, spread deceit among the people with every word they said and wrote in the newspapers. They rushed to confirm that which was not and disputed that which was, were naïve and ignorant, putrid with self-assurance, and didn't make the slightest attempt to establish the facts before giving the benefit of their views.

Professor Mertens was a short-sighted man but he could see well in the dark. He went to his wardrobe and put on a warm dressing gown and slippers, then he wandered through the three rooms that until now had been his billet, opening and closing drawers. He searched his desk for a particular object, eventually found it and put it to one side, looked in the bedroom for things he might need and laid them out. There was no point in maintaining illusions in the last hours of a year when his eyes had been opened, even with regard to his dearest and most firmly held values, for example about his father. Would the venerable Gotthold Mertens, descendant of protestant pastors and Mecklenburg officials, have rejected the illusions established by the Fatherland to conceal and justify all the horrors brought by its lust to conquer? Of course not. Let's not kid ourselves. At the outbreak of war, the great man would have rallied the young men and sent them into battle. Throughout the first year of the war, operating from a deep sense of justice, he would have championed Germany's actions as a necessary mission. In the second year, he would have invoked his country's destiny, called for stout hearts and endurance in the face of a holy necessity, certain that he was fulfilling his duty, dealing with reality and promoting the survival of the nation. And if his son, who now knew how things stood, had then set out what he knew, what was the best

Gotthold Mertens might have done? Said nothing in public and approached his former pupil the Imperial Chancellor in private. Then he would have given up in the face of the Army Command, taken comfort from past glories and dark allusions to the spirit of European legal history, whose aim was to tame the passions, establish inalienable civil rights, provide peaceful citizens with security, improve public morals, and promote intellectual enlightenment and the cultural heritage that alone made life worth living. But he, his son, no longer believed in all these wonderful claims and illusions. A sapper lieutenant had opened his eyes. During the past half year, he'd learnt to look more closely, and his suspicions had grown. And now he knew more: the gaps had been filled in by that same sapper lieutenant and by his murdered brother in the shape of two brief reports.

When he looked back on that whole period, he realised that, oddly enough, his art books had helped to sharpen his sense of the authentic. Painters' creations don't lie. Their absolute devotion to what is real, their powerful desire to reveal form, in the landscape as much as in figures, had simply made him more sensitive to the embellishments, calculated lies and biased quarter truths that people made do with day after day, month after month, in politics as in the army bulletins. But he could no longer make do with that. Faced with the incredible he had begun to investigate. And once his eyes had been ripped open he couldn't shut them again. Until he reached a point where it became blindingly clear to him that he couldn't go on. Until his disgust with the whole business knocked him over – literally. His life did not have many roots. He had no interest in women or the usual male enjoyments and distractions. His father had both replaced such pleasures for him and devalued them. He had loved travelling, but after the destruction of this war there wouldn't be many places a German could go without feeling ashamed. He had thought himself to be in the service of the intellect and truth but had seen them abused and defiled. Only music remained to him, and that tragic existential force was no longer enough to keep him going. Beyond the soft lit walls of the concert hall, a world of barbarism began; beneath the alluring strains of 50 violins and cellos echoed the groans of the exiled, the slain and the dispossessed, and he would never again be able to look at a conductor's raised baton without thinking of all the compliant minds that studiously marched in time with the lies fed to the public, all those who heard the beat and followed. *Followed, followed, Volk, follow, follow.*

When Sergeant Kroysing's case first came before him, he was initially surprised, then scandalised. He wasn't deterred by its difficulties. He believed amends could be made; it would be difficult, but not impossible. For about a fortnight now, he'd known it wouldn't be possible. The letters forwarded by the sapper lieutenant hadn't given him the necessary leverage, and then he vanished after the fall of Douaumont. His unit provisionally reported him missing, as the fort's garrison had been blown to bits in October. Subsequent weeks of searching ended hopefully: Lieutenant Kroysing was alive. There had been a confirmed sighting in a dugout in the Pepper ridge lines. The sapper commander had received Kroysing's report and knew where he was. Until a fortnight previously when those German lines also fell in the fresh French attack. Since then there had been no sign of him. The last news of him had come from one of his NCOs, who had seen him disappearing into an ice-covered shell hole during a French bombardment. Lieutenant Kroysing was again missing, but this time the tone was hopeless. Hard to see how he could have reached safety in an area under continual French machine-gun fire. No, the Kroysing brothers were dead, and justice was unattainable even for an individual within his own nation. What hope was there then among nations? None. 'None,' said Judge Advocate Mertens under his breath in the darkening room, and he heard the strings of his piano vibrate slightly with the echo of that terrible word.

Yes, C.G. Mertens had grown ears. He no longer believed people's claims or their denials. They did not give the complete picture. No one cares to admit that a loved one's case is hopeless – not metaphorically but literally. And this wasn't about a beloved person but about the prerequisite for all that one loved: the homeland, the land of one's birth, the Fatherland, Germany.

This clean-shaven man, with his scholarly head and fine gold-rimmed spectacles, shivered. Headquarters had installed an ugly but efficient little coal stove in the black and white stone fireplace, the same sort as currently heated many a German home. Mertens pulled his armchair nearer to the reddish glow flickering through the vents in the nickel-plated door, sat down and warmed his splayed hands. He relaxed back into the low padded chair. Meaningless scraps of verse ran through his mind from poets who were still alive or whose work has been much discussed when, as a young student, he began to suck up the joys of knowledge and intellectual life: '...it will not be long/ Till neither moon nor stars/ But only black night stands above us in the sky... The crows are cawing/ And flapping homewards towards the town/ The snow is near at hand / Happy is he that has a home still... We listen gratefully to the rustle of the wind/ Gleams of sunlight flicker through the leaves/ And we look up and listen as one by one/ The ripe fruits patter to the ground...'

He didn't have a home any more. Why kid himself? He could have chosen another day to resign once and for all. But now was as good a time as any. No one would disturb him until midday tomorrow. And if the officers went on the lash, as they usually did, probably not then either. Koschmieder, the doctor, was fond of saying that a man who really needs a doctor will send for him two or even three times. As there was no need to worry about medical bills behind the lines, officers became ill just to pass the time. He'd have time to consider his options and reach a decision.

The Kroysing case had opened his eyes. Then from somewhere or other he'd heard a report – disputed and denied – that the Germans had also committed arson and murder when they invaded defenceless little Luxembourg, which had almost been an ally. This news had awakened the historian in C.G. Merten, who doesn't believe any statement until he has checked his sources. Luxembourg was close by and he had the use of an official car. He'd spent many Sundays and weekdays in the areas of Luxembourg where the Germans had broken through, first in uniform and then in civilian clothes. At first he only saw ruins and rubble, which could have been caused by military action. But he began to find the iron silence of the local mayors and residents disturbing. They obviously thought he was a spy. But he found the information he sought among the crude ironwork crosses in the churchyard, adorned with offensively ugly porcelain medallions of the departed created from photographs. A great many of these worthless memorials were from August and September 1914... In Arlon he had finally met a reasonably friendly American professor, who was travelling through the ravaged area, escorted by an officer, as a delegate of the American Red Cross. His job was to collect information to counteract the incredibly skilful horror stories with which Reuters and the British press were bombarding right-thinking American citizens, in particular American Jews who were fond of Germany. It took Professor Mertens four hours, from 9pm until 1am, to convince Professor Mac Corvin that unlike other German scholars he'd remained loyal to the truth. Then Professor Corvin opened his heart. In Luxembourg alone over 1,350 houses had been burnt to the ground and at least 800 people shot. In Belgium and northern France, the same methods had brought much worse results. The newspaper correspondents might have exaggerated certain details, but the reports were basically true.

Still in deep shock from this, Professor Mertens then had to deal with the case of Corporal Himmke from the Montmédy field bakery, which seemed to confirm his worst fears. While drunk, the man had boasted about his heroic conduct during the battle of the Marne when the village of Sommeilles was burnt down. He and two comrades had burnt six people alive, a grandmother, mother and four grandchildren, who had taken refuge in the cellar of their house. In his naïvety, this blabbermouth had thought it would help if he could prove that what he'd said was true and call witnesses to show that the men had been ordered to burn the village in terms that put little value on the lives of the peasants and their womenfolk. Judge Advocate Mertens saw it that way too and conducted the investigation with a certain hidden fervour. But the officers from Himmke's unit who were to attend the court martial saw things quite differently, and the communications inspectorate, as the highest authority, backed them up. The man wasn't to be punished because he'd committed a crime, though they did condemn his crime, but because he'd boasted about it, with the result that the unsavoury matter became widely known, bringing Germany's conduct of the war into disrepute.

'We all know that all kinds of unpleasant things went on,' said one officer privately, 'but that that bastard should talk about it – he definitely deserves a good thumping for that.' And a couple of days later when Himmke was collecting the rest of his things from the bakery at nightfall, he was taken from his Landsturm escort by some unknown cavalrymen, and the following day he appeared in the Montmédy garrison hospital having been beaten to a pulp. What was that? It was war. From the point of view of legal history – and at this Mertens, who was warmer now, smiled to himself – there were two strands to justice: inviolate legal certainty, which came from outside, and the laws of revenge and retribution, based on the best interests of a given fighting unit or group. The two were cunningly interwoven such that to the outside world a façade of European civilisation was formally maintained, while behind it raged the impulses and passions that the process of civilisation was intended to control. The Bible and the human conscience demanded one sort of justice. Several other sorts were permitted by contemporary professors and current conditions. Elements of legal practice that countries had surreptitiously allowed before 1914, but had been ashamed of and disclaimed, now shamelessly reigned, though they were still disclaimed, and there seemed to be no restraining power to punish the abuses and put a stop to them. There was gruesome evidence of this in the story of the Belgian deportations, which had upset the European public in recent months, and Judge Advocate Mertens with them, in the punishment camp in Montmédy citadel, the Kroysing case, the submarine war – everything. Hundreds of thousands of civilians arbitrarily removed to Germany to provide slave labour for the law and peace breaker. Hopeless protests from neutral states against these abductions, conducted in the style of Arab slave traders or African rulers, designed to benefit German industrialists and army units short of men. Dark rumours about hundreds of deaths caused by shell fire, malnutrition and disease in the concentration camps. Was that commendable? How could you square that with German culture, with the polished performances of classical dramas put on in the theatres of Berlin, Dresden and Munich?

Well, you could square anything, it seemed. Fur coats and no knickers, his Auntie Lottchen used to say when she saw her little nephew's neat desk, then pulled out his messy desk drawer. The punishment camp in the citadel had been set up in retaliation for the abuse of German prisoners of war that certain correspondents were supposed to have observed in France and as a way of applying counter pressure. The French government had denied the reports, and the German military administration had believed the reports blindly and ordered one of the courtyards in Montmédy citadel, which was about three-quarters the height of a man, to be covered over with barbed wire and used for French prisoners. They had to bend over double to move about. It was unwatchable.

Mertens, who as a judge advocate was not without influence, had tried to have the camp closed down, but in vain. First, he was told, the French must learn how to treat Germans properly. The idea that information should be checked had entirely disappeared. When he asked if there was any proof, they just shook their heads. With his Moltke-like face, he was seen as an old traditionalist who was obviously overworked and had better grab some leave. No worries, he was going to grab some— the only question was how. The world exuded horror and could only become more horrific, because it no longer contained any cleansing, atoning force: no church, no prophets, no reflection or repentance – and no notion that such things were needed. The world was inordinately proud of its own existence, and it would remain so in peacetime, if peace ever came. He, Mertens, had to go. He was a stain on this world that was so gloriously in agreement with itself. There was a level of shame that was deadly, because it didn't come from one event or action, but from the very source of one's existence: the era, the nation, the race – call it what you will. Plenty of people would pass from life to death in cities large and small this New Year's Eve in the normal course of things – why not him too? There was no shame in standing and falling for the civilisation you loved, silently and with no fuss. He just wasn't sure how to do it.

He stood up, feeling better now. He was a man who needed clarity. He lit the shaded lamps, the candles on the piano and the night light. He drank a glass of the French liqueur he kept for visitors, then a second. It tasted good. He collected together the things he'd laid out earlier. He took his matt black service revolver, a modern pistol, from his open desk drawer and placed it on a silver platter beside the poisonous sleeping pills he'd gradually accumulated. In Germany, you could only get them with a doctor's prescription. Citizens had more freedom in France, even when it came to death. As a Prussian officer, it was his duty to choose the weapon. If he was going to die, he should do it properly. But as an intellectual man, averse to violence and destruction, he preferred poison. As his father's son, he had paid his father far too much regard while he was alive, silently conforming to his wishes. Should he pay him regard one last time and do as convention demanded? Or should he perform this last of all human actions as he saw fit? To ask the question was to answer it. If he had paid his father less regard, been less the well-behaved son, been less sensitive to the rough and tumble of life, had engaged with the world as vigorously as many of his boyhood friends had done, then who knew what his life might have been like and if he would now be facing the silence of eternal rest. Great was Diana of the Ephesians and Cybele the Great Mother, but great too was the consolation provided by music, the mysterious source of existence that was expressed both in the remarkable ratios of planetary orbits and in the simple metrics and proportions of harmonies, through which the unknown could be measured. Vibration and gradation were all. Physicists said everything could be reduced to movements in the unknown ether, in its force fields, which themselves could transform masses and solids into pulsating, substanceless and therefore spiritual matter. Then why not into something akin to music? Why not into music itself? Wasn't there something in those remarkable sequences of resonant air, vibrating strings and complex interrelationships that went beyond noise and air? Didn't we see behind the secrets of advanced mathematics when we lost ourselves in music? Physics had a great future, he sensed, though he understood little of it. The physicist Einstein, raised in Switzerland but whom he'd known in Berlin, had changed our world view, freeing it from the physical and introducing with his spiritual concepts a new way of thinking, akin to that of Husserl in Göttingen. And he loved music. Perhaps music and the solace it provided led us to an existence more real than our earthly existence of flesh and nerves, making us aware, through the physical instrument of the ear, of a wider universe, the other stars and better worlds that Shakespeare, pointing to the night sky, had described as 'patines of bright gold' that move 'like an angel sings'. Be that as it may, he knew how he was going to move: while making music. He would put a sleeping draught on the piano and drink it when he felt like it. It would be a sort of deathly refreshment, and then he would pass into a world of unknown consonances and harmonies, through the portal of those he loved the most, because they were dark and ambivalent, but also modern and glorious: Brahms' quartet in A minor.

The piano they'd put in the house for him came from Paris. It was old and some notes were a little tinny but on the whole the sound was soft and warm. He made his drink with hot water from a vacuum flask, stirring it slowly as he thought about his nephew, to whom he'd bequeathed most of his worldly goods, and about the humble library in a small university at the foot of a little visited range of hills where he'd spent some happy months, which was about to become an important seat of learning for legal history and the development of legal theory through the priceless bequest of the Mertens library. A lot of other things went through his mind too, for example that with a little more knowledge and skill he could have rigged up the stove to give off carbon monoxide, removing any need for action on his part. *Next time,* he smiled. Then he opened the piano score for the Brahms quartet and began to play. The music echoed softly in the quiet house and out through its rustic windows, and a passer-by occasionally looked up or stopped for a moment before the damp, icy weather drove them on.

Mertens' fingers flew over the keys, a blissful smile lit his face and he moved his head, his whole body, in time to the rhythms of the overture. His heart filled with inexpressible joy. The man who had brought these sounds into being, before they were inked on the page, was a stout, long-haired cigar smoker with a beard and a snub nose, but an angel had clearly possessed him – for this to have sounded within him, his soul must have been lovelier than Rembrandt's or Grünewald's most splendid creations. It was indescribable, other-worldly, the highest joy, a revelation scribbled down for 16 strings of gut stretched on a hollow wooden frame – a dance of blessed spirits performed by 10 fingers that soon would hang rigid and numb. But for now they played. All the sweetness of a spring breeze rippling over a meadow of flowers was there in those notes, as well as the dark, putrid source from which the flowers, like the soul, sprang. This music was the world all over again, but better, flawless, free from the terrible savage urges of our animal nature, which smother everything that is light and pure. How good it felt to bring it to an end, to leave and go through the unknown portal into the unknown land on the wings of the only joy that had never let him down. He drank from his glass, to which he'd added a sweet liqueur, and began the second movement. The deep solemnity of farewell... his fingers slid lightly over the keys, his ear caught every note, his mouth was set and grave. The earth curved away from him; all the people and trees rose up from a mountaintop, but he didn't see them. Swaddled in the swirling atmosphere, he saw himself on the edge of space, which began above his head and stretched unbroken to the planets. A musician sensed such things. Writers, too, had a sense for what was behind their backs, above their heads and beneath their feet. Had he ever heard as clearly as today? And then the master, in the midst of his wonderful art, bowed before the genius of a young Austrian named Franz Schubert, quoting one of his songs entitled 'Numbness': 'I search the snow in vain/ For the trace of her steps...' Which trace of which steps did a man seek when, the numbness finally over, he softly opened that last of all doors and set upon a new path, leading to new meadows and new towns built of spiritual materials by unknown residents, of gratitude, service and kindness, of valiant solitude, genial companionship and the joy of giving – everything that was great and noble in the human soul and that might just as well, or even better, exist within a Negro savage as within the emperor Napoleon or the philosopher Nietzsche? It felt good to be tired, tired of life and death, tired of being and not being, tired of what lay above and what lay below, tired of colour and the absence of colour... The opening of the minuet required a certain effort from the player, but then a threshold was crossed and the dance of the ghost-lit sylphs was consummated. It didn't matter if the player's fingers obeyed him in the allegro. The meaning was clear before the notes were struck, before the opening and progression. But it seemed only natural that Maestro Brahms, pot-bellied with a cigar butt in the corner of his mouth, should come to the aid of his pupil and passionate admirer C.G. Mertens, take a seat at the piano in his black frock coat and apply his soft hands to playing his own music as it was meant to be played, while Mertens rested for a moment. Was it any different from Socrates sitting and drinking with his friends? A solemn sweetness surrounded Mertens' heart. The spirits of the strings danced a silver, moonlit minuet, caressed by a night breeze, on a hilltop, scented by seaside pines. Foothills and coves swayed before him... 'and their heads began to sink onto the upholstery/ a young man came – I can remember...' He walked, grave and lovely, from behind the gathered bedroom curtain supported by two slender, flute-playing women, and Maestro Brahms looked at him questioningly and said in Latin: 'You have loved justice and hated iniquity and so...' *What does he mean?* thought Mertens in alarm. *I'm not dying in exile! No one could fall asleep more blissfully than I am doing in this armchair.*

BOOK SEVEN

The great cold

CHAPTER ONE

Pelican

THE EARTH WAS a stone disc under a sky of ice.

Winter had bitten across the whole continent and now held people and objects in its pitiless grip. In Potsdam, for example, where Frau Bertin's parents were able to heat two rooms in their villa, the thermometer had registered 34 degrees below zero one night. But that was little help to their son-in-law. In France, particularly in the Meuse hills, the cold was less extreme: 17 degrees below, but it was still plenty. Since the beginning of January, the company's gods and demigods had all returned from leave and been rather depressed by the reception they'd received from various quarters and by the changes that had taken place. Having already been dismantled and reinstated once, the depot was now dismantled again, this time for good. It was relocated to Mureaux Ferme wood, a dense, undamaged woodland behind a hill, which meant a new railway line was required to connect this sheltered spot to Romagne station. By the time that would have been done, the French airmen would long since have spotted, photographed and reported the clearings in the wood with predictable consequences, so that the whole facility would have to be moved again – chop, chop – this time to the gorges near the village of Etraye, but that was still some way off; work first began on the standard-gauge railway.

Under Sergeant Schwerdtlein's reliable direction, a construction squad of heavy labourers was transferred from Romagne to work opposite the Mureaux Ferme men. He lived in a stone house and didn't see the company on weekdays or on Sundays. At daybreak, in a heavy frost, the ASC men loaded one lorry with the heavy 6m full-size rails, another with oak sleepers and a third with loose chippings, before climbing on top of the cargo to travel to their place of work. The lorries were then unloaded – the heavy rails dug into the men's collarbones – the ground levelled, the sleepers laid and the rails set in place. The screwing in place of the 'joints' with fishplates and nuts was the job of the Württemberg sappers, Landsturm men who had come from Damvillers, and they performed this duty with sober exasperation. For the greater part of the day, they all helped the Russians, who were preparing the track. The Russians? Absolutely. Russian prisoners, over 70 men in all, had been attached to the ASC men, and no one knew where they were billeted. Gaunt men in earthen coloured coats, patient and quick on the uptake, they were guarded by men from the Prussian Landsturm, if possible ones with a smattering of a Slavic language. And did we already say that Private Bertin was part of the Schwerdtlein working party too? As it was not a congenial working party, it's hardly worth mentioning. However, there he was, more patient than ever, apathetic even, no longer hoping for an Iron Cross, but with the demeanour of a man who has escaped death twice in a row. He'd spent five days in the Karde working party, which was in charge of a small testing station in the cartridge tent for shells damaged in the bombardment. On the sixth day, he was sent to Romagne in the morning, and at midday one of the shells burst, killing his bed neighbour, Biedenkapp, a farmhand from Upper Hesse and father of three. And only two days later, an aeroplane had dropped its load on Steinbergquell depot, and although it only destroyed the officers' latrines, the barrage of shell splinters perforated the outer wall of barracks 2 at the narrow end where only Private Bertin ever slept. Such coincidences made a man think and promoted patience, especially as rumour had it that the same aeroplane had visited Montmédy as well and taken out a high-ranking military official – or possibly several. Happy, then, was the man who could sleep safely in Romagne at night and warm himself up working with a pickaxe during the day. The frozen clay was as hard as marble and could only be broken into small fragments the size of mussel shells. In this terrible cold, the men sometimes warmed themselves by a fire, which the weakest of the Russians were allowed to tend. An undamaged copse of deciduous trees stood outlined against the sky. The new railway line's course was marked by felled trees, blown-up roots and a levelled ridge. By the time the men had removed 10cm of frozen crust and reached the softer clay underneath, the sun would be setting. In the night, the earth froze again to a depth of 10cm, and the next day the game restarted.

But the worst job of all, feared by everyone, was unloading the loose chippings. The men stood on the trucks, almost unable to feel their feet because of the cold, ramming a broad shovel into the recalcitrant stones and then throwing them with a wide swing into the new stretches of track. Whoever was assigned to beating them flat with a mattock was lucky, because he could move and get his circulation going. No more than three men could fit on to one truck at once without getting in each other's way.

That day Privates Lebehde, Pahl and Bertin were unloading loose chippings. Lebehde was strong enough to wield the heaving shovel without overstraining himself, but Pahl and Bertin were in agony. They had taken off their coats, canvas jackets, tunics and sweaters, and were sweating and freezing at the same time in their flannel shirts. They shovelled on in grim silence. They were friends, and Karl Lebehde wouldn't have turned his sharp tongue on the two weaker ones if they had left the bulk of the work to him. But precisely for that reason, decency demanded they not give up. The metallic twang of the shovel and the rattling of the stones was interrupted by shouts of encouragement and cursing. Thus a whole day would pass, from sunrise to sunset, during which the men hardly thought about the task in hand. They thought instead about the unconstrained U-boat war, which was inevitable, and the declaration of war from America that would follow it, which Bertin stupidly misjudged in line with the views imposed on the newspapers by German Army Command. The three men thought about all sorts of special plans, wishes and ideas. Some of their wishes were strange. For example, Private Bertin would have been very shocked if he had realised how seriously his comrade Pahl was considering sacrificing one little bit of his fragile body in order to get the rest home safely. That was why Pahl and Lebehde had not let him in on the secret. Although they thought he was a decent man, they considered him to be a loose canon – and weak, weak. He'd recently bought a tin of fat substitute from some crooked big shot in the kitchen staff and now quietly shovelled it down without offering any to his comrades. He hadn't been like that before, and they'd have to rub his nose in it at some point. But, as Karl Lebehde pointed out, everyone was in dire straits and men even stole food parcels from each other within the squad, so there was no point in getting too moralistic. Pahl took a dimmer view of Bertin's conduct, because he had to overcome his disappointment. Fat substitute was a good thing, but solidarity was a better one; Bertin had taken to eating his evening meal on his bunk and no longer showed the same comradely attitude as before. Well, that would change too. As a starter punishment, they told him that he'd been overlooked for the task of caring for a certain letter, which Sergeant Süßmann, now missing, had given to Comrade Lebehde in December. Instead of getting upset or being offended, Bertin had calmly asked if the thing had been duly forwarded. He seemed not to care about things that he would have cared about three months previously. Yes, life was hard. It was no jolly jig with pancakes and New Year's Eve punch.

Pride, sensitivity and honour all got moth-eaten. The fur on the jacket of high ideals and good intentions wore thin, leaving nothing but a scabby rabbit pelt, blue and bald.

Private Bertin really was in a bad way and every day it got worse. The back-breaking work in icy conditions had used up his last reserves of strength, and the occasional pleasant interlude, of which there were some, didn't seem to help.

One evening, when he was already dozing on his bed and the rest of Schwertlein's squad were doing their mending and playing cards, a stout man with glasses, a flat nose and bulging eyes marched into the barracks, bringing a gust of cold air behind him. He looked around in the bright carbide light, taking in the iron stove, the long pipe with drying laundry and the bare windows, which the men had labouriously covered with newspaper to keep out the wind and cold, and wheezed out that he was looking for a certain private named Bertin who was a trainee lawyer and had obviously come to the wrong place. Nearly all of the men had stood up when he came in, as in his fur coat he looked like an officer come to carry out an inspection. But Sergeant Porisch waved this aside and said there was no need for any fuss. He saluted Sergeant Schwerdtlein, put a packet of cigarettes on the table and had everyone won over.

In the meantime, Bertin pulled himself up, looked at the stranger with sleepy eyes and said he was the man he was looking for. At that, Sergeant Porisch explained that although he was from the court martial in Montmédy, he wasn't there to cause Bertin any trouble, but simply wanted some information for a current case. And as the main purpose of his journey was connected with a secondary purpose, he asked Bertin if he would kindly put his boots back on and accompany him to the station, where a friend of his, also a Berliner, was on duty. At the words 'Montmédy court martial' Bertin had brought his feet to the floor and said: 'Aha.' Suddenly, he was moving more confidently and within a minute he was standing at the door ready to go.

'Let's get one down us,' wheezed Sergeant Porisch, making a drinking motion with his fist.

'Just don't send him back plastered,' said Sergeant Schwerdtlein. 'Work starts again tomorrow morning at 6am sharp,' and the other men sniggered maliciously.

They walked carefully down the slippery, dimly lit staircase. The icy streets lay deserted in a vicious easterly wind. 'Let's get into the warm,' groaned

Porisch. 'These thin shoes of mine are not suitable for polar expeditions.'

Bertin, who had completely revived in the biting night wind, laughed a little: the man was wearing nicely cut civilian shoes of fine leather. 'Where are you actually taking me off to?' he asked as they walked.

'To Fürth, an old friend of mine from university,' panted Porisch, breathing heavily through his flat nose. 'But we'd better keep our gobs shut or we'll freeze our throats off.'

Bertin knew Sergeant Fürth slightly, and had always taken him for a dislikeable big mouth. There were plenty of wisecracking know-alls from the city in the army, but in his own billet Sergeant Fürth made a much less offensive impression than he did outside.

He used the informal *du* with Sergeant Porisch and shook Bertin's hand as warmly as if they were old drinking buddies. Two fine scars ran across his right cheek, one straight and one jagged – *tiercé* and *quarté*, thought Bertin, surprised that he hadn't forgotten these student fencing terms from his school days. In any case, they fitted with the way Fürth had done out his billet. A huge sofa of yellowish wood upholstered in tobacco brown wool occupied the back wall. Above it Fürth had hung a sort of coat of arms painted in red, white and black diagonal stripes with ornate writing in the centre that conveyed the mysterious message: 'To A.J.B. the banner!' Beneath it an embroidered student cap hung from a nail, and beneath that were two crossed sabres of French origin with coloured ribbons from various academic associations woven through their hilts. To the right and left of it pictures of bearded men in drinking garb, cut from magazines, were fixed to the wall with drawing pins. Bertin realised with amazement that this had all been swept here from the forgotten world of German universities, where young men joined associations seemingly in order to drink, fence and enjoy their youth, but in fact to smooth their future career path with the connections and patronage provided by the 'old boy network'. As the various layers of the German bourgeoisie excluded young Jewish men of similar social standing, on transparent pretexts of race or faith, they had formed their own associations, with or without Christians, unless, like Bertin, they preferred to join the army of free, self-reliant academics, where what mattered was not a man's origins or how wealthy his father was but his abilities, commitment and personal dedication. So Bertin now stood in the billet of an A.J.B.-er, who wore colours and fought with sabres like a member of a corps or fraternity, but who, as a member of the University Jurists' Club, had known many club mates and protégés of weighty professors from the time of that great old man, Gotthold Mertens, who for his part had first seen the light of day in a modest parsonage in Güstrow in Mecklenburg.

Tea stood steaming on the table beside a bottle of rum for grog and a box of cigars. Sergeant Fürth himself was smoking a short pipe. 'I feel,' he beamed, 'as if I had a drinking jacket on and this were a house party in Munich or Freiburg. You get these kinds of Arctic nights with no snow there too. It's very decent of you, Pogge, to come to say goodbye like this.' Bertin guessed that Pogge was the sergeant's drinking name – a Low German word meaning frog, which given Herr Porisch's appearance, wasn't at all inappropriate.

'Hardly,' said Porisch. 'I came to see you and I came to see him' – he pointed to Bertin – 'but above all it suited me to come. Because I need to talk. Because I can't keep the thing to myself and I know that I won't find a single soul in Berlin who'll believe me or understand: people don't dare use their heads in our circles because they're so intimidated and so patriotic. And in the War Materials Department, where I'm being shifted, I'll obviously have to act much more stupid than elsewhere – do your walls have ears, Pelican?'

Pelican – Bertin had to laugh. Again, the name wasn't a bad fit with Sergeant Fürth's big nose, small, round, bird-like eyes and receding chin.

'Pull your chairs in closer...'

'But first let's fortify ourselves with a slug of something to help against this polar chill,' said Pelican.'

'Slug is the right word,' said Porisch, noisily blowing his nose. Was Bertin mistaken or were the fat man's eyes a little moist?

So, Carl Georg Mertens, the erstwhile judge advocate in Montmédy, had poisoned himself. He had not, as had been reported in the papers, died in an accident, neither a car crash nor an aerial bomb. 'It was too much for him, you see,' snivelled Herr Porisch. 'He wasn't used to the brutality of this world, and so he threw in the towel so that men with thicker skins and coarser hands could pick it up – men who had a better idea how to shovel muck than him. He was a gentleman. No one apart from me realises quite what a gentleman he was. And to boot his father had equipped him rather poorly for this life – had crushed him, in fact. Being old Mertens' son was a job in itself.' And then Porisch unburdened himself of the pressure that had weighed on him for weeks, and the words tumbled haphazardly from his mouth, mixed with cigar smoke and interspersed with unclear insinuations and terrible jokes. He talked most about the Belgian deportations, because he had helped to collect information about them. Fürth showed himself to be much better informed about this than

Private Bertin, who seldom saw a newspaper, and it was years since he had felt so keenly that he was still training to be a lawyer. He'd removed his tunic and sat in his blue sweater with his elbows on the table. Agreeable sips of grog warmed him inside. Now he understood what he'd seen around Romagne: civilians in thin, black Sunday clothes standing motionless on the road with their shovels stuck in the icy ground, not working to warm themselves up. He had been told they were Belgian civilians by the Landsturm guards, who had long since give up trying to make the Belgians work. They starved, they froze and they didn't move a finger. It had left a deep impression on Private Bertin. It was called forcible recruitment, but that expression hid the reality. However, he had also disapproved of the fierce contempt in which the Belgians held those of their countrymen who crawled to the guards in Flemish, made fires and heated coffee for them in return for some bread. This is war, he'd thought; people shouldn't be so sensitive and proud. The conquered had to come to terms with the conqueror and not increase their own suffering unnecessarily. Now, coloured by the outrage of the dead Mertens, these things appeared differently to Bertin.

But Porisch carried on. 'The judge advocate was dealing with the Kroysing affair up until the end. So, this concerns you,' he said, and his expression clouded. 'You didn't give a sender's name, but your name was mentioned in an enclosure among some papers written in the hand of the elder Kroysing – that enigmatic lieutenant who remained so vivid in Mertens' memory and in my own. He said that you, as his dead brother's friend, would help out with your testimony if needs be. Then we heard nothing more from him. Our enquiries returned a message of 'missing'. Then, four or five days after Mertens' body had been transported to St Matthews churchyard in Berlin in a freight car, Kroysing got in touch from the field hospital in Dannevoux, where he was being treated for a broken shin bone, and said he wanted to pursue the matter once he'd recovered.'

'He's alive!' shouted Bertin, sitting bolt upright.

'Amazingly, yes. And now I have one question for you: are you the man whom young Kroysing got to know the day before he died?' Bertin nodded silently, wondering what was coming next. 'So you're not part of his company and you didn't actually see anything?'

'No.'

'Thank you,' said Porisch wearily. 'Then that won't help him, for my professor's successor is just your average circuit judge and he consigns any unnecessary bits and pieces *ad acta*, that's to say to the devil. No lieutenant can fight that – not even that one. He seems to be made of iron, Kroysing, doesn't he?' he added, shaking his head. Bertin nodded to himself; that was definitely true, he was made of iron – and mad and obsessed to boot.

Pelican, who was in fact a lawyer called Alexander Fürth with an office on Bülowstraße and an apartment in the Wilmersdorf area of Berlin, demanded an explanation, saying he couldn't be doing with Pogge speaking in this insider's code. Porisch and Bertin told him what they knew and what they thought about the case. Pelican shook his head at them. 'Just be glad this matter has been buried. What good would it do anyone if some dog came along and dug up this particular bone?'

But Porisch blew out his cheeks. This case was the last legacy of a just man, a man with completely clean hands, and he didn't want simply to let it disappear into the great murky heap of injustice that was growing each day.

'Well,' said Fürth, 'that does change things. But we should really warn our guest,' and he turned fleetingly to Bertin, 'to keep his fingers out of this dodgy butter sauce in case he gets a blister. I've often seen you heading off in the morning and wondered why you don't apply for a better job, but that's another matter. For you, dear Pogge, all I can do is pass on a piece of news that may or may not help.'

'Stop,' interrupted Bertin, seduced by the rum and the cosy atmosphere, and transported back to a time when he felt sorry for students who belonged to fraternities, seeing them as throwbacks in human development, tattooed savages with artificial scars and garish dancing clothes. 'The most important thing is to find out exactly where the Dannevoux field hospital is.' Pelican glared at him, but Porisch said he was right. Fürth silently fetched a map from the cupboard and spread it out. They found Romagne, Flabas, even Crépion and Moirey, but nowhere called Dannevoux. They looked at the coloured sheet in bafflement, at the town of Verdun, Douaumont, the winding course of the Meuse, then Pelican laid the sharp tip of his pinkie nail on Dannevoux. 'How could anyone get there?' cried Bertin. 'It's on the left bank.'

It was true that the world continued on the other side of the snaking black river. But as another command started there that was of little use. Pelican leant back solemnly and folded his arms. 'I don't know if this is lucky or unlucky for you, Pogge, old boy. Either way, I'd best tell you that Mopsus is judge advocate over there with the Lychow Army Group. Do you know Mopsus?'

Porisch stared at him in astonishment. Of course he knew Mopsus, actually a lawyer called Posnanski, not just from the old boys' list, but personally from the bigger club parties and from fleeting encounters in the corridors of the Berlin courts. 'How did you find out he was over there?' he asked, to which Pelican retorted that he perhaps didn't read the A.J.B. newsletter as carefully as he should. Porisch said he barely glanced at it, and Pelican gloated that it was then no surprise he didn't have a clue what was going on. 'On the left bank,' said Porisch pensively.

'In Esnes or Montfaucon, I expect,' said Pelican.

'I don't have much time,' explained Porisch, 'but I'm going to go and see this lieutenant and advise him to speak to Mopsus. If anyone can advise him, it's Mopsus.'

'Yes,' Fürth confirmed. 'He'll advise him.'

Bertin yawned. He was getting tired. And at the end of the day, these men with their ridiculous names weren't his concern. The next day, he'd be hauling rails about again. 'I don't give much for your lieutenant's chances,' said Pelican in the meantime. 'I won't hide that from you. His opponent has a head start.'

'I would very much like to see,' said Bertin, yawning again, 'how the Prussian Army would resolve a case like this if the points balanced each other out.'

There was no reply; they were waiting for him to go. To fill the pause, Porisch said that there was a black notebook of his brother's among Lieutenant Kroysing's things, which no one could read because Mertens' pupils were famously never allowed to learn shorthand. And they laughed together, remembering how the old bearded man at the lectern used to lose his temper with new students at the beginning of term when they tried to take notes during his lectures. He'd thunder that he hated that kind of Mephistophelian wisdom, which Goethe had put in the Devil's mouth purely in irony. What they took home written in black and white was irrelevant; it was what stayed in their hearts that mattered and his courses were for law students not for clerks.

Bertin started, wondering what time it was. Sergeant Fürth confirmed that it was nearly curfew and he'd better hurry. He spoke gently and didn't sound at all like the big mouth Bertin had taken him to be, telling Bertin he was welcome to warm himself up in his billet whenever he wanted, pressing a couple of cigars on him and lighting his way down stairs, after Porisch had shaken his hand sympathetically several times and said he hoped he'd make it through the winter in good shape. Pelican returned, shook some railway coal into the little stove and filled his pipe. 'God knows he needs our good wishes.

We always know what's going to happen to those ASC men a bit before they do themselves.'

'What is your actual job here?' Porisch asked.

'Theoretically, I'm a railway NCO,' Pelican replied. 'In practice, I'm Railway Transport Commander for Romagne and I run the show. My lieutenant drinks, lets me do the work and signs everything. It suits us both down to the ground, and I know everything and get a princely amount of leave,' and he laughed loudly. 'That lad and his squad are going to be relieved next week by the Fourth Company from the same battalion, then he'll disappear from my view. They're joining a really horrible detachment under a sergeant from Hamburg named Barkopp. How do I know that? I heard it from Barkopp himself. He was knocking back schnapps in the mess last night precisely on that account. They're going to be trained to look for duds and may count themselves lucky.'

'What will they be used for?' asked Porisch, as if he had never worn a soldier's tunic.

'And to think that you're going to be working in the War Materials Department, my dear Pogge!' retorted Pelican, 'They're going to be used for shooting, of course, for the final victory against America and the rest of the world!'

'Well, cheers, then,' said Porisch.

Meanwhile, Bertin ran through the icy night, his footsteps echoing. The sharp air revived him. The tea with grog had done him good and he'd found the unusual Pelican amusing. He would nurture that relationship. In any case, he'd had the great consolation that evening of learning that Eberhard Kroysing was alive and well. Humanity was in a strange state when a serious injury was the admission price for some peace, and people were glad to pay it. He'd write to Kroysing as soon as he could. Perhaps not immediately but when he was feeling better, so he wouldn't sound like a professional moaner. When it got a bit warmer and the work was easier and he got some of his 1917 leave, he'd take Kroysing's advice to heart and keep his chin up. Sweating, he made his way up to the hut just before 9pm. The men were snoring peacefully inside, unaware of what was in store for them because the gods had quarrelled and cast lots over mortal men.

CHAPTER TWO

When the gods quarrel

IF LIEUTENANT VON ROGGSTROH had been an experienced officer as well as a well-meaning one, he would have checked whether Bertin's superiors had all been furnished with sufficient medals before setting about actioning his good intentions, when he had a moment to do so. Unfortunately, he didn't do that. His request arrived in the battalion orderly room in Damvillers shortly after New Year, via the depot orderly room, with the result that Colonel Stein and Major Jansch were informed almost simultaneously that they were to procure an Iron Cross, Second Class for Private Bertin.

The two officers, who, as we know, couldn't stand each other, were also diametrically opposed types. An old cavalryman, Colonel Stein was stout and short-tempered but fairly good-natured; Major Jansch was a thin, bitter man and very restless, though self-controlled up to a point. Naturally, they both had the black and white ribbon of the Iron Cross, Second Class in their buttonholes. But reading the report, written by Lieutenant von Roggstroh, nephew of a influential landowner in East Prussia, setting out Private Bertin's deeds and achievements, they both had the same thought: with careful handling it shouldn't be too difficult to turn this into an Iron Cross, first class – and for themselves.

'Look here,' said Colonel Stein to his adviser and adjutant, 'with all due respect to your prophetic gifts, this is impossible. It's out of the question for some little ASC major in Damvillers to claim an Iron Cross, first class. We were at the depot. We went through the bombardment. Our ammunitions expert Sergeant Schulz issued Lieutenant von Roggstroh with 300 contact fuses and 50 time fuses. We were the most affected, and no one can take that away from us.'

We means you, thought Lieutenant Benndorf, but he didn't say that. Instead, he said: 'And the man whom the lieutenant expressly mentioned?'

'Will go away empty-handed this time,' said the colonel gruffly. 'We come first. He'll prefer some leave to an Iron Cross. What have those ASC men got to do with me anyway? I don't know them, and they don't know me, and if anyone here is to get a birdie, it's going to be me.'

'Hmm,' said Lieutenant Benndorf, walking over to the window of the gloomy room where they were billeted, 'that's not quite true, Colonel. You do know this man.'

'Don't remember having the pleasure,' muttered the colonel, whose leg was hurting him.

Lieutenant Benndorf continued, not out of malice, but because he wanted to say something to smother the nagging pain he felt at the assumption he would step aside. 'You've seen the man. You even had him punished back when that flock of Frenchmen were marched past and the ASC men gave them water. Don't you remember, sir? There was a good-for-nothing among them with a black beard who let a Frenchman drink from his canteen without the slightest compunction. He was called Bertin.'

The colonel remembered him dimly and without rancour. 'Oh, him,' he said, lighting a cigarette. 'Yes, he was a right one. But if you really think that Jansch is after the prize, I suggest we pay him a visit and talk him out of it. I'll give him a box of chocolates, and he'll be so thrilled he'll forget the Kaiser and our dear Lord, never mind the Iron Cross, first class, which isn't edible after all.' And he laughed loudly at this notion, while Lieutenant Benndorf merely smirked and nodded. The truth about Major Jansch couldn't be hushed up in a village such as Damvillers; he had the sweet tooth of a teenage girl, which made it easier than he realised for his enemies to manipulate him, as he was soon to learn.

When his enemy, the colonel, was announced, Major Jansch got the picture immediately. His eyes flashed like a weasel's, and his hair almost stood on end. He had been busy drawing a map of the future German Empire for *Army and Fleet Weekly*, which reincorporated Lutzelburg, Nanzig and Werden into the motherland, as well as Holland, Switzerland, Milan and Lombardy, Courland, Livonia, Lithuania and Estonia as far as Tartu. Currently – and shamefully – Lutzelburg, Nanzig and Werden were called Luxembourg, Nancy and Verdun. But members of the Pan-German Union and the 'Association against the Domination of Jewry' felt duty bound to reintroduce the honourable old German names. He folded his map up, smoothed his Balkan moustache, straightened his Litevka and went to greet his visitor.

The major's room was overheated, and the colonel found it stuffy. Smiling pleasantly, he asked if he might open a window. Major Jansch consented with a sour look. Now they would argue and the whole world would know about it straight away, because the colonel liked to talk in a booming voice. Well, so be it. He, Jansch, was ready and would not weaken.

Within three minutes, those two roosters were at each other, feathers flying. The colonel could not believe that the major seriously thought the medal should be bequeathed to him. Everyone knew he never left the pretty stone village of Damvillers, and no one earned an Iron Cross, first class in Damvillers. Herr Jansch's quiet, icy retort was that every man must fight at his assigned post – not turn up in Damvillers while the ammunitions depot of which he was in charge went up in flames.

Colonel Stein clutched his stomach laughing. That was priceless! Now the major was preaching morality and criticising others for sensibly retreating, when he himself had never put his nose anywhere near a shell. It was enough to make you want to climb trees!

Major Jansch said it had nothing to do with trees. Lieutenant von Roggstroh had recommended a man from the battalion for a medal, not a man from the depot personnel. Did the depot command propose to take possession of all the medals I/X/20 had won? That would take the biscuit. He was tired of all this incessant interference and grasping. No one needed to tell him how to do his job, and he would decide who in his battalion got a medal – and no doubt about that.

'What a pity you're so intransigent, my dear friend,' said Colonel Stein, staying comfortably put in his chair. 'And I had planned a friendly swap with you for a box of chocolates. You'd have got more from that than from a medal, which after all you can't put in your mouth.'

At that, Herr Jansch blew up. Unfortunately, Colonel Stein was sitting with his back to the window and so the large tin box of Belgian sweets sitting resplendent on the floor to the major's right did not escape his notice. Jansch slammed the lid shut and hissed angrily: 'Did you just come here to talk nonsense? Intransigent! Swap! Is the German language not good enough for you to say what you mean? Can't we even manage to get rid of French muck in the middle of a world war?'

Colonel Stein turned to Lieutenant Benndorf in astonishment. 'What does the gentlemen mean by such idiocies?' he asked as if Herr Jansch weren't in the room. 'Is old sweet tooth trying to insult us? Then this little outburst of his might have some kind of meaning, because there's only one person talking nonsense here.'

Major Jansch went pale, then red and blotchy, then pale again. He gasped for breath. He knew he was unpopular and until then he hadn't cared a jot, because men of intelligence couldn't avoid being disliked by fools. Now he must control himself, play for time and wait for his friend Niggl, who would shortly be returning from leave. And so he tried to be more conciliatory. The colonel already had a lot of medals, he said almost pleadingly. It wasn't as if he were trying to rob a widow of her lamb. The man named in the communication belonged to I/X/20, and any duty station would be able to see that he had defied the shellfire not for Colonel Stein but for the honour of his company. If a gunner from the depot were to perform deeds that got noticed by officers from elsewhere, then Colonel Stein would be first in line. If this was about what was right and justice...

Colonel Stein leapt from his chair, inexplicably enraged. Only later did Lieutenant Benndorf understand why the depot boss had become so angry: he secretly recognised a kernel of truth in the drivel emanating from the small major. 'The widow's lamb!' he screamed. 'Right and justice! We'll soon see what sort of unit you command, sir! According to right and justice, I should have had this man who's now come to the attention of an external officer court-martialled back in July. That little traitor should have avoided coming to the attention of his own superiors and refrained from fraternising with a French prisoner and allowing the swine to drink from his canteen – in full view of the depot commanders, in full view of me, sir! In full view of hundreds of men, sir! Against my express orders! Back then Benndorf here persuaded me mercy was the better part of justice. But if you're going to mess with me, as we say in Berlin, then I'll hang that story from the biggest bell I can find round here. And then, my dear chap, you'll be had up for not keeping proper discipline.'

Major Jansch turned pale again. He felt his stomach cramp in rage. What was this? Had something happened in the summer he'd not been told about? If this old lush was telling the truth, and if he used the information he'd just screamed at him, then his Iron Cross, first class would go flying out of the window. Because you didn't mess with indiscipline and fraternisation. Jansch turned to Lieutenant Benndorf, who was leaning against the wall with his arms folded like a spectator. As they both seemed to be the calmer ones, perhaps the lieutenant could explain what had happened.

'Nonsense,' interrupted Colonel Stein. 'Ask the men in your own company.'

But Lieutenant Benndorf, who wasn't entirely happy to see matters resolved long ago being revisited like this, asked to be allowed to speak and set out the by now entirely trivial incident.

Jansch listened attentively. The matter wasn't at all trivial, he said gravely. It should never have been kept from him, and he would ensure that it was dealt with in the proper Prussian manner. But he certainly wouldn't be relinquishing the Iron Cross, first class on that account, and they would see how it all turned out.

Colonel Stein stood up. So we shall, he said imperiously, adding that he'd bet a tonne of chocolate against a single schnapps that he and no other would emerge from the race victorious. And then he put his cap on, saluted and left, already reproaching his adjutant in the hallway for not backing him up properly and saying they'd never sideline the old nutcracker like that. What did it matter to them if that ASC private got it in the eye? And in all sincerity he added: 'You and your kind-heartedness, but can you please explain to me what this so-called Bertin has got to do with my Iron Cross, first class.' And to his astonishment the lieutenant stopped on the stairs and burst out laughing. Then the colonel clapped his hand to his forehead and joined in, because of course this was his reward for that beard he'd quarrelled with Herr Jansch about.

Up in his room, Major Jansch closed his window, exhausted. Then he stuck a sweet in his mouth – a long, pink, raspberry-flavoured lozenge. He marched up and down, and the orderly room knew that boded ill. The staff sergeant had to sit and listen, as did Diehl the clerk, Behrend the post orderly and even Kuhlmann the messenger, and they all came to their own different conclusions about how best to behave. They were sitting in a nice, heated room, their feet were dry and their food was as good as it could be that winter. None of them wanted to slip up and get moved back to the bloody ASC, where the men slaved away day after day in the old shelled area. The staff sergeant and the messenger, a couple of real slaves, were ready to play along with whatever mood the major might be in. The other two just wanted to keep out of it. Because that Bertin was bad luck, and anyone who tried to help him would be marked. First, there'd been the water tap business, then the screw-up over his leave, and now there was this Iron Cross story, which would have been good news for anyone else, and the water tap business was being reheated, so to speak, in a rumpus between those two bigwigs – it was enough to finish off the strongest man.

There was no need for Jansch to wait for his friend Niggl to return. There he sat in his chair whispering urgent advice in broad Bavarian – or at least there sat a dreamt-up Niggl, or better still a remembered Niggl, which the major's imagination had magicked up. For the major was an habitual and lavish fantasist. It was a gift – or rather an escape – he'd had since childhood. In his mind, during long day dreams, he took revenge on his enemies, generously pardoned those who'd misjudged him, gave advice to the Kaiser, which that short-sighted prince did not follow, with the result that Jansch, a humble major, had to rescue the Fatherland. He had long since worn an imaginary Pour-Le-Mérite, the highest order of the Prussian state, which he had won for an imaginary strategic masterpiece that had destroyed the Italian army – the traitors – with an aerial bombardment of poisonous gas, such that the German divisions could break into France through Turin and Savoy and were currently destroying the cities of Lyon and Avignon. Furthermore, an unknown major in the Supreme Army Command had performed the inestimable service of stirring up a revolt among the oppressed Little Russians in the Ukraine, who were now summoning the Germans as liberators. No one knew who had come up with the clever plan. Its author remained modestly anonymous, content in the knowledge that he had saved the Fatherland and performed some small service for its esteemed leaders. It didn't bother the little man marching back and forth that reality ran alongside his dreams undeterred. For example, Colonel Stein, whom he often cursed for his disdainful conduct towards a worthy colleague (namely himself) and had reduced to the command of a punishment battalion, had in reality just left the house unmolested having spoken to him in the vilest terms. Jansch sucked honey from his fantasies and rarely set foot in the dangerous world of reality.

At that moment, he saw Private Bertin of the ASC tied to a tree for hours in a biting frost, hanging unconscious in his bonds, and gloated at his just punishment. At the same time, he envisaged that shrewd Bavarian paragon who had so easily got rid of the trouble-maker in his own battalion. Conjured up by Jansch's imagination, Herr Niggl sat there, whether he liked it or not, the fine cloth of his tunic rubbing against the wooden chair back, modestly offering advice in his agreeable accent to his much cleverer, much more elevated comrade, the genial Major Jansch. His chubby-cheeked visitor sounded innocent as he advised Jansch to return Lieutenant von Roggstroh's submission with the curt observation that the person in question had remained at his post in the field gun depot on the express orders of the battalion commander. He, Captain Niggl, could then duly draw attention to Major Jansch's merits over a few beers with Group Command. But Private B. of the ASC would have to disappear into a working party near the front, one not entirely without danger. And he would have to stay there until his human vulnerability was tested. Because that Jew knew how to express himself in writing and could presumably talk too, and so, if asked, he was quite capable of spreading all kinds of plausible lies. Better he wasn't asked then.

Cheeks flushed and still stalking up and down, Major Jansch listened to the advice coming from the empty chair. Just such a working party was about to be formed and stationed close to the left bank of the Meuse. Its task was to collect stray ammunition, duds and discarded shells, examine them and send them home. The depot had already started the work on a small scale under Sergeant Knappe, and a ghastly explosion a few days earlier had left two dead and seven wounded, among them Sergeant Karde, a decent, hard-working man and a patriot, whose left leg had unfortunately been blown off beneath the knee. This incident had left an unpleasant impression, and the depot had decided to move the operation much further forwards and put it under the command of Sergeant Barkopp from the First Company, a marked man from Serbian days. B. would fit right in there. Smiling, Herr Jansch accompanied his fictional visitor to the door and shook his imaginary right hand gratefully, feeling hugely encouraged. He even opened the door for him and shut it behind him. Then he marched back to his desk and scribbled on a scrap of paper: 'Think about B.' He laid the scrap of paper in an obvious position in his drawer and rang for Kuhlmann the messenger. It was dinner time. The major had worked hard and was hungry in spite all the sweets he'd eaten.

CHAPTER THREE

The purchase price

DUD IS THE term used for shells that don't explode because of faulty manufacture or simply by accident. They lay about the country like giant, elongated Easter eggs – sometimes more in one place, sometimes fewer – waiting for whoever might be fortunate enough to find them. At certain times a lot came over, most other times hardly any. For that reason, the detachments had to spread out wide, remember or mark the places where they found a shell and then get an expert to look at each one and say whether it was safe to touch it. The shells were formed into small piles, and the small piles formed larger piles near the railway tracks. The shells were then examined thoroughly at the testing station and put in a freight car, gradually filling it. When two or three cars were full it was worth transporting them home. In the heady days of the first year of the war, looking for duds had been a private enterprise undertaken by gunners and ASC men who made all kinds of war souvenirs from the sometimes very heavy copper screw rings. The lively trade in these artefacts compensated for the risks involved in knocking off the red-gold bands. In the meantime, as is so often the case, a state monopoly had replaced individual enterprise...

Sergeant Barkopp's ASC men spread out across the high plateau, whose craters and shell holes offered a good place to search. Admittedly, the French could see what was going on and sometimes blessed the proceedings with shrapnel or shells. Only a couple of days previously, they had found the grinning corpse of Franz Reiter, an infantryman from Aachen, lying peacefully on his back with nothing but a postcard with his name on it in his pocket and of course without boots. Lebehde, Pahl and Bertin, all members of the working party, had lingered by Herr Reiter's corpse deep in thought, until Karl Lebehde encouraged them to move on with the melancholy observation: 'Wherever we go, someone has always been there first. You're out of luck Wilhelm.' This was a reference to Wilhelm Pahl's footwear, which had become completely useless. His boots had been with the company cobbler in Etraye for weeks but hadn't been repaired because, like the rest of the Barkopp working party, their owner lived in a barracks at the so-called railway station of Vilosnes-East and therefore couldn't come round to kick up a fuss. In the meantime, his lace-up shoes had worn through at least 10 days before. The soles weren't hobnailed and the ridges and grooves of the rock-hard clay had finished them off. Pahl was now walking on the insole under the ball of his left foot and the big toe of the right. Starving as he was, he now went about his duties rather turned in on himself and didn't seem bothered by his shoes. But appearances deceived.

In fact, Sergeant Barkopp's entire working party was in a desperate state. The men's underwear, constantly in need of darning because it was washed in caustic soap, no longer provided any warmth. Their tunics had taken on the colour of clay, and their trousers were ripped to pieces from climbing over barbed wire and had been patched with different coloured wool and twine. They now hardly bothered to fight their infestations of lice and no longer wondered what the next days might bring, for what could they bring? They didn't read or play chess, and there was no mouth organ or accordion to create a mirage of cheerfulness when work was finished. When darkness fell, ending their work, they crawled back into the barracks together and played cards, squabbled, or wrapped some warming rags round their heads and went begging. A battalion's rations are first sifted by the headquarters staff, then by the companies' staffs and their favourites, then by the kitchens and the companies themselves, and what's left wends its way over to the external working parties. This meant the men had to beg if they wanted their stomachs to be full. The stronger among them scoured the area night after night. They asked for but didn't give information as to the whereabouts of battery field kitchens, reserve infantry companies, railway sections (they always had it best), transport depots or, best of all, field hospitals. Field hospitals were a sublime oasis and cause of delight, and no one turned his nose up at barley stew laced with scraps of beef should a comrade happen to let it fall into his canteen. Good judges of character such as Karl Lebehde soon understood what made the kitchen NCOs and their underlings tick, as well as all the kitchen high-ups in the units nearby. They knew where they could simply queue up and hold out their pots in silence, where it was better to ask nicely, where a few jokes got things moving and where you had to offer a cigarette in exchange for a meal. Bertin provided cigarettes to barter with and got a share of the food as a result. Wilhlem Pahl always got his for nothing but had to put up with Lebehde the inn-keeper watching him and making comments, which didn't exactly cheer him up. Pahl was in the throes of a difficult decision. All the men were under pressure. They all knew the German army was starving but the end of the war was nonetheless nowhere in sight. They all felt they were in pitiless hands, and the only happy man was Naumann II, the company idiot. Yup, that poor little grinning devil, with his gigantic hands and feet, massive ears and watery blue eyes, had been shunted into the Barkopp working party too, no doubt on account of his sharp mind and skill at handling explosives... Well, the former warehouse packer from Steglitz was an idiot, and Sergeant Barkopp had clapped him good-naturedly on the shoulder, had Knappe the ammunitions expert take a photo of him grinning from ear to ear with a shell under his arm, and assigned him to barracks duty with the words: 'Make yourself useful with the broom, my son.' Despite the handicap of his impaired glands, Naumann II did so loyally and dutifully and with unswerving devotion to authority in the form of Sergeant Barkopp and all those whom life had treated less harshly than himself.

Barkopp, a publican at a seaport in civilian life, proved an excellent working party leader. From Sergeant Knappe he soon learnt all the signs that distinguish dangerous duds from harmless ones: open fuse holes and whether the shell is at an angle or level. His sharp eyes were everywhere, and he soon had a handful of practical-minded men trained up too. 'Better to leave one too many lying than to pick one too many up,' was his motto. Small fences were put round particularly dangerous ones – there were branches and rusty barbed wire everywhere – or if necessary they were sunk in flooded craters where the damned things rotted away. Because of this there had been no accidents. Emil Barkopp particularly looked out for small ammunition dumps abandoned by batteries that had retreated or been destroyed. These were sometimes found in sheltered spots in the ravines. Germany's national wealth lay strewn across the war zone, recklessly abandoned, as if the units that had left their supplies behind wanted to give their successors something to do. Having fallen into disfavour and been transferred frequently as a result, Emil Barkopp had seen a lot; he'd seen with his own eyes how the gunners laid down a layer of shells in the mud after the first rainfall, put cartridge baskets on top, then another layer of shells, carefully defused, and ate, drank and slept on that. Now they had to track down that treasure. His scouts were everywhere. Where were the best spots? None of the men knew apart from him and Sergeant Knappe, a thin, pensive man with a goatee beard. None of them had maps or the skills to make an exact evaluation of the set of the sky and the ins and outs of the front. All the ASC men knew was that they were next to the Meuse and would soon shift from one bank to the other. Most of the men from I/X/20 were stationed in the gullies by the village of Etraye, where the depot command had finally established its ammunition dump. But the working parties were spread across the whole sector to the east of the Meuse, and Barkopp's was the furthest west. Vilosnes and Sivry were connected to each other by a bridge but were otherwise cut off. The French had been firing all summer long from the right as well as from the high ground on the left bank, where the watchful enemies faced each other.

Pale ochre light suffused the high plateau. Private Bertin had strayed too far on his search, and it would soon be nightfall. He trotted on, jumping back and forth, then found a path and continued slowly, catching his breath. But the French batteries in the former German positions knew the path and before it was completely dark they flung a few well-meaning shells in his direction. In the deathly cold air, he heard the discharge at once. By the time the shell had exploded, Private Bertin was pressed to the ground, flat as an insect. But as the splinters from the explosion flew over him with the muffled drone of a giant beetle, a mighty battle was going on within him. Why was he taking cover in this idiotic way? What was the point of extending his life from one incident to the next? Wouldn't it be as well to help fate remove him from here, never mind to where, by sticking his backside in the air so that one of the splinters might tear into his flesh? He'd often considered letting his foot be crushed under a wagon but hadn't been able to resolve to do it. But if things continued as they were for another couple of months, there was no telling what he might do. For now, however, he pressed himself into the earth and clung to life. Then the evening blessing was over. He knocked the dirt from his clothes, pulled his cap down over his woollen head protector and trotted off for dinner and some warmth. He hadn't realised it yet himself, but there was no denying that in his overall demeanour the one he resembled most of all his comrades was that poor idiot Naumann, Ignaz.

An icy wind from the northern glaciers and eastern plains whistled across the churned-up land. Every gust cut across the area, whining and crashing against tree stumps, howling upwards then whooshing on. Between the dun-coloured earth and the ceiling of uniform grey cloud, the wind held sway. Harried and tormented, it lacerated its airy body against the rusty teeth of the barbed wire in a morbid frenzy. There were 10,000 km of barbed between the stormy English Channel and the leaden stone walls of Switzerland, leaving plenty of scope for the wind to whip itself up against the the barbed wire spikes, and this it did. It cut against the knife-sharp edges of old food tins, moaning there. It couldn't stop – it was in too much of a hurry to reach the warmer climes of the western ocean – but it pulled at every scrap of rotting cloth, chased pieces of paper into the bottoms of shell holes, not caring about the rats that peered restlessly out of their holes and were starving because the whole world had suddenly turned to stone, and rampaged on over the plains, through the narrow gorges, magnificent as an heir squandering the last of his inheritance, knowing it will soon be over.

Two ASC privates had sought refuge from the wind and found it in the bottom of very large and deep shell crater. They thought they were sitting on a thick sheet of ice but they were wrong. They were in fact sitting on the bottom of an ice cone that pointed downwards to the centre of the earth, and frozen within it, like an embryo in the womb, lay a dead German solider, waiting for the midsummer thaw. Then he'd be discovered, earth would be thrown over his fleshless bones and the rags of his uniform, and a wooden cross would be erected over him reading: 'Here lies a brave German soldier'. That's if anyone went to so much trouble, for by that time the first tank squadrons would be appearing on the horizon, the first American air squadrons would have relieved the French and things would be looking quite a lot livelier in the western theatre of war. But the two ASC men knew nothing of this as they spread out their legs, trusting their thick layers of clothing to protect them from the ice. To be absolutely sure, one of them, Karl Lebehde, had brought some newspapers with him, which he shared with his friend. As all beggars know, newspaper protects against the sharpest frost and the iciest of seats thanks to the gauze-thin layers of air between the sheets. And the two muddy, unwashed men bundled up in grey clothes looked like beggars, with their frozen faces poking out from their dark grey head protectors, their bluish noses and reddened eyes.

Wilhelm Pahl and Karl Lebehde were speaking to each other in hushed tones – not whispering exactly but speaking in such a way that no one outside could hear their voices. The tension in their faces and their quick, furtive movements suggested they were doing something untoward. Karl Lebehde had a sharp, rusty tool in his hand – a filed nail, which must have lain about in the damp for several days after it was filed, for the point was covered in rust too.

'Jesus, Karl,' groaned Pahl. 'If only I wasn't so bloody scared. First there's the pain, and I don't have a high pain threshold. Then there's the hospital, and if they have to amputate, they probably won't have any chloroform to spare.

That means more pain. And then who knows if you can walk about or stand at a type case with a missing toe?'

'Listen, lad,' replied Karl Lebehde, 'if you want to buy something, you have to pay the price. There's no other way. Come on now, son, give me your foot and we'll give it a wee tickle.'

'Shout a bit louder, why don't you?' said Pahl. 'Then we'll have Barkopp or old Knappe over here watching you operate on me.'

Karl Lebehde knew neither Barkopp nor Knappe nor anyone else was nearby. But since mutilations such as the one he was about to carry out at his friend's request were the only really effective way to escape the vengeance of the class state, the bourgeois Prussian Army pursued those who performed them with blood-thirsty rancour, and so he stood up, clambered up the sloping earthen wall, set his face to the wind and looked around. It was 9.30am, and there was no one around to see his head and freckled hands suddenly appear. Reassured, he slid back down. 'I don't know why I always fall for your tricks. You just wanted to put if off, didn't you, old pal?'

'Yes, I did. I'm scared stiff. God knows how this'll all end.'

Karl Lebehde's voice took on the reassuring tone of a mother persuading her child to go to the dentist with her: 'Listen, Wilhelm, you're welcome to forget it as far as I'm concerned. I don't fancy your chances or have any faith in the stuff you talked about during those long winter nights. You think the German workers are too dozy, but it takes someone like me who was brought up behind a bar listening to the rubbish they talk year in, year out to know just how dozy they are.'

'You can't say nowt against the Berlin workers, Karl.'

'Yes, you can, Wilhelm. Yes, indeed. Our Party Comrades are all right, and the Comrades in Hamburg are all right. The core is very capable – nothing against them. And they're probably in high dudgeon at the moment because their stomachs are empty, and so they'll listen to you and the couple of men working back at home, and maybe they'll walk out and jack in work and demand peace. And what will happen then? They won't be put up against the wall. Thousands will be called up, 80 or 90 will end up in the nick and the rest will get bigger rations with a bit of ham thrown in now and then for heavy labour – and that'll be the end of it.'

'So you think the German workers don't know the score and are going to let themselves be given a showing up by the Russians? If the papers are to be believed, they've put a bit of a bomb under their Duma with those massive strikes and hunger riots outside bakeries.'

'Yes, I do think that.' (Karl Lebehde tried to be as verbose as possible in order to distract Pahl.) 'I know as little about the Comrades in Russia as you do. But what I do know, my dear Wilhelm, is that unless the Party newspaper *Vorwärts* had been making things up, there are a few little differences between us and them. For example, things were always worse in Russia than at home, they faced starvation, Siberia was just around the corner, the bourgeoisie had had enough of Tsarism and world opinion was against it too. Then there were those spectacular defeats by the Japanese in 1905. And clear distinctions between the classes provide an excellent training for class war: we're here and you're there with no bridge between us. But everything has always been hunky dory at home. Socialists were only persecuted a little bit under Bismarck and that's long since been forgotten, and the labour movement was so full of victories and dreams of the future state it didn't realise that a proletarian on Sunday still stands a bit lower than a bourgeois on a weekday. And when the men in standy-up collars started talking the red, white and black of the flag, the proletariat couldn't afford to ignore it and no less a man than August Bebel bust a gut to demonstrate his patriotism, shouldered a musket and marched against Russia, and the men in standy-up collars just laughed. But why did they laugh? He was speaking the truth. And that was in peacetime when we had a small, modest army, and the Party's coffers were full to busting. That's the difference, do you see? From nowt comes nowt.'

Wilhelm Pahl had been listening carefully, both legs stretched out, thankful for the delay. The tear in his sole under the ball of his left foot gaped, and the right sole was worn through under his big toe. Convinced he'd distracted his friend, Karl Lebehde surveyed the bald patches with his small, glittering eyes. Surreptitiously, he took hold of the rusty nail. Early that morning he'd attached a wooded handle to it made from an elder branch.

'From nowt comes nowt,' repeated Pahl meanwhile. 'That's why I've got to get going and come to the aid of the Party Comrades at home. The signs from Russia says it's time, which is why I asked you to do this to me. I thought it would be easy. But when I first tried to step on some rusty barbed wire, I noticed immediately that the first step is the hardest. I just didn't realise how hard. Laugh if you like, Karl, but I'm starting to wonder if it wouldn't be better if I did it myself after all. It's like shaving. If someone else cuts you, it hurts more.'

Karl Lebehde smiled. 'Sure,' he said. 'Do it yourself if you want.'

Wilhelm Pahl sat hanging his head with his back to the wall of the shell crater wearing an agonised expression that made his friend feel very sorry for him. 'We're so weakened,' he said. 'No fat on our bodies, and the constant cold and stupor, and the lice don't let you sleep at night, and there's no hot water to do washing in – it's a pile of shit, Karl.' He closed his eyes. 'If it weren't for you doing the rounds of the field kitchens I wouldn't have had the strength to get up in the morning for ages now. Ow!' he screamed suddenly, ripping his eyes open. 'What are you doing?'

Karl Lebehde pointed to the spike in Pahl's shoe. 'It's all over,' he said gently. 'It's a good centimetre inside you, my son. Don't move for the next five minutes. The rest is in the hands of the dear Lord, who created blood circulation.'

Pahl went belatedly pale and shuddered. 'Good that it's over,' he said. 'You handled that well. I feel a bit funny, but it had to be done. I'd thought it through and... People who find it easy don't really know what they're letting themselves in for. At the same time it was really nothing. The cause of the proletariat is worth a bigger sacrifice than that.'

'The colour's coming back to your face, Wilhelm. The spirit is willing, but the flesh is not cheap,' Lebehde joked. 'And tonight you'll tell old Barkopp you stepped on some barbed wire...'

'I asked him for new shoes or boots the other day for the third or fourth time. He just grinned. "New boots."'

'And if you can't walk tomorrow morning, you'll be put on barracks duty and you'll have to scour the muck out of that lice-infested hut with Naumann II.'

'I will be able to walk tomorrow. It doesn't hurt that much any more. Do you think it's bad enough?'

'Don't worry about that. It'll start to fester like nobody's business in two or three days' time. And if the doctor tells you off for not reporting sick earlier, Barkopp will have to explain that we men in the working parties are such orphans we don't even have a paramedic to look after us. And that's nothing but the truth. Besides you don't feel much pain in your toes if they're nearly freezing off.' And he yanked the nail out of the wound, looked at it, threw away the elder wood shaft and hammered the iron spike into the splintering ice sheet with his heel. 'Don't you betray us now, little fella,' he murmured.

Wilhelm Pahl's normal colour was returning. His face was still grey but not quite as bloodless as before. Cautiously, he tried to get up and walk; he could. He'd hobble a little, partly from the wound and partly for the benefit of the sergeant and later the doctor. The two men climbed out of the shell crater, shivered in the wind and tramped off to look for shells.

'And you really do want to take Bertin back to Germany with you?'

Pahl nodded. He had to grind his teeth as a twinge of pain ran through him. 'Haven't you noticed how he's slowly going to pieces? He can't take much more. And I'll eat the sole of my shoe if he doesn't make a very useful Comrade when he's awoken from his stupor.'

'Hold on for a bit, Wilhelm, and you won't have to eat any shoe soles, neither roasted nor boiled, because you'll be living it up. Apparently, there's a really good leg doctor at the field hospital in Dannevoux. I'm a regular at the kitchen back door there, and if I let the kitchen NCO know that you're a friend of mine, they'll feed you up good and proper.'

An aeroplane sped eastwards above them, braving the bitter cold. A young French sergeant, bent over the cockpit with his camera ready, peered through the dry morning light. He didn't miss the two ants trudging across the abandoned field; he could've taken them out with a rifle. But his remit for that day was to photograph Vilosnes-East station, which was being used for ammunitions transport. Of course that was only part of his remit and it would take him further afield. The loops of the Meuse, and the slopes and valleys of the hills also repaid photographing – and later bombing based on the photographs. Jean-François Rouard, a young painter, was in no sense a bloodthirsty person. He would have much preferred to be sitting in a well heated atelier in Montparnasse or Montmartre, helping the further development of French painting, which had gone in new directions since Picasso and Bracque. But as he was now a soldier he had to make the most of these barren war years. Even once pull a bomb release handle and hear and see freight cars blown to bits. Below was his target for that day. He sighted it with his sharp eyes, clicked the shutter and the plates, adequately exposed, fell into the container. The line of Dannevoux roofs up against the tiny wagons on the railway track would look quite odd in the picture. That was because of the perspective in aerial photography, which had its own rules, as yet untested, and offered great possibilities to cartographers. Painting wouldn't benefit. He knew that. But from a military and aeronautical point of view, the Sivry-Vilosnes-Dannevoux triangle, with the loops of the Meuse and its bridges, was a tough nut to crack. The airman given the job of torpedoing the ammunitions train at night would have to bloody well watch out.

CHAPTER FOUR

A winter walk

A MAN'S POWERS of resistance are limited. However, it often takes a while for him to realise that; others usually notice first. Certain types who retain a sort of nostalgia for suffering from their childhood sometimes astonish the world with their martyrdom and heroic endurance. When they break, however, they break completely – it comes as a surprise because their intellectual and spiritual capabilities have been eroding away imperceptibly.

A man was strolling along the road from Vilosnes to Sivry, enjoying the soft of golden light of a late February noontime. He grinned quietly to himself and whistled along with the sparrows, yellowhammers and tits. He had a job to do of course; he wasn't just walking about enjoying the charms of nature. It was too cold for that, for the frost was relentless. The nature of this happy man's business was clear from the objects in his right hand: an oval French hand grenade and a long, mushroom-shaped shell fuse of pure brass. 'Take these to Herr Knappe,' the bewhiskered Sergeant Barkopp had told Private Bertin. 'He can have a sniff at them. Mind you hold them up the way I've given them to you. You know why.' Private Bertin did know why. The fuses were awkward customers. They'd explode on you if you changed their position such that the needle inside fell forwards or backwards of the angle at which the damned thing had lain since it was fired or thrown. At first, Private Bertin walked along with the two deadly objects in his right hand. The frost bit into his immobile fingers, and a glove was no help. After a while, Private Bertin started to think this was stupid. Besides, he wanted to be able to swing his arms and jot down any ideas or lines of poetry that might occur to him on such a lovely, clear day. Suddenly, he decided to shove the two explosive machines in his trouser pockets, one in the right and one in the left, making sure that up stayed up and down down. But what if he slipped and fell? The road beside the Meuse was frozen solid and icy, making a slip possible. And he had to cross the river at Sivry on a long wooden bridge, a pontoon bridge to be precise, resting on boats and often pretty slippery. But what the heck? Private Bertin wanted to have warm hands and to feel free and to be as comfortable as possible. Between leaving Sergeant Barkopp and reaching Sergeant Knappe he wanted to open up as a private person. It was a wonderful thing to be alone. All a person needed was to be able to walk and dream.

His thoughts came thick and fast. The street followed the Meuse, an idyllic river, lined with trees and bushes and frozen solid. From the far bank, came the occasional clear, metallic rattle of gunfire or an explosion – both far off. The left bank was known as 'Hill 304' and 'Mort Homme'; on the top the French and Germans faced each other with hand grenades. However, a recent report had said that the Frogs were bombarding Romagne, as the railway station there rankled with them. Whatever, Romagne still glimmered back there somewhere, and the men from Bertin's working party could still buy fat substitute and chocolate there. Those 30 or so men were starving, like the entire army. When the two-wheeled limbers had been blown to bits somewhere on the way to Etraye and there were dead horses lying about, infantrymen, sappers, gunners and ASC men had rushed towards their still-warm carcases from craters and dugouts all around and used knives to tear the spare flesh from their skeletons, then carried the meat triumphantly back to their small iron stoves in buckets and canteens to roast. But that paled into insignificance compared with one company excursion this side of Etraye when the occupants of the large barracks had feasted on roast meat from a forbidden and much more disgusting source. There was a knacker's yard down there a few kilometres to the rear, which gave off a dreadful stench all day long. Long dead horses with bloated stomachs were burnt there for manure, glue and grease, and their hides were used for leather. Eating their flesh was forbidden. But, guess what, it was eaten, for the cold kindly kept it fresh and the ASC men preferred a stay in hospital with meat poisoning and attendant torments to their regular lives. Hence the bonds of comradeship had long since frayed away; anyone who got a food package now was best advised to eat it as quickly as possible, because he wouldn't find it in his rucksack or bed or wherever he'd hidden it when he got back from work. That's how life was now, and it somehow had to be endured. It wouldn't last much longer though. A miracle had happened in the meantime. By all accounts, Russia was no longer heading towards a crisis; it had collapsed. The German attacks had taken their toll. The Russians had had enough. They were making democratic demands, and that was the beginning of the end. Of course pessimists such as Halezinsky, know-alls such as Lebehde and scardy cats such as good, old Pahl maintained that the French, British and Japanese military missions would now get the upper hand in Russia and step up hostilities. But the Russians wouldn't be so stupid. They'd tell their allies to get stuffed and throw down their arms. Yes, they'd all be home by Easter, and if not by Easter then by Whitsun. Private Bertin smiled to himself thinking about it as he stumbled over the deep frozen ruts in the road.

The Meuse now lay before Bertin. He had half a mind to walk across the ice so he didn't have to go the long way round to the bridge. Surely he'd be able to slide over very easily on his hobnailed boots. 'Skidding' they called it at home in Kreuzberg. Ha, ha, ha, he thought, where are Goethe and his friend Klopstock now? He really felt like putting on a pair of skates and sweeping through the meadows and alder trees, rapturously free, composing poems in praise of ice skating. The French would get a bit of a shock if someone came sweeping straight into Verdun in a great arc! Surely they'd be chivalrous enough to let him go on his way unharmed. But he walked obediently along the river's edge to the wooden bridge and sticking close to the hand rail crossed into another command, a completely different zone. As he crossed, he tossed some twigs on to the ice, and there was a dull echo deep beneath the surface as they bounced. On the other bank, a square of ice had been cut away and you could see the black water moving past, icy and silent.

Since the dismantling of the Steinbergquell depot, Sergeant Knappe had been living in a barracks at the bottom of a gully overgrown with bare bushes and trees, and was in charge of the field gun ammunition. His eyes widened in astonishment when Private Bertin nonchalantly handed him the two explosive devices to examine. Bertin must be off his head, he muttered as he carefully carried them through to the testing tent, which was kept apart from the ammunition, telling Bertin to disappear for half an hour. Bertin longed for a heat and some hot coffee and he soon got them from Knappe's assistants, a couple of artillerymen. Little Herr Knappe had always been thin, but his cheeks had never been as hollow as they were now, and his goatee beard had grown appreciably. *They're starving here too*, thought Bertin, as he said goodbye. *You can see it.* But Herr Knappe's emaciation was actually due to quite different reasons than hunger: love of his country and despair. He was an excellent design engineer and using a couple of pictures from newspapers had designed one of those all-terrain combat vehicles with caterpillar tracks instead of wheels that the Entente alliance had been using recently. He had sent the drafts to the Supreme Army Command and had received, through Colonel

Stein, a scornful reply: such toys could happily be left to the enemy. Let them crawl into those iron dustbins and bring their coffins with them. German infantrymen had no need of such vehicles and the ammunitions expert should get on with his job and leave the rest to the Supreme Army Command. This grieved Herr Knappe, and ever since then he'd been sleeping badly and had lost his appetite and interest in playing chess; where would it all end?

Half an hour later, Private Bertin, now warmed up, reported back to him. The hand grenade was gone, but Knappe handed him the fuse by the tips of his fingers. 'There,' he said simply. 'Drop it in the water from the bridge. But watch out it doesn't turn round, lad, or you'll have drunk your last cup of coffee on this earth.'

Somewhat sobered by the little bearded man's stern tone and serious eyes, Bertin trotted off. On the bridge, he did as he'd been told, but as the water closed over the accursed thing, his thoughts darted off in a completely different direction. The gunners, who knew the area well, had given him a piece of news whose importance none of them could have understood. There was a relatively unscathed village on the hills above Vilosnes-East – what was it called again? It was called Dannevoux. And the barracks on the perimeter above the railway tracks, where the Barkopp working party loaded and unloaded its wagons and which you could just see from the Meuse, formed the large Dannevoux field hospital. There in the immediate vicinity lived Eberhard Kroysing. Bertin would have to go and see him, shake him by the hand and find out how much of him had emerged healthy and unbroken from the darkness of the December battle. His comrade Pahl had been sent there three days ago with blood poisoning in the foot, and that would provide a good excuse for his superiors. Visiting Pahl could easily be passed off as his soldierly duty – a duty to which Eberhard Kroysing had always attached such importance. A good day, a good walk, a welcome hand grenade, a nice chat over a cup of coffee.

BOOK EIGHT

The eleventh hour

CHAPTER ONE

The blessed island

THE BATTLE FOR Verdun had been fought and lost, but nobody said that. The German communiqués had revised the aims of the operation, invented the 'battle of attrition' and recast the truth, and there were a lot of big kids who believed this fairytale. Raw materials and supplies essential for life were stretched to the utmost, diluted and mixed with substitutes. But what had just about sufficed in the second winter of the war failed in the third. Not enough butter, not enough meat, not nearly enough bread, although it had been 'extended' with bran and potatoes; hardly any pulses or fresh vegetables, no ham, almost no eggs, and no noodles, millet, oatmeal or semolina delivered from abroad. Leather was running out, as were linen and woollen cloth; you only got clothes if you had a ration coupon, and they were often made with unsatisfactory new materials. When fruit and sugar disappeared into the jam factories, notices were put up encouraging children to collect fruit kernels for their oil. For the same reason, sunflowers were planted, and linseed and beechnuts crushed. Wool to darn stockings and thread to mend shirts were precious goods hunted down by anxious housewives. And just as plant compounds and chemical mixtures appeared in tins and tubes as sham food, so paper masqueraded as clothes, twine, bags and shoelaces. Newspapers and cookery books were full of recipes for conjuring up tasty dishes out of insipid mixtures of potatoes, turnips and brine. No vitamins, no carbohydrates, no protein and still fully fit for work – that's what the physiologists and doctors preached in order to secure final victory in a war that had long since been lost. Germany was trying to triumph over the whole world, all reason and the course of history and development in the last century. That diabolical instrument of war, the British blockade, was at last being countered – so said the powers that be – with something equally effective: the torpedoing of all cargo ships on the seas. In half a year, Britain would sue for peace. And the nation believed this. Unaccustomed to measuring their rulers' speeches against reality or demanding accountability for spilt blood and the wasted years of their lives, the people worked in the factories, fields and cities, sent their children to be soldiers, washed themselves with clay soap and paper towels, travelled in unheated railway carriages, froze in lukewarm flats, sunned themselves in the glow of future glories and unverified reports of victories, mourned their dead, spied on the healthy and patiently allowed themselves to be ridden into destruction.

There was still a last streak of smoky red in the evening sky, as Bertin climbed up to Dannevoux field hospital, with Sergeant Barkopp's permission, to find out how Pahl was getting on (but above all to see Eberhard Kroysing again). From the rear, a minor road wound up the hill to the plateau, then past some barbed wire and wooden fencing to the hospital offices. Several wings enclosed a large open square, and the barracks loomed like a headland above a plain. It was outside visiting hours, and Bertin was greeted curtly and told he should kindly keep to the prescribed times displayed on the gate. After much explaining and a bit of toing and froing he was finally admitted through a back door at the top of a small wooden staircase. It led into a white corridor that clearly went through the section for seriously ill patients. Bertin's heart contorted with anxiety, and the groaning he heard pierced his thin layer of self-protection. The smell of iodoform and lysol wafted towards him. When a nurse squeezed past him with a covered bucket, the sudden proximity of pus and rancid bodily fluids nearly made him sick. Through an open door, he glimpsed thick, white bandages, a row of beds, a leg suspended in a pulley, the backs of two nurses. He might have grasped then the full terrible significance of it all, but instead he closed up like a mussel caught in an unwelcome current of water and carried on looking for men's ward 3, which he found at the end of the second long corridor on the left, and on the right room 19.

Eberhard Kroysing greeted Bertin, who looked shy and unkempt, with undisguised joy. Kroysing sat up in his bed beaming and stretched out his powerful arm to Bertin, letting the ASC man's hand disappear in his. Kroysing's deep voice filled the room. 'Wow!' he exclaimed. 'Bertin! This is definitely your best deed of this fine New Year, and you'll be richly rewarded for it in heaven, which, like the rest of us, you seem to have to dodged so far. Now get some of those layers off, you old grey onion. Hang that lice-infested gear in the corridor. There's a coat stand on the right outside the door.' When Bertin asked suspiciously if things didn't get stolen even here, there was a roar of laughter from all three beds; he could still hear it through the closed door.

Obediently, he took off his head protector, coat and canvas jacket, returning in his tunic.

The room smelt of bandages and wounds, cigarettes and soap. But it was warm, light and clean – to Bertin it seemed like an enviable, heavenly existence. He might easily have thought that the times must be pretty crazy if pain, blood and wounds were the price to be paid for such modest comforts. But he had no such thoughts; he was much too steeped in the world of war with its twisted values. Besides, Kroysing immediately commanded his attention. He told him to sit on the bed, introduced him to the two lieutenants, Mettner and Flachsbauer, as a friend he'd inherited from his late brother, failing to notice that Bertin was starving, freezing and miserable. Bertin asked Kroysing how he was – 'Great, of course,' he replied – and to tell his story, but he was reluctant. Storytelling wasn't his game. It was Bertin's game, and everyone should stick to what they knew. The last time they'd met had been on the other side of Wild Boar gorge. Since then, he'd been in the thick of it. They hadn't got Douaumont back, but they had dug themselves in quite nicely up on Pepper ridge and laid a load of mines, but just as they were about to let the Frogs have it, that 15 December business started, putting a stop to their fun. He, Kroysing, must have spent too much time sitting in the fort and the trenches because he'd lost the knack of doing a break in a field battle or he wouldn't have had the misfortune to throw himself into a hole that was much too shallow when the advancing battery's damned shells reached him. The shell hole had been deep and steep enough in itself but it was frozen and full of ice, and so Kroysing ended up with his great knuckle of a right leg sticking up in the air and it was caught by a shell splinter that sliced right through his puttee and shin bone, though it didn't bisect his calf bone. He'd hobbled over to the dressing station on his stick like some demented grasshopper and had passed out there. Well, now he'd paid his debts to the French in full and could relax. He had an excellent doctor here in the hospital, and the care was first-class. For now, he wanted for nothing. The bone was healing nicely, and a piece of ivory had been inserted to replace some damaged fragments – as he'd said, the head physician was a hot shot and had worked miracles. He'd not yet decided what to do when he was better – there was still plenty of time to think about it. And now it was time to hear Bertin's news. He must have a lot to tell too. Above all, how was Kroysing's old friend, Captain Niggl? Here they were under the Western Group Command – west of the Meuse – and heard about as much about the eastern sector than they did about Honolulu, although they hadn't crossed the river, geographically speaking.

There was indeed a lot to tell, said Bertin, and he began with Captain Niggl's advancement and the great fame he'd acquired.

'The Iron Cross, first class!' shrieked Kroysing. 'That cowardly swine! That shuddering pile of dirt!' And he burst into a fit of laughter, then nearly coughed his eyes out from choking.

Someone yanked open the door, and a forehead and a couple of strands of blonde hair appeared. In a pleasant Rhenish accent a voice said: 'Boys, keep the noise down, would you? The boss will have a fit.'

'Sister Kläre,' cried Kroysing. 'Stay here! Listen to this!'

The nurse waved a hand and said, 'Maybe later.'

Kroysing sat in bed, pale and wild-eyed. 'I'll be hanged if I'm going to put my dog tag back on after this,' he said. And he described to his two room mates, battle-hardened front-line soldiers like himself, how he had ensnared the ASC captain at Douaumont – a man who'd have done a bunk if he could have and would never have gone near the front of his own free will.

The two lieutenants jeered at his fury. 'You're so provincial,' said Lieutenant Mettner equably. 'I always suspected as much. Instead of being upset because some squit is getting a medal, you should be amazed you managed an Iron Cross.' Kroysing's caustic reply was that he wasn't yet as philosophical as that but would no doubt learn to be in due course.

Bertin sat on the edge of the bed, silent and gaunt. With a smile he told them what had happened when Lieutenant von Roggstroh made a recommendation on his behalf. Kroysing was only half listening. 'So that thing is to be promoted to major as well?' he asked wearily. 'And there's nothing we can do about it? Just wait!' And he clenched his fist. 'And you, my dear chap, have only got what you deserved. Why are you still hanging around with those lousy ASC men? When will you realise that His Majesty's sappers need new blood, leadership material, officers? Aren't you ashamed to stick at that job, sir, as if your being in the ASC was God's will rather than a temporary measure? No, I've no sympathy for you, my dear chap. You could be out of it in five minutes. All you have to do is apply to my esteemed regiment, formerly battalion, in Brandenburg an der Havel, and I'll take care of the rest. Then you'll have a lovely spell near Berlin first of all, which, if I'm not mistaken, will please your young wife. You'll get a nice new tunic and leave as a sergeant. After all, you've already been at the front for 12 months.'

'Fifteen,' corrected Bertin. 'If you include the Lille forts.'

'And the next time we see each other, you'll be wearing a sword knot like your friend Süßmann... Sergeant Major Bertin, soon Lieutenant Bertin. Have some sense, man! Take stock!'

Bertin listened to him talking, and what the wounded man said now seemed sensible, compelling even. What was he doing among slaves? Wasn't there a better way to rediscover his humanity? Naturally, Lenore would give up her apartment and join him in Brandenburg for weeks or months, unless she used her father's influence to get him into a Potsdam regiment... For a few sparkling moments he plunged into such dreams: what a heavenly escape from this endless, unmitigated torment...

Kroysing saw his words had made an impression. 'Let's get on with it,' he cried. 'Say yes.'

Lieutenant Flachsbauer, in bed by the same wall, watched Bertin's expression eagerly, entranced by this show, which that old devil Kroysing had pulled out of his sleeve.

'My dear sir,' countered Lieutenant Mettner from the bed opposite, 'don't let him talk you into anything. Wait until you've seen our bandages being changed before you make up your mind.' And he stretched out the misshapen, bandaged stump of his arm to Bertin with a melancholy smile.

'Mettner!' cried Kroysing. 'Is that what you call camaraderie? Alienating a recruit already three-quarters won over! I wouldn't have thought you capable of such a thing. It's unforgivable.'

'Nonsense,' countered Mettner phlegmatically. 'Forgivable or not – if you're going to play the recruiting sergeant, you should at least offer your victim something to put in his stomach. Or do I misunderstand our candidate's wishes?'

Bertin conceded with a smile that he was absolutely famished and could certainly go some hospital food. And while, half jokingly, he described the tinned soup called 'crown prince soup' that was dished out to the men day after day, Lieutenant Mettner left the room – now just one man among others in his blue and white striped hospital pyjamas.

'He's the only one of us who can walk,' said Kroysing by way of excuse.

Flachsbauer observed with some amusement the contrast between Kroysing's self-confident gestures and imperious bearing and the humble demeanour of the gaunt ASC man he wanted to seduce into playing the officer.

The one-armed man reappeared at the door with a white bowl and rapped with his foot. Bertin opened it, thanked him and started eating. The soup was made from poor quality beef provided by an elderly war cow past her best when slaughtered; the chewy morsels of her flesh sort of swam in the broth – the delicious broth. And the bright yellow noodles were war-time fare. Not much egg had been used in their manufacture, and their yellow hue came from a colouring agent, probably saffron. But this concoction, liberally seasoned with salt, parsley and leeks, constituted a meal the likes of which Private Bertin had not tasted since his wedding leave and it brought tears to his eyes – tears of shame at the happiness that flooded him, at the humiliation and indignity of being as moved now by beef soup as he once had been by music or poetry, and because he felt he could be a different man if he always ate like this. He sat head bowed, the soup bowl on his knees, his face in shadow, silently spooning the soup into his mouth, and each of the three men watching him noticed how much he was enjoying it and that his dark brown hair, greying at the temples, was going on top. But no one guessed what was going through his mind, or if they did they didn't show it.

'I knew,' said Bertin, laying his spoon down in the bowl and looking up, 'that I had found the Island of the Blessed here.'

'But the entrance fee isn't cheap,' nodded the rather fat Mettner.

'Not as dear as yours,' replied Bertin briskly.

Lieutenant Mettner looked at him. 'That remains to be seen,' he said carefully. 'What's your line of work?'

'Lawyer,' replied Bertin.

'Don't be so modest,' broke in Kroysing. 'He also writes books.'

'Good,' continued Mettner. 'In me you may admire a mathematician, pupil of Max Klein, Göttingen, and not a bad one either. We have plenty of free time now, and so I tried to solve a cubic equation recently to pass the time. Do you know that I don't understand them any more. I hardly know what a logarithm is. That's how far I've sunk.'

The others laughed. But Mettner continued undeterred. 'Consider this, young man: you will probably have sunk even lower than us, and so you'll have to start again from the beginning. We're out of practice, our minds are dulled, our judgement is gone and our professional know-how has evaporated. And we'll have to relearn what civilisation means. Believe me, it's going to be quite a task. Or do you think you'll still have respect for human life after everything that's gone on here? Won't you just reach for your pistol if your landlord doesn't want to fix your shutters? I know I'll at least want to. And when the postman rings in the morning, I know I'll secretly want to open the door and chuck my water jug in his ugly mug. That's how I, Hermann

Mettner, feel – born in Magdeburg and not the least bit bloodthirsty. But you, my dear legal friend, have spent the last 20 months standing to attention and saying 'Yessir' even if the man in front of you is an absolute baffoon. You'll definitely go to the dogs. Let's assume the worse that happens is that you're still in that tunic at the end of the war. When you're released, you'll be used to obeying. No matter what you're asked to do, you won't complain, and if people ask nice and politely, you'll melt like butter. You're sure to find people who'll save you the trouble of making your own decisions. And once the lovely business of making money starts again, in an office or wherever, one fine day you'll realise you lost whatever scraps of personality you had in the war and you'll remember a certain Mettner, who only gave his right arm, and there'll be much wailing and gnashing of teeth – or worse.'

'How! I have spoken,' joked Kroysing, quoting Karl Mays. 'My dear Mettner, you're an intelligent man, and we're sure to hear more from you as the days get longer. And it's brilliant that you're trying to put my good friend Bertin off being in the rank and file. But don't be offended if I take issue with you on certain points, for I'm a military man through and through now, and if I don't stay in the sappers I'll do something in the air force. This gentleman here has no right to think about himself and his personality. For now, he should think about Germany. Comrades of his and ours are being killed every day, and sometimes it's necessary and sometimes it isn't. If a man is courageous, devoted to duty and able to lead, then God damn it he belongs in His Imperial Majesty's most prestigious Officer Corps until the peace bells ring out. As to what happens to him afterwards, Germany will take care of that; our country will do things properly. And now, goodnight, gentlemen, and please close your ears for a bit. I have some private matters to discuss with Bertin.'

Flachsbauer and Mettner turned to the wall. Lieutenant Mettner had long since given up trying to influence Kroysing, who was older than him but still such a boy, and he knew that his friend Flachsbauer always agreed with the person who'd spoken last – in this case the old warhorse. Just don't rush things, he thought, as he snuggled down in his blankets. It was spite on Kroysing's part, if not something worse, to want to get that bright, left-leaning dreamer with his jam-jar glasses into an officer's tunic. But they'd cross that bridge when they came to it. Now it was time for sleep. A man always saw things more clearly after a good sleep.

Bertin stared at Mettner's back. Waking up with that wound must have been like coming round after a drinking bout; he'd have liked to know more about him. He'd been thinking about his Kroysing novel and felt uneasy about it, unsure whether it was good or bad. Perhaps it was bad – and he couldn't see it. For his two years as a soldier had taken their toll, eroding his education and character... What would become of him? He was suddenly overcome with fear. *Don't think about it*, an inner voice cried. S*ave your soul! If you start to think about it, you won't do your job properly tomorrow. You'll drop a dud and blow yourself up. You only have one duty: to stay alive. Eat lots of soup like that one, listen to Lieutenant Mettner and stay true to yourself...* Montmédy? Ah yes, Kroysing was asking if there was any news from there. Bertin ran his hand through his hair. He hadn't heard anything for weeks. The papers Kroysing had sent him via Süßmann had certainly been forwarded and would be there now. But since Judge Advocate Mertens' fatal accident...

'It's always the wrong ones who get it,' growled Kroysing, lying back, his nose casting a sharp shadow on the barracks wall. 'Why couldn't that bloody aerial bomb have blown the heroic Niggl through the roof? No, it had be a decent man and one of the most indispensable.'

Bertin nodded and said nothing. Something made him want to tell Kroysing the wild hunter the truth about that indispensable man's death, but he let it go out of respect for the deceased. He'd heard nothing further, he lied.

'Well, I have,' said Kroysing. 'His sergeant came to see me, Herr Porisch from Berlin. A queer fish, but well-meaning, no doubt about that. First of all, he made it clear that Herr Merten's successor would not want to open the dead file. Then he gave me a piece of advice.'

Bertin had instinctively put his pipe in his mouth and was sucking on it. He saw Porisch's pale, puffy face, brash Sergeant Fürth – Pelican – the billet at Romagne with the crossed sabres. Poor Christoph Kroysing's affairs were in disarray, and that couldn't be allowed to go on.

'Porisch is clever,' he said.

'So he is,' growled Kroysing. 'He suggested I make a complaint against Niggl to the judge advocate of the Western Group Command, whose jurisdiction we fall under here, Lychow Division, German Field Post and so on – I've got it written down. He said I should address it to Judge Advocate Dr Posnanski, confidentially in the first instance, outline the case briefly, cite you as a witness and ask for a meeting between the three of us to discuss the matter, so that I don't get a reputation as a troublemaker with my unit if the evidence doesn't conform to the rather exacting standards of the military judiciary.'

Bertin said that seemed like a very sensible suggestion to him. 'I think so too,' continued Kroysing, 'but before I pursue it, my young friend, I must warn you that it could create unpleasantness for you. An ordinary ASC private who picks a fight with a battalion commander is letting himself in for it. I didn't have your postal address and besides I had to deal with my leg and I learnt patience in the Prussian army. But now that you're here, I must ask you: are you in?'

'Certainly,' replied Bertin without hesitation. 'I'll never go back on the promise I made to your brother. And now I must go if you don't mind. My comrade Pahl is over there in ward 3.'

Kroysing reached out his hand. 'You're making off before I can say thank you. Fair enough – I know how it is. I'll send the letter tomorrow. Where can I find you?'

Bertin, who'd already stood up, described his barracks under the hill near the goods siding at Vilosnes-East – very close on the map, but a good 20-minute climb on the ground. He told him his duties were always finished by dark. 'And what happens,' he asked, buttoning up his tunic, 'if it's not possible to pursue Herr Niggl in law?'

'Then I'll take up the chase alone and hunt him until he drops. As long as we both live, there will be no let-up and no mercy, even if I have to drag him from his orderly room or his bed or some latrine he's crawled into. A man who kills one Kroysing has to face the other's pistol or pitchfork, and that's the end of him. And now go and see your comrade. What's he called?'

'Pahl,' Bertin replied. 'Wilhelm Pahl. It would be nice if you could look out for him. Goodnight.'

When Bertin had left the room, Lieutenant Mettner turned on to his back. 'You'll destroy that young man, my dear Kroysing, if he acts as a witness against a captain.'

'May I turn out the light?' asked Kroysing politely in reply.

Mettner smiled, not at all offended. 'Please do, my dear Kroysing. That lucky fellow Flachsbauer has been asleep for a while.'

CHAPTER TWO

Suffering flesh

'HOW NICE THAT he's got a visitor,' said Sister Mariechen, who was on duty in ward 3 – minor cases. And her small blue eyes twinkled amiably as she greeted Bertin. 'He simply doesn't want to get better. He seems preoccupied. Tell him it was really nothing. Now hold the fort for me a moment,' she said, 'and I'll get you some nibbles.' And with a maternal shake of the head, she bustled out of the dismal ward to have a chat with Sister Annchen and Sister Louise in the kitchen.

Fourteen of the 18 beds were occupied, and Pahl's bed was next to the window. Three electric light bulbs hung over the central passageway. The one furthest away was turned on and shaded by a blue bag. 'Come and sit next me, my friend,' said Pahl weakly. 'They're all asleep and the old bird's gone out. We might not get another chance to speak privately.'

Bertin felt moved as he looked at Pahl the typesetter's strangely alien face as though he'd never seen it before. He looked like one of the executed men in those big depictions of the Deposition from the Cross from the Middle Ages – pallid and extinct. There was a frizz of grey-brown stubble on his cheeks that emphasised his stubborn brow, squashed nose and remarkably bright eyes. The thin moustache above his lips repeated his eyebrows and underlined the set of his mouth. He'd pulled his blanket up round his chin, such that his short neck was hidden from view and all that remained of his familiar form was a face etched with pain.

'Everything's fine here,' said Pahl. 'The people have been quite decent so far, and the food is edible. But I absolutely cannot get over what they did to me, nor will I until the day I die.'

Bertin shook his head sympathetically. Wilhelm Pahl really wasn't the man he'd been. What had happened? Exactly what had happened to nearly all the 'minor cases' over the past year: slish-slash, the doctor had chopped off his big toe – it was high time, he'd said. The blood poisoning had already spread to the middle of his foot. They'd laid Pahl on a scrubbed table, tied him and held him down, and then operated. 'I was fully awake, my friend, completely conscious.

They showed no mercy or compassion.' To the contrary. The medical officer had yelled at Pahl the typesetter for kicking up a fuss over such a trifle and had told him he'd be lucky to get off that lightly, since his leg was swollen and discoloured below the knee and if they had to take more off there wouldn't be any chloroform for that either. Happily, the first intervention was enough. But – and the medical officer could not get over this – Pahl was not getting better. He took an iron hold of himself when the bandages were being changed, ground his teeth and didn't say a word, but his whole body trembled and he nearly passed out. Some kind of inner turmoil was how Dr Münnich, the medical captain, explained his unusual condition to his assistants and the more intelligent orderlies and nurses when the word 'malingering' was mentioned. A psychic trauma, he called it, for which the ground had obviously been laid by childhood experiences connected with his deformity. But for his recovery to make better progress he would have to regain his lust for life and direct his will, which clearly had not dissociated itself from the experience of pain, forwards.

'Boy,' said Pahl, 'it's unbelievable that there are such things in the world, that people can inflict so much pain on you, that the pain can go right through you to your heart and brain and back again... It doesn't really fit with the world of blue skies and bogus sunshine and birds singing to order that we've all been sold. But it fits with a society that's harder than hard. It fits with the situation of the oppressed classes. With how a man can be condemned from birth to toil and go without, even if he has great gifts that could benefit humanity...' He stopped talking and closed his eyes. 'The slaughterhouse,' he said shaking his head, 'is always there, it's just that now in war time we see it everywhere. We're conceived for the slaughterhouse, brought up to it and trained for it, and we work for it, and then eventually we die in it. And that's what's called life.' His breathing grew heavy, and he put his waxen hands on the bed cover. Bertin instinctively looked for the red lacerations from the nails. A couple of tears seeped out from under Pahl's right eyelid. *My God*, thought Bertin, *and I had tears in my eyes earlier over a bowl of soup.* 'We must stop supplying the slaughterhouse,' Pahl continued in a low voice, while around him the others snored, 'starting with the one we can see all around us.'

'So far as that's in our power,' agreed Bertin cautiously.

'It's in our power alone. Only the victims of injustice can stop injustice. Only the oppressed can put an end to oppression. Only men who've been shelled can bring the shell factories to a standstill. Why would those who profit from the torment want to abolish it? No reason.'

Bertin was glad to be able to distract Pahl from his sorrows by contradicting him. A sensible man would willingly give up one-third of his power in order to be able to enjoy the remaining two-thirds in peace, he said. But Pahl said no. That had never happened. Everyone preferred to grasp hold of three thirds and be killed for it. And so the proletariat would be forced into a reckoning with the capitalist class.

Pain hardens you, Bertin thought. Aloud, he said there were some very decent capitalists.

And in a whisper Pahl rejected this objection. First the world had to be rid of collective injustice. 'If you had a finger hacked off, you'd spend your whole life wanting to abolish finger hacking. It's good to get this all off my chest. This place is full of butchers and pious old women, and the patients only think about next lunchtime's soup and whether the nurses are sleeping with the doctors or officers. Sometimes it drives me nuts. The ruling class certainly has finished us off.'

Bertin stole a glance at his watch. Pahl noticed and said he should go: duty required sleep. 'That game old bird will be back in a minute, so we'd better decide quickly what we're going to do.' Would Bertin allow himself to be requested if Pahl could get him a job somewhere when he'd recovered and was back at work? He'd be able to work his way up from typesetter to copy editor, and it was a secure job as no administration could afford to ignore newspapers, whose job it was to titivate the national mood morning, noon and night.

Bertin looked away. This tormented man was so sure of his cause and so convinced he'd be able to spirit Bertin away. Bertin asked if he hadn't perhaps underestimated the difficulties.

'No,' said Pahl impatiently. 'And once you're in Berlin, perhaps you'll come and talk to a works gathering or a members' meeting. And then maybe you'll write me up a few leaflets that'll get the ammunitions factory workers thinking. Agreed?'

Bertin looked into the drawn, waxen face of Pahl the typesetter, now more than ever a cripple and resolved to resist evil. For a moment he bridled inside and wondered why they were all drawn to him: Kroysing from the right, Pahl from the left. Why did no one leave him in peace to listen to his own inner voice? He suddenly clenched his fist and thought, *Let me come to myself!*

But Pahl misunderstood the gesture. 'Good,' he whispered. 'Bravo!'

Sister Mariechen came up behind them, and Bertin stood up. 'See if you can fix it, Wilhelm,' he said with a smile.

288

'Come again soon,' said Pahl with a similar sort of smile.

And Bertin thought how much better he looked when he was smiling. The nurse waved a little package at him: a ham sandwich as a thank you, she explained.

'No one could resist that,' said Bertin. 'I'll eat it on my way down.'

'Reward for your good deed,' said Pahl.

CHAPTER THREE

Man and justice

THE STAFF OF the 'West of the Meuse' Army Group were each week reduced to despair by the breadth of Judge Advocate Dr Posnanski's knowledge and his propensity to share it. How were they to know that their billet of Montfaucon had provided the poet Heinrich Heine with an opportunity to lampoon his colleagues Fouqué, Uhland and Tieck in 'Mistress Joanna of Montfaucon'? Posnanski, in his graciousness, didn't expect that others might be educated in these matters too, but no one likes to be made to look like an ignorant boor, and less tolerant men than Lieutenant Winfried, the general's ADC, found the judge advocate's blethering rather offensive. 'I've got nothing against Jews,' Brigadier-General von Hesta (whose family had migrated from the Hungarian to the Prussian service in 1835) growled on one occasion. 'Nothing at all, so long as they knuckle down and keep their gobs shut. But when they worry away at this book stuff like a dog in a sandpit – out with them.' Should Dr Posnanski learn of such remarks, the corners of his mouth, much wider apart than those of most men, would twitch, he'd close one of his eyes, look heavenwards with the other and drily note: 'That's what comes of letting newcomers into the ways of the Mark. Let them play the Prussian as long as the likes of us have. They weren't there at Fehrbellin, they fought on the other side from Mollwitz to Torgau, and I didn't see them at Waterloo either – and that little chicklet wants to say his piece.' Indeed, his friends admired in him a certain philosophical calm, which came from an understanding of how slowly civilisation progresses and that people absorb that progress at a snail's pace. 'If I thought life under our changing moon would always remain as it is now, I'd breakfast on rat poison tomorrow and greet you in the evening from the fourth dimension.'

He said this one morning to Lieutenant Winfried. They were sitting in the cellar dugout of the Mairie in the village of Esnes, both on urgent business. It was to do with the relief of the division – a weighty matter. As Hill 304 and Mort Homme could testify, the Lychow Army Group had done its duty, and when it returned to the Russian front that had been its home since the start of the war, as it was about to do, it would be able to inscribe certain names from the Battle of the Somme in its group register. While in France, it had bored a couple of tunnels in the rock – the Raven, Gallwitz, Bismarck and Lychow tunnels – and it would be leaving the 'West of the Meuse' sector in excellent condition. For as everyone knew, from the infantry to the general staff, who were inclined to make up their own minds about army commanders, General von Lychow asked a lot of his men but nothing unnecessary. Yes, Old Lychow still enjoyed the confidence of the men. And when the French took the left bank of the Meuse in August 1917, and those tunnels were full of dead Germans, a number of the officers around the crown prince expressed the view that it wouldn't have happened under Lychow...

The two men were occupied with completely different matters. While Lieutenant Winfried was to inform His Excellency of conditions in the sector that was to be evacuated next, Posnanski was to investigate a break-in at the provision stores in Esnes; responsibility for it was being passed back and forth among units, and no one wanted to admit it was them. 'From the point of view of who's hungry, it was all of them,' said Posnanski earnestly, 'but the main culprit was probably the name of the place. Because although that's not how the French say it, our men pronounce it "Essen". And having said the German word for food, they want to have some.'

'Posnanski,' groaned Winfried, 'have you no sympathy?'

'I do indeed. For example with my clerk Adler who's quaking with fear in case he is sent to be medically re-evaluated for active service.'

'Is he going to be re-evaluated? God help him.'

Posnanski's bald, knobbly head bobbed in concern: 'It's a shame because he was a good lawyer and it's a double shame because he had training. I suppose I'll have to find another one.'

'There's plenty of choice,' said Lieutenant Winfried. He was studying the battle history of a particular battalion whose commander was to be put in charge of the rear guard.

'Less than people think. I require certain moral aptitudes, and they don't grow on trees.'

'Seek and ye shall find,' murmured the ADC, trying to decipher some reports written in half rubbed-out pencil: 12-18.XII.16, extremely critical days...

'I hope you know how the quotation continues,' said Posnanski, getting ready to go.

'How?' said Winfried, his pale eyes meeting the dark grey ones of his stout friend.

'Knock and it shall be opened unto you.'

Winfried laughed. 'Right. Have a private word with Sergeant-Major Pont. I'll be in reserve.'

'Thanks,' said Posnanski cheerfully. 'And as you're in such a giving mood, when can I have the car for a little official trip? I'm hearing strange noises from the Dannevoux field hospital.'

'Laurenz Pont is the man for that.'

'Good afternoon, then,' said Posnanski expansively.

As he climbed the narrow staircase, moving slowly in the gloom because of his extreme myopia and astigmatism, he steeled himself for the distressing interview to come. Waiting upstairs was his clerk Adler, once a barrister at the High Court in Berlin... he quickly pushed the thought aside. Odd how things happened in pairs. He'd had two enquiries from the same field hospital on two successive days. First, the medical officer wanted to complain about the shoes issued to a particular ASC private and asked how best he might do this; secondly, a wounded lieutenant asked for a interview regarding a serious miscarriage of justice committed against his younger brother, killed in action. As he grasped the handrail then make his way across the rubble-strewn courtyard, Posnanski marvelled at people's inextinguishable need for justice. In the middle of a war, when civilisation had long since broken down and was about as dilapidated as that Mairie over there, people still railed, in defiance of the gross injustice all around, against incidents that might have screamed unfairness to the heavens in peacetime but now counted as little more than minor irregularities. And it was good that they did so. For that unswerving compulsion provided the only means of bridging the abyss of the war years and creating a world worth living in.

'Good afternoon, Herr Adler,' said Posnanski.

Judge Advocate Posnanski's uniform had a high collar, purple tabs, officer's epaulettes and a dagger. His tunic strained almost as tightly round his stomach as did Colonel Stein's, and he wore the same leather puttees round his calves. For these reasons, Bertin stood to attention in his presence, which rather turned Dr Posnanski against him.

The medical officer, Dr Münnich, a man in his fifties with bristling grey hair and grey eyes, had cut his interview short by producing the shoes in which Private Pahl had been admitted to hospital: a hole in the middle of the left sole and the tip of the right one as good as gone. Dr Münnich had a tendency to flush, which made his duelling scars stand out. He spoke in a very controlled way but liked to tear the objects of his wrath up by the roots – which, as can be imagined, had made him a difficult but respected colleague in Liegnitz in Silesia in peacetime and wherever his division was stationed in wartime. He explained that he considered it unnecessary to increase the hospital population in this way and considered a battalion commander who allowed this to happen unnecessary and would like to make that clear to the gentleman. However, the division in question came under the 'other bank' – headquarters in Damvillers. How to bridge that gulf?

Dr Posnanski smiled thinly. There had been tensions between the Eastern and Western Groups since His Excellency von Lychow had stated that no captain under the command of the General Staff should have risked confining the attack to the right bank, even if experienced corps commanders had said that their Brandenburgers could manage it on their lonesome. This tart criticism, uttered on the evening of Pierrepont, had been instantly conveyed, as is customary among comrades, to the commander of the Eastern Group. He had merely sniffed contemptuously and asked what an Eastern front bunny rabbit like Lychow was meant to know about operations in France. Since then the two officers had been rather off with each other, had avoided meeting and enjoyed putting little difficulties in each other's way. Dr Posnanski was generally considered to be a peaceable man, but he understood how power worked. If His Excellency Lychow happened to be in a good mood, then it would be easy to free his clerk Adler from the clutches of the murder commission. He'd just have to be transferred to a fighting regiment, the radio operators or telegraphists. If that happened straight away and with his Excellency's blessing, then none of his well-meaning colleagues would have time to denounce him. If Posnanski introduced these boots in a joking way, they might amuse the great man, who could then forward them to the proud gentleman on the right bank with an appropriate dedication. And so Posnanski had the offending objects wrapped up and told the doctor he'd see to them. That done, he asked for somewhere to have a conversation with Lieutenant Kroysing undisturbed.

Undisturbed would be difficult, explained the medical officer. Every corner of his barracks was in use. But then something occurred to him. One of his nurses, the most able as it happened, had asked for a room to herself when she joined them – just a little corner with a window and a bed, so that she could be by herself from time to time. And as she was actually a colonel's wife and therefore enjoyed a certain influence, they had cleared out a room for her that the hospital orderlies kept their buckets and brooms in. A window was cut in the barracks wall, and Sister Kläre had gladly taken up residence. 'She's one of the quiet, warm-hearted ones, who's been through a lot herself and therefore understands what other people need,' explained Dr Münnich. As they were busy and it was all hands on deck, the small room would definitely be free. Luckily, the cold snap had broken a few days ago, as well it might have given the time of year, so the gentlemen wouldn't freeze – there was of course no stove in the room.

Sister Kläre wasn't exactly overjoyed when asked for her room. But she nodded, went in first and turned a picture to the wall that was hanging above the bed. The crucifix at the head of the bed stayed where it was. The patient Kroysing could lie down. One of the gentleman could sit beside him, and the other would have to stand. The other, naturally, was Bertin, who had been phoned for in plenty of time and had just arrived from work, dog tired and still starving. But he was so intimidated by the presence of this high-ranking officer called Judge Advocate Posnanski that he initially said nothing at all, only stuttering out a shy request for bread and to be allowed to sit down. This too made a bad impression on Posnanski. This man who was of the same religion as him was lazy and greedy as a pig. He was a pathetic sight sitting there on the floor with his legs stretched out in front of him, shamelessly shovelling soup out of a large bowl and crumbling bread into it, all the while preventing more civilised people from smoking and getting comfortable. With his sticky-out ears and damaged front teeth, he was hardly an adornment to the Prussian army. Furthermore, in his excitement over this decisive meeting, Kroysing had laid so much weight on Bertin's testimony when introducing him ('...and this is my friend Bertin, who spoke to my brother the day before he died and will tell you what he learnt from him...') that Dr Posnanski, never much good at remembering names, had completely failed to note this one. Lieutenant Kroysing, whom Posnanski had liked at once, began to speak, and the lawyer listened. The room was as white and narrow as a ship's cabin, and as soon as the witness laid down his spoon it was also equally smoky. For Posnanski had put his cigar case on Sister Kläre's bedside table for people to help themselves. Kroysing's deep voice vibrated through the clouds of tobacco smoke. Posnanski asked questions, and Bertin listened. This was the story of Sergeant Kroysing and his brother, Lieutenant Kroysing, who had done battle with that dwarf Niggl in the dripstone caves and hideouts of Douaumont mountain, only to have the pesky little gremlin snatched away from him by the French attack, overhasty orders and thick fog. And now Bertin was smoking a stogie such as he hadn't enjoyed since his wedding, and that wedding seemed to belong to another world beyond the River Acheron, the world of the living where his sweet and lovely wife was getting thinner and thinner because even gods and goddesses starved in those iron-hard times. How did those verses go that he'd read at university from the ancient Norse Edda about doom fulfilled? 'I was snowed on with snow, and smitten with rain, And drenched with dew; long was I dead.' Did that apply to Christoph Kroysing, Sergeant Süßmann or Paul Schanz? In any case, there he was squatting like a beggar on the floorboards of a strange woman's bedroom, ready to fall asleep... The weariness of spring, the waxing moon, and the goods train on the siding at Vilosnes-East station growing longer...

'Hm,' grumbled Posnanski. 'Our witness is asleep.' Bertin really had sunk forward, arms round his knees supporting his head.

'Please don't wake him yet,' said Kroysing. 'He hasn't got much to laugh about.' And he quickly explained how and where he'd met Bertin, about the work he had to do, the injustices he'd suffered and his visits to Kroysing. It was a mean sort of life for a lawyer and a writer; no one liked to fall outside their caste.

At the words 'lawyer and writer' Posnanski pricked up his ears like a startled hare. 'Bertin?' he repeated incredulously, almost in disgust. 'Werner Bertin?'

'Hush!' whispered Kroysing, but the sleeping man had started up at the sound of his name as if he'd been kicked. 'Yessir, Sergeant,' he said, and then opening his eyes: 'Oh, please excuse me... We were hauling wet crates of powder on our backs. There are still clumps of earth on my boots.'

Posnanski was still looking at him in shock. 'Did you write the *Man called Hilner*?'

'How come you know it? It was banned.'

'And *Love at Last Sight*?'

'Well, what do you know!' said Bertin, suddenly cheering up.

'And *The Chessboard: Twelve Stories*?'

'The judge advocate is the first person I've ever met who's read that book.'

Posnanski nodded. 'Lawyers, stockbrokers and ladies: they read everything, you know.'

Bertin laughed happily and said he'd thought the reading public was mainly school children and students. If that were the case, writers would starve, said Posnanski, and that must be avoided at all costs. 'And now, my dear colleague,

I'd like to hear your report. What happened to Sergeant Kroysing and what do you know about him?'

When Bertin had finished silence hung in the room as heavily as the smoke. 'Don't get your hopes up,' said Posnanski. 'As a private individual I believe you and Herr Bertin implicitly. As a lawyer and judge, unfortunately I must alight on the flaw – if I may mix my metaphors – that the witness can only state what he heard from your brother, but who can prove that your brother described the situation accurately? That he didn't embellish and see enemies who wanted to persecute him in a perfectly standard military order? Had Herr Niggl signed a confession but then convinced the court that you had forced him to sign in fear of his life, then we could have countered that objection and supported your brother's subjective view with Herr Bertin's testimony and statements from the Third Company, and thereby proved what we are convinced is true. Think about it,' and he rose, agitated, and stomped the four paces from the window to the door and back again, hands behind his back, his bald pate thrust forwards. 'We're up against it. We have the truth, and it's believable and convincing. You both strike me as entirely reliable witnesses who have described the incident accurately, and God knows the incident itself is as clear as Pythagoras' theorem. But to prove what you say to a reluctant court of the accused's officers and peers: that's another matter entirely.'

Kroysing sat up in bed, letting his bandaged leg hang down, which he was not supposed to do. 'So is the whole business going to come to nothing? Bloody hell!' he almost spat. 'What's the point of society supporting lawyers, then?'

Posnanski leapt to his profession's defence. 'It's definitely worth society's while supporting lawyers and supporting them – as you insinuate – rather comfortably. But let's not fight, Lieutenant. Let's try to work this through because compromise is the best lawyer. Give me the file from the preliminary enquiry. I'll send for the papers and look into the case. In the meantime, think about whether you want to bring a complaint against Niggl and his accomplices for abuse of military authority resulting in a man's death. Eat well, sleep well, get well and recover your spirits, and then write and tell me your decision. If you want to fight for justice, then do so, and I'll help you and so will this young gentleman, though he will be taking the biggest risk of all of us. But it won't be an easy battle. If you cannot prove your case, you'll be in a terrible position and the stain of it will stay with you for the rest of your life. Right, now get me the file.'

Kroysing raised himself up, his good foot in a slipper, his wounded leg bandaged up to the knee, his torso slung between the crutches from the padded supports under his armpits (to Bertin, it was a pitiful sight – Eberhard Kroysing on crutches!) and left the room.

'Now as regards yourself,' said Posnanski in a businesslike tone. 'You obviously can't stay where you are. Are you fit for active service?'

'No, I was declared unfit long ago on account of my eyes and my heart,' said Bertin.

'Good. I'm having to give up my clerk. I shall ask for you.'

Bertin sat there wide-eyed in his overcoat and scarf, his worn cap beside him. 'But,' he stuttered, 'my training, my situation... I struggled to understand your exposition of the case earlier.'

'My good man,' cried Posnanski, 'say yes and be quick about it. You don't get a chance like this every day. Can you type? No. You'll learn in two weeks. Give me your unit's address. And then this evening won't have been a complete waste of time.'

And as Bertin was still staring at him in confusion – could something so incredible happen so easily? (*He's been driven demented*, thought Posnanski compassionately) – he added: 'But please don't mention this to anyone or it'll go wrong, as we superstitious types know. How much leave do you get at the moment?'

'Four days,' replied Bertin, touching the floor. Still made of deal floorboards, so he wasn't dreaming. 'As a thank you, sir,' he said falteringly, 'may I offer you a report about my meeting with young Kroysing? It's actually written as novel,' he added almost guiltily. 'That's to say, it's going to be a novel – the only thing I've written since I've been a soldier. If you would like to keep these few pages here..'

Posnanski extended a grateful hand. 'I won't keep it. No gifts, my dear man. But I'll definitely read it.'

CHAPTER FOUR

Sister Kläre

THERE WAS A knock. Sister Kläre appeared in front of Kroysing, but recoiled in mock horror, crying in Russian, 'My God' (*Bozhe moy*), then asked in her Rhenish accent if there was actually anyone there as it was impossible to see. She yanked the window open and flung the tarboard shutters wide.

'Turn the light out, toad face, if you want to see the view,' growled a deep, angry voice. And Kroysing turned the switch.

'You're not in Douaumont now,' said Sister Kläre sharply. 'The French airmen have got better things to do than to mess about here.'

'If only she weren't so pretty,' said Kroysing apologetically to the others.

The landscape beyond the small window was bathed in the soft glow of twilight. From the ridge, the hospital overlooked the valley, which was shrouded in the spring night: the half-risen moon, mysterious stars glittering in the haze and the winding Meuse, glowing faintly between its dark sloping banks with their flecks of light. Only a faint flicker and rumble betrayed the existence of the front. The four of them crowded round the window and hungrily breathed in the pure air of approaching spring. The Meuse was still spectacularly frozen, but the warm breeze was unmistakably from the south. Sister Kläre folded her hands. 'If only people weren't so insane,' she sighed. 'I always have to remind myself that it's not the Mosel, somewhere behind Trier. Why can't the enemy just give in? Then we'd all be home by Easter and we could start to forget the war.'

'Better not,' said Bertin, then seeing Sister Kläre's wide eyes: 'Forget, I mean. People forget much too quickly.' He stopped talking, realising he wouldn't find the right words.

'No, no,' joked Posnanski, 'we won't forget this one. We'll dress it up in patriotic colours and nice little rosy cheeks for future generations.'

'I'll be interested to see how you're going to manage that,' blinked Kroysing. 'But beforehand, let me share my humble experiences with you. In the spring of 1915, on the Flanders front, we were facing the British and were pretty close to them when we installed our gas canisters – we had the honour of being the first gas company. From February to April we slept cosied up to those large iron canisters. One time one of them leaked, and I saw the damage in the morning in the shape of 45 sappers, dead and blue. And when we did a test explosion with the bloody things on the drill ground and carried the pieces home, every man who'd touched them entered the hereafter too. They died slowly. When I was in the hospital at Jülich with my first wound I met some of them. They died off, and no one really knew why. The doctors were very upset about it, but, hey ho, they still died. End of the line, alight here. Anyway, there we were waiting in our waterlogged trenches for a favourable wind. We kept having to relocate the canisters because they kept getting stuck in the clay. There were no gas masks back then. We were supposed to protect ourselves from the bloody stuff by shoving cotton wool in our noses. The Tommies kept throwing over cheery little notes, asking if the big stink was ever going to start. They were bursting with curiosity, they wrote. And then finally an east wind came, and we blew our gas over and the Tommies were curious no more. Their trenches were full of blue-black corpses when we walked through them. Blue and black, Tommies and Frenchmen, lying peacefully side by side. There were at least 5,000 dead on the Poelkapelle cycle track, and the lucky ones, who'd only got a bit of the stuff and were still choking and spitting, they expired in Jülich, without ceremony, slowly, one by one. Well, it was an unpleasant episode, best buried as quickly as possible. We'll revisit it next time, when the only ammunition will be gas.'

'You're horrible, Kroysing,' said Sister Kläre. 'You always have to spoil everything. Haven't I got enough on my plate looking after your filthy wounds? Can't I spend five minutes soothing my soul with God's creation without one of you butting in? The next war! There won't be another war! If anyone threatens to go to war again after this massacre, our womenfolk will beat them to death with their brooms.'

'Let's hope so, sister,' said Posnanski with conviction.

'There won't be another war,' said Bertin, nodding. 'This is the last one. Our rulers can fight the next one on their own. We men won't be there.'

'Quite right!' cried Sister Kläre, wiping away a tear with the back of her index finger. She had been thinking of her husband, Colonel Schwersenz, a once proficient staff officer who had been sinking ever deeper into depression since the winter of 1914 and was now being cared for by her mother, the elderly Frau Pidderit, in a small hunting lodge in Hinterstein valley in the Bavarian Allgäu. Only the medical officer knew Sister Kläre's story and real name. She was generally thought to be the plucky wife of a captain somewhere on the Eastern front, and there were whispered rumours about a flirtation with a very high-ranking personage.

Kroysing, towering above them all, his mouth set in a sarcastic line, shrugged his shoulders: 'Then we have the honour of living through the funeral of the last war. It didn't really have a very long career, war – a mere 5,000 years. It was born in the time of the Assyrians and ancient Egyptians, and we're putting it in its coffin. The world has been waiting for us. The people who ran the Thirty Years' War, the Seven Years' War and the Napoleonic Wars didn't know what they were doing. We folks from the 1914 war are the ones to sort it out – we of all people.'

'That's right,' said Sister Kläre and Bertin in defiant unison. However, Bertin couldn't help but see a grave and them all as grave diggers standing round it, spades in hand: Kroysing, the nurse, the fat judge advocate, and he himself, outlined against the cloudy sky, hacking at clods of earth. Below them bulged a bloated belly and a plump, hairless face with a grin across its chubby cheeks beneath its closed eyes – perhaps portentous, perhaps a sign of contentment at its own demise.

Meanwhile, Sister Kläre closed first the shutters then the window. 'Now put the light on and then you can go,' she said.

They all blinked as the light bounced off the walls. 'We'd all like to thank you for your kind hospitality,' said Judge Advocate Posnanski, bowing over Sister Kläre's long, strong hand, calloused by work. A strand of ash blonde hair escaped from her nun-like head covering. Beneath it shone her beautifully set eyes. Her alluring, tender lips were obdurately closed. *Hell of a lovely little thing with her Madonna face and pert lips*, thought Kroysing. *Very likely she did have a thing with the crown prince.* He felt the need to improve his standing with her. 'What would I get, sister—'

'You'd get nothing,' she interrupted, eyes flashing. 'You'd get a punch on the nose.'

'—if I dished up something extra nice for you? Allow me to introduce you to my friend Werner Bertin...' – Sister Kläre stopped in the middle of the room, her lips slightly parted and her hands outstretched as if to push him away – '... author of the much-read novel *Love at Last Sight.*'

Sister Kläre's trained eyes took in Bertin's grey-brown face, drawn cheeks, bristly chin, the rim of slack, dirty skin above his worn and muddy lice-infested collar. When he laughed in embarrassment, she saw he had a gap in his teeth and a broken front tooth and that he was going bald on top. And yet there was something about his eyebrows, his forehead, his hands, which suggested that Kroysing wasn't joking. This man had written that tender love story! 'It's you,' she said quietly, offering him her hand. 'I can't believe it. And my friend Annemarie in Krefeld wrote to me three months ago to say that she had met the author and he was a Hussar lieutenant and a charming man.'

Bertin laughed in disgust at this, and Posnanski and Kroysing laughed at his disgust, and they all left Sister Kläre's nun's cell like a cheerful party breaking up. Now she could sleep in the room again, she said, adding that Bertin should visit her the next day when she would be off duty.

'Well be in touch,' said Posnanski, bringing the memorable meeting to a close.

CHAPTER FIVE

Counterproposal

THE BLACKBIRDS WERE singing as Judge Advocate Posnanski got out of his car at Montfaucon castle. After some thought, he had decided to let the package with Private Pahl's shoes in it disappear without trace so as not to complicate his request for Private Bertin to be transferred to the Lychow division court martial of the Eastern Group. But he could have spared himself these reflections. Sometimes documents such as his request took weeks to arrive, other times only days. This one was passed very quickly from the Western to the Eastern Group, where it was eyed suspiciously in the ADC's office and a query scrawled across it in blue pencil: was ASC battalion X/20 in a position to give up any of its men? That meant: kindly say that you are not in a position to do so. As well as the usual hostilities, the transfer of the Lychow division to the Russian front played a decisive role in this. The rivalry between the fronts was gathering momentum. The new Supreme Command had not been able to change this, and the two staffs rejoiced – General Schieffenzahn's word – only in each other's setbacks.

When the imposing folio sheet with the teal and violet seals of the two quarrelling army groups was placed in front of Major Jansch, he first removed a yellow sweet from his mouth and stuck it to the edge of a saucer on his right. When he realised that behind the polite, typewritten text lay an attempt to wrest one of his men from him, and furthermore this particular man, he gave a hiss of fury that made his clerk Diehl's blood run cold. However, the blue-pencilled query, whose meaning Jansch immediately divined, calmed him down. 'Take this down,' he said to Diehl, standing up and striding round the room with his hands behind his back as Bonaparte was said to have done. Eventually, after many improvements and deletions, he dictated the following text: 'Returned to sender with the following remarks: the battalion's First Company occupies the area between Mureaux-Ferme and Vilsones-East, and its working parties large and small are scattered across it. The company is so weakened by casualties and illness that it cannot countenance the departure of a single healthy man fit for work if there is no replacement. The battalion proposes that Private Pahl, currently in Dannevoux field hospital, should, when recovered, be detailed for the required duty at the court martial. P., a typesetter by trade and exceptionally able, knows how to use a typewriter and is unfit for anything but office work due to the loss of a toe.' He felt the distinguished gentlemen had miscalculated.

The clerk Diehl left the major's room and descended the stone steps to the orderly room. As far as he was concerned, his most important duty was to get through his servile existence under that sweet-guzzling old whinger until peace came and return to his wife and child in Hamburg come what may. He felt a lot of comradely sympathy for Private Bertin and wished him well. Anything would have suited Bertin better than collecting duds with Sergeant Barkopp, and now he was going to be done out of a good opportunity in that smooth, hypocritical way that powerful men's protégés could be pushed aside by those who were protected by equally powerful men. Diehl stopped at the landing window halfway down the stairs, looked at the court martial's application, which he'd been the first to read that morning, and carried on out into the pale spring light gilding the streets and roofs of Damvillers. He knew nothing of the war between the two army groups, and the Eastern Group's request seemed reasonable to him, though he spotted the guile in Jansch's reply. It couldn't be helped, he decided, walking on: once jinxed, always jinxed, poor lad. Even a blind man could see that he'd pulled some strings to get this transfer. It he found out quickly enough that it had been refused, then he could perhaps – perhaps – think of a way round it, though Diehl couldn't think what that way might be. He was a primary school teacher, a man with a great deal of respect for books and writers of books, and he felt he should try to help. As he rang the doorbell and stepped into the overheated orderly room, which smelt of men and tobacco, he decided what to do. He opened the typewriter. But before slipping the folio page of the Western Group's court martial through the roller, he laid a sheet of blue copy paper and a thin sheet of carbon paper beneath it, as was normal practice. If someone sent the carbon to Bertin at lunchtime, he would know what to expect. The typewriter tapped, tinkled and tapped again. The folio sheet was taken out and slipped into the file for signature and the thin carbon copy was placed in a drawer. Everything was going like clockwork. Diehl didn't even notice that he was breathing more heavily than normal.

In the meantime, Major Jansch telephoned his friend Niggl. Yes, they had become friends. They had eradicated the Main frontier, and Prussia and Bavaria had risen as one empire, dedicated to the overthrow of its malign adversaries. Every morning, they congratulated each other on the recently sunk merchant tonnage and thought they heard the edifice of the British Empire cracking within its boundaries. Every morning, they agreed that French discipline was weakening, the Italian attacks were making them a laughing stock and one could only shrug at the Americans' big talk. The Russians were on their knees and would soon vanish from the map of Europe: the revolution had finished them off. No danger of bumping into them again in the Balkans or the Near East. Victory was finally within Germany's grasp. When the concentrated might of the German army was unleashed on the Western front and that of the Austro-Hungarians on the southern front, that would be it – and then it would be the turn of those who pulled the strings behind the scenes: Free Masons and speculators, Jesuits, socialists and Jews.

Niggl listened to his clever friend with profound admiration. He was quite right, said Niggl. You couldn't argue with a word of what he said. And there would be a remedy that got rid of the Free Masons and Jews just as there was for everything else.

Yes, replied Herr Jansch, sounding both triumphant and concerned, but it would require quite a bit of work, because they were as thick as thieves and if you wanted to see what they could do you need look no further than the fiery warning of the Russian revolution. Jewish bankers had vowed to bring down Tsarism at the behest of the Alliance Israélite and had armed the Japanese against the mighty Russian empire 10 years previously. That time they'd failed, but they didn't mean to fail this time.

So, asked Niggl naïvely, had Germany been doing the Jews' work against Russia?

Major Jansch, for a moment nonplussed, said you couldn't exactly say that. The situation did indeed shed a bright light on just how devilishly clever the Jews were, but also on their basic stupidity, because in the Germans they had finally found a superior adversary, who saw through them and would make sure they were cheated of their profits this time. That very day, he, Jansch, had, not without difficulty, repelled a Jewish attack. Some Jew, a scandal in itself, was judge advocate for Group West. No sooner had he found a little Jewish writer within the ASC than he had wanted to pick him out, probably at the expense of a decent German, and the unsuspecting army commander had given his blessing to this scheme. Jansch was vigilant, however, and Bertin, the author in question, would be blue in the face before he'd be allowed to skive off useful work and loaf about. It was the same man who'd already put on a little show for them, as his friend Niggl might remember. That time he'd wanted to go on leave; now he was trying another ruse.

At the other end of the line, Captain Niggl, soon to be Major Niggl, cleared his throat, stuttered something in reply, and asked to be excused for a moment as someone had just come in with a question. The combination of 'Bertin' and 'court martial' had momentarily taken his breath away. All too clearly did he see again the dreadful vaults of Douaumont, the gaunt figure of the dastardly Kroysing, who unfortunately hadn't been killed but was lying in a field hospital with a harmless leg wound. *Damn him, damn him*, he thought. *By the Holy Crucifix, may he never rise again, the miserable dog.* He would donate a candle as big as his arm to the Ettal monastery or the Pilgrimage Church in Alt-Ötting if Kroysing and all his cronies came to horrible end. Then he picked up the receiver again and said he couldn't wait to hear how his comrade had sorted the Jew out.

Moving his yellow sweet over to his left cheek, Herr Jansch described with a giggle the replacement he had generously offered – a decent man who'd been wounded, a Christian typesetter. In any case, it was well known that His Excellency Lychow was moving back to the east again. In a fortnight, or even 10 days, it would all be over.

CHAPTER SIX

Night-time reading

JUDGE ADVOCATE POSNANSKI received the Kroysing files from the Montmédy court martial and ASC battalion X/20's negative decision on the same morning via the staff records office. Every man in Montfaucon who came into contact with that piece of paper had a laugh at it. Sergeant Major Pont laughed at it as he put it in the judge advocate's in-tray, and the judge advocate himself laughed, as did his clerk Sergeant Adler, despite the pressure he was under. Even the orderly, Gieseken from the Landsturm, burst out laughing when he saw the document, observing: 'Whoever wrote this is some man. We've got a hard neck here in the Prussian army – and that's for sure.'

The only man who didn't laugh but was furious was Colonel Winfried, Excellency Lychow's ADC and nephew. He was angry at the lack of respect for his uncle, at the sheer insolence of the ASC major on the other bank and above all that the refusal would have to stand. 'If Dr Posnanski thinks we're going to let this matter detain us he's got another think coming. Another time, we might have taken it up, but we don't have the time right now to start doing callisthenics and going on the warpath against Group East. He'll have to magic up a replacement as his clerk.'

Sergeant Major Pont, a thickset master builder from Kalkar on the lower Rhine, smiled a knowing smile and said: 'I'm of the view that we will not be spared this Herr Bertin. That's what my nose tells me.' And he pressed his thumb to his squat nose. 'Lawyers can work magic.' And as proof he told the story of an advocate in Cleves who had fought a firm of brick makers for a year and a half over two lorryloads of bricks and had nearly ruined it.

Lieutenant Winfried carried on going through some documents on the of the division's step-by-step transfer. 'Posnanski will have to handle it himself. I'm not going to bother His Excellency. He's already back in his beloved east, sniffing lakes and pine woods from his window. If the French don't put a spoke in our wheels, we'll be gone in a fortnight and Group East can... shed a tear for us.'

Sergeant Major Pont stuck out his lower lip and murmured something about how far away they'd soon be from the lower Rhine, then veered into saying he'd like to go on a three-day official trip so he might visit his mother. Lieutenant Winfried replied crisply that the sergeant major's desire was God's desire, adding only that he would like him back five days before the staff departed.

Pont thanked him profusely and immediately consulted the railway map to work out the best place for him and his wife Luise to meet. He loved her, and she was the centre of his life.

In the early evening, Judge Advocate Dr Posnanksi sat at the round table in his chilly living room, which actually belonged to the pharmacist Jovin and his wife but had been removed from them by the town headquarters at Montfaucon and given to the judge advocate as his billet. The room was full of solid, old-fashioned furniture and artefacts. The lamp stood on a high alabaster pedestal and shed a mellow light through a pleated silk shade. The paintings on the wall were rustic renderings of members of Madame Jovin's family, peasants, who had not been slow to seize their chance when the aristocracy's estates were partitioned immediately after the revolution. The Jovins had a son in the field and a married daughter in Paris and under constant threat from enemy Zeppelins. Their interaction with their compulsory lodger was limited to a dozen words daily. But compared to some of his predecessors, they found this German officer tactful and not unlikeable. Madame Jovin occasionally remarked to her husband that the way he lived was almost French, praise which Monsieur Jovin felt he must circumscribe with an 'Oh là là'. But Dr Posnanski was at home a lot, he drank black coffee and red wine in the evening, and he loved books and took his work back to his quarters, which he had left unchanged. He was domesticated, frugal, moderate and industrious, and he didn't have the dreadful habit of smoking cigars, which left the curtains, tapestries and carpets hopelessly saturated with tobacco. Madame Jovin could not have wished for a more agreeable intruder for the duration of this dreadful war.

Posnanski, in an old brown tweed house jacket, laid his cigar in its white holder on the pewter ashtray from time to time and stretched his slippered feet under the table. The only military item in his clothing were his long, grey trousers with red piping. His thick neck bulged from an open shirt with no buttons or collar, and the Kroysing files lays scattered on Madame Jovin's elegant walnut table. The Bertin affair glimmered on the edge of his awareness; it would be sorted out later – or not. As intellect was not held in respect and there was no demand for men of good will, it would probably fall through. A lawyer had to be well-versed in injustice and not let it disconcert him. But this case was about the fundamentals of coexistence. He had already established the legal facts in conversation with the brother and accuser. There was no conclusive proof in these papers that the younger Kroysing had been deliberately got rid of because of misappropriated foodstuffs – because meat, butter, ham, sugar and beer had not ended up in the right stomachs but the wrong ones. If there were no other cases and he'd had all the time in the world to become obsessed with this one, he would have questioned the men individually, forced the NCOs to confess, artfully pumped the orderly room and the company and battalion commanders for information about the normal duration of outpost duty and how often men were relieved, and then examined the question of why young Kroysing had not been given leave to appear before the court martial and why the files had been sent to Ingolstadt. All that having been established, the witness Bertin could have marched in and read out young Kroysing's letter and testament. With his advocate's oratory, bolstered by genuine conviction, he could then have forced the judges to see that such activities could not go unpunished as that would only encourage them. Advocate Posnanski was confident he could have brought such a case to a happy conclusion with the public behind him and the nation avidly following the matter for weeks, passionately debating whether there had been a cover-up or the officers were just carrying out their duties – in other words in peacetime.

Peacetime! Posnanski leant back in his chair and snorted derisively. In peacetime, this Kroysing case would have been a sure-fire route to victory and fame. Could something like that happen in peacetime? Of course it could. If you replaced the ASC battalion with a large industrial concern that clothed and fed its workers through its own canteens and shops, housed them and provided medical care, then the opportunities for corruption and profiteering at the expense of the mass of the workers would be just as great as in the Prussian army. If you put Kroysing in the overalls of an apprentice and future engineer, assigned him to dangerous work until his knowledge of a crime was extinguished by an industrial accident – an industrial accident helped along ever so slightly by cunning people in the know – then you pretty much had the exact sequence of events as Posnanski was convinced they had occurred. But woe betide the employers if such a thing happened in their company. In a well-governed nation they'd go to jail; in a nation where the exploited were on the march there would be a mass uprising whose effects would be felt deep into the middle classes; in Britain or France new parliamentary elections and a change of government would be required. Even in the German Fatherland, such a case would have far-reaching political consequences; none of the ruling groups would dare to back the guilty parties. An experienced reader of Berlin newspapers could easily imagine the tone that the conservative, liberal and even social democratic press would take. In peacetime.

It was very quiet in the house. Somewhere a mouse rustled behind the ancient wallpaper. Posnanski drank a mouthful of wine – he was using a porcelain beaker on three lion's feet that made the wine look a darker red – and rose to move about as he thought.

That was all true for industrial areas, cities. But what form would the case take if it happened among farm workers out in the sticks on the big estates of West Prussia, Posen, East Prussia, Pomerania and Mecklenburg? He brooded over this, his hooded eyes half closed, stopping on a woven shepherd's scene from the 18th century in which he could make out nothing but a narrow mesh of different coloured stitches, until gradually it revealed itself to be a representation of a human foot above a leafy plant. In a country setting, clarification would be more difficult and there would be more of a threat to the lawyer and witnesses. Some of them would be discredited as Jews, but the conclusion would be the same. The conservative Protestant landlords of the region east of the Elbe, the feudal Catholic landowners of Bavaria: they wouldn't aid and abet such rash employees either and in the end would sacrifice their incompetent peers. But in wartime injustice piled up, committed by one nation on another – violence unleashed by one group on another – and became such a mountain that a bucketful of filth simply disappeared. The naked interests of life were so fully at play, the question of the existence and survival of the ruling classes, and therefore, admittedly, the ruled as well, that an individual's right to life and honour was postponed until further notice – shifted on to a siding until civilisation was reinstated. Of course that signified a relapse into the times of the migrations, a decisive defeat for the Mosaic Convenant. Captain Niggl's reckless dirty tricks, his trading in human life, was currently being carried out (if the mutual recriminations in the war bulletins were to be believed) with little better justification on the largest possible scale and on all fronts by many of the great nations – don't bother asking after individuals, dear lawyer. And as all the groups concerned daily affirmed that they were fighting only to save their existence and human culture, a civilian such as Dr Posnanski had no influence at the moment. All he could do was advise Lieutenant Kroysing to wait until peace was re-established, get the names and addresses of as many of his brother's comrades as possible now and bring his case as soon as the German nation, its lust for victory notwithstanding, was ready to rekindle the memory of Christoph Kroysing.

Dr Posnanski was now haunted by his figure. He'd read his letter and taken it on board. Then in deepening silence he'd studied his black notebook, which contained drawings, scraps of verse, thoughts, opinions, impressions, questions. To begin with Posnanski had been interested in the notebook because of a particular hobby of his: he loved shorthand, which he considered to be a valuable and sensible invention; he knew all the systems and ways of abbreviating and even at school had excelled at deciphering unknown handwriting. Even the style of Kroysing's pencil strokes appealed to his inner being. An honest, clear-minded man had made those marks, and his good opinion was confirmed on every page by the content of the notebook. Young Kroysing had been someone. He had campaigned against injustice not with a particular end in mind, but simply because it was injustice – an ugly blemish on the body of the community he loved. A pure and wonderful love of Germany spoke from that young man. He didn't have an heroically distorted vision of his nation. He saw its weaknesses. 'I don't understand,' he once complained, 'why our men let themselves be manipulated. They're not dim-witted or without a sense of justice, but they're almost more sensitive than women. Are we a feminine nation? Is it our fate simply to know what ails us and express it? If so, I don't want to join in.' He clearly realised that the high moral development of German writers and thinkers had its roots in the nation. '...but it seems to me that root is long and fibrous and takes a convoluted route and only sends up a beautiful plant to the light much later and somewhere far away. I wish we had a short, strong tap root that sent up healthy growth full of spikes and stings against violence.' Another time he complained 'that the beauty of life as expressed in a sunset, a starry night or even just ordinary daylight doesn't seem to have any influence on the ways of the Germans. They enjoy nature for a couple of minutes and then fall back into old habits that might just as well have been developed in underground caves. But Goethe and Hölderlin, Mörike and Gottfried Keller, seem constantly aware of plants, wind, clouds, streams. The air of the countryside goes with them into their studies and offices, and to the lectern. That's why they're free. That's why they're great.' *Yes, my young friend*, thought Posnanski, *what you say there is very true and important. Such things cannot be learnt from working life. It's a shame that we can't talk about them any more. Men like you will be missed. Your verses are lovely and sensitive, though still very juvenile. But let us imagine that Hölderlin, who was a volunteer for a year, Sergeant Heinrich Heine, Lieutenant von Liliencron or Sergeant Major C.F. Meyer had been killed at your age – with assistance or otherwise, it doesn't matter – or that the little cadet von Hardenberg had died at 14 of a cold caught on a training march – to say nothing of officer trainee Schiller drowned at 18 while swimming in a mountain stream in Swabia: would those young men's legacy have looked much different from yours? Not at all. But how much poorer and more miserable the world would have been! We wouldn't have known what we'd lost.* 'Yes,' he sighed to himself, 'it's not an easy problem, and whoever can solve it for me gets a thaler and five Pfennigs: whether the people live for the gifted, or the gifted live for the people, so that any old Niggl has the right to abuse them. That's why I'm going to have a look and see what Herr Bertin made of his meeting with you.'

CHAPTER SEVEN

The Kroysing novella

AT THAT HE opened the manuscript that Bertin had sent him. He poured another glass of wine, lit another slim Dutch cigar, looked disapprovingly at Bertin's rather cramped handwriting, began to read the story, holding each sheet up to the light, and was quickly absorbed and captivated. The light cast a soft glow, the mouse rustled behind the wallpaper, people passed the window, talking, but Posnanski was now in Fosses wood in a hollow full of shot-up trees where two abandoned guns raised their long, mournful necks to the sky and amongst a group of workers in field grey he saw the tanned, friendly face of young Kroysing, his curved forehead and calm eyes. The work could hardly pass as a novella, since it contained no artful characterisation or surprising plot twists. Sometimes the language wasn't very polished, which could be excused by the speed of writing, or was too bold where a more restrained expression would've been more powerful. But it did invoke the figure of the man as perceived by the author and it showed what had happened clearly and pitilessly, shaking the world from its sleep so that it could not just snore on as a French shell dispatched the writer's recently won friend. And it made it quite clear that the burden of this death did not lie with the French. No, behind the miserable ASC chiefs lay the gigantic outline of the owners and unleashers of violence – all those who were planning and carrying out the suicide of Europe, those backward types who saw their neighbours only as something to attack and whose last trump card in international competition was: the gun.

The fact that Bertin had not invented names in this draft created an unusual and convincing effect. The hero was simply called Christoph, and other names were indicated by initial capital letters. At the end of the fourth page he found a note from the author to himself: 'Improve names.' But however essential it might be for artistic effect to invent credible characters and refine real events to bring out their essence, the relaxed handling of names and events meant this first draft spoke all the more directly to the lonely reader. Posnanski groaned in agony and also in satisfaction; under no circumstances should he let the unprepossessing Bertin get away. He belonged to the same group of men as young Kroysing and Posnanski himself: those who tried to sort the world out and using the right tools for the job – justice, reason and informed debate. It might seem laughable but it was true: whoever used those tools inevitably excited the anger of the evil principle and its minions, the men of violence with their feverish thirst for action and desire to oppress. And as Posnanksi buttoned his housecoat over his rotund body, because it was a cold March night and he was tired, to his amazement he found himself marching over to the fireplace at the far end of the room where embers still glowed. Marching because the glow embodied the enemy, the eternal foe of all creativity, the opponent and the opposition in one, the blocker, Satan himself. He literally saw him squatting there with claws, a beak, bat-like wings and a dragon's tail, casting around with his ambiguous basilisk's eyes, always on the brink of shrill laughter. It was this rash, devouring element, allied with ubiquitous steel, that had given birth to every technology and forged every gun, and whose omnipotent laughter lay behind every explosion. It had killed young Kroysing and wounded his older brother. It threatened Bertin in the form of duds, it had killed Judge Advocate Mertens in the form of an aerial bomb, it lurked over him, Posnanski, over Winfried, over that old Junker Lychow – over every man and every woman. Man had made a bad job of taming the fire that had fallen from Heaven; reason too, the light of Heaven, and morality, born on Mount Sinai, he had handled like a schoolboy. In that dark hour before bedtime, Posnanski was inclined to give the human race as a whole a mark of three minus. That made Pupil Bertin all the more indispensable. Fire had consumed Pupil Kroysing, and the same thing happened to countless others every day. It was sheeplike logic to plunge into the fire in ever greater numbers because of that and not bother about individuals because that had no purpose in such times. But Pupil Posnanski knew that there was a purpose and that it was the only purpose because it was always at hand; it didn't wait for the fire to go out but quietly smuggled the creative principle away from the destroyers. At present there was nothing to be done about the Kroysing case, and Posnanski carefully laid the various sheets of paper in the orange folder with a Montmédy file reference. He put the Kroysing novel in there too.

But the Bertin case was one to fight. He'd used the first half of the night well and he'd use the second half even better, because people were always much cleverer and more whole when asleep than when awake. And as Posnanski opened the window to spare Madame Jovin the worst of the bother, he said to himself: there are serious ways to rescue a man and funny ways, direct and indirect, honest and dishonest. They're all allowed. The only way that is proscribed is the one that doesn't work and puts him in more danger. Common sense and what he remembered from his last conversation with Lieutenant Winfried told Posnanski that he wouldn't be able to count on Lychow in this instance but should turn to his ADC (which he was wrong about). The only one he could rope in fully was Eberhard Kroysing, because it would be easy to make him see that the future shape of his campaign against Niggl stood or fell on Bertin's testimony. Sitting on the edge of his bed in his underpants, groaning, flushed and tight-lipped from the effort of reaching his sock suspenders over the bulk of his stomach, Posnanski came to a final decision: the main thing was to sort out the Bertin affair.

Then, when he was already in his pyjamas under his soft clean coverlet and had turned off the lamp, he noticed to his annoyance that he'd left the light on in the living room. Fire always resisted him, he thought, mocking himself grumpily, as get got up, fussed about with his slippers, went out and turned the light off. He noticed with amazement how bright the moon, now sinking in the west, shone through the window.

Once he was asleep and dreaming, he was transported to a fabulous landscape and there came to him the face of Christoph Kroysing, whom he'd never seen. It appeared surrounded by luxuriant southern foliage like the face of a man pushing through a jungle, and in the middle of the jungle resided the sleeping man – Posnanski, in rejuvenated form, fervently engaged in regulating the traffic on an anthill and in reaching, with the help of white termites, the ideal offered by the round public square and the Kaiser Wilhelm Memorial church outside his window. As if seen from the perspective of ants, the young sergeant's countenance hung like a large orb in the midst of bayonet-like agave leaves, which ended in a spike and were ridged with narrow little points, and palm fronds seemed to grab at his visored cap. Beneath the red ribbon and visor of his cap, Kroysing's steady, dark brown eyes were trained on Posnanski, who was busily working away, and there was a smile on his lips beneath his broad forehead and arching brows. 'As you can see, I was unfortunately detained, my dear colleague,' his voice said from far above the earth, and Posnanski, a chubby schoolboy crouched in the sand, replied: 'I hope you've got a note from your parents. You brown-eyed types are always playing truant and leaving us to do all the work. It's a typical sixth former's trick.'

'Oh, you poor thing. You've really changed,' said the young sergeant. 'Can't

314

you see that there'll be no leave for me?'

And then Posnanski recognised the fire burning among the plants: iron and oxygen had combined to set their green cells ablaze. 'A hundred years of purgatory will pass in no time,' he said reassuringly. And the man held prisoner by the plants agreed: 'War years count double.'

'I'll be your representative in the meantime, my dear colleague,' said Posnanski into a telephone attached to a green silk cord that he was now holding in his hand, and from far above, now transformed into a sort of moon but still connected to Posnanski's desk lamp by a long, twisted root, the prisoner spoke into the receiver: 'Affirmative.'

CHAPTER EIGHT

A cry for help

IT WAS A lucky thing for Private Bertin that the First Company's postal orderly never arrived from Etraye-East until the early hours of the afternoon. Otherwise he would have come to grief that day. There wasn't much left to crush in his soul, but such miserable little scraps of optimism and presence of mind as remained were obliterated by Diehl's carbon copy. He understood immediately what had happened and saw what it meant. This was the end. He'd had a bit of wild good luck and been applied for by a court martial – but because it was him, things didn't follow their natural course, and an ASC major was able to turn the request down and suggest a replacement who was no replacement at all. It was disgusting, it was enough to make you puke, to make you mutiny, to make you want to die. Would anyone keep trying after such a rebuff? Surely not. There was only one way out. He'd better go at once to Kroysing, to Sister Kläre, to people who knew him and wished him well, and who thought that he wasn't meant to hump crates of wet explosives around and break his back under a load that made the blood rush to his head and weighed 89 pounds even when dry. He gave himself a cursory wash, told Sergeant Barkopp he was going out and ran rather than walked up the familiar hill path, which was getting muddier each day but luckily froze over at night. Blind to the misty beauty of the early spring evening under a jade sky, he trudged on, getting worked up over a long letter and cry for help he was composing in his head to his wife Lenore – as if she were in a position to help. To the rhythm of his footsteps, his troubled heart let rip, spilling forth a confused, accusing mixture of self-pity and entreaties, based upon a pathetic overestimate of the influence his father-in-law could wield on his daughter's behalf.

That was how he consoled himself as he wished the hospital porter good evening, exchanging remarks about the weather. And although his cry for help showed a certain childishness, this sort of daydream did him good. It put him in a position to describe the matter to Eberhard Kroysing and his two room mates with the kind of casual self-mockery needed to maintain and if possible increase his esteem with the young officer.

In the meantime, because they shared a room and a common fate, Lieutenants Mettner and Flachsbauer had been let in on the matter that bound Bertin and Kroysing, gradually at first then completely – and during the long conversations that filled the endless expanse of days, some of Bertin's other experiences had been discussed, for example the bizarre outcome of Lieutenant von Roggstroh's medal recommendation. The two young officers roared with laughter, recognising the way the military worked; both of them had been robbed of the credit for valiant actions while some 'lazy bones' or other benefited. They thought that Bertin had behaved impeccably and warned him that he should under no circumstances make a hasty complaint or do anything stupid. He could safely leave the next move to the judge advocate, whose division would hit back at such a rebuff as a matter of honour if nothing else.

The white-washed barracks room with its three metal beds looked more homely than it had a few days ago. A vase had appeared, containing pussy willow, alder and some early greenery – a sign of the interest Sister Kläre had lately started to take in the three lieutenants – all three of them. She was careful to resist a mild impulse to favour one of them, a sturdy, big-nosed lad whose exceptional character shone through. As a result, a humorous undertone of jealousy had broken out among the three, who half liked and half couldn't stand each other, and this new tinge to their lives, with its attendant rivalry and competition, provided a vigorous spur to healing. For her part, Sister Kläre, a grown woman, was delighted by the beneficial effect she was having on them and appeared to take all three young men equally lightly, learning various details of their lives and sometimes bringing in work to do while she sat with them.

Now that the good weather had started, there was no need to worry about keeping the windows shut, and the men could smoke to their hearts' content. At the same time, the wounded men, who'd been patched up in a pretty makeshift way, found the arrival of spring very tiring. And so an hour of bed rest had been prescribed from 5pm to 6pm before the evening meal for all rooms and wards with no exceptions: no talking, no smoking, no reading – only dozing. After months of overexertion, soldiers can sleep like babies – any time and with enjoyment. Bertin sat rather unhappily on his stool, wondering what to do in the meantime as Pahl would be sleeping too. The lieutenants, who already had their bedclothes pulled up to their chins, consoled him that Sister Kläre would soon appear. She had threatened and promised to check if they were obeying orders. She might let Bertin write his letter in her room during the period of bed rest (and the letter would now come to him in more considered form than on the way up the hill).

Sister Kläre came in with her light step. Some nurses stamped about like dragoons. Sister Kläre had all the beauty of a nun, Bertin thought, as she paused for a moment in the doorway, surprised to find him there, yet pleased: she blushed slightly. 'That's nice,' she said, 'but you'll have to leave.' Bertin obediently stood up and made his request. What beautiful shining blue eyes this woman had, or rather this lady, to use an expression that had gradually lost all relevance in his life. 'I have a much better idea,' she said. 'Come with me. Goodbye, gentlemen. See you in an hour.'

Bertin had to take his coat and cap with him. Then he followed Sister Kläre through the half rectangle of the barracks' corridors to a special wing that was damp and smelt of warm steam with a whiff of sulphuric acid. Opening a door, they stepped on to wet decking as in a bathroom. From a chair rose a giant of a man dressed in the overalls of a hospital orderly. His left hand was missing and had been replaced with a hook.

'This is my young charge, Pechler. Give him a bath fit for a general and smoke out all his bees. He's to be back in room 19 in an hour or so.'

'Bloomin heck, Sister Kläre,' chuckled Herr Pechler, 'I've never had a general in before.'

Bertin lay in a bath full of hot water, a dark grey zinc tub in a dim cell. He could hear Herr Pechler outside going about his business, and it flashed through his mind to give him 50 Marks as a thank you. He hadn't enjoyed the deep pleasure of a bath like this for nine months; the only chance he'd had to rub the old skin off his body had been in streams or the very occasional shower. He was trained to accept this, and only now that he was enjoying such civilised amenities again did he feel their lack since the start of the Glory Days. The immeasurable joy of a hot bath – which he'd taken as a matter of course every morning in the first winter of the war. How wonderfully relaxing to sink into it and ease out his limbs, how like sleep it was to abandon himself to it, only much rarer! And how nice it was to meet a woman, who wanted nothing from him and from whom he wanted nothing, but who simply wanted to show her thanks for a book, which he happened to have written.

Would he ever write again? Would the frost that had gone right into the marrow of his bones ever melt? Would he ever be able to write convincingly of all he'd experienced, the enormous misery and his bitter rage at the infernal stupidity and evil he'd encountered? They'd managed to reduce him. Like all the others, he'd been brought up to stand in the breach for the homeland, to remain steadfast, not to shirk the common fate. But now he was tired. All he wanted was some peace, to turn his back on the mountain of crap that kept threatening to engulf him, to escape from all the unchecked hostility directed at undermining the intellect and intellectuals in order to bring them down and bury them. He no longer cared what lieutenants and his class comrades thought of him. He didn't want to see or hear any more about the demands of service; he wanted to crawl behind books and plunge into fantasy, to dissolve the world as it had been shown to be into farce, into a smile at the state of things that should linger like a soft reflection from the sky on the ragtag creatures of the earth. Over there, not very far away, lay the Ardennes forest, which Shakespeare had peopled with immortal beings, locating among its trees fugitives and exiles, melacholics and lovely maidens, youths and old men, dukes and minstrels. How he suddenly longed for that world as he lay there sweating in the warm steam. Ah, but he no longer knew a single verse of that heavenly music off by heart; none of the dialogue now resonated within him, all forgotten. He did, however, know how an enormous weight breaks a man's back, tightens his shoulder muscles and pushes his torso down on to his pelvis. He had, however, learnt all the labourer's arts, how to use tools and his hands and all his muscles, lots of tricks, and he had become the Comrade and sleeping companion of those upon whom society builds its entire way of life. He had, however, witnessed all manner of destruction, men's tenacity and endurance in the face of sludge, hunger and the threat of death, mutual killing on an industrial scale, mountains of rubble, rivers of blood, frozen twisted corpses, wounded men in the grip of fever shivering by a fire, and the mysterious impossibility of finding a way out that led not to death but to peace. He knew that it would all have to mature within him, year after year, the way a good ham is smoked. Could it be given expression? Would it resist being shaped, like the water in this bath as he opened and closed his hand? The novella was no good; he suddenly saw that. It had been stupid of him to show it to Dr Posnanski. He'd better stand up now, soap himself like some dingy old underwear, shower off and go back out into the world refreshed, turning his back on past and future dreams as soon as his foot hit the clean decking, the way you walk away from a shower that's run cold, and deal with the stupid little private matter on which his life unfortunately depended.

Everything is hunky dory

DURING THE REST hour, Sister Kläre sat in her room and wrote to her two children, who were being better looked after and brought up in a countryside boarding school than they could have been within a marriage destroyed by war. She wanted to write to her husband too, whom she still held very dear, although a shared life had become impossible since he'd started to react in a threatening way to any dissent. And who could listen with equanimity to him berating the Kaiser for joining with the lunatic Austrians in unleashing a war that was already lost because he was afraid of the Pan-Germans? Who could remain silent when a once highly gifted man fumed that German misanthropy was to blame for the war and whoever was a slave to that would pay the price into the third and fourth generations, as was written in the scriptures? Perhaps later they'd find a doctor who could remove the burden from Lieutenant Schwersenz's mind and the poison from his soul. Klara Schwersenz would then gladly take him by the hand again, start a new home, bring the children back, rebuild their life together and forget the whole dreadful nightmare. Until then, everything had to stay as it was: he buried away in Hinterstein valley, and she working in the service of the Fatherland. Klara Schwersenz, daughter of the well-know Pidderit family from the Rhineland, now simply Sister Kläre, didn't see herself as a martyr. She had a found a second youth in the tumble of war, had become freer and at the same time more capable, loved her work, and also being a woman, and knew that you got but one transitory life. She wrote to her children in clear, pointed handwriting. Later she would do some ironing in the lieutenants' room.

There was a gentle knock at the door. An orderly brought the confidential news that a gentlemen called Judge Advocate Kostanski, or something like that, wanted to say goodbye to her. She raised her eyebrows, shrugged her shoulders and said to show him in. A moment later, Posnanski's bulky figure filled the front of the room. Sister Kläre sat on the bed, offered him the wooden stool and asked if the time had come for him disappear to the east.

Posnanski blew out his clean-shaven cheeks, rolled his frog-like eyes at her, and, thinking how attractive she looked and that she should always wear this nun's costume, began to speak in a very skilled and humane way: yes, he said, he was here to say goodbye, but that was really a side issue. Much more important was a question he had for her, a request in fact. They were both adults who had seen something of life and so there was no point in beating about the bush. Through Lieutenant Kroysing, he, Posnanksi, had learnt of a shocking abuse of justice to which Kroysing's younger brother had fallen victim. In connection with that, Private Bertin had come to his attention. He believed the man had been shunting ammunition around long enough and that it was time to think about the country's intellectual nourishment after the war and make sure a few talented men were saved, and he'd tried to act on that belief. He'd noticed that Sister Kläre had taken to the writer as well.

'Very much so,' she agreed with a smile. 'I'm letting him soak in the bath right now, the poor lice-ridden chap.'

'So much the better,' replied Posnanski. 'Then perhaps you've heard what happened to my application to have the worthy gentleman transferred to our nice little court martial?'

'Not a sausage,' said Sister Kläre.

Right, said Posnanski, in that case he'd better begin at the beginning with the Trojan War. And in an easy, good-humoured way he described the simmering resentment between the army groups east and west of the Meuse, and how, against this background, Bertin's battalion had refused his request, and that the matter now looked completely hopeless. If the division had not been about to move off and if Excellency Lychow's mind had not already been in the east, then the Western Group Command would certainly have had its way. Because right was on their side. A request from high-ranking personnel to have a man who was only fit for limited service to perform office duties ought not to be refused when men fit for active service were being released. After a bit of back and forth, ASC private Bertin would have been transferred from his unit to the Lychow Divisional Staff and given his marching orders. But when the gods were busy, dwarves came out on top and that's what would happen now, unless higher powers intervened.

'Higher powers than a divisional general?' asked Sister Kläre in astonishment. 'Where will you find them?'

'There's one very near at hand,' replied Posnanski.

Sister Kläre blushed, deeper and deeper. 'That's a lot of silly gossip,' she said and got up.

'Gracious lady,' said Posnanski, remaining seated, 'let me ignore that rejection for two minutes. You may yourself have noticed that Herr Bertin has held out under considerable pressure for quite a long time and is now in a parlous state. He might survive another year if a dud or shell doesn't wipe him out before then. We can get him a decent job in the next few days. Why pussyfoot around with something that is simple and humane and in everyone's best interests. Of course I know it's all gossip. People can't live without gossip, and the higher staff echelons constitute their own social zone and have their own interests and gossip. But there's always a grain of truth in such gossip, and so I assume that the crown prince has had the honour of being introduced to you and taking tea at your house. Would it be asking too much to suggest that you telephone the exalted gentleman, not today, not tomorrow, but, say, this coming Sunday, and ask him for a favour, which we believe would benefit the collective intellectual good and not just a personal acquaintance? Wouldn't you do it without a second thought if you were in Berlin?'

Sister Kläre had sat down again. The flush on her cheeks had faded to a rosy glow, and she looked pensively at the tips of her shoes and her ankles in their coarse black woollen stockings. 'I shouldn't like to meet you in court as lawyer for the other side, Dr Posnanski,' she said.

'My dear lady,' replied Posnanski soberly, 'I hope I'd know better than to do that. No one can win a case against Saint Genevieve.'

Sister Kläre shook her head impatiently. 'We're talking like monkeys,' she said. 'This isn't Berlin. The crown prince isn't a gentleman, and I'm not a lady. I'm a nurse, which makes me a sergeant at best, and the crown prince is a general and commander of an entire front. I hope that lets you see that what you're asking me to do is quite monstrous.'

'I'm afraid, my dear, gracious lady, that you're talking to a civilian, a Prussian civilian but a civilian nonetheless. I'm completely convinced that the crown prince, who is a person like you or me, will gratefully kiss your hand if you dare to do the monstrous, as you call it. After all, what are you asking of him? That he get his adjutant to write a couple of words to rescue the situation. Words from on high, like in a fairytale.' And when Sister Kläre didn't reply, he suddenly added in a different, more nonchalant tone: 'We don't want things to be dictated by a bunch of bourgeois philistines after the war. I'm interested in your view – you don't want that, do you? Surely the novel *Love at Last Sight* is worth conquering your compunction for.'

For a moment, silence reigned between them. Sister Kläre looked calmly into her companion's ugly face, and he looked equally calmly into her beautiful face. She sensed that this frog knew no prejudices and understood people's ways. For him there was no shame in admitting what one had had the guts to do. Nonetheless, it was unpleasant for a sensitive woman to realise she was the object of tittle-tattle and that her private life, which was of no concern to anyone else, was a source of entertainment for others. If she consented now – all right, I'll phone the crown prince – she would be confirming the gossip around her and betraying the relationship to this lawyer whom she didn't know. Caution demanded that she not do it, tact demanded it, femininity, the social contract. No one who counted would blame her for having a friendship with such an agreeable and high-ranking man, a prince and son of the Kaiser, who set every German girl's heart a-pounding when he carried the white Borussian standard through the streets of Bonn, her home town. Every woman who knew of the liaison envied Klara Schwersenz, formerly Klara Pidderit, or stared up at her in awe. But she must not confess it openly. She must preserve an impassive countenance and the family honour. And this lawyer in uniform wanted her to confess it openly. He sat there girded in tan leather with a look on his fat face, a Socratic look, that exhorted her not to kick up such a fuss when she was so beautiful. Not to erect a cardboard façade between them. Not to act more stupid than life already was. Hadn't it been really rather a nice experience? And even if it hadn't – if the best she could say was: it was okay; it was fine – shouldn't one be extremely grateful for any small pleasure when the whole world faced a doubtful future? Sister Kläre realised she was smiling openly at her own inhibitions, gently mocking herself. She reached her hand out to Posnanski and said: 'Thank you, Dr Posnanski. I'll think it over, but for now I must fish our charge out of the bath.'

But when Sister Kläre went into Pechler the bath orderly's room, the bird had, as he put it, flown. Bertin had hurried off to see Pahl, reproaching himself for neglecting him and saying that he really should put his own worries aside for once and think about him. He was concerned, however, about how he would justify his desire to be transferred to the court martial to Pahl.

Thus two ASC men met by Pahl's bed: Lebehde and Bertin, both currently troubled in mind but physically comforted; for one of them had emerged newborn from the bath and the other had been in the kitchen, which also had its merits. They were unanimous in their view that Wilhelm was changed beyond recognition. He was sitting up for half an hour at a time, putting on weight and felt himself to be on the mend. 'I bet you're surprised, aren't you?' he grinned. 'Yes, I'm feeling better. It's not getting me down so much any more. The worst is when they change the bandages in the morning.' He frowned. 'Just lying there knowing you're going to be put through the mill and there's no help for it – that's what knocks the heart out of you.'

Karl Lebehde caught himself wanting to stroke Pahl's hands. Bertin wondered anxiously what he'd say to this martyr if he started to talk hopefully about their future work together in Berlin. Diehl's carbon copy rustled in his pocket. Perhaps there would be a way to give a funny twist to the whole application story, which thanks to Major Jansch's kindness now affected Pahl too.

'Now I'm going to talk as much as I want,' joked Pahl. 'My bed is my castle, and we can spin a few yarns.' He said that since his bandage had been changed he knew how prisoners must have felt in the Middle Ages when they were waiting to be tortured – tomorrow at 9am I'll be interrogated again – or executed. It was horrible to have to hold still and let people do as they wanted with you like some kind of overgrown baby. The terrible pain, the intrusion – it was all awful. You didn't need to experience an actual execution, be hanged or have you head chopped off or be shot, to realise that the death penalty was the lowest of all human ideas; it was enough to have your own body reduced to a passive object. Abolishing the death penalty was a natural step for people who had electricity and could spread the truth through print. Then he asked if there was any news from Russia. What he missed most here in hospital was the chance to discuss that earth-shattering event.

No, said Bertin and Lebehde. They only knew what everyone else knew. The three of them marvelled at the speed and consistency with which things were moving in Russia. They all admitted that they hadn't thought the Russians had it in them. Bertin in particular, who had twice crossed the Russian border with his school class and had taken an optional Russian class at school, repeated several times that no one had expected it because the people were so passive and had such meek faith in the Tsar. It had seemed as though the sun rose and set at the behest of the 'Little Father', and now, look, it had carried on doing its duty and was still shining down on Little Mother Russia although the double-headed imperial eagle was gone .

'One day every beer glass will be full.'

'Ours too,' said Pahl firmly, looking at Bertin.

But Bertin didn't want to follow him down that path. Fortunately, he remembered something he'd witnessed when he was working with the Russian prisoners during the weeks at Romagne. One of them, a lad with teeth like a fish and a full blonde beard, was sitting at the fire in the lunch break distributing pieces of bread amongst his comrades, not out of kind-heartedness but for money: 10 Pfennigs a slice, quite costly. A young Russki with his cap pushed back and a blonde fringe, handed him a coin, received his slice, held it in front of him for a moment, opened his mouth as if to take a bite but then calmly said: 'When we get you home, you miserable Kulak, we'll batter you to death and that's a promise.' Then he took a bite. You could see the bread seller turning a lighter shade of grey beneath his dirty, tanned skin, and his small, light-coloured eyes were fixed on the other man's as he replied: 'If such is God's will, Grigori, I'll have you shot first.' But the younger man, chewing away with his mouth full, just laughed and shook his head. 'Did you hear that, my friends? We'd better watch out for those Kulaks.' Muttered laughter ran through the group, but many of them clearly didn't want to queer their pitch with the profiteer, who calmly went on selling his wares, checking coins and shoving them in his pockets. However, he did throw a quick glance at the guard's bayonet, which didn't escape Grigori's notice. 'No,' he laughed, cleaning his hands on his coat, 'there won't be any Cossack there to protect you from us then.'

'If God so wills it, then no one will protect me,' the bearded man replied patiently. He was a gaunt, middle-aged man, who obviously had to exercise great self-control to hold on to the bread in order to sell it. This scene, which Bertin had observed during a cold snap worthy of Russia in the middle of France, had stayed with him because it was so savagely strange. Since the outbreak of the Revolution, it had taken on a deeper meaning. 'If it has gripped the peasants, then it'll succeed and it'll last,' he said pensively. 'It started with the peasants in France too in 1789. They were crawling across the fields like animals, looking for something to eat – ragged beings reminiscent of people, as a writer called Taine wrote. The lord of the manor had sold the crops in order to live *bon* in Paris. It might succeed in Russia too, but what about at home,' said Bertin doubtfully, 'where everything's so well organised?'

'We've invented organised famine,' said Pahl.

And Karl Lebehde, his fat fingers folded across his stomach, said in a measured voice: 'My dear man, has the phrase "grubbing trip" never come before your esteemed eyes? According to my old lady, whose letters are quite uplifting, Berliners go swarming across the Mark with rucksacks on Saturday evenings, sort of like older versions of the youngsters from the *Wandervogel* rambling club, and curse like blazes if a gendarme asks to look inside their packs. And I'll tell you something for nothing, there aren't many gendarmes that take the stuff off them, and it's easy to see why. If this goes on for another year...'

'Another year!' cried Bertin and Pahl as one. 'Listen,' said Bertin, overcome by the dreadful prospect of an endless war and and full of good will towards the comrades who shared his fate. 'For a couple of days, I've been mulling something over, and sometimes it makes me hopeful and sometimes it fills me with dread. I want you to tell me what you'd do in my place. It actually affects you quite deeply too, Wilhelm,' and he described what had happened, or what he could guess had happened, between his first conversation with Posnanski and the present moment. Pahl's hands trembled slightly as he held the carbon copy in silence. Lebehde bent his copper head over the pillow and read it too. Bertin waited to hear what they would say as if it were a court judgement. Then Pahl tore the thin paper into long strips. 'What they want won't happen,' he said, 'and what they don't want will. You've no idea how well this suits us, my friend. I had a long chat with Karl about it the day before yesterday. I was still woozy when we had our first talk. I had completely forgotten something that my agent only wrote to me about in detail in January. And now you appear like an angel from Heaven and put everything straight again.'

Bertin looked uncomprehendingly from one of the two hardened agitators to the other and listened while Lebehde explained all the preliminaries that had to be gone through before a man could be transferred from the front back to Germany. A detour via the court martial would reinvigorate the plan and make it realistic.

'No,' said Pahl, shaking his head, 'unfortunately, the major's got it wrong. I'll be buzzing off back to Germany with my toe, and you, dear chap, had better get some help with this even if you have to go to the moon for it. We'll soon prise you out of a court martial.'

Bertin felt suddenly ashamed of the initial caution that had made him want to keep quiet. He needed to be open with those who trusted him and discuss with them how best to proceed. He was ready for the fight now and armed against the potential vicissitudes to come. That was why he just laughed when a nurse came up to Pahl's bed, asked rather curtly which of the two of them was Bertin and said he'd been expected him for some time in room 19.

The two men left behind watched his retreating back and thinning hair. 'We did him an injustice that time back in Romagne, Karl,' said Pahl. But Karl Lebehde observed impassively that it was better to do someone an injustice than to suffer one and that he hadn't noticed anything.

Judge Advocate Posnanski took a while to say goodbye to Kroysing and was almost paternal in his warmth. The room mates listened with amusement to the fat man talking but thought that what he said made sense. For Lieutenant Kroysing didn't want to accept that his plan to send the sappers a replacement in the form of Bertin simply wasn't going to work. Posnanski spoke only of how important Bertin was as the only witness in the future trail of retired civil servant Niggl from Weilheim in Upper Bavaria. Kroysing could not deny the logic of his analysis, though he growled in reluctance: 'You want me to start fighting private battles like everyone else in this war.' This 'you' encompassed Lieutenants Flachsbauer and Mettner, who supported the judge advocate's plans. 'The man is capable of commanding a company, and you want me to put him in a display cabinet.'

The man was born for the court martial, Lieutenant Flachsbauer cried in reply. And Lieutenant Mettner asked sarcastically if he'd ever thought of letting him choose for himself.

'Choose?' said Kroysing haughtily, though he was laughing. 'Oh, that'd be great.'

'You tyrant,' teased Lieutenant Flachsbauer.

'Slave driver,' added Lieutenant Mettner, who was often genuinely annoyed by Kroysing's tyrannical and commanding manner. And in order to irritate him he told the story of a minor and not particularly relevant incident he'd seen a few weeks before he was wounded. It demonstrated a lack of backbone which showed the average officer clearly represented the average German, as Mettner had come to know him. As a liaison officer with Group West he had passed on a complaint made to him by an officer who had poured his heart out to him during a inspection in a neighbouring sector. The officer had said that because of the relay stations it was impossible to get the high ups to understand that each of his companies in the front line ('in the shit,' as he put it) had a combat strength of barely 40 rifles at its disposal and not over 110 as was continually reported. 'And then the high ups wonder when we take a pasting. Sick and transferred men are always counted in too.'

Mettner promised to deal with it. But when one of the inspectors from the Lychow Group appeared to check it out, the officer denied it all for fear of making himself unpopular with the regiment, and Lieutenant Mettner was left in the lurch. 'And he did only have 40 rifles when the French suddenly attacked.

And you want to throw your unsuspecting friend in among that lot where he'll always be putting their backs up? Well, I'd sooner not have you for a brother.'

Kroysing started up, upset by the word 'brother', but controlled himself: he had always put the common good above his own interests, he grumbled. Was that a problem?

'But you can see that in this case circumstances require a different response,' said Posnanksi soothingly. 'So let me have Bertin or rather help me to get him, for—' But the three men in the room explained they'd already heard the whole story from the jinxed man himself. 'So much the better,' twinkled Posnanski, 'then you can be my representatives.' And he said that he had found a champion for Bertin in Sister Kläre, who was going to telephone a high-ranking personage and ask him to intervene. 'Keep at her. Don't harangue her but don't let it go either. If she gets annoyed, don't push it. Maybe you can bring it up in 12 hours or so, eh? All she promised me was to think about it. You look as though you won't leave her in peace until she gets on that phone, dear chap.'

Kroysing flushed and said he would do what he could, just as Bertin walked in eager to hear from Posnanksi if his cause was lost. They laughed at him, mocking his downbeat attitude. Speaking in the tone of a regimental commander, Kroysing announced that Bertin was to be transferred to the court martial because of lack of bottle. Posnanski assured him that effective steps in that direction had already been taken. When Posnanski finally set off, he left behind a happy party and Bertin was much reassured. Posnanski shook Bertin's hand warmly and said he was counting on him and was only going on ahead in order to spend his leave in Berlin.

'Have a good time, then,' said Kroysing, 'and say hello to the old place for me.'

'I will,' said Posnanski. 'Any particular part?'

'The part between the Technical University and Wittenbergplatz,' said Kroysing. 'Where there are always so many girls' legs on view.'

'Right, so Tauentzienstraße and the Kurfürstendamm,' said Posnanksi, pretending to make a note on the palm of his hand.

'Stop,' cried Bertin. 'Where are the files?'

'You'll make an excellent clerk, my legal friend,' said Posnanski gravely. 'I'll leave them with my representative.' And then he finally pushed off, accompanied to his car by Bertin.

When he returned, Kroysing asked him in passing if frog face had told him anything important. No, replied Bertin innocently, he'd just told him a bit about the people in the staff with whom he might come into contact. Kroysing seemed happy with this reply. None of the four initiates had let on to Bertin whom the judge advocate meant by his representative. Posnanki had worked on the assumption that people usually come over best when they act naturally. However, the three officers, who had all been rather taken aback by Posnanski's disclosure, kept the information from Bertin out of a curious kind of *esprit de corps*. They were from the hospital, and so was Sister Kläre. Bertin wasn't. The person to be telephoned was a hospital secret. Outsiders didn't need to know about it. But above all, they liked the idea of at least sharing a secret with this woman, if nothing else. Until that day, the idea that she'd had something with the crown prince had just been talk. Now it seemed it was real, and each of the three young men envied the general. For some time now, none of them had seen Sister Kläre as a nurse. They all felt themselves to be enveloped by her sparkling charm. For in a long war, however manly a soldier's behaviour may be, he falls back into childhood in most important respects. He no longer eats with a knife and fork, but instead spoons gruel into his mouth. He no longer goes to the toilet on his own, but sits on a public latrine like a child in a nursery. He suppresses his own will to an extraordinary degree, obeying blindly and unconditionally, as a small child obeys adults whom it trusts or who force it to comply. His feelings of love and hate, of liking and aversion, are directed at his superiors, who replace father and mother, and at his comrades who represent siblings. In this seamlessly childish existence, where destruction plays as big a part as it does in the nursery, there is no room for relationships between men and women except in the imagination. Furthermore, soldiers like children are spared the struggle for their daily bread and do not have to deal with the relationship between earnings and productive work, with the toil, labour and rewards that are such an integral part of adult life. And so the erotic impulse is much stronger in the creative environment of peace than in the destructive one of war, where it can easily be diverted to the same sex, completing the analogy with childhood. But after the shock and physical agony of the first weeks in hospital, there is a rebirth, a sort of maturing such as follows the torture of puberty in primitive communities, and the young men start to look around themselves with new eyes, discover that there are women and are thrown into turmoil. But towards Bertin, who was denied the blessings of this rebirth, they were unconsciously patronising, like 15-year-olds to a nine-year-old, treating him like a lower being, harmless and inadequate. What did he know of adult secrets?

The misanthrope

AS SISTER KLÄRE made her way to room 19 to do some ironing as promised, who should be carrying her ironing board, a joyful smile of farewell on his chubby face despite the white bandage round his neck, but Father Lochner. As before, the divisional Catholic chaplain from the other bank sported flying coat tails and a violet collar. 'Lieutenant!' he cried, more Rhenish than ever, 'Ah'm mad happy to see you, so I am.' (The phrase 'mad happy' could cover a wide range of insanity.) And as he carefully laid the white-covered board, which was almost as a tall as a man, against the wall, he took Kroysing's right hand in both of his and shook it for such a long time that Kroysing almost began to look uncomfortable. He briefly greeted Bertin then introduced himself to the other two patients, sat down on a bed, slightly out of breath, and watched as Sister Kläre erected a bridge between the table and the window frame, while Bertin, kneeling on the table, carefully plugged the iron into an adaptor. For a moment, the room was plunged into darkness. He heard a voice whispering in his ear: 'I won't leave you in the lurch.' When the light bulb flashed on a second later, Sister Kläre was busily arranging her washing as though nothing had happened. It was very nice of the nurse, thought Bertin, as he sat down on a stool in the corner and listened to Kroysing and Father Lochner's talking – it was really very nice of Sister Kläre to console him and offer him her help. But she had clearly overestimated her range, to use of a favourite word of Kroysing's. Posnanski had had to leave the matter with a representative, and by God they needed one, and he was sure to be a more powerful man than anyone Sister Kläre might be able to produce. Well, he wouldn't agonise about it any more. The judge advocate had probably meant his divisional commander or someone else who had enough influence with Group East to reverse Herr Jansch's cocky refusal. In any case, it was very nice to sit here freshly bathed and lice-free, to doze a little and enjoy the moment. Because the lice would get stuck into him again that night. His undeloused sleeping bag or his neighbour Lebehde or the man under him would see to that. Lice were as unavoidable as fate, and as long as you were ensconced in communal accommodation and the misery of war you couldn't get away from them. And he mustn't forget that Sister Kläre had asked him to write a dedication in her copy of *Love at Last Sight*.

Father Lochner was at the hospital to be treated for a carbuncle, an ugly deep red swelling on his neck. He'd made the difficult decision to have it lanced and he'd have to prevail on the doctors' kindness a few more times. So, even godless doctors were doing God's work with their dexterous hands.

Kroysing was almost irritated by the priest and his good mood. What was this outsider doing breaking in on this private hour? It was bad enough to have to share the vision of Sister Kläre with his comrades, her coming and goings with the ironing board, those duties of a maid – a maid he could regard more directly and desire more keenly now her secret had been revealed. But Father Lochner was so overjoyed to find Kroysing unhurt after all the adventures around Douaumont...

'Unhurt!' cried Kroysing indignantly, pointing to the thick bandages on his foot. 'Hind paw.' That was nothing, insisted Father Lochner, nothing at all compared to the dreadful possibilities he'd escaped. 'Thanks,' said Kroysing. 'It was quite enough for me.'

Not to be deterred, Father Lochner pointed to the thousands upon thousands of men who had given their lives for the Fatherland. Kroysing had fared extremely well and now he would see the homeland again and return to his profession in one of the factories essential to the war effort... 'Definitely,' Kroysing nodded. 'I can't wait to return to my profession. My profession is being a soldier, and I'm going to transfer to the air force.'

'Oh,' said Father Lochner startled, that was very admirable but he had more than fulfilled his duty and should now think about himself and his future.

'Rubbish!' retorted Kroysing, as the others listened intently. He wasn't talking about duty; he was talking about his own enjoyment. Surely the priest knew that he was a heathen, an avowed disciple of the religion of killing. Instead of hobbling around on the ground, he wanted to soar up into the clouds and rain avenging fire down on the heads of his enemies.

Father Lochner hung his head sadly. He had hoped Kroysing's afflictions might have mellowed him. And his private dispute? he asked. He didn't know if he could mention it openly?

'My quarrel with that scoundrel Niggl? Say what you like. Everyone in this room knows about it or is a fellow sufferer. Nothing has changed, Father. I'll hunt him down. And if he's promoted to major soon...'

'He's been promoted,' Father Lochner broke in.

'...then he'll be over all of us as a result of his actions.'

There was pause. Sister Kläre let the iron rest on its tripod for a moment. They all looked at him, this wild hunter, who admitted his vendetta so openly, simply pushing aside the New and Old Testaments, both of which replaced individual and clan vengeance with the rule of law and public justice. Then the iron began to steam again. Father Lochner folded his hands in resignation: in that case the matter must be left to Providence and hopefully it would turn out well for Lieutenant Kroysing. He just hoped that when the time came he'd have as peaceful an end as that little sergeant from Douaumont three days ago in the field hospital at Chaumont... Kroysing, who'd been lying down, slowly pulled himself up. 'Do you mean my friend Sergeant Süßmann is dead?'

Yes, Father Lochner nodded. That was the name. *That young sapper who guided you to the infantry position, the very same.*

'Impossible,' groaned Kroysing hoarsely, clearing his throat. 'He went to a training course in Brandenburg.'

But, quietly implacable, the priest insisted: he must have been sent back into the field in the meantime. Since the beginning of the year, training courses had increasingly been held in the communications zone. As though drawn by a magnet, Bertin had moved past the ironing nurse and now stood at the head of Kroysing's bed. 'Süßmann,' he said simply. 'Our little Süßmann.'

According to Father Lochner it had been an accident during grenade throwing training for recruits and had happened very quickly. One of them, an elderly man, couldn't get to grips with the grenade, and Süßmann stepped out of cover to show him how to handle it one more time, having been assured by the future sapper that he hadn't taken the pin out. Then as Süßmann walked towards him the man dropped the hand grenade and ran away. Immediate explosion, half of which caught Süßmann, the other the unfortunate recruit, a hireling from Mecklenburg. He died immediately, but Süßmann lasted until the evening after he was admitted to hospital and didn't suffer much. Dr Baer, the military Rabbi, had been with him at the end. Between two morphine injections, he'd dictated a few sentences, including one for Lieutenant Kroysing. 'Write to my parents that it was worth it and to Lieutenant Kroysing that it wasn't. It was a swindle.' Apart from a few wild utterances in his death throes, an exemplary soldier had gone to his final rest, and his memory would certainly be preserved by the grateful Fatherland.

Kroysing turned to Bertin. 'Our little Süßmann,' he repeated sadly. 'Escaped twice from the hell of Douaumont only to be done for by some hick from Mecklenburg. And he was so sure – so sure – that death had spat him out once and for all and he'd probably outlive the Wandering Jew. No, I don't want to hear any more today.' And he turned to the wall.

Bertin stared down at him, arms hanging. No one was safe, and it was always the wrong ones who got it. Every minute a man was taken, and no one cared. Yes, Pelican and Sergeant Fürth had been right. There'd be nothing but rubbish left in Germany if things went on like this. And eyes full of dread, he looked round the comfortable room where the smell of ironed sheets now mingled with that of cigarettes. They all had plans for the future. He was trying to be transferred to the Lychow Division court martial, Kroysing wanted to join the air force, Lieutenant Mettner wanted to return to his study of mathematics and Lieutenant Flachsbauer wanted if possible to join the world of commerce where his father's company was eagerly awaiting him. Sister Kläre and the priest no doubt had clear plans too, just like Pahl down the corridor, who wanted to organise strikes in Germany. So many decisions and ideas! 'Nothing is final as long as we live,' was how his novel ended. Existence was always uncertain. A tile could fall on your head at any moment; an electric cable might snap and kill you. In Upper Silesia a parson had been killed when the fly wheel broke loose at a pumping station, flew through the air and crashed into the roof of the parsonage, crushing the parson at his dinner. But in war such accidents became part of a malicious system that multiplied them tenfold – a hundredfold at the front. Death wasn't unusual; survival was unusual.

Just then someone knocked at the door. 'Are you coming?' asked Karl Lebehde.

Spring is sprung

A FEW MORNINGS later, full of longing, Sister Kläre opened the tar paper-covered shutters of her little cell; the next day was 21 March, the first day of spring. In her cosy, candy-striped flannel pyjamas, she stretched out her arms, folded her hands behind her thick ash blonde plaits and leant out to look at the great silvery star set in the green dawn to the east: Venus. She could see right across the countryside to the golden streaks above the horizon and the misty river valley, and on the left to the woods of Consenvoye. She noticed that the beech trees were already covered in green shoots and didn't hear a couple of metallic strikes that drifted across from behind the hills. If only this year would fulfil its promise. *It's Tuesday today,* she thought. *Father Lochner will be coming about his carbuncle for the last time. If I want to speak to him it'll have to be today.* The week before he'd said that Kroysing was an extraordinary man, and that he had presented him with the news of his friend Süßmann's sudden death in that unvarnished way in order to give him a shock, make him understand humanity's limits and force him to reflect. But unfortunately it hadn't done much good, and that steely soul would have to experience much worse before it learnt humility in the face of the unfathomable and opened up to the sorrows and splendour of natural life. Yes, Kroysing was quite someone, but so was Father Lochner. He was well schooled in the contemplative as well as the active life, and it was a pleasure to listen to his feisty debates with those atheist savages, Kroysing and Pahl. Father Lochner found Pahl almost more compelling than Kroysing, but Sister Kläre wasn't with him on that one; she found Kroysing much more compelling than Pahl, than Mettner, than the medical officer – although he did put forward spectacularly gloomy views about life on earth – than Bertin, dear God, whom circumstances had reduced to a sheep, than Father Lochner himself. So far there had been no declaration or even a hint of one between herself and Kroysing, the enemy of God; the odd embarrassed glance had done the talking. Was it possible to marry a man like that? She was reserving judgement on that point until she'd heard the priest's view. But how to get out of her current marriage, that cross she had to bear, or at least have it annulled on account of her husband's condition? Conscientious Peter Schwersenz was in the grip of a disastrous depression, unable to cope with experiences he bore and answered for in silence. He sat there in Hinterstein valley, like a hermit in his cell, poring over maps, files and cuttings from French, British and Swiss newspapers, like a man eternally damned to fight the Battle of the Marne over and over again, to replay what ought to have happened and what, through his actions though not his fault, had in fact happened.

Well, she understood nothing of that, or very little. She had always been glad of her husband's intellectual superiority. But she, Kläre Schwersenz, had given birth to two children, had aborted another one and prevented the conception of countless others, but she had never felt as fulfilled as a woman as she did now. The last decade of her womanhood had begun. She didn't want an intellectual man, a kind, pleasant man who was unsure of himself; she wanted a real man, a man who bristled with energy and crackled with fire – who was dangerous, facetious and opinionated and who if necessary was prepared to spit in the face of death. She knew too much of life to claim that she couldn't live without Kroysing, but she knew that with him she would be twice the woman she was now. And for him, as an engineer, an alliance with a daughter of the Pidderit family would open doors he didn't even know where there. The workers at the Pidderit plant would naturally respond quite differently to the man who wouldn't surrender at Douaumont than they did to her brothers and the directors, and they would be ready to obey him. After the enormous sacrifices of this war, the workers would quite justifiably make demands on the state that would be hard to resist. Only those who understood them and appealed to them as soldiers would be able to deal with them. Her father, Blasius Pidderit, a great old man who loved her as much as he was capable of loving another human being, after visiting the Great Headquarters of the crown prince (with whom she was still on close terms at that time), had spoken contemptuously of the idiots who were mad enough to try to curry favour with the Junkers by blocking the workers' most basic demand: equal, secret and direct suffrage in Prussia. The old man and Eberhard Kroysing – they would get on. She could see Kroysing in the bosom of her family, a tall man with a deep, resonant voice that captured people's attention. Then shaking her head at herself, half laughing, half disapproving, she pulled her small window shut and went over to the washstand, wishing for the first time that her mirror weren't so tiny, and got ready to face her day's work.

For Eberhard Kroysing having his bandages changed was no longer horrific. He began each day with breakfast, which he enjoyed less each morning, but that couldn't be helped. In his mind, he replaced the weak coffee, meanly spread slices of bread, and porridge or rye flour soup with the dishes he would have when the the war was won and he had an adequate wage that allowed him to breakfast properly. It remained to be seen if Sister Kläre, were she to become his wife, would know how to reconcile the modest income of an engineer with his lavish requirements. Either way, breakfast at the Kroysings must and would comprise an apple, a Calville apple, crisp, yellow and fragrant; it would also comprise two eggs in a glass, fresh butter, toasted bread or white rolls, and coffee – coffee such as the Austrians were supposed to make, although compared with the breakfast coffee of Eberhard Kroysing's dreams they didn't even know what coffee was: small beans, round and silken as pearls, freshly roasted, which, after they'd been ground, would have no contact with metal; hot water would slowly be poured over them and they'd percolate for three minutes, after which a drink would be poured into the master of the house's cup whose aroma would pervade the entire apartment and the master would enjoy it with a spoonful of thick cream and some good-quality sugar. Resplendent upon the fluffy white rolls would lie either properly salted steak tartare mixed with chopped onion and goose fat and very lightly peppered, or that ivory coloured cheese you got in Switzerland and the Allgäu, that dark yellow cheese from Holland, that reddish cheese from England, a flat Brie or a runny Camembert.

If you had to lie in bed as he did, though admittedly he was no longer a cripple, but an airman and an eagle, you could happily spend half an hour dreaming about cheese – and in wartime the whole world dreamt with you. People must have learnt how to use milk properly very early on – the people of the steppes would have known, horsemen with their mare's milk, and the herdsmen races with their cow's and goat's milk, their sheep's and ass's milk. It was funny to think that they had only make these nutritional discoveries in order to have them taken away from them by warriors: Semites and Ancient Greeks, Teutons and Mongols. They had all gloried in the desire to take from others, to rob and kill, and no one understood that better than Eberhard Kroysing, as he stretched out his legs and flexed his toes. For some time now it had been his turn to kill and conquer, and now it was his chieftain's privilege to steal the most desirable woman – the sweetest and loveliest in the whole tribe.

The world had not come as far as it had through the fist alone, and to win her he would have to be considered and persuasive, and use all his will power and guile, combined with the ardour of courtship. He would do it. The only other serious contender had been removed from the field, that sneaky Mettner. He was to leave the next day for a German orthopaedic hospital, where according to his papers he would be fitted with a prosthetic arm. But perhaps the downy-haired mathematician had sensed that Kläre felt nothing more for him than friendship and sympathy, and no doubt that wasn't enough for Mettner. Well, buzz off then, old pal. You'll soon find another girl to suit you, and there'll be no Kroysing to queer your pitch.

Lieutenant Mettner was in fact in his uniform watching the orderly Mehlhose strap up his luggage and carry it out. 'I hope I'll hear from you again, Kroysing,' he said. 'I think it's a shame you're not going back to civilian life too. You're a talented man. In different times, that is in peacetime, you'd have become one of those crusading engineers who travels round the world doing battle with wild rivers and waterfalls – creative warriors, or warlike creators, if you prefer. But nowadays—'

'I'm going to be an airman,' said Kroysing curtly. 'And I'm quite happy with the division of labour we've come up with. You work on the future, and I'll take care of the present.'

Mettner shook his head. 'I'm very much afraid flying won't agree with you.'

'Rubbish,' cried Kroysing. 'I'll only get back to full strength and put some weight back on when I'm regularly sat behind a machine gun inside one of those bloody boxes chucking lovely bombs down on my fellow men. Then those little Frenchmen won't wander about so brazenly down below.' And he pointed through the window to an aeroplane flying at a considerable height across the beautiful blue spring sky like a black insect.

The painter Jean-François Rouard was to bomb the ammunitions train and the barracks at Vilosnes-East that night, then bear right to blow up the railway line at Damvillers. He'd received the order half an hour ago; it was to be a beautiful full moon that night, but the weather might break the next day or the day after and it might rain. He knew that stretch of countryside but was doing a test flight to check the times. The Germans would try to retake Bezonvaux, which had been a terrible loss to their line. They had sent in two regiments from Baden. Two men with the numbers 83 and 47 had been taken prisoner – crack regiments that hadn't suddenly appeared there for fun. Well, they were going to disturb those gentlemen's plans and extend them a warm welcome before they'd prepared their new positions. Jean-François Rouard was a go-getter – canvases, women, railway stations, it was all the same to him. He was all keyed up, pipe in his mouth, in a leather jacket and trousers, listening to the beat of the plane's plucky engine, as he made signs to the pilot and noted his times.

In the meantime, Lieutenant Mettner had taken his leave of Kroysing. He was to take the train around midday from Sedan or Montmédy depending on the connections and couldn't wait any longer. His parting from Sister Kläre took place in men's ward 3 and was brief, cordial and non-committal, and from now on Flachsbauer and Kroysing would share the room alone. Eberhard Kroysing eyed Mettner's empty bed with philosophical calm; he'd be able to use it to spread out his maps now. Today was a good day. He'd got rid of a rival, and furthermore it was spring. The window could be left open, and the beginnings of certain songs were coming true: 'Balmy airs approach, blue and flowing.' He felt like getting a flute out and giving a spirited rendition of Mendelsohn's air. And later in the day he would present a certain lady with an either/or decision. And as a sign that she was breaking definitively with her past and making a full-scale transfer to a certain Herr Kroysing, she would finally find time that evening to phone a certain high-ranking personage, a shy and silly boy at best, who would then probably turn up the following afternoon and sit about looking miserable. But it had to stop sometime.

The ASC men in the Barkopp working gave the arrival of spring a muted welcome. Half of France was stuck to their legs, to quote Karl Lebehde. Great clods of earth clung to their boots as they ranged across country. Because of the thaw, a cache of shells and crates of ammunition, which the gunners must have used as a platform for their guns, had come to light in one of the ravines. It was going to be bloody awful job to dig them out of the muck and get them to the nearest field railway. But Sergeant Barkopp had promised them the following day off, as they'd have filled the last freight car with the new find by the time they finished work that day. Together with the three French goods wagons, which were filled with gigantic paper bags whose content was unknown, a train would be ready to leave that night, 16 axles, enough to add to the next empty transport. The ASC men were sometimes called 'shovellers', and the five men working on the new find justified their name that day, shovelling away layers of clay to expose the shells, carefully scraping out the loose earth between them with picks: yes, the caps were still on the fuses and so the steel cylinders were as harmless as babies' bottles, but freezing cold, slippery and heavy, and very hard on the hands. But men who'd warmed their hands on their own urine during the great cold didn't think twice about grasping hold of the cold, slimy earth.

'Did you know we're on guard duty tonight?' Lebehde asked Bertin, who was beside him.

'It's all one to me. Who's the third?'

'That tall lad from Stuttgart. They're going on about the cases of explosives. He already told me he wants number one so he can hit the sack before midnight.'

Bertin laughed at the scorn in Lebehde's voice. 'He's welcome as far as I'm concerned,' he said. 'I'll take number two.'

'Then I have no choice but to take number three and be the first to greet the new spring,' grinned Lebehde. 'I'm honoured to meet you, I'll say. My name's Lebehde. With whom do I have the pleasure of speaking? *My name's spring.* The pleasure is all mine, Mr Spring. I've already met your worthy family about 40 times. I hope you won't bite me. In that case I won't go up to see Wilhelm tonight. I'll take a sniff round the new field kitchen for the Oldenburgers. They're supposed to be relieved at the front tomorrow. How about you?'

'I'll definitely make a flying visit,' said Bertin, trying to lift the rear part of a shell.

'Oh well,' said Lebehde, 'maybe I'll have a heart and come too. Who knows how much more we'll see of Wilhelm. The old joker's supposed to be sent to Berlin soon. I'll be jolly glad when he's safely out of here.'

'Would you swap places with him?' asked Bertin, curious.

Grasping the shell from his end and effortlessly lifting it up, Karl Lebehde said: 'I can't answer that just like that. Sometimes I might say yes, other times no, depending on my mood. If Barkopp has annoyed me, I might want nothing more to do with that bloody Hamburg bastard and be thinking: "Get a grip, man. Give yourself a hernia and follow Wilhelm." But if I've just had a good bowl of soup, then I might think about how I can get things from the field hospitals cheaper than he could and stay put. Then sometimes I worry about all kinds of things when I think about the poor, old lad. What if there were a fire in those stupid barracks for example – what would happen to that baby then?' And he shook his coppery head crossly. 'Right, you take number two then and hoof it back down with me now.'

Guard duty in the Prussian army involved two hours at your post and four hours of sleep. As number one started at 8pm, number two was at the sentry from 10pm until midnight and from 4am until 6am. If French planes flew over, they usually did so around 11pm, sometimes a quarter of an hour earlier, sometimes a quarter of an hour later.

Post

PRIVATE PAHL'S CONFIDENCE and lust for life had increased markedly. Certainly, the hospital, just as expected, had all the characteristics of the class state: doctors, officers and nurses over here, rank and file patients over there, and in the middle the hospital orderlies, who were gradually, albeit much too slowly, realising where they belonged – with those who stand to attention, third-class patients, health insurance cases in uniform. But the things that were good were: they weren't treated any worse than need be; efforts were made to make the food wholesome; and the general tone of the place was cheerful, though in a hearty way that was a little too Christian for Pahl's taste. But better Christian than Old Prussian. It was getting easier to face the early mornings when his bandage was removed and the wound that had replaced his big toe was sterilised and dressed again. Only paper bandages had been delivered from the homeland, with wood pulp instead of cotton wool, and so no one needed to feel he was being treated worse than his neighbour in the officer's room: they were all subject to the same law of the blockade. They were fed five times a day on the kind of food that had long been but a myth for the brave men in field grey: milk, not from a tin but from a live cow, white bread made with real wheat, real sugar and even real ham. The day before yesterday one of the hospital pigs had been killed by its faithful carer, Pechler the bath orderly, with a shot behind the ear. Until its death, it had proudly borne the lovely name of Posemuckel and now it was buried in numerous people's stomachs. But there would be successors among the pigs – and among the rabbits, which the hospital fattened up on the patients' leftovers so they didn't go to waste. Pahl loved pork and he loved rabbit meat, and the nurses and orderlies were delighted to see that Pahl the typesetter had started to make jokes at which his ugly face with its staring eyes lit up in a childish laugh.

Pahl had also come into conversation with officers for the first time since his training, namely the acquaintances of his comrade Bertin. They had visited him. A certain Sister Kläre had warmed to Private Bertin's friend and had got others interested in him too, and thanks to his unique character Pahl was the last person not to merit such attention. People were captivated by his knack of saying exactly what he thought, without anger, and by his newly discovered smile, the smile of a man reborn. That engineer Kroysing was a strange fish. Pahl knew what had happened to his younger brother: that he'd been a little bit shot to death because he'd stuck his neck out for the men in his company. But his brother, this Kroysing engineer chap, was a clever man and worldly wise. So what conclusions did he draw from the incident? Did he rise above the purely personal element? Was he able to see the structure of the society he served in the case? Not bloody likely! That strong, well brought up man who ought to have known better was heaping his hostility on some miserable retired civil servant from Bavaria and his subordinates. Not even in his wildest dreams did it occur to him to ask if this Captain Niggl had not simply been carrying out society's instructions when he pinned young Kroysing down in Chambrettes-Ferme – unwritten instructions to get rid of strike breakers in order to put the wind up their successors, to cleanse the ruling class of traitors and elevate the interests of the state above those of so-called humanity.

Although he was mentally focused on his wound, which was healing slowly but healing nonetheless (the skilful surgeon had folded artificially long strips of skin over the site of the operation), Pahl had been curious to meet the tall lieutenant and was delighted when Kroysing came by every day after his first visit to chew the fat with him – i.e. to have a chat. Pahl's reputation as a thinking man had spread much more quickly in the hospital than in his company. For in hospitals people have a lot of time and few distractions. Authors could easily write novels about the conversations that take place among patients, whereas busy people usually talk to hide their thoughts and advance their aims. Kroysing wasn't an engineer now but a patient, and he thought carefully, moving his head slowly, as he engaged with the questions that the recumbent typesetter put to him in a polite but facetious tone – very tricky questions. What, for example, did Kroysing, as an engineer, think about the fact that if he invented something while working for some company or other, the patent would not belong to him or the general public but to the company? Did he think that was reasonable? Sitting on Pahl's bed, Kroysing the engineer did not think that was at all reasonable. He took the view that engineers around the world, though perhaps initially in one country, should band together to make sure they got a share of the profits from their inventions. However, Kroysing was under no illusions as to the viability of such lovely ideas, because it was almost impossible to get engineers to cooperate on anything as they were so competitive. That meant people had to be persuaded that they needed Kroysing the engineer as much as Kroysing the engineer needed them; it would then be possible to rely on the well-developed self-interest of those industrial lords.

It was all very entertaining – the patients in men's ward 3 listened avidly as the little hunchback presented arguments and counter-arguments, and the tall lieutenant answered him back, glowing with pleasure. Finally, backed into a corner, the lieutenant said that he didn't give two figs for cooperation and if a man didn't know how to help himself then he must be left to flounder. He, personally, was not one to be discouraged, and that was the main thing. A real man was a lone wolf, as in the old saying: God helps those who help themselves, and if not there's always the fire brigade. Whereupon Pahl had pointed out that solidarity and mutual assistance in life and death situations were an essential prerequisite for a fire brigade. Neither of them was prepared to give in, and it became increasingly clear that reason and the facts were on Pahl's side. He was right and that was all there was to it, whereas Kroysing, snapping around him like a sheepdog, was his own argument and his own person was the best evidence he could offer for this thesis.

In the end, they laughed and agreed to continue their discussion after the war, Pahl at the head of a horde of power-hungry slaves and Kroysing as satrap of the rapacious captains of industry – to use the language of opposing newspapers. Then they'd see who was right – who was stronger and more forward-looking, and could be relied upon to replace all the human lives that had been destroyed. Kroysing wanted to bring in the military; Pahl thought the military would long since have been transformed inwardly into proletarians in uniform. And so they parted on good terms, each with much food for thought, though they didn't show it.

Pahl's thoughts, as he tossed from side to side turning his face to the blue sky in the window, were as always focused on the essential dilemma of how to reawaken in the engineer and his kind the sense they'd had in their youth that they mustn't squander their gifts. How could you teach them to see beyond their education – their training to act as faithful servants to the religion of private property as manifest in all the raw materials and natural forces that had been torn from their original owners – everyone? On the horizon Pahl saw a vision of suffering humanity awaiting its freedom and felt dizzy because he wasn't strong enough for the enormous task that awaited him at home. Because life on the breadline – cramped housing, poor food, lack of time and education, insufficient schooling, monotonous work, lack of hope and longing for the comforts of the middle classes – paralysed or perverted whatever ideas, talent and special qualities slumbered in the vast army of the exploited. Bertin had once explained to him that Christianity had triumphed because it had awakened self-awareness in women, slaves, prisoners of war and children, had unleashed and unfettered their abilities to the benefit of the community. In this, as in so many other respects, Christianity was a precursor of socialism. Would he live to see a time, 20 years after the war, when one or two liberated nations had been able to show what colossal creative forces lay within them, after this frenzy of destruction?

When Kroysing returned to the room, Sister Kläre was clearing up and Lieutenant Flachsbauer had been taken down to the massage room to try out a few simple appliances and would be gone for half an hour at least. Kroysing was bristling with tension, and the engine of his will crackled and sparked. He sat on the bed and looked at this woman sluicing the floor with a pungent solution of Lysol. 'Well, Kläre,' he said abruptly, 'what's to become of us?'

Frau Colonel Schwersenz turned her beautiful nun's eyes on him in shock. Had she hidden her feelings so badly? 'What can I do for the young gentleman?' she asked in servant's mode, mocking both of them.

He looked at her sadly. 'Come off it,' he said. 'Let's put all that nonsense to one side and look at the matter honestly. If I were a foreman and you were a maid we'd have come to an agreement long ago and we'd now be considering how and on what basis to get married. Our situation is more complicated because we're distinguished people.'

Sister Kläre felt herself flush with fear. 'Lie down, Lieutenant. Rest your leg and don't say things you can't answer for.' At the same time, she was ashamed of this inhibited avoidance tactic.

Kroysing lay down obediently, watching her fixedly. 'Kläre,' he said, 'you know how things are. There were three men in this room who loved you. One of them has trundled off, the best and weakest of them, and now sleepy old Flachsbauer may dream of you his whole life long, which will do him good as he won't get you. I'm the one who's either going to marry you or snuff it.'

Sister Kläre made as if to push him away. 'You're a blackmailer. You're like a mad vice.'

But Kroysing shook his head: 'I'm just telling it as it is. I'm mad about you Kläre, not just in that way but in all conceivable ways. When I think of having you beside me day and night for the next 20 years, I feel I could jump on to the ceiling and bang the walls. You know that. You're not a coward. You're a real woman and your heart's in the right place. I'm not trying to blind you with romance. I'm not producing flutes and violins. I'm not trying to stroke your leg or put my hand on your breast...'

'You'll get a cuff round the ear if you do, Lieutenant.'

'...but I can't sleep for asking myself how I'll feed us and arrange accommodation. As long as the war lasts, I have to go where GHQ sends me. At the moment I'm just an ordinary sapper lieutenant but in nine months I'll be a famous airman – or a pile of ashes.'

Sister Kläre looked at him wide-eyed, then she closed her eyes, took two steps towards the bed, opened them again, realised she had a wet cloth in her hands, wrapped it round the scrubbing brush and finished mopping the room.

He carried on talking as she mopped, and she felt his eyes following her every movement. 'When the war is over and we've both come through it, you without having caught any diseases and me without having broken my neck or my big nose – when we're back in Germany and everyone's celebrating victory, what can I offer you then? That buckled lad Pahl next door is no fool. What prospects does an engineer have? As a boy, I always dreamt of being a ship's captain in the merchant navy. I thought it would be wonderful to stand on the bridge and command some great white tub from port to starboard, from the top of the mast to the bilge – to be responsible for it. Of course it never occurred to me that the captain doesn't own a single rivet on the ship. Now I know that a captain is really a modestly paid transport engineer with few options for advancement, even if his wife can travel round the world first class. So what do I really have to offer you apart from myself? A nice four-bedroomed house in Nuremberg or Augsburg, a couple of lovely old people as in-laws and with a bit of luck a car if the company provides one? I think I'll manage to get one.'

Sister Kläre suddenly fell back into the cockiness she'd rediscovered in the field after 15 years of marriage. 'Really?' she said innocently. 'Well, that would be necessary. For without a car – I'm afraid I couldn't be happy without a car, Lieutenant.'

Kroysing fell for it. 'That's just it,' he said despondently. 'I imagine you couldn't be. I don't know how you lived before you came here. People say you're from a rich family and your husband was a staff officer. We'd have to cut right back, Kläre. Not everyone can live like that.'

Later, Sister Kläre often remembered the absurd, sweet joy that flooded her during those morning hours on the 20th of March – the calm, collected way the young man wooed her, which he seemed to find as natural as the healing gun wound in his leg.

'It's nice of you to acknowledge the existence of my husband, Lieutenant Kroysing.'

'There's divorce,' he answered curtly.

'And there are Catholics,' she said in the same tone.

Kroysing sat on the bed and peered at her. 'Kläre,' he said hoarsely, 'you're not going to tell me there can't be anything between us because you've been married for a few years.'

'A few years!' said Sister Kläre. 'Fifteen years!' And that numeral inspired her to think of all the terrible difficulties of the situation. 'You don't just separate after that long because you've found someone younger who wants you. You've had a life together, and that deserves respect and consideration and a place in your heart. I'm not some kind of hussy who skips from bed to bed with no baggage. No, my dear friend, there's a lot to think about, a lot of dissenting voices that must be considered, a lots of barriers. And if I'm to take your proposal seriously—'

'Kläre,' he cried, standing up on one leg with his injured leg bent under him, supporting himself on the bed with one hand and reaching out to her with the other.

With a happy but wistful laugh, she backed towards the door. 'I'll have to think about it,' she said firmly.

'I'm sick of thinking,' he cried almost angrily. 'First she wanted to think about whether she could make a telephone call and save my friend, and now she wants to think about whether she can end her marriage and marry me. Well, my extremely thoughtful lady, I believe in acting quickly. If you're prepared to marry me, phone the crown prince before midnight tonight. If you don't want me, all you have to do is say tonight that you'd prefer to phone him in the morning. Agreed?'

She nodded and was about to repeat his final word, but Kroysing made two sudden hops across the room on his good leg, wrapped her in his long arms and pressed his mouth to her parted lips, felt her go soft against his chest then stiffen, let her go and said: 'To have is to hold,' and hopped back to the bed like a long-legged grasshopper. She took her bucket and scrubbing brush and left the room without a word, like a pretty housemaid who's just been kissed. Kroysing felt his heart hammering against his ribs. *She'll telephone*, he thought triumphantly. *She'll telephone tonight and her name will be Frau Kroysing as surely as mine is Herr Kroysing.* Immediately afterwards it occurred to him that she'd definitely ask Father Lochner's advice. He'd have to get the priest on his side. He could not deny that Niggl had become completely irrelevant to him in that moment. He laughed inwardly. It would pain him, but if Sister Kläre married him and Father Lochner helped her to get her present marriage dissolved he'd abandon his vendetta against Niggl.

In a fairly large field hospital, the staff working to relieve human suffering and return wounded men to full strength are kept fully occupied in the morning. That underlying reality doesn't change whether you view the process as a way of rehabilitating slaves to work and fight for the ruling class, as Pahl did, or a way of summoning all Germany's strength in the battle for her very existence, as Kroysing did. The sometimes terrible ceremony of changing bandages, with its groans, clenched teeth and curses, its snarling and coaxing, passed on, which is to say it moved from room to room. Nurses carried buckets of festering wood pulp out to be burnt. Sometimes, if the healing process had gone wrong and there was excessive granulation in the wound rather than firm, new flesh, cauterisation was required. Then the silver nitrate probe or small, sharp scrapers were brought out, and great suffering ensued. Other, more fortunate men toiled in the gym where their injured limbs were gradually restored to the purposes for which nature intended them through exercise. Once it has realised its potential, human material, that baffling, growing, animate cell tissue, is doomed to rejoin the Earth's surface – that underlying impulse is inherent in its target form, just as butterflies, flies and bees are driven to fertilise flowers. Sometimes it seemed as though the planet itself wanted to be stimulated to preordained levels of performance – a frenzy of raw materials and forces – so it might offer ever-improving living conditions to rational beings. Perhaps that was why it incited the nearly two billion cells called humanity to excessive activity and conflict. It wanted to spur the higher, more rational, more forward-looking ones on, while provoking resistance from the lower, wilder, more instinctive ones, so as to squeeze as much as possible in the way of inventions, discoveries and harvests from both. Aviation, chemistry, medical science, warfare – all had advanced in leaps and bounds. New means of communication had brought communities together that previously had hardly known of each other's existence. Biased social systems had come crashing down, and those who did not understand how to deploy all available forces within their borders in the struggle for existence were doomed to defeat, whatever the existing privileged classes might say. Services rendered could always be repaid with ingratitude, promises could be turned around and chartered rights rescinded. Why not? People did not have a very well developed sense of civilised behaviour. They barely understood what it was for. It was easier to appreciate technology. It helped with killing.

On this basis, the engineer and the priest understood each other very well. Each considered the other to be the champion of a weaker cause. Happily, their meeting took place in an atmosphere of vague agreement that members of the global household had an important duty to respect the individual. For they knew that nature only works in species, kinds, races and large groups; the requirement placed on men by nature to respect the individual was thus all the greater. For as it battled to enrich its homeland, humanity had need of individuals as if they were the purpose of earthly fertility and the battle for existence. And while the engineer and the priest conducted their cheerful argument, the medical officer sat with some wounded man who had been put in special rooms to test whether water promoted natural healing. The water did help. Man's fluid composition seemed to respond gratefully to it. Out in the courtyard, flocks of white and tan chickens cackled, pecked and fluttered, commanded by a couple of cocks, pigs grunted by a row of sties, and enormous long-haired Belgian rabbits with soft eyes and fur hopped about. March light sparkled down on them, and their animal hearts thrilled with joy. They did not divine their purpose, which would bring their joyful existence to an end, or that it was only because of that purpose that they existed in the first place. In certain rooms, wet laundry was being rubbed down on corrugated iron; in others, food was being cooked for several hundred people. A ruddy-faced matron bent over a ledger and noted down figures. A horse-drawn wagon panted up the hill, bringing tinned food, ration bread and the post in a large sack. That created a lot work; it had to be sorted, distributed and read – but it also radiated healing. Pahl the typesetter received a letter, which he read with a strange smile. His application was already in progress and would doubtless be successful. His unit, the replacement ASC battalion in Küstrin, had emerged from obscurity. Once it had established what pension the grateful Fatherland owed him, it was going to order that he be sent home, formally and solemnly discharged, transferred back to civilian life and his profession. As a typesetter doesn't exactly need his toe, the compensation for his wound wouldn't be very high; nonetheless, Pahl was now a pensioner, and so there was a limit to how bad things could get. The soldiers sang that this campaign was no express train, but for him it had come to a halt. For the others it would rattle cheerfully on. It had been as little detained by the Kaiser's peace initiative as by President Wilson's messages or Pope Benedict XV's prayers – this capitalist war about the redistribution of world markets. You couldn't say that the capitalists had started it, but they had made the aristocratic land-owning class in the three empires into masters of a military machine so strong that once it had been set in motion it could only come to a standstill when it had extinguished them and itself. Capitalists couldn't make peace. Neither could feudal states. They paid for it with their own collapse. Only nations could make peace, when the blessings of a lost war had made enough of an impression on them. The Russians would prove that.

Lieutenant Flachsbauer also received a letter, read it, sighed and placed it under his pillow. So did Lieutenant Kroysing. His letter was from his mother, as his father had delegated letter writing to her some time ago. She was looking forward to him being transferred to a Nuremberg hospital and asked him to hurry the process along. She was having nightmares and clung to every bit of news from him. She felt that he would only be safe from the murderous claws of war when he was in her arms. Kroysing frowned: people at home really knew how to lay it on thick. Claws of war! That kind of talk should be left to washerwomen. He wondered what exactly she thought was going to happen to him here. The Verdun front had lost its importance, and there had been no more talk of long-range guns from the Frogs. And the Red Cross flew its flag and had painted a cross on the roof to prevent air attacks. He decided he'd better wait to tell his parents about his transfer to the air force in person when he had some proper leave.

'We're counting on you remaining in Germany from now on, my beloved child, and returning to your profession if possible, hopefully somewhere very nearby. We both very much regret that we weren't always close before the war. Perhaps that was just part of your growing up, but now, darling boy, now, my dear lanky Hardi, you must remember that you are our only child and help us to take some joy in life again. A family home is only a family home if the children call it home. And we've already had to part with our dear Christel. I have to confess that I'm not a heroic mother. I could weep and weep over your dear, kind, talented brother, just as I would have wept inconsolably if it had been you and our tall, proud, manly Hardi were never to dash up our steps again. I don't cry because it's useless and it just breaks your father's heart, and he can't do anything to help me. If the Fatherland really needs further sacrifices, then other fathers and mothers will have to make them because we have suffered enough. Sometimes I wonder if I'll ever lift a grandchild from its crib – that's the only real joy left to an old woman like me. *Yes*, thought Kroysing, *a grandchild would give her a new lease of life*. He should write to her and say that. He'd been right to offer Niggl's scalp to Father Lochner as they philosophised together earlier – provided Lochner agreed to help with certain difficulties that Sister Kläre would tell him about after dinner. It was a fair exchange, and Lochner seemed to acknowledge that.

And so he replied to his mother immediately. He felt unusually warm towards her. The resentment she'd alluded to was completely forgotten. Tender, cheerful words poured from him as he bent uncomfortably over the table and wrote his forces letter in bold handwriting – his last.

BOOK NINE

Fire from heaven

CHAPTER ONE

A helping hand

FATHER LOCHNER TRIPPED into Sister Kläre's nun's cell with excited little baby steps. She'd invited him for a coffee before the end of the lunch break. 'What's this I hear, Sister Kläre – and not from you, but from the wild hunter himself!'

The little room smelt pleasantly of real coffee, the one luxury Sister Kläre did not deny herself and her friends. She sat calmly on the bed looking at the agitated priest with a direct, almost stern expression. 'It doesn't matter who you heard it from, and if our tall friend exaggerated, then I'm here to set things straight. So, will you condone it or not?'

The chaplain had lowered himself on to the stool and was stirring his sugar with a small spoon, his pinkie delicately raised. 'That's what I call taking the bull by the horns. That's vintage Sister Kläre. Do you know, you could have been abbess of a great convent. A thousand years ago, you might have shed light and consolation upon a whole area or province.'

'Now you're just talking rubbish, Father Lochner, complete and utter rubbish, and you're doing it to avoid answering. But you must answer.'

'Do you like him?' asked the priest carefully.

'Yes,' replied Sister Kläre. 'I like him. I like that tall young man a lot. But I also like my husband and children. I'm not some daft wee girl. My liking for him is not so ingrained that I couldn't cauterise it like a granulated wound if need be. If you think that the practical difficulties are too great and that it would be too painful for my husband and children, I'll tell Kroysing we can't have what we want and that we'll have to form a different kind of friendship if we survive the war or go our separate ways.'

Father Lochner raised his eyebrows, secretly shocked at the down-to-earth way this lady from the highest echelons of society, in nurse's uniform with the face of a lovely nun called Klara, expressed herself. 'Do you think then,' he fumbled, 'that Colonel Schwersenz will ever get better? Do you think you'll ever be able to live with him properly again and mean something to him?'

'No, I don't think so,' said Sister Kläre. 'My mother writes from the house in

Hinterstein that he sits there surrounded by maps and papers, more shut away than ever. He's completely obsessed by his role in the Battle of the Marne and is dead to everything else. He only takes the vaguest and most distracted interest in what's going on around him and hardly ever asks about the children, whom he calls his grandchildren. But he's strong physically and has a healthy appetite. He goes for long walks – route marches – and sees nothing but sectors and strategic, tactical problems. The old lady, who's the wisest person I know, says she's become quite a military expert. Her main concern is that Schwersenz will try to leave so he can explain his role in the Battle of the Marne to the Kaiser and the Reichstag, or even try to address the nation from a public square, in which case he'd be transferred to a closed institution.'

'Dreadful,' said Father Lochner. 'O, what a noble mind is here o'erthrown!'

'That's Hamlet, isn't it? It's only too true. What if I can never really connect with him again?'

'Then a Christian marriage with him is no longer possible,' said the priest, draining his cup. They were both silent.

Sister Kläre wondered whether she should say any more. Then she did: 'It's not that I'm complaining. But neither do I particularly care what people think. What I would like to say is that the current state of affairs is just the last stage in a process that began years ago and always looked like it might end this way. My husband lived for his work like a scholar or a monk. He was a soldier body and soul. Otherwise a man of his class would never have embarked on such a career. No living creature was ever good enough for him, me included. Before the war I thought that was just how it was, particularly as my father and brothers were no different. Now I don't think that any more.'

'I understand,' said the priest, as he watched the steaming coffee fall on to another cube of sugar and began to look forward to a second cup. 'The war has shown you humanity in all its myriad forms. It has revealed the kingdom of the world to you in all its abundance and misery, as well as the relief work you perform. You no longer want to lie fallow. But, Sister Kläre, how do you think a new marriage would affect your children?'

Sister Kläre took off her head covering and smoothed her hair into shape with her strong hands. 'I'm convinced,' she said, 'that a younger, more active stepfather such as Kroysing would be good for them – as far as one can humanly tell. But children are passionate, impulsive and unpredictable, and so you never know how they will react. I know only too well that growing children are people in their own right, inscrutable to a certain extent and not easily swayed. That needs to be taken into account.'

'People are not insurance companies,' said Father Lochner, dabbing his bald head with a handkerchief. 'If they have good intentions and are convinced their actions are right, that's enough.'

'God knows I have those,' said Sister Kläre.

'Then in my opinion your marriage to Colonel Schwersenz may be declared invalid, and if that's what you want I'll do everything I can to support you.'

'Yes,' she said. 'That's what I want.' And she replaced her head covering.

'My God.' He looked at the clock. 'You must get back to work. And I had better say goodbye to all those poor lads who want to ease their souls, whether they're Catholics or not. I'll start in ward 1 and try to finish in ward 3. I must find time for that Pahl. And the boss man has invited me to share a bottle of wine after dinner as a reward for my abstemiousness during my treatment. That's my little timetable for today.'

Sister Kläre buttoned on her apron. 'Then we'll be bumping into each other.' She did up the buttons at the back, and almost as an after-thought added: 'You know Kroysing's a Protestant, don't you?'

'Oh,' said Father Lochner, raising his hands to table height as if to fend off this objection, 'it's best if we stick to the matter in hand. If your marriage is dissolved or declared invalid, a new page will be turned and this is not the time to decide what will be written on it. But I must confess,' and he smiled a little guiltily, 'that I shall not perform this service without misgivings. As he will tell you himself, Kroysing has promised me he will behave like a Christian rather than a heathen and pardon an enemy, or at least to let him go, avoid a dreadful court case that would have caused uproar in Bavaria and embarrassed our Church, and for that reason, Sister Kläre, I thank the Holy Virgin that things come together for the best and no one will suffer for your happiness.'

'Here on earth we can expect no more.'

CHAPTER TWO

The man

BERTIN APPEARED LATE in the afternoon, accompanied by Karl Lebehde. They found a strange gathering at Pahl's bedside. A lot of patients were standing around, sitting on beds or leaning on the wall, listening. Kroysing, looking like a referee, sat on a stool with his bandaged leg stretched out on Pahl's mattress. He had in mind the unnecessarily strident arguments from his student days, which ended in mutual insults. But Father Lochner, who'd worked in the Ruhr mining district, the Cologne docks and the button-making factories of Elberfeld, had no intention of playing that game. As a Rhinelander he was used to dealing with city folk, and in a few minutes he had started a conversation, which he expected to control, watched expectantly by Pahl with his magnetic gaze. However, it proved not to be so easy. When Kroysing arrived, accompanied by the medical officer in his white coat, they were arguing about the origins and meaning of the Easter festival. Pahl saw reflected in it the general joy that people and animals felt at the return of spring, and for him the symbolic egg represented fertility rites and resurgent life. Father Lochner, by contrast, took an historical, materialist view of the festival's meaning, taking it back to the struggle for freedom – for example, that of the Jewish proletarian nation from Egyptian exploitation – under a civil servant or member of the ruling class, such as Mirabeau or, at that moment, the lawyer Kerenski in Russia. So they've swapped sides, thought Kroysing in amusement. The priest had been too clever, and Pahl was as ever Pahl, bright-eyed and calm. But when Bertin and Lebehde joined the friends, the conversation took an even more general turn. They discussed redemption, martyrdom on Calvary, 'evil' and human nature, and the divine. There was a fervour in the air, said Lochner. With each passing month, all of humanity was yearning ever more deeply for peace, since the Kaiser had, so to speak, stamped the imperial eagle on the word. The Pope, the Kaiser, Professor Wilson and international labour leaders were united in their efforts to restore peace to the world, but it didn't happen. What was going on? What was barring the road to salvation? Definitely not the soldiers.

They'd all had enough, and if the bugles sounded the ceasefire at 12 noon that afternoon, it would be pretty to difficult to drum up a German, French or British soldier for a game of skat by 12.30.

General laughter. General agreement. Only Pahl didn't laugh. He'd sat on his pillow, his back against the bedstead, and in his slow but direct manner advanced the counter argument: 'Unfortunately,' he said, 'the ruling masters' peace overtures all have conditions attached that the other side must meet, just as a dog catcher will keep a dog that he's just caught on the lead. He doesn't know the dog, and guess what, it turns out to be wild and won't do what he tells it, and so the conditions are not met and peace must unfortunately stay in the box.'

'No politics, please,' said the medical officer. The wide space between his eyes, his square forehead and bouffant hair gave him a decisive air, which was softened by his husky voice.

'Nonsense, doctor,' said Kroysing. 'Let the tormented flesh talk politics if it wants. We won't lock horns.'

'I should hope not,' said Father Lochner. 'Please note that I'm the only man in this group wearing anything approaching a military tunic...'

'The militant Church—' interjected Kroysing.

'...I'd find it difficult to raise an army among all these white coats. And yet I'm in favour of war – and a militant Church. Not war with guns and infantry, but war against the indefatigable adversary – the only one who can chase peace from the world and impede redemption.'

'Yes, when I look around me the world looks pretty darned redeemed,' said the medical officer without bitterness.

'And yet me must believe that Christ died on the cross to save us from the worst of our bestiality,' said Father Lochner almost passionately, 'or we might as well pack up and suck gas.'

'Do you mean that if that hadn't taken place things would be even worse,' said Kroysing. 'Assuming it really did take place?'

'No religion, please,' said the chief physician, not without a little self-irony.

It was relatively immaterial whether something had happened or not, compared with the faith it inspired, said Pahl. There was therefore no need for a theological dispute, since faith was a generally recognised fact and could not be denied by Christians, Jews or atheists. So the priest could happily carry on. But, he said with a joking twinkle, they should really hear what their comrade Bertin had to say about it. Because the Exodus from Egypt and the trial of

Jesus of Nazareth before the Roman military governor of Judea had all taken place among Jews.

Bertin gave an embarrassed laugh. He was the only Jew in the room. He was proud of the urge for redemption and the messianic impulse towards a better organised world that had dominated the spiritual history of his race since the days of Nebuchadnezzar. Before he'd been able to talk at length about the prophet's tirades against the potentates and the multitudes, which were intended to instil morality in organised society. *But now my mind is so dulled*, he thought, as he prepared to answer Pahl's question. Yes, he said, the struggle with fate, expressed by the Greeks in their tragedies, had been played out in real life for the Jews in the prophets' struggle against the reluctant flesh of their own nation. They had not spared that nation and had even made a bad name for themselves on account of their obstinacy. But in truth all nations were just as obstinate; they just didn't talk about it, or so it seemed. There was something there, he said, staring glumly into the middle distance, that impeded redemption. That was why the devil played such an important role in all cults and in every age, even if Christian teaching said that the worst of his teeth had been knocked out. You had to concur with the poets, Goethe for example, who said that his remaining powers were enough to be going on with.

Pahl and Kroysing protested, and Father Lochner wasn't happy either. The first two didn't want to hear such superstitious nonsense, while Father Lochner wanted more recognition to be given to the reality of the devil.

'Oh dear,' said Bertin, 'I'm in hot water now. They don't want to acknowledge the devil's existence, and for you, Father, he's not real enough. What am I to do?'

'I'll tell you what you can do,' muttered Kroysing. 'Let's forget the bogeymen, eh? And we don't need any riddles either.'

Pahl said nothing more, but made a mental note to box Comrade Bertin's ears for coming out with such embarrassing antiquities, which would've made any young worker roar with laughter.

Karl Lebehde opened his mouth, which he'd thus far not done in that company. If the gas man came demanding payment for January in March and there was no money left to pay the bill, he explained, his wife would say the gas man was the devil incarnate. For there was only one gas cooker in their flat, provided by the state, and if the supply were to be cut off she wouldn't be able to cook or eat. For his wife that would be the devil incarnate appearing. 'If my wife were stupid,' he said, 'she'd have a go at the gas man, as if he could do something about it. If she weren't so stupid, and I don't think she is, then she'd work out where the real devil lies. For there must be one. She'd just have to ferret him out. Is he at the gasworks? No. In the city of Berlin? Again, no. At the provincial administration? Who knows. In the State of Prussia? That's what the British think, as if their gas men were angels. Among the whites? That's what the Indians and blacks are saying now. And so we come back to the Father's view that he's got the whole world firmly in his claws.'

'Slow down,' said Pahl. 'I think you skipped a few stations there.'

'No,' broke in Father Lochner. 'Our Landstürmer hasn't skipped any stations at all. The harshness of life, the lack of brotherly love, our un-Christian society: the spirit of the nation expresses all that in horns, hooves and the hairy tail of a cold, jeering monster, and there's no point getting angry about it. The wise old Egyptians wrote in pictures, and nations are like children and Egyptians and poets: they think in pictures. The only fools are those who take the pictures literally and act as if the others were stupid. And yet no one thinks that lightning is really a jagged, shining wire thrown down from on high, even if that's what it looks like.'

'That's one way to redemption,' observed Kroysing drily.

Some of the men laughed. They always enjoyed listening to the tall lieutenant. He didn't let these boring speechifiers pull the wool over his eyes.

'So the devil is the capitalist system.'

Father Lochner frowned. That was trivial, he said sharply. Any economic system that knew no charity could degenerate in exactly the same infernal way. They'd been discussing fundamental forces, which were the message of Easter and the objective of religion when it tried to look after people's souls.

Suddenly Sister Kläre pushed through the circle of seated and standing men, radiantly white in her apron and starched head covering. She whispered a couple of figures to the medical officer, which she read from her chart, a long slip of paper that trembled in her hands. The doctor nodded at most of them, frowned at a couple and shook his head angrily at a few: 'The devil is our stubborn flesh,' he said. 'Our accursed organic state that we'll never fully understand. And redemption, if I may speak bluntly, is and remains death. As long as flesh lives it suffers, and our tricks for deadening pain turn out to be a swindle when the chips are down.'

And, guess what? At that, the adversaries of a moment ago suddenly united in protest. 'Impossible!' they almost shouted.

Death, wheezed Father Lochner fiercely, was a gigantic folly that had first been brought into the world by sin. It crushed everything under its clumsy feet. It had trampled Novalis into his grave and destroyed thousands of fresh talents and new beginnings.

Yes, agreed Kroysing, it was a point of honour with soldiers never to have a good word to say about death. In the trenches, death was the ultimate treachery and desertion. A man who died left the Fatherland and the cause in the lurch, so to speak. He couldn't help it if war was eternal and men were imbued with an inextinguishable desire for conflict, and all warrior religions had to take that into account. Given the choice, he at any rate would prefer to roam the earth as the Wandering German, like the Wandering Jew, plunging into every conflict and joining in every victory.

Pahl's pale eyes lit up. That was fine so long as there were an idea behind it, if it were about liberating a vast, productive section of humanity from oppression, exploitation and injustice. It was for those kinds of ideas that the fighting spirit should travel the earth, building a new platform so that future generations would have a better starting point and every Pahl, Bertin and Kroysing would be able to fulfil their talents to the benefit and redemption of humanity.'

'There it is again,' said Kroysing. 'Redemption.'

But Bertin, pale and trembling, said that if anything were the devil it was the use of violence, trampling people underfoot in a murderous, silencing frenzy. Death wasn't evil. Death had wonderful, alluring depths – to lie down as your ancestors had lain down, to understand nothing, answer nothing, ask nothing. It was the business of murder that was infernal, the thousands of ways of achieving extinction, the executioner's axe crashing down. If everyone's life ran out as a candle burns down, then there would be nothing to say against death. But if an individual – or a whole generation – had his life and rights ripped out from under him like a chair wrenched from him by a stronger person, then we should combat that with all available means, join the fight and ally ourselves with those who, like ourselves, were under threat.'

The man's gone mad, thought Sister Kläre. He's talking himself into trouble. 'Bed rest!' she cried. 'Time for quiet!'

The men muttered. They wanted to hear more. The man was right. Everyone had the right to live.

'You'll make yourself very popular with the Prussians with those opinions,' said Father Lochner sharply but with respect.

'If you're against violence, then you must be against life, young man,' added the medical officer. 'I'm afraid your indignation is blinding you to the facts of life. People create suffering; it's the first thing they do. Before birth, during birth, after birth – it's all the same. A baby makes its way into the world by force, or more correctly, is thrust into it when its time comes. There's force, pressure, blood, screaming. That's how a young hero appears – you, me, all of us. And if these basic facts mean anything to you, how does he reply? What does he do to greet existence?'

'We scream?' asked Bertin. 'We scream furiously, rebelling against our delivery?'

No one listening knew why he was so eager to hear the answer.

The doctor had an inscrutable smile on his face. 'I don't know,' he said, speaking slowly in the silence, 'if you'll be satisfied with my answer. You want me to verify the revolutionary principle, and I will in a certain way. But it's not very appetising and it's bound be too much for you. In order to make a newborn baby cry, we slap it. Blows are the first thing it experiences. That's the only way to get it to take its first breath.'

A couple of soldiers laughed appreciatively. Blows created a bit of atmosphere.

'And yet,' continued the doctor, 'even that isn't the beginning, the first utterance. For as the baby passes through the gateway into the world, it suffers fear; how much remains to be established. And in order to express that fear, it shits. That's how it greets life. The name for this calling card is "meconium", young man. I knew you wouldn't like it. It's not very heroic, is it, this revolutionary act? But our nation retains the memory of it one of our vulgar expressions for mishap.'

Four men opened their mouths to speak then shut them again. Objections flared within Bertin: hadn't reason and intellect been applied to alleviate the natural pains of childbirth through obstetrics? But he didn't feel he could say that. The doctor had struck a commanding tone that must be allowed to fade away. And so the group fell back respectfully to let the doctor through. As he left, he turned round one last time: 'I hope that what we've been discussing won't go beyond the four walls of this room,' he said.

'It's not a room,' laughed Sister Kläre. 'It's a miserable barracks. Throw a trouser button on to the roof and watch it collapse.' And with that she followed him out.

The others followed her example and began to leave. Pahl shook Bertin's hand as they said goodbye. Bertin, looking pale, said he was on guard duty that night, as was Lebehde, and so they'd better get back pronto. 'Get your guard duty over with, my friend, and come and see me again soon,' said Pahl almost tenderly. 'You really stuck it to them, my friend. You and me together: we'll shake that baby up.'

Lebehde made a mental note to advise Bertin on the way home to be more careful, although he was less surprised than the rest by his outburst. It was an accident waiting to happen after everything he had been through and seen.

'Wait for me outside, Lebehde,' said Bertin. 'I'd better go and calm my lieutenant down or he'll bite my head off the next time I visit him.'

As Bertin made his way slowly out of the room with Kroysing on his arm, he apologised, saying he didn't understand why he'd flared up like that. Priests had always infuriated him before, but it was the first it had happened for a while.

'You're a right one,' snarled Kroysing. 'It seems you're not as daft as you look.'

They had reached the corridor. The door to the broom cupboard opened and Sister Kläre came towards them. 'You're quite a ball of fire,' she said, looking at Bertin. 'You'd better tone it down and sharpish. I'm going to be making a telephone call on your behalf this evening.' And she nodded and went off down the corridor.

Kroysing stopped and pressed his fist into Bertin's shoulder painfully hard. 'There is going to be a redemption, then,' he said, breathing heavily. 'Yours, I mean.'

CHAPTER THREE

Bread for the hungry

LEBEHDE THE INN-KEEPER, disguised as a Landstürmer, his grey oilcloth cap with its brass cross tipped over his forehead, a leather belt round his hips, handed Private Bertin a long rifle, infantry issue 91 with an improved lock, at one minute to 10. 'Right, my friend,' he said a little shiftily, 'take this shooter and have a ball.'

Both men were wearing their overcoats. Lebehde's stuck out oddly at the hips. As they walked a little way together towards the barracks where the Barkopp working party was billeted, Lebehde explained in passing why: he'd taken the liberty of feeling the gigantic paper bags in the French freight cars and had been very pleasantly surprised. 'Have a taste,' he said holding something hard and sharp-edged in front of Bertin's mouth.

Bertin bit in to it cautiously. It was white bread, a hard old roll. He looked at Lebehde in astonishment. He nodded solemnly. 'White bread, my lad. For the French prisoners in Germany, so they don't starve. The Red Cross provides it. But it doesn't provide for our wives. We have to sort that out ourselves.' Lebehde tapped his pocket. 'I've got a whole load of it.'

'This rock hard stuff?' asked Bertin.

'Listen, lad,' said Lebehde kindly, 'dunked in coffee and fried up with a wee bit of butter and artificial honey it'll make great French toast. And if your wife can get hold of some of raisins and whisk those in and bake it in a mould, it'll make a better pudding than the Easter bunny himself could wish for. It's great quality wheat. Ask the Kaiser's wife and if she's in a truthful mood, she'll tell you she hasn't had wheat that good for ages.

And chatting away in this vein, Karl Lebehde grabbed the door handle. But then he swung round and whispered: 'If you hadn't sorted out that lot up there, I wouldn't have let on about this, because there have been too many times recently when you didn't share your tin of fat with us.'

Stunned, Bertin made his way back in his jackboots, shouldering his gun, to his beat between the two sidings at the tiny station of Vilosnes-East.

The mild glow of the spring night spread along the valley to the river. On top of the steep slope to the right, out of sight, sat Dannevoux field hospital. The earth stuck to his boots, but the damp air was pleasantly soothing compared to the smoke and stink of the barracks. Vilosnes-East station! It was there that Acting Lieutenant Graßnick's labour company from Serbia had alighted and marched behind him in a kind of dream, past the muzzles of the Bavarian field guns almost stumbling into range of the French guns. A year had passed since then, slightly longer even – and what a year! He looked back on it the way he must have looked back on himself as first-year schoolboy when he left school: a moustached teenager in slacks, schooled in dancing, looking down on a trusting little squirt in short trousers. And he wasn't even sure if the year was over. But Sister Kläre had promised to telephone someone for him tonight. He was no longer as naïve as he had been when he first met her, when she was ironing in Kroysing's room, for example. From snippets he'd heard, it seemed there had been something going on between that lovely woman and the crown prince, which of course put a different light on things. Well, why not? Adults' private lives were their own business. The crown prince was not well liked in the army. He refused to endure the hardships that hundreds of thousands of men were commanded to endure in his name. He paid the price for that. Packets of cigarettes were left lying in the mud on the Moirey-Azannes road. But he was also meant to be gallant and incapable of being unkind to a woman with whom he'd been on intimate terms. If Sister Kläre took up his cause, things looked promising – thank God. Even if that poisonous little toad Major Jansch stood on tiptoe and spat as far as he could, he wouldn't reach this particular bowl of soup.

Bertin felt hopeful as he climbed over switches and sleepers on his beat between the two trains: on his right were the five closed rectangular freight cars full of damp powder, damaged shells and collected duds, on his left the open wagons of the bread train covered with large tarpaulins. He shoved his hands in his pockets and strolled on. He was glad of the chance to think for a couple of hours. He was damned if he understood what had happened up there. Like any soldier, he often grumbled. Grumbling went together with discipline. But never before had he lost his temper like that in front of strangers and superior officers to the point where Pahl had congratulated him and the medical officer had asked everyone not to repeat what he'd said outside ward 3. What was happening to him? He was 28 years old but he felt about 100. He'd gone to war full of enthusiasm for Germany's cause, thrilled that he'd experience the Glory Years, worried only that he might miss it because of his physical infirmities. And now, barely two years later, all his hopes had turned to ash. The world around him was bleak and leering, and violence ruled – the plain and simple violence of the fist. It wasn't the justice of the cause that held sway but the size of the boot. This war was a stamping of boots: German boots kicked French boots, Russian boots German boots, Austrian boots Russian boots, Italian boots Austrian boots, and the British, with their lace-up shoes that were sturdier than them all but more elegantly cut, helped out where they could, sticking in a few kicks of their own – and he understood that. Now American shoes had appeared, and the world had become a madhouse. Everything from peacetime had been swept aside. The world was now run by sergeant majors and you were a lucky man if you survived in it.

Sunk in such thoughts, Werner Bertin reached the bread cars, which were sealed with grey and brown tarpaulins. He pulled up the open flap on the middle car and felt inside. Fantastic! The papers bags had been slit on one side and some of the contents were already gone. Bertin, the sentry, hurriedly stuck his hand in and began to fill his coat pockets, hunching his shoulders guiltily and glancing round. But there was only the moon to see him, small and faraway, shining down through a hole in the mist high up in the sky on to the wisps of fog in the valley.

Bertin was wearing gloves so he didn't need to put his hands in his pockets, the deep sack-like bags of thick lining material inside his coat. The next day he'd send the rolls to Lenore with that recipe Karl Lebehde had magicked up. Things weren't good at home. How could they be? And it seemed they weren't any better elsewhere in Germany – or so he'd heard. His last few weeks' post had given him a great deal of food for thought, only he didn't have the time to think. But today he did, and his thoughts turned to his brother-in-law, David, a future musician, who had sent his sister bitter letters of complaint about their parents from the training camp, because they'd knowingly let him participate in the whole swindle. 'We're forced to do things that can only be done voluntarily, and to round the whole dirty trick off we're called volunteers though we're slaves.' David was sharp young man, thought Bertin, and not just when it came to musical notation and the five-line staff, which he'd once called Beethoven's telegraph wires. The news from his brother, Fritz, wasn't very joyful either: the regiment had left Romania again and was now inexplicably stationed in the Adige valley in the South Tyrol, which was bad news for all concerned, including the Italians. The old Kaiser Franz Josef had died, and his successor, Karl, had, as they said, betaken himself to the front, but the bulk of the task still fell to the Prussians (who might be from Bavaria, Württemberg or Hessen). In short, there was little to gladden Frau Lina Bertin's heart – to the contrary. At least soon she wouldn't need to worry about her eldest son, even if little Fritzel was undeniably her favourite. Sister Kläre, a grateful reader, was going to make an important call that night. She might already have done it, in which case Frau Bertin could soon put her mind at rest.

Small was the room, and narrow was the bed. And yet two people successfully squeezed into them with surprising regularity. Even Lieutenant Kroysing's long legs somehow slipped under the covers quite easily, although one of them was swathed in stiff bandages. Lieutenant Flachsbauer slept across the way blissfully alone.

'Should I go and phone now?'

'Why would you do that?'

The tinkle of a woman's laugh: 'Because I promised you that I'd phone tonight.'

'The night is still long. It's only just begun.'

The woman laughed again, a light, charming laugh, such as may never before have been heard under that flat roof. The glow from a wick floating in an ugly glass tumbler of oil played on the ceiling. It shone on Sister Kläre's quiet eyes and across Kroysing's forehead and the bridge of his nose. 'We have to be sensible. Don't forget your sweetheart is a maidservant, Lieutenant. She has to get a good night's sleep and be up early. I need seven hours.'

'Sweet maidservant. Couldn't you make the call after 11?'

'How about between 10 and 11? Okay, just before 11. And then you really have to hit the sack, all right?' She sat up and looked at him sternly, her plaits hanging down, a laugh on her lips. The exquisite line of her shoulders seemed to start beneath her ear lobes and flow down her arm, inviting caresses.

Kroysing let his long hand slide down her skin. 'Kläre,' he said. 'Kläre.'

'What is it, sweetheart?'

'I'm so stupidly happy. Bertin in his entirety does not merit you taking your beloved leg out from under the covers and putting your foot on the cold floorboards.'

She stretched her leg out and wiggled her toes, and their shadows flickered on the wall.

How quickly does time pass on guard duty? As quickly as the guard wants. He can think about his own life, the movements of the stars or whatever he chooses as he paces back and forth. The one strange thing is how a veiled thought will sometimes know how to keep battering away inside his head until it finds a weak spot and breaks through. Bertin looked around happily, drinking in the moonlit night, the vast stillness and indistinct sounds wafting over. Somewhere very far away a lorry with iron tyres was driving past. If there was anything happening at the front, it was out of earshot, for the guns barely fired now and the rifle fire was swallowed by the steep ridge. It was so very light. He could make out every sleeper, the points over the way, baskets of broken shells and the gravel between the rails. Should he have filled his pockets with that stale, unsalted bread? Hadn't Lebehde committed a serious crime by stealing goods he was commanded to guard? And had not Bertin now committed the same crime? A military offence of the first order – if it were discovered. At the same time, most officers would just laugh if someone accused him or someone else of such a crime. For what was the harm in stealing a little food in the middle of a war? War was one long, uninterrupted looting spree. They'd been thieving from the homeland and neighbouring nations for three years now, day and night, every second of every day. Stealing a little food did no harm. A soldier's needs had to be met. An army needs a lot over the duration and as it doesn't produce anything it has to steal. If it's judicious in its stealing, it can last for a long time, but if it isn't, if it's too greedy, it won't last. Just as Sergeant Major Pfund, who had suddenly disappeared a couple of days previously, had been sent back to Metz with a fat black mark against his name. For the winter of starvation had reached its peak. Major Jansch had been forced to cough up his hoarded supplies. He had sought and found a victim. Herr Pfund and his cunning Christmas purchases became: embezzlement. The result was the company had no money and couldn't offer its men the same supplementary food as other canteens – cheese, pickled herrings and chocolate. The doctor had complained and the depot had complained, but these complaints were viewed very unsympathetically by Army Group East, and according to the postal orderly Behrend, a pair of dilapidated shoes had arrived with a snide letter enclosed – all most helpful for sending a sergeant major into the wilderness. A new man had been put in charge of the company about three days previously. Who was he? Sergeant Duhn, a quiet man with steady grey eyes, who didn't draw attention to himself but had achieved the dagger and badges of the regular army that had been denied to pushy Glinsky. Lost in his own thoughts, Bertin hooked his thumb under his rifle sling and wandered the long stretch back to the bread wagons.

There they stood, the covering loosened in one place, laying them open to the guard who was supposed to protect them. *Excellent*, thought Bertin, *and how typical of human society. The state, which is supposed to protect the weak against the strong, comes down firmly on the side of the strong and steals from those it's supposed to protect, but in a limited way, so that the starving don't go too hungry, throw down their tools and band together against the thieves. Organised protest is forbidden. The weak have to present their complaints individually. I believe in organised protest and want to join cause with the weak but here I am with my pockets full of white bread for my wife, which I've stolen from the very weakest. Deal thy bread to the hungry, it says in the Bible. Steal thy bread from the hungry more like in wartime, and I'm cheerfully joining in.* For what had actually happened? Private Werner Bertin from the ASC had just stolen eagerly awaited food from French prisoners, which had been collected for them by their wives. Despite this realisation, he made absolutely no move to put the stolen goods back. For his wife was starving too back home. Back in late summer and even at the beginning of October, he had disobeyed officers' orders and given some of his ration bread to the Russian prisoners who at that time were doing menial jobs in the depot. He clearly remembered a gaunt soldier in an earth brown coat with earth brown skin who was scraping around on the platform outside the third platoon barracks. When he saw Bertin stop, he whispered: 'Bread, Kamerad!' What a look of joy had crossed that starved man's face as he whisked the hard black bread into his coat pocket. Bertin slung his rifle back over his shoulder but put his hands behind his back and continued on his beat bent over, eyes to the ground, astonished and disgusted. *Bloody hell*, he thought. *Bloody hell.*

Far beyond the burnt, half-destroyed city of Verdun, an aeroplane was at that very moment being readied for take off. Pale in the moonlight and feeling tight round the chest, the painter Jean-François Rouard, together with the mechanics, was checking the wing struts, altitude and directional controls and bomb fixings. The bombs hung head downwards under the belly of the aeroplane like giant bats: two on the right, two on the left. *These old crates always look pretty rickety*, he thought. No wonder. It was not yet quite eight years since Blériot had flown across the channel. And how long was it since Pégoud had horrified the world with his loops, dives and upside down flight? With his hands in his pockets, Rouard shook his head and marvelled at people, for what had once been considered disgusting was now a wartime pilot's bread and butter. *Down with war*, he thought. *It's a filthy mess, but as long as the Boche wants to trample over France, we'll have to drop the necessary on his thick, wooden skull.* And then he asked about the petrol. All being well, he hoped to be back in half an hour and he knocked three times on the leafless apple tree next to the hangar, whose branches were silhouetted like veins against the sky. From the half shadow of the nearby barn Philippe appeared, his friend and pilot. He'd been answering the call of nature before being strapped in. He was the son of a Breton fisherman and approached with a rolling stride. From his hand swung a rosary of ivory beads that he always hung on a little hook to the right of his seat at the front of the plane as a talisman. Rouard nodded to him and he nodded back. There was a calm affinity between the two friends, who had already faced death together under an aeroplane's blazing wreckage, and no more was required.

Lieutenant Kroysing stretched his long legs over the edge of his hard-won woman's bed, got dressed, kissed both her hands, wished her good night and hobbled the couple of steps to the room across the corridor as quietly as he could. It was completely dark, Lieutenant Flachsbauer was snoring and a similar sawing could be heard from many of the men in the ward across the corridor. Kroysing felt his way along the wall to his bed, stowed his crutch and hopped into the sack with practised ease. His heart was full of joy and a contentment as deep as the voice in his chest. He had bent fate to his will. By taking possession of that woman, he felt quite sure he had given himself a head start on all other men. Now he could become whatever he wanted: air force captain, chief engineer, the driving force at the head of a global company. That woman was now rummaging about in her tiny room, getting washed, and in a moment she would open her door warily and hurry down the corridor by the light of her pocket torch to put in a word for a friend at his request with a man of whom he was not the slightest bit jealous. Because henceforth he would just be a memory to her. That woman who had hesitated so long and laughed at him, even when he took her in his arms, would propel him on and be the wind in his wings. He couldn't imagine a higher state of bliss. He hadn't been able to hold Douaumont because imbeciles had intervened, but he would hold on to that woman and with her the path into the future. He closed his eyes, completely at peace, and let himself sink back with a smile. He actually wanted to stay awake so he'd hear her come back. He still felt very awake; he'd just doze for a moment. The following day she'd have to clear up the squaddies' festering bandages again. No matter, that was part of life too. He hummed a tune in his head, a song from his student days by the poet Friedrich Schiller. It began with the words: 'Joy, beautiful sparkle of the gods...'

As Sister Kläre walked down the long corridor in barracks 3, turned the corner and made her way down the much longer ones in barracks 2 and 1, she wondered if it had been silly of her to leave the electric light on in her room. She'd opened the window. She didn't want to sleep in the fumes from the oil lamp and had left the room to air until she came back. She wished she could find a new way of breathing that would let her to suck the happiness she felt right down into the tips of her toes along with the God-given breath of life. She hadn't felt as alive as this for a decade. If only she were sure she'd closed the shutter. There was enough of a draught between its wooden edge and the barracks wall. And there was no point in being too careful. Sister Kläre was an old soldier and knew you sometimes had to be careless. Nonetheless, it would be cleverer and better, more sensible and more careful to go back and turn the light out. But – and she laughed internally – we don't always do what's careful and sensible; we usually do what's sensible and sometimes what's easiest. And she was very tired and she'd need be on the ball for the conversation to come and it would probably take a while to get put through, and so she'd best save those precious minutes. And what if the shutter were gaping open? And someone went past precisely in the quarter of an hour when she was away and noticed that Sister Kläre had disobeyed the regulations and left her light on and not sealed the window? Was it that nice lad Bertin who'd told a story about seeing a general when he was on guard duty driving through an ammunitions dump with his headlights on full beam? *Come on*, thought Sister Kläre as she went into the telephone room, *leave it. I'm so happy. I've got such a fine specimen for a husband. Nothing can go wrong for me now.*

For obvious reasons, the Dannevoux field hospital telephone exchange was located in that part of the large barracks complex closest to the approach from the village. It was operated by severely disabled soldiers with eye injuries; before this war they would have been called blind men. One of them could made out a certain amount of light and shade, the second only had the use of part of his left eye and the third could only see things on the edges of his field of vision – everything in front of him dissolved into darkness. The medical officer had selected these three almost blind men from among his patients and made them telephonists. They were happy with their work and accommodation. All three had been cavalrymen: an Uhlan from Magdeburg, a cuirassier from Schwedt and a dragoon from Allenstein. None of them wanted to go back to Germany and tap around as blind men, and they had all easily mastered the tasks associated with their new work. Their hearing had sharpened and their memories had improved. The telephone service in Dannevoux field hospital functioned smoothly. When Sister Kläre opened the door, the room reeked of smoke from the men's tobacco. By the faint light of the lamp she saw Keller the cuirassier sitting knitting – a sense of touch was more important for that than sight. He recognised her by her voice and was surprised and pleased to have her visit at this late hour. As he'd been working at this job for while, he often made the connection Sister Kläre requested and as usual he said: 'Sit yourself down, sister. It might take a while.' Then he began to negotiate with people far away. He'd never seen them but was on highly confidential terms with them. Discretion is part of a telephonist's job.

In the circle of light from the small lamp, Sister Kläre waited to hear the results of his efforts. With her arms propped on the table and her slim wrists either side of her chin, she watched him. She felt for her cigarette case, pulled out a cigarette and began to smoke. She smiled as her eye lit upon a small monogram on the hammered metal with a tiny coronet under it. That golden thing was quite appropriate here; the man who gave it to her would soon be on the other end of the line.

The crown prince of the German Reich was a particularly genial host and that evening he was in radiant mood. He'd had a Swiss military author to dinner, and they'd enjoyed a long, technical chat about the movements of the 5th Army during the last days of the Battle of the Marne – a discussion that would one day bear fruit. Also at the small, round table were a war correspondent and an artist, both from German newspapers. The crown prince's personal adjutant completed the company. There were no women. When an orderly entered and whispered something to the adjutant, and he turned to his host and said, with a particular emphasis that remained opaque to the guests, that there was an official telephone call for him, the slim gentleman leapt up, excused himself with a few polite words and hurried into the room next door. He didn't know exactly who might be calling him, but it couldn't be anything unpleasant. Perhaps it was the crown princess, perhaps one of his boys, but before he'd sat down at the writing table with the telephone on it, his adjutant caught up with him, said two words to him and disappeared again. 'But how delightful,' were therefore the first words he spoke into the telephone.

No woman is immune to such graciousness, especially not a German woman, since German women are not very spoiled in that department. Therefore, Sister Kläre immediately made a joke and said he should find out who was on the line before squandering his charm like that.

He laughed softly calling her by a pet name he had for her, seemingly unaware that they hadn't seen each other for nine months. He asked if she couldn't come over for a little while. He had some good friends round, unfortunately there were as usual no ladies present and a car could be on its way to Dannevoux in two minutes.

Sister Kläre laughed. The blind telephonist was beside her, but he got up and went out to look at the stars. She could then speak more freely and assure the crown prince that while he might be a great general he clearly had no idea what it was like to work with her boss. She'd be delighted if one of his cars came by one day, but she'd expect his Imperial Highness to be inside it on a benevolent visit to the field hospital. Then she'd be able to introduce him to an officer, a sapper lieutenant, who could tell him the most amazing things about the last days at Douaumont.

The crown prince asked teasingly if Sister Kläre had a personal attachment to this gentleman and received a scornful rebuff. He couldn't see her blush. Then he asked after Colonel Schwersenz – was there anything he could do for him? – and heard with regret that there was nothing new to report or to be expected as long as the war continued. Sister Kläre then said that she had rung up to ask a favour – not for one her intimates but for a man of intrinsic worth. And in her charming Rhenish accent she described the whole situation with Bertin the author and lawyer, his major and the court martial at Lychow, which needed a replacement for a man who'd been transferred to active service.

The crown prince was overcome with liking for the woman on the other end of the line, whom he could visualise very clearly. With his mouth very close to the receiver he said he wished she would think of him again with such warmth and eloquence. Anyone who didn't know Sister Kläre very well might imagine all kinds of silly things about her.

Oh, Sister Kläre replied innocently, in a field hospital where there were so many 'departures' at certain times you learnt to have more regard for the individual than did the authors of war reports. (In the heartless language of the doctors, departures always meant deaths.)

The crown prince pretended to be shocked by Sister Kläre's vehemence but said that doing something for an author fitted in very well with his plans that evening as he happened to have three newspaper men to dinner, and he noted Private Bertin's name and unit on his writing pad.

Pleased to have got to that point, Sister Kläre now metamorphosed into a charming but bossy governess. He mustn't dawdle over it as was unfortunately his wont. He must get on to it straight away, brook no refusal and remind the major who was actually in charge of the 5th Army.

The crown prince was tickled; she really was a clever woman. He'd arrange to see her again in the next couple of days, visit Dannevoux field hospital and look up the sapper lieutenant. And he'd put the telegram through to the labour company that night. As he told her this, speaking in a warm, endearing way, he remembered his guests. He stood up and leaning over the telephone began to bring the conversation to a close, saying he would visit the following Sunday, and then he heard Sister Kläre's calm voice thanking him repeatedly and asking to be excused: she'd have to hang up as the line was urgently required on account of an air raid warning.

Somewhat startled, the crown prince said he hoped the anti-aircraft batteries and M.G.'s would give the blasted Frogs hell and hung up. He lit a cigarette and, deep in thought, wandered back to the small, atmospherically lit dining table where the Sekt glasses were being filled. These air attacks were making the war ever more unfair.

For the last few seconds, Keller the almost blind cuirassier had been standing beside Sister Kläre pointing to the light for the second line, which had suddenly lit up. Discretion aside, it had been the whinny of a horse that had drawn him outside earlier. Horses were his passion, and it was a source of great regret to him that there were no riding horses in the hospital stables. He'd recognised the whinny. It was a chestnut called Egon, an average gelding, well kept though undernourished, upon whose back the field chaplain with the lanced boil came and went. Keller wondered if he might perhaps get a chance to hold the chestnut by its curb strap for a minute, stroke its soft fur and breathe in the warm odour that every rider knows and loves. And sure enough, there was Pechler the bath orderly leading the horse, which was looking forward to getting back to its own stable, through the pale moonlight. Father Lochner, meanwhile, was warmly shaking the medical officer by both hands, saying how much those hands had helped him, and heaping blessings and prosperity upon the doctor and his admirable institution. Then, despite his bulk, he swung himself nimbly from the stirrup into the saddle. He looked like a cowboy now protected against the night air by a riding coat, his wide-brimmed hat cocked at a jaunty angle. And off he rode towards Dannevoux where he was to spend the night. The Sauterne wine had been splendid, and they'd had a stimulating discussion about the deeply sceptical views on the value of life the doctor had expressed at the bedside of that ugly but rather bright typesetter – what was he called again? Pahl, that was it. Yes, when you had to abstain for a couple of weeks even the smallest amount of wine went straight to your head. But it gladdened the heart, as the Holy Scriptures said, comforted those who mourned, gave hope to the lame and helped the righteous to a gentle sleep. And furthermore 20 minutes' slow riding – it was nearly 11pm – should be enough to ensure a good night's sleep. The moon shone so beautifully. Up ahead the road forked into two shining bands that stretched into the distance: one towards Dannevoux and the other downhill to Vilosnes-East on the right. Dr Münnich, now in a Litevka and looking more like a major than a surgeon, watched the peaceable rider's bold silhouette for a moment; then he sent his men back inside and went in after them. And still smiling to himself at the contrast between the dashing figure the good father cut on his horse and the silver cross around his neck, he didn't notice how hastily Keller opened his office door and pulled it shut behind him.

Keller really was in a hurry. He'd already heard the phone's urgent ring from outside. He pushed the plug in impatiently and received a report from further up the line via the switchboard at Esnes that an aeroplane was approaching and to pass the news on. When telephonists and sentries received air-raid reports, they passed them on to the nearest exchange.

Meanwhile, the telephone was also buzzing in the shed that served as a station building at nearby Vilosnes-East. It was definitely buzzing, but no one heard it. After an exhausting day's work, the railwaymen who ran it by, older men from the Landwehr, were sleeping the sleep of the righteous. They had a sort of arrangement with the ASC men that their sentries would wake them if anything happened. But did the ASC sentries hear the desperate clamouring of the old telephone? No one was sleeping nearby. The railwaymen liked to be comfortable. Both they and the ASC men preferred the roomy barracks on the other side of the station. There were dugouts in the hillside to be used in case of air raids, but the men had to be woken in plenty of time to reach them. The telephone buzzed and squawked. Where the hell was the sentry from Barkopp's working party? Did he want to consign his sleeping comrades to eternity if that bloody aeroplane did fly over?

Bertin, with his rifle, was still between the tracks deep in thought – not so far away that he couldn't hear, but too distracted to be alarmed. He was full of self-pity in that moment. If he'd had any sense, he have been like the other grown-ups in the company and wouldn't have trusted the sergeant major back in the barracks yard in Küstrin. He'd have let himself be transferred to the east rather than insisting on making a voluntary pilgrimage west. That way he'd have remained the decent lad he used to be and he'd have been able to do his duty just as well in the east. But he'd been afraid of the east, hadn't he? In the east there was the threat of lice, snow and cold, uncivilised towns, horribly degraded roads, and in the towns lots of Jews – Eastern European Jews with nasty habits, steeped in an embarrassing, over-the-top kind of Judaism designed to make him, Bertin, feel as uncomfortable as possible. He'd been honest enough to admit that to himself and he admitted it now too. He just felt the punishment was a bit harsh for such a small misdemeanour. Why should a Jew not be able to admit that he didn't like certain other Jews, but did very much like the Prussian military: its discipline and order, its spruceness and drills, its warrior dress and spirit, the military might of its proud traditions and its invincible strike power? Hadn't he been brought up to feel like that?

And now, after two years of service, here he stood a miserable thief of bread for the hungry. In such circumstances a Berliner would joke that something was a bit fishy. A lot of things had been revealed as a hoax in the last two years, for example the idea that it was sweet and honourable to die for the Fatherland. Well no, actually, it was always nasty and awful to sacrifice a young life before it had come to anything. But sometimes, by God, it was necessary. You couldn't just leave women, children and old men to be overrun by brown barbarian hordes, such as the Mongols and Tartars who had repeatedly attacked the his Silesian homeland. *Well, Mr Bertin,* he told himself, *you've been a sheep with your Prussian patriotism, you've behaved like a wee laddie going off on an adventure and failed to noticed that you were in fact in the service – and in the noose – of the enemy of all people: naked force, the adversary incarnate.* It was a bit late to be discovering this. In the meantime, he'd sunk to the level of the plundering Bashkir nomads held up in horror in the history books of his childhood. For they had only plundered food from the Silesian peasants and townspeople because they were hungry and needed to put food on their own tables. Bertin

Bashkir – what a slap in the face!

And then he heard the ringing. He jolted awake and was back in the present. Pushed the shed door open, flashed his torch around: no one there. Grabbed the receiver from its cradle and listened: air raid alarm, pass it on! A sudden, glaring memory of the five wagons of explosives. Fifty living men dependent on his watchfulness. Get a move on!

Bertin bounded like a hare over the rails and sleepers. Shoving his gun aside, he stormed into the railwaymen's barracks. 'Get out! Air raid alarm!' He left the door open so the air would help to rouse the sleeping men and rushed out again to wake his comrades. He had no fear for himself. He was alive with sensations, engulfed in the excitement of this extraordinary night. He stood in the doorway, heard Sergeant Barkopp curse the draught and banged on the floorboards with the butt of his musket, cruelly driving out the last vestiges of sleep: there was a reason why a certain private had once blissfully slept through an air raid alarm. Back then, there had been 150m between the men and the ammunition; now there were just 30m.

He looked to the sky and listened. A very faint singing could be heard, unmistakable and evil. A searchlight had already swung upwards from the Sivry area, its chameleon tongue, broader at the top, licking for insects. A second joined it, apparently from behind the main railway station at Vilosnes, then a third from Dannevoux. And then the anti-aircraft guns started yelping. They boomed out from behind the hill on the other side of the railway, and heavy machine gun fire clattered from the side of the hill. Shafts of light swung across the sky. Dark puffs of red shrapnel burst around the plane and bullets ripped towards it. Watch out, Froggie! We'll punch holes in your wings or arms, engine or heart, petrol tank or lungs – it's all one to us. You must be brought down before those terrible Easter eggs of yours can be sent crashing to earth. A flock of inadequately clothed ASC men trotted past in the moonlight towards the dark hollows of the dugouts. Most of them tried to push through to the back where it was safest, but the railwaymen were already there, smoking cigarettes. The ASC men had to take cover further forwards.

One man stayed outside: Bertin. He had to stay and see what happened. Sergeant Barkopp barked at him good-naturedly to come inside as it was about to rain. Bertin, shading the visor of his cap with hand, stayed where he was, saying there was time yet. Where was the Frenchman? Had he cleared off to Stenay, where the crown prince was supposed to have his headquarters? Woe betide you, Frenchie, if you take out a certain someone before he has arranged my transfer to the Lychow divison court martial.

One thousand two hundred metres up in the air, Jean-François Rouard leant out of the cockpit and peered down with his night binoculars. The landscape beneath him was completely different from in daytime. The silvery light of the moon is a poetic lie. Beneath him lay a shrouded, grey expanse, and he could barely make out the course of the Meuse. He shouldn't have let himself in for a bombing raid so soon. On the other hand, orders were orders and he had to stop taking childish photographs sometime and get down to the real business. There were four pointed bombs hanging from the belly of his plane. They looked like sleeping bats hanging head downwards from the eaves of a barn. He couldn't wait to get rid of them. God in heaven, where was that bend in the Meuse and the target valley with the railway tracks? He flashed his torch over his time sheet, map and watch: still straight on. He didn't hear the shrapnel bursting in the noise of the engine, but he saw it when he leant out of the cockpit again searching for some sign that would bring this paralysing uncertainty to an end – the hot, wild confusion of his first night-time bombing raid. If the time sheet was right, they should fly on for two seconds and then downwards to get a better aim, and then a jerk of the lever, and to hell with the mess he'd be creating. Life was one big mess, you just had to accept that and make sure you hit the target. Perhaps he'd get hit himself. There, a light ahead on the left, a bright speck on the ground. Probably someone stumbling along between the tracks. He tapped the pilot's left upper arm, and he changed course almost imperceptibly.

Below a witches' Sabbath had reached its peak. Guns crashed. Shells howled up and burst. Machine guns rattled out their violent worst. Searchlights groped around. The hum of the plane's engine and propeller grew more distinct. Bertin was trembling with excitement. He was pressed into the entrance of the dugout, all his senses alert. The mad frenzy of battle tearing the night to shreds engulfed his soul. Madness gripped him. A few hours earlier he'd been attacking violence up at the hospital and now he was in raptures over it. *How is that possible?* he wondered. Could the two go together? Didn't you need to be a sergeant major to tremble with bliss, as he was now doing, at the volley of explosions and the air man up there, chasing his target undeterred, which included Bertin? *Have I become a savage as well as a thief?* he wondered. *Did I even need to become one? Haven't I always been one? Didn't I bully my little brother, just as Glinsky bullied me. Didn't I throw a weaker and worthier person than myself to the ground and rape them, just as Jansch did with me? I mean my wife. I mean Lenore.*

Where was he now? Low pine trees, greyish green under the dull blue Brandenburg sky. The clearing between Wilkersdorf and Tamsel. Yellow sand and fields waist-high in rye. He was in the uniform of a warrior, which he'd been wearing for three months by then, and he had to prove his manhood because she'd refused him under that clear sky. He'd gone for her and pressed her down into the moss by the shoulders. She struggled furiously. He'd forced himself on her and frightened her as he'd earlier frightened a boy who'd tried to follow them. Had that rape, and all the misery, pain and unpleasantness that followed, been a manly act? No, it had been the act of a sergeant major. Crushing someone instead of winning them over, throwing them down instead of seducing them, ordering them about rather than persuading them – that was how a sergeant major behaved. Tons of steel, volleys of explosions, desolate swathes of poisonous smoke, careening mounds of earth, cracking joists, howling and whistling bursts of splinters and shells: they were all the result of a kind of exasperated weakness. Anyone could press a button. On 14 July, he, Bertin, had not pressed the button. But on 15 July, do truth the honour...

Bertin clung to the dugout post. Suddenly he felt sick and dizzy. The outlines of the wagons standing calmly on the tracks not 40m away, treacherously quiet in the treacherous moonlight, swam in circles before him. But before the sergeant could ask him what was wrong, a dull thud shook the hill above their heads, then a second. Splinters of stone fell from roof. The anti-aircraft fire doubled in intensity. The machine guns grew frantic. But the roar of the propeller was still there, though more distant. The railwaymen sat against the wall, and the ASC men further forward in the darkness. Bertin the sentry, suddenly completely exhausted, crouched beside them on the wooden edge of the wire bed. Excited chattering until the conclusion was finally drawn that it had been a lot of noise about nothing. He'd missed the ammunitions wagons and been disorientated by the counter fire. He must've dropped his bombs somewhere on the ridge behind or in front of Dannevoux. From the sound of it, the second bomb had probably ripped a hole in the hill path.

Bertin stretched his aching knees slowly. Only half an hour more of sentry duty and he could go to bed and spend four hours wrapped up in his blankets like a chrysalis undergoing metamorphosis. His second round from 4am to 6am might be restorative, with bird song, sunrise and a chance to pull himself together. But this last half hour would be hard. His limbs were trembling. He hurriedly lit his pipe and felt better, letting the men's talk wash over him. Sergeant Barkopp pushed off to bed: tomorrow was another day – and an off-duty one at that. Bertin carried on smoking, in contravention of the rules, as he made his way out of the shelter with Karl Lebehde and Hildebrandt, who was on sentry duty after him, and stumbled across the rails past the ammunitions wagons towards the middle of the valley. Karl Lebehde stopped, turned and peered up at the hillside. A flickering red glow. An old barn or pile of wood was burning up there, said the tall Swabian. A bomb must have hit it. Karl Lebehde said nothing, wagged his head on his short neck, looked round again and finally went to bed. Bertin shivered. His musket suddenly felt like it weighed nine pounds. It had been a long, exciting day, and around midnight nature said: enough! But he was still on duty. That couldn't be helped. His bulging pockets dragged at this shoulders.

CHAPTER FOUR

A tile falls from the roof

LIEUTENANT KROYSING, IN bed by the outer wall of his room, was already fast asleep. Only a tiny spark of consciousness connected him to the earth's surface; his reality in that moment was that of a dream. He was flying, he, Flight Lieutenant Kroysing, was flying over the Channel. He was surrounded by roaring: from the sea, the wind and the thrum of his engine. The North Sea heaved beneath him. But its waves couldn't hurt him and neither could the long-range guns on the ships below: their shells fell back down, yelping and powerless. In his dream, the missiles climbed towards him, pointed end first, hovered for a moment, bowed before him and hurtled back down. The cheeky little machine gun bullets were another matter. They flew up at him like bees and settled on his wings, making curves and star shapes, and transforming his plane into a butterfly. But it wasn't like other butterflies. It was a huge death's head moth, a bomber that threatened cities. Beneath him lay an English city full of English people, with a layout similar to Nuremberg. There was the castle where Alfred the Great had lived with Christopher Columbus – they were going to drop a bomb on its chimney. His hand was already reaching for the bomb release handle. Then a shell burst beside that hand and with a start Eberhard Kroysing woke up.

Noise filled the lieutenants' ward. It seemed that an aircraft was actually paying a visit to the station down below. For all the batteries and M.G.'s in the area were letting rip at it. At first he wanted to jump out of bed and alert the barracks. But then he felt ashamed of that impulse, for this was a hospital not a... He couldn't follow this thought to its conclusion. Sitting bolt upright, all ears, he tried to imagine the enemy – the enemy, who was really a comrade. *Just you wait, old chap*, he thought. *In three months, I'll knock you out of the sky and pay you back for this night-time visit with pleasure.*

Through all the noise he heard the engine approaching in the darkness, despite Lieutenant Flachsbauer's snoring. (The poor man wrapped himself up in sleep as though it were a thick quilt. His bride was seriously ill with septic appendicitis. It was an almost hopeless case, and he'd become suspicious, as soldiers do in hospital, and thought it wasn't her appendix but septicaemia in another organ.) What a healthy racket the anti-aircraft guns were making! Out of bed. Yank the window open; white ribbons streaking across the night sky. Flashes as the anti-aircraft guns opened fire. A black-red puff of bursting shrapnel, then a second. He heard the aircraft engine very clearly through the frantic rattle of the machine guns. Kroysing peered up, half leaning out of the window; nothing but sky, ribbons of light and a couple of stars. A figure almost as tall as himself ran past underneath and returned a couple of seconds later. A muffled voice almost as deep as his own cried out to him: 'Kamerad, take cover!' And the man disappeared. Kroysing paid him no mind. This visit would be on little Bertin's watch. Wasn't he on guard duty? Of course he was. It was nearly 11pm, and he had number two. Well, that boy had a cool head. Kroysing had seen how he handled different kinds of situations. He would wake the barracks up.

But hadn't the sound above him changed? It certainly had. It was fractionally louder and getting closer. He couldn't see much out of this bloody window, which faced Dannevoux. And was it appropriate for an old soldier with an injured leg to go running out into the night against doctor's orders? A little sobered, Kroysing straightened his pyjamas and was about to go back into the room. But what was that? That guy up there just kept heading downwards. Was he still dreaming or what? Had his dream spooled on and flipped over, as sometimes happens? *This is a field hospital*, a voice screamed inside him. *You can't drop your bomb on our beds.*

He listened intently and suddenly the realisation struck him like a bullet to the heart that the guy must have made a mistake. He was going to blow the field hospital to pieces by accident and it would happen any second now if the anti-aircraft guns didn't take him out.

Bring the devil down, you morons! Shoot, you lazy bastards, shoot!

Suddenly, the engine cut. Had they got him? They'd got him! Kroysing dropped his arms in relief. No more comradeship with the airman. Hostility ruled the world.

And then, as he stood in the darkness clutching the window in his pale pyjamas, the experienced soldier in him who'd seen it all before heard a faint whistling – the wilful whistling and shrill shriek of a falling bomb. The inescapable drone of fate lay within that sound: I'm coming to snuff out life and ignite fire... The plane had glided down with its engine cut, now it thundered back up. Fire from Heaven was a good thing, in the hands of Prometheus, benefactor of mankind. Watch how I crash as ordered, I, the hammering thunderbolt, obedient destroyer. A bomb takes nearly six seconds to fall the 180m this one had to travel. But it wasn't falling on a leaderless sheep pen. A man, who suddenly had two healthy legs, tore open the door of men's ward 3 and yelled: 'Air raid! Get out!' After the men, the woman. He grabbed the door handle. Empty – the room glaringly bright, the window half open. And as ward 3 erupted in screams and the electric light blazed on, a figure appeared at the end of the corridor, and just before the crash Kroysing heard death's messenger clamouring above the roof. In a furious frenzy, he grabbed the water jug by Kläre's bed, totally beside himself, and hurled it up at the ceiling, into death's ugly mug: 'You cowardly bastard!' Then the explosion above his head ripped him to bloody shreds.

Flames, flames. The bomb had landed in the corridor right between room 19 and ward 3. Seven or eight of those who'd fled had simply collapsed in a heap. Flying all around were corrugated iron, splintered beams, burning wood and flaming tar paper, and almost in a single moment the entire outermost wing of the barracks flared up like a bonfire. With fists and kicks and their whole bodies the wounded fought their way out through the furthest of the three doors despite their bandages. From beneath the poisonous, choking fumes of the billowing black and white smoke came the shrill screams and primaeval whining of men who'd collapsed and been crushed, and the ghastly howls of those licked by flames. Those who'd been killed outright by splinters from the bomb were lucky.

In bed, surrounded by burning floorboards, lay the body of Pahl the typesetter. Only his body: his clever head, of which the workers had such desperate need, had been crushed by the explosion like a hen's egg under a horse's hoof. It had got him in his sleep this time, just as it could so nearly have got Bertin nine months previously but hadn't, to his and Karl Lebehde's astonishment. This time he'd slept through the noise. By the time the noise started to wake him, he was already gone. There would be nothing left of him. For his brain and crushed skull had been spurted somewhere, and his disfigured body would be reduced to ashes by the slow, tenacious blaze, as would his bed and that entire section of the barracks. In the meantime, the medical officer, Pechler the bath attendant, the night watchmen and orderlies had rushed over. A bit of luck, thought the medical officer, as he pulled the fire extinguisher from its bracket and let the hose unfurl – a bit of luck that it had hit ward 3 with all the minor cases. In ward 1, no one would have been able to escape. Wrapped in blankets, the occupants of the burning wing crowded into the safe side of the courtyard and the southern terrace with its deckchairs.

The chief nurse did a roll call to get an idea of how many were missing and who they were. Streams of carbon dioxide from the red canisters were already hissing on to the blaze, and men with minor injuries helped the telephonists to pull the hose out further. The bath orderly, in his capacity as a water supply expert, soon had a sharp jet raining down on the burning timberwork, dashing the debris aside and sending the ruins flying into the air. 'Watch out, roofing!' cried one of the rescued men for whom the disaster had quickly become exciting entertainment.

Sister Kläre lay on the matron's bed, passed out. It was a mystery why this woman who normally had such presence of mind had been shocked to the core like that. No doubt she'd been overcome by belated horror at her miraculous escape from death. That corner had suffered the worst. No one had been rescued from there. No, not true: Lieutenant Flachsbauer had survived. The explosion from the bomb that had crashed through the roof into the corridor and set the floorboards on fire had spared him. It had only shaken him wide awake, warning him that something was happening. He'd climbed out of the window as the hut went up in flames above him. He'd lowered himself down the outer wall. He'd been very calm and phlegmatic and hadn't got as much as a splinter in his skin. *That was what happened,* he thought, *when you didn't give a monkey's about life, when it made you sick, because a wee lassie at home had got some old quack of a woman to abort a baby that wasn't yours.* As if any of it mattered: pregnant or not, a baby by Mr X or Mr Y, trouble from the parents or people talking. All that mattered was to be alive, to continue to breathe, to have eyes to see, ears to hear, a head to think, a nose to smell, even if all you smelt were tar fumes and burning flesh. A miracle that he'd been saved, really and truly. He must write to that silly little goose immediately the following afternoon and make it clear to her that she should get well, for God's sake, and not give a toss about anything else.

Twenty minutes after the bomb had fallen, drivers arrived at the scene of the blaze from the Headquarters at Dannevoux with men from the large billets there, sappers with picks and axes and infantrymen with spades. The front part of the men's ward and the nurses' rooms across the corridor could still be saved, though they'd be too water-logged and full of debris to be used.

The second bomb... A solitary rider on the way to Dannevoux had stopped, rigid with shock, and turned in his saddle as white arcs cut across the dome of the sky and the deafening play of the guns and rifles began. Father Lochner, under his wide-brimmed hat, was admittedly quite convinced he was in no danger up there. His fear was for the others, the ASC men down below, who didn't belong to his division but whom he'd intended to visit before Easter. Apparently there were a couple of Polish Catholics among them.

Suddenly, a shrapnel case hurtled to the ground beside him. 'Watch out!' it said. This nice little show, which mere mortals had cribbed from the magnificence of God's thunderstorms, was not without its dangers. For a precious second, Father Lochner remained undecided as to whether he should spur his gelding on and gallop over to Dannevoux or turn back and take refuge in the hospital for a few minutes until the attack was over.

Unfortunately for him, he did neither. He stopped where the road forked, sorely tempted to take the one that led downhill and shelter against the hillside in the round black shadows cast by the summit. The gelding Egon, much wiser than his master, pulled impatiently at the reins; he wanted to go. This dark field surrounded by banging frightened him. A horse has a long back to protect if things fall from the air, and the rider had no sooner given him the direction than he flew down the muddy path at a canter. Father Lochner had a job bringing him to a standstill when they reached a point that deceptively seemed to offer cover. For the horse, ears laid back, wanted to bound off as behind him the hill began to roar and flash. Across the road, down the slope – he just wanted away. (It was because of his nervous disposition that the heavy machine gun company had exchanged this otherwise lovely animal for a more placid one.) Lochner, a fearless man with a heart both kind and wise, held the trembling horse by its bridle and spoke to him soothingly, looking to the sky when he jerked his neck up. And there he saw the body of the aeroplane in the glare of the searchlights, barely 100m above him, roaring over the hill large and white, the curve of its belly, the pale cross of its wings, the circle of its insignia, its struts: it all appeared before the eyes of the solitary priest with ghostly clarity, as the Frenchman prepared to complete his attack, ascend and veer away.

Few people see the bomb that kills them before if falls, but Benedikt Lochner from the Order of St Francis, Catholic chaplain on the western front, was one of those few. A road was nearly as good a target as a railway line, and that was why the little painter Rouard yanked the lever when he got a clearer view of the area the plane was crossing. And Lochner saw it. In the beam of the searchlight he saw a bright drop detach itself from the dreadful monster, as if it were sweat or dirt, and fall. And he fell to his knees. He knelt at his horse's feet with his hand clasped round his small silver cross. The aeroplane had long since vanished into the night. With his eyes firmly closed, while his horse Egon chewed and stretched his neck out above him, he filled the space inside his chest with prayer: that the Father in Heaven preserve him, that the Virgin take him into her gracious protection, that the Son of God, who had suffered so much, shelter and receive his soul. 'Father, into thy hands I commend my spirit,' cried his inaudible voice and then it spooled frantically into that great old prayer made up of snatches from the Holy Scriptures that is called 'Our Father'. He didn't pray in Latin, as was his habit. German words welled up inside him and drowned out the shrill approach of the falling bomb. And as he prayed, he saw pictures from his childhood of the majesty of the Trinity enthroned on painted clouds, the Father, bearded and in flowing robes, his hands spread in a blessing, to his right the Son, and above their heads doves with halos. And when he got to the line, 'And forgive us our debts as we forgive our debtors', a red blaze crashed down in front of him. A good 12m from him, Rouard's hanging bat had burst a hole in the road surface, sending mounds of earth rolling downhill and scattering cascades of splinters all around. They hit the dead wall of the hillside with as much force as the trembling flesh of the man and the horse. Lochner was struck in the chest, the horse in the neck and leg. A scream was the last thing Lochner heard – it wasn't clear if it came from him or the animal, which now collapsed on top of him. Their gasps and groans and blood intermingled.

The next morning infantrymen would arrive from their position nearby shaking their heads at the size of the holes an aerial bomb could make and saying, good heavens, it's taken out a field chaplain this time. And then they would calmly get out their canteens and knifes and cut off the tenderest parts of Egon the gelding's flesh to make a delicious roast for their evening meal.

CHAPTER FIVE

The survivors

MAJOR JANSCH PACED round his office, very pale, with slippers on his feet – thick felt slippers as there was a draught through the floor. He'd blanched in fury and hissed at his batman Kuhlmann that he was going to transfer him back to his unit because his cocoa was too hot. He'd blanched in fury and trampled on a spider because it had the temerity to cross his path. He'd blanched in fury... The orderly room beneath him was in no doubt as to his state of mind; if his friend Niggl didn't come and mollify him no one would dare to go near him that day. No one perhaps except Corporal Diehl, the primary school teacher from Hamburg. He was in restrained high spirits for the same reason that Herr Jansch was beside himself. For Diehl had learnt that the world was not always as evil and nasty and it sometimes seemed. Even in the Kaiser's army, the weak sometimes found succour. Such a miracle encouraged backbone. If necessary, Diehl would venture into the lion's den.

But it wasn't necessary. Outside the spring weather looked moody and changeable. But Herr Jansch didn't notice. His indignation prevented him from noticing. First, there had been a dreadful air attack the night before. Damvillers station had suffered a service breakdown, and you could see why. Even in his cellar, Major Jansch had heard the two bombs crashing down. And furthermore, it had been proved that the Jews were omnipotent. Even in the Kaiser's army. Even if they knew how to act powerless for a year or two. When it suited them, off they floated. And just when an honest German thought he'd backed them into a corner, they pressed a button and a Hohenzollern appeared through a secret door to play the rescuing angel of Judas, disappearing with his charge as the orchestra struck up the march from Handel's *Messiah*: 'Daughter of Zion, rejoice'.

Jansch pressed his chin into the collar of his Litevka, tugged at his long moustache with both hands, bit into a raspberry flavoured sweet and cut a deep shaft in his world view. He'd always known the Hohenzollerns weren't up to much. They were erratic people, those descendants of the Burgraves of Nuremberg, and their blood was far too mixed for them to produce men of steady character, true sovereigns and rulers. Again and again, this inborn mushiness broke through the little bit of toughness and character they had painstakingly cultivated in Berlin and Brandenburg. All of them had signed despicable peace treaties, all of them had made bad bargains, and all of them had had dealings with Jews. After Frederick the Great it had got worse, not better. The Guelphic and French blood that had produced him had only really been properly felt in his descendants. Wilhelm II and especially his son, grandson of the English woman, they had been the business. When Frederick III succumbed to cancer of the throat after 99 days – his father had told him this – the citizenry mourned in its entirety, but Old Prussia secretly breathed a sigh of relief: that bearded liberal would only have let the country down. And then, barely two years later, that which ought never to have happened happened: Bismarck's dismissal. A logical chain ran from that act of betrayal to the overthrow of the Old Prussian constitution, which, as the Pan-German Union admitted through clenched teeth, seemed inevitable now, and right in the middle of a war. A man who could chase out the Iron Chancellor as though he were a disloyal lackey deserved that Bethmann-Hollweg, that chancellor made out of philosophy papers, and the rubbish that came out of his mouth every time he opened it. So much for the father, but the son wouldn't improve things, wouldn't rescue the situation, however much he seemed to applaud the Old Germans. That frivolous man always did the opposite of what might have been expected, as the present example showed. Such things came back to roost. Any reasonable man could see that, even in sunglasses at midnight. Those people were played out.

Major Jansch paced round the stone walls of his room, which was hung with maps and lay in a house wrested from the conquered French. Solemn music resonated within him, based on the funeral march that tended to be played at burials, which, regrettably, had been written by a Pole, a certain Chopin. He filled up inside with sorrow at Germany's destiny, at the decline that always threatened that which was most noble. Some lines of verse sounded within him, heroic lines from his favourite poet Dahn:

> Give place, ye peoples, to our march:
> The doom of the Goths is sped!
> No crown, no sceptre carry we,
> We bear the noble dead.

So ended the conflict between the noble Gothic nation and those sly, shifty sons of the Eastern Roman Empire, the Byzantines. Innocence, nobility of mind and trusting heroism had no place in that world, which belonged to the descendants of dwarves. The riff-raff always triumphed because internal German discord smoothed their path.

There it lay, the document that represented the end of all hope; printed in blue on German Army notepaper, the telegram from the Commander-in-Chief of the crown prince's Army Group, sent via his Quartermaster General, said that Private Bertin of the ASC was to be transferred forthwith from the First Company to the Lychow Army Group. Confirmation was to be telegraphed when the order had been carried out. All over, Jansch. No Iron Cross, first class will ever adorn your breast. If that Jew ever learnt of your intentions and were asked questions, he'd only have to laugh and tell stories and the game would be up...The First Company orderly room was on the line, literally a-quiver with awe and excitement. A telegram from the crown prince! The order would be carried out that day. Private Bertin would be summoned to Etraye-East that very morning. His papers had already been drawn up, and his travel documents were being prepared. He could leave that evening and then the battalion could report up that the order had been carried out.

Life had taught Major Jansch self-control. 'Whoa, whoa, hold your horses,' he said, acting casual. Was it not the case that the First Company, like so many others, was considerably below strength? And would not the staff first have to find out the current position of the Lychow Army Group? The battalion could pass on the whereabouts of the court martial during the course of the day. The man would manage fine if he left the following morning, or afternoon, or sometime during the day. In the meantime, he could do his duty, night duty for example. He could relieve one of his comrades of that arduous task. Perhaps rations were due to be transported to the front that night. Did Sergeant Major Duhn understand his meaning? He did. The major hung up. Sometimes miracles happened. He was entitled to clutch at any straw. The French were still shelling both the standard-gauge and light railways. Maybe Herr Bertin would take a hit.

His other source of disgruntlement, admittedly, continued unabated. Easter was drawing inexorably closer. In a fortnight – at the behest of the Frau Major – Herr Jansch would have to go on leave. What for the overwhelming majority of soldiers in Europe was the greatest pleasure imaginable he viewed with dislike. What was missing from his life here in the field? Nothing, or as good as nothing. He was a master. He had lackeys and servants who trembled before him. A whole outfit was geared towards him. The population of a subject land had to speak respectfully to him and his like or there'd be hell to pay. Here he need fear no dissent. Even if people didn't like him personally, a whole caste closed ranks behind him. But at home... He sighed.

There was no peace. He was constantly disturbed by trivial bills. He had to fight each day to preserve his inner composure in the face of the silliest disruptions. He didn't like women. They were in every sense inadequate. And their nagging voices got on his nerves. A three-room apartment on Windhorststraße in the suburb of Steglitz – a street name that infuriated him every time he thought of it – brought no happiness when it was run by Frau Major Jansch and the maidservant Agnes Durst from Lübchen in Saxony, and a man had to constantly rescue his papers from their concepts of order. For they didn't understand his work at Windhorststraße. They treated it with contempt. Within the family, his work was judged according to money and monetary value, and they were unable to hide their mild disdain. They – the girl, his wife and even his son. His son Otto would also be home on leave and that increased his discomfort... Lieutenant Otto Jansch was from one of those nameless infantry regiments that fight and die in enormous numbers without distinction. However, during the fighting at the end of 1915 on one of the rivers in southern Poland his son had distinguished himself, perhaps more by accident than through exceptional merit. Since then, he'd possessed an Iron Cross, first class, and his father did not possess one – and therefore had hardly any authority over his son any more. Even though his friend, Major Niggl, had done everything he could to bring the officers at the depot round to his side, he still didn't possess one and he never would, although news had been received from the hallowed domain of the Artillery High Command that a certain Lieutenant von Roggstroh had fallen, killed in a small but successful action against Bezonvaux that had unfortunately led to considerable losses. He was supposed to have been a nice, blonde chap, little Roggstroh. Now he wouldn't bother anyone any more. The day before yesterday, actually even yesterday, it had seemed that the longed-for decoration was about to appear on the horizon like the morning or evening star. But now it was all over.

Major Jansch grabbed the telephone, then let his hand drop. There was no point. He needed to get out, shake off his agitation, go and see his friend Niggl, get some fresh air about him. He rang for his batman and told him he wanted to get dressed and ride out.

The streets of Damvillers bustled with spring. Sparrows chirruped in the bright sunshine. Swallows shot across the light sky, and men hurried past without coats. From his high steed, Major Jansch checked whether they were saluting properly. Drills were taking place on the meadow on the other side of the village, and from the machine gun practice range came the rhythmic tap of blank cartridges. Major Niggl was not at home. In fact, he had ridden over to see Captain Lauber, the sapper commandant. Major Jansch hesitated for a moment and then, under pressure from his news, decided to fetch him from there. He didn't particularly like Captain Lauber. Swabians were all democrats – adversaries in other words. But in his present mood he overcame his aversion, turned his chestnut horse, and rode back at a walk and over to the sapper headquarters.

Captain Lauber sat crestfallen at one end of his sofa and at the other sat Major Niggl, full of concern. An armchair was pulled up for Major Jansch, a rare visitor, and he was given a glass of cherry brandy and offered a cigar. Indeed no, Captain Lauber wasn't smoking that day either. He didn't feel like it. He'd received dreadful news from the Dannevoux field hospital via the brigade headquarters: the plane that wreaked havoc on Damvillers station had smashed up Dannevoux field hospital beforehand. Definitely a breach of international law. Of course the French would maintain it had been an accident if representatives of the Red Cross raised a complaint. They'd punish the airman or replace him, and they might not even do that. But that wouldn't bring back Lieutenant Kroysing, who had been killed with a number of other wounded. Major Niggl nodded his head sympathetically. His little pale eyes were full of deepest condolences as they sought the captain's dark eyes. Surely not the Lieutenant Kroysing he'd fought beside at Douaumont, he asked. And Captain Lauber nodded. Of course it was him; there was only one lieutenant of that name in the army. And there weren't many officers of his calibre. He'd had high hopes for him and expected him to go far. It was from such tempered steel that the bonds had been forged that held the front together. Such men guaranteed the nation's future: affable, always ready to listen to the men's concerns, relentless in the pursuit of duty, completely and utterly committed. And to think how happy they'd been that the lad had escaped unharmed from that lice-infested pile of rubble that was Douaumont and had come through that mess on 14 December without serious injury, and now a stupid aerial bomb had landed on his head and killed him off. Well, today was a black day.

Today the world felt like a speck in his eye. This war in the air reduced war to a kind of trade for mechanics, photographers and hurlers of bombers – it was time to abolish it and replace it with something more sensible, something that didn't mean it was always the best men who got destroyed. It was a great and wonderful thing to defend the Fatherland, to use intelligent means and brave men to prevail against an intelligent and brave opponent. He used to have joking quarrels with his friend Reinhart about whether the heavy artillery had spelt the end of that. But when it came to this flying business, there no was point in wasting breath. It wasn't proper; it was bloody idiotic – be done with it. So, Lieutenant Kroysing was gone too; maybe it would be his turn next. That would be fine by him. Let the next airman crack his skull the way his little boy cracked walnuts at Christmas. But until then one had carry on working, do one's duty, look neither right nor left. His two visitors got up. Major Niggl shook the Swabian's hand, all innocence. He and Lieutenant Kroysing had not always seen eye to eye, he said. That could happen among comrades. But that he'd now been taken from them was enough to make a man spew, and he hoped that his friend Lauber would soon recover from the knock and take a more cheerful view of the world.

Shaking his head and almost bowing, he walked to the door and went out to where the two horses were tethered, nuzzling one another trustingly, the neck of one laid against the other's mane. Open-mouthed with admiration for his friend Niggl, Major Jansch followed him out into the open air. For many decades to come, he recalled that feeling whenever he met the Bavarian.

CHAPTER SIX

The legacy

IN AN EMPTY barracks, words echo uncomfortably. For that reason, it's best to speak in a hushed voice. During the morning, Private Bertin was informed by Sergeant Barkopp himself that he was to pack his things and return to the company. Private Lebehde went with him; he wanted to help him. The things that had happened the previous night, whose consequences were visible that morning, made the two men want to stick together. It was a beautiful day outside; the march to Etraye-East would be tiring but enjoyable. Lebehde the inn-keeper and Bertin the lawyer had spread Bertin's coat out on one of the bunks and folded the arms in accordance with army regulations, and now they were rolling it up into a sausage that was as tight and even as possible: no wrinkles, no knots. Both men had been on sentry duty and looked pale. The news about the havoc the enemy aircraft had wreaked had been brought to them by the railwaymen around 8am. Both of them had scarcely begun to digest the fact that Wilhelm Pahl was no longer in the world. Bertin shook his head inwardly as he performed his tasks and sometimes he actually did shake it to the surprise of uninitiated observers. A banner kept running through his head upon which nothing was written but three words: Pahl and Kroysing... Pahl and Kroysing... had he looked more closely, he'd have observed within himself a child's amazement at the immense forces of destruction available to life on earth. Kroysing and Pahl... Pahl and Kroysing... A peculiar world, an extremely funny world.

That day Lebehde's freckles stood out particularly clearly on the pale skin of his round face. His thick fingers rolled the coat up with peerless precision. 'I imagine they might dig a mass grave in Dannevoux cemetery tonight for the men from last night. They won't take up much space now.'

'A load of flaky skin,' said Bertin senselessly. 'To the earth it'll just be flaky skin.' In his mind he saw a confused mess of white and charred bones, skulls with no jaws and jaws with no skulls, the skeleton of a foot lying in a ribcage. Pahl had exceptionally small hands for an adult, Kroysing exceptionally large ones. 'Do you think they'll put the lieutenant with the men?' he asked.

'Hmm,' replied Lebehde. 'The way I see it, yes, they will. The medical officer is a sensible man, and one grave is less work than two. And at the Resurrection the angel on duty will be able to sort them out. You're lucky,' he said, changing the subject. 'You're getting out of here, which is the best thing you could do.'

Bertin shrugged his shoulders and hung his gaunt, wasted head. He felt guilty that he was leaving his comrades in the lurch. He couldn't deny that he had a bad conscience.

Meanwhile, Lebehde contemplated their handiwork: the long tube of coat. Even the Kaiser wouldn't be ashamed to buckle that to his pack. Then with Bertin's help he bent it round the rucksack – they had to keep an iron grip on the ends as they did so – and slung the right strap round it, while Bertin slung the left one round. He'd always been surprised that Bertin hadn't cleared off well before now, he said in the meantime.

'But you're my company,' murmured Bertin, as he secured the upper coat strap round the middle of the sausage.

Lebehde looked at him wide-eyed. What good had his staying there done them or anyone else in the world? And who had asked him to invest so much in their comradeship?

Bertin stepped back, shoved his hands in his pockets and looked at his rucksack, his head to one side. That was how he'd always felt, he said slowly, and after a pause he added that he had no explanation for it. He didn't say anything about his inability to change things once he'd got himself into them; Lebehde wouldn't think very highly of that.

Lebehde helped himself to one of Bertin's cigarettes, which he'd been going to leave him anyway. He said he thought those kinds of feelings were inappropriate. A man encumbered by those kinds of feelings could wind up in Hell's kitchen. 'Wilhelm,' he said suddenly, 'would have understood that very well. Feelings are for toffs. Sometimes I think they've standardised all our feelings for their own ends. Let me tell you something, my friend. What's important for the likes of us is to think. The more we think, the more clearly we see things, the better it'll be for us. I take it you're not offended by me including you with us, Comrade?'

Bertin wasn't offended. To the contrary, he was deeply moved and greatly satisfied by his inclusion.

'All afternoon I've been asking myself where we went wrong, Wilhelm and I. Where was the mistake in our calculations? And I said to myself: we shouldn't have jumped so far ahead. You and I, we're sitting here safe and sound with our heads intact and ready to use. But for Wilhelm all that's left is a mass grave, and the workers of Berlin will have to get on without him. And it's a comfort to know that they will get on without him. It would have gone quicker with Wilhlem, no doubt about it. That boy had a good head on his shoulders, and he did what a man could, even if he was a bit careless in his choice of parents, and he knew that the bosses wouldn't give anything away, and that we would hand them a box of cigars in return for a match. And yet, you see, he miscalculated, as events have shown. Where did he go wrong? Can you answer me that?'

Bertin had started folding his blankets, which had to be strapped under the flap of his rucksack. He was reluctant to answer Lebehde's question, because his thoughts were of Pahl the living man, his way of smiling, his fondness for a well-turned phrase, for the newspaper quarter in Berlin with its machine rooms and great rolls of white paper held together by wooden battens, for the smell of printer's ink, the aroma of paraffin from the freshly printed sheets; his fondness for Sunday outings to Treptow, to the Müggelsee, for the high banks of the Havel by the Great Window in Wannsee, the silvery green pine trees of the Mark. How could he possibly identify the mistake in Wilhelm Pahl's calculations that had cost him his life? Were there actually any calculations?

There certainly were, said Lebehde. Wilhelm hadn't lost his toe by chance, but thanks to meticulous planning and a sharpened nail that had been carefully made to rust.

Bertin received this news open-mouthed.

They hadn't told him about it at the time – they could talk about why until the cows came home, but, said Lebehde, there wasn't much point now and so it would be better to skip it. Wilhelm had wanted it done, and Lebehde had stuck the thing in, and so it was him who'd started it and he shared responsibility for how it had turned out.

Bertin was amazed at himself. Eberhard Kroysing had suffered the same fate as his brother. He would never see him again, and he would never see Pahl again, who had had himself maimed, nor Father Lochner – and what had become of Sister Kläre? It was far too much for one person, who only had two ears and one heart, and whose soul was still preoccupied by all the things that had been going through his mind when he was on sentry duty. He would need time, a lot of time, to make sense of it all. He looked at his dirty fingernails and finally asked whether Lebehdhe required people to factor chance into their calculations, because air men didn't usually drop bombs on hospitals and so it must have been chance that directed the bomb.

Lebehde immediately said that he did. It wasn't that he required it. The cause required it, as the facts demonstrated. It required absolute vigilance, for the opponent was ruthless and exploited even the smallest advantage, to say nothing of big advantages. They had underestimated their opponents – the capitalist world order and its wars – and now the goose was cooked.

'Listen, my friend,' he whispered confidentially, 'you made all kinds of pretty speeches against violence up there, but did violence listen? Not a bit of it! It struck and made us into survivors. Perhaps that teaches us a thing or two. And if I hadn't neglected to pay due attention to my profession, which I should have done, I might have realised it sooner. For what does a good inn-keeper do? You're thinking he sells beer and cheers people up. If you like. But calling time and throwing out troublemakers – once they've settled their bill – is also part of his job, and I've always been a stickler for decency and good behaviour. And so I have used force for the collective good. Do you follow?'

And because Bertin thought too long, he shook his broad head. 'But carry on speaking out against violence by others. The fewer bouncers there are for my competition, the better it is for me, especially as I've always got to be my own bouncer. The longer this war lasts, the more stupid the world will become. But an order backed up by a gun – everyone understands that. That's what a certain Lebehde has learnt, and now he's going to head back to Germany as quickly as he can. I'll be out of here before the month is out.'

And that was why he thought it was quite right and the best thing for the cause that Bertin was pushing off to the court martial and to the east where there were no air attacks. Bertin had learnt first hand what the score was. And now he'd have an important position and learn more. The question for the future was whether it was possible to eradicate the great injustice in society. A man who worked in a court sat behind the bar where right and wrong were dished out. He was very happy about this change in Bertin's career. 'For what could you have written in the newspapers that would have been of any use? A load of crap. And how long would you have been able to carry on speaking to the workers while the war was going on? Three months at most. Then they would have got you by the collar and thrown you out, and the whole mess would have started again. No, my friend, you scarper off to your quiet little corner right away, keep your eyes peeled, keep your gob shut and try to reduce injustice. Wanna hear how it went when we see one another again after the war. Holzmarkstraße 47, Berlin East. I'll give you a nice glass of Patzenhofer beer on the house and I imagine you'll meet some people. And now get going. I'll represent you at the funeral. And while the priest is babbling on, I'll have a consultation with myself and try to work out how to create the force that will eventually make all force redundant.'

They shook hands, a thick hand and a thin one. Karl Lebehde had a chin that was twice as strong as his, Bertin noted with surprise, and his narrow mouth sat embedded between it and his nose, giving him the look of a painting or bust of one of the great commanders.

CHAPTER SEVEN

Full circle

PRIVATE BERTIN WAS nobody's chump now. He didn't even consider walking to Etraye-Ost. Wasn't that what horse-drawn and engine-powered lorries were for? It was one of the laws of life for the soldier that it was better for someone else to get his boots dirty than to get your own boots dirty because no one would clean them for you. And the drivers were always happy to have a passenger for company. Bertin was a monosyllabic passenger compared with many others, but the carter, a Frisian from Oldenburg who'd grown up with horses and always worked on the land, had a concept of conversation more akin to a city dweller's idea of silence.

In blank astonishment, Bertin realised that fate – or coincidence, if you preferred – was taking him down the same road that he had travelled when he first arrived in the Verdun area, from Vilosnes-East, where they had been detrained, through Sivry-Consenvoye, then left through the woods where the signpost still stood that read: 'Not under enemy observation'. And then uphill and back down through the beech trees, which formed muddled green thickets on either side of the road. It was almost exactly a year since a marching solider had opened a letter from his bride-to-be here that said she was pushing through his marriage leave; and at that moment the first heavy gun had sent a shell roaring up into the air like some kind of primaeval forest dragon. Spring had been more advanced that year, and the winter had not been so bitterly cold. But looking at it from the outside that was the only difference.

The feeling that everything was repeating itself reached its zenith in the orderly room when Sergeant Major Duhn informed him rather drily that he was to go to Romagne-West that night with four wagons of explosives, picking up three wagons of flares and light ammunition from Damvillers sapper depot on the way. That meant he had the right to sleep through the afternoon if he wanted, and that's what he did after he'd had a look round the depot and camp. The Etraye depot, which was built into the valley in tiers, was a lot more difficult to run than old 'Steinbergquell' on the road to Moirey, but it was also harder to shoot to pieces. Bertin bumped into a lot of old acquaintances; one minute he was shaking Halezinsky's hand, the next Sergeant Böhne's. In the field gun ammunition section, he looked for Strauß, that clever little lad from the Mosel valley, and when he found him, Strauß, who was deeply depressed by the long winter and the seeming impossibility of peace, squealed with delight and congratulations. Bertin had a refreshing three hours' sleep on Strauß's bed, ate a dinner of roast horse meat from the private kitchen of the moustachioed ammunitions expert Schulz, borrowed a coat so that he didn't have to unbuckle his beautifully rolled up coat, and reported to the orderly room and then at the depot.

The moon was in a completely different position in the sky to the day before when the little narrow-gauge train moved off. Strauß had also pressed a blanket on Bertin. He sat on a sort of recliner made of smoothly planed crates of explosives, with his cold meerschaum pipe between his teeth. Almost in dismay, he felt the helix come full circle: the narrow-gauge railway ran through the sheltered terrain to Damvillers, where the sappers attached their wagons. And then, metre by metre, rail by rail, the train slid back into the past, into what was dead and gone, taking with it a man bundled in blankets, who no longer knew if he was awake or asleep, who kept forcing his eyes open only for them to close again. Bertin had stumbled down this road in October when Major Jansch cancelled his six days' leave. This was where the crown prince's car had taken the bend and disappeared from view. Wilhelm Pahl, earmarked to die in a bomb raid, had spent the night in those dugouts when air raids made the camp unsafe in July and August. Wasn't that him stepping out of the dark and bowing, his hands crossed over his chest, a spectre made of smoke, smiling wryly because he was now under ground? All around ghosts wafted up, whitish trails of smoke, the souls of dead men. Poor little Vehse, good-natured little Otto Reinhold, Wilhelm Schmidt, the illiterate farmhand from the Polish borderlands, and Hein Foth, the ship's stoker from Hamburg who had such terrible lice. Over there had stood the cartridge tent where they'd worked so hard and argued so vociferously. It wasn't there any more, but the ghost of it was, built of grey air against the dark grey sky. Above it a pennant made of Sergeant Karde's blown-off leg fluttered merrily and a couple of dead ASC men formed a grinning guard of honour by the door, because the inspection tent for damaged ammunition had later stood on the same spot awaiting the blast that destroyed it. Up on the right the abandoned camp's barracks still loomed against the night sky. But where was the field gun depot and the bubbling brook that flowed through it? There was a pond there now, and the new barracks of a delousing station or laundry crouched in the valley.

And then the small railway followed the course of the Theinte, and to its right disappeared the road to Ville and the approach to the ravines of Fosses wood. From the left above Chaumont little Sergeant Süßmann nodded, no longer a sergeant, his clever monkey's eyes shining in his singed face, and then the puffing locomotive came upon Artillery Lieutenant von Roggstroh wafting past with his boyish face and short, straight nose; and Bertin suddenly understood that he too must have been killed, which was hardly surprising. But rising above the hills like a gigantic pillar of smoke, lit by a reddish glow, was the figure of Sergeant Christoph Kroysing, waving from Chambrettes-Ferme where the French had long since installed themselves. *God, God*, thought Bertin, snuggling into the crates of explosives and wondering why young Kroysing had that strange form, like a candle flame, sharp and snapped off at the top. Of course – he recalled the balloon observers who'd been shot down and the two columns of smoke that had then unravelled against the sky. Then a ghostly aeroplane crossed the sky, the pilot's back covered in a handful of dark bullet holes. Poor young lad with his handsome tanned face.

On the right, they'd reached some ruined trees with disintegrating tops – what was called Thil wood. Suddenly, shells were exploding among them. Dark red flames, yellow lighting. Bertin got a real shock. He had slept through the gunfire. But before he could jump down from his crates of explosives, the sapper on the wagon furthest back reassured him that the gunfire was 150m to the right and would stay there. The Frogs couldn't get any closer however hard they tried – God damn them.

Still feeling somewhat wary, Bertin remained present and alert, but only a couple of rounds of machine gun fire broke the silence and the even chug-chug-chug of the doughty locomotive. He leaned back again and surveyed the black bulk of the land stretching off to his right. Over there was the road to Azannes and Gremilly. There by a fire that didn't really exist, a red shell flame, crouched the young farmworker Przygulla, blowing on the flames and warming his hands. His mouth hung open as always because of the growths in his nasal cavity, and his fish eyes looked questioningly at clever Herr Bertin, who proved so much more stupid than Przygulla, when his belly was slit open and Private Schamm carried him into the medical dugout dying like a little child. Yes, said, Lieutenant Schanz, we lads from the Prussian school have to go through some pretty stiff tests before we see sense.

Bertin shuddered, buttoned his coat tighter and put his collar up.

The train stopped for a moment. The line branched off here to Romagne in a continuation of the section that the Schwerdtlein party had constructed with the Russian prisoners during the Great Cold. The sapper had to carry on alone with his wagons into unpleasant territory. The front part of the train, with Bertin and his four wagons, went round the corner into the darkness.

Bertin looked back at the three sapper wagons. Stalking over to meet them was a tall, lean figure in breeches and puttees, who revealed his wolf's teeth as he laughed and waved his long hand in goodbye. In the end, thought Bertin, he really did choose to haunt Douaumont. 'Not as unpleasant as you might think, my new state,' he heard Eberhard Kroysing's deep voice purr from the distance. 'I decided to skip the whole air force bigwig business and go straight for that pile of rubble. You won't forget me, will you, my little joker?' *No fear of that*, thought Bertin.

Then he jumped up as the train braked with a jolt. From a dugout cut into the hillside a railwayman appeared and took Bertin's papers. He said the dugout was called Romagne-West and that Bertin could wait in the warm and cruise back to his depot around 5pm with the empty wagons. Below, in the harsh light of an acetylene lamp, a little stove pumped out heat and there was the smell of coffee. Bertin was handed a mugful. He asked how long this new system had been needed. Since the French had gradually shot the old train station at Romagne to pieces, came the reply. During one of their fireworks displays that big-nosed Berliner had been taken out, that capable sergeant from the Railway Transport Office: had Bertin known him? Of course, replied Bertin. Anyone who had anything to do with the railway had known him. He was the soul of the whole operation and the railway transport officer's right-hand man. So he was gone? Poor Pelican! That night seemed to belong to the dead. It would be better not to ask after anyone else, for example Friedrich Strumpf. It felt bloody spooky to be leaving this place alive.

And so goodnight.

About 8am, freshly shaved and having shared a good breakfast with little Strauß, Private Bertin of the ASC finally received his travel papers in the orderly room: railway warrants, ration card, delousing warrants, identity card. In his identity card it said that he was to report for duty with the court martial of the Lychow division at Mervinsk. He would find out where Mervinsk was – and how to get there – at the Schlesischer train station in Berlin. Because it was a long journey, he was even authorised to take an express train. The arrears of his wages and his ration money, calculated exactly, were handed over to him in brand new five and ten mark notes; he waived his share of the accumulated canteen money and donated it to the gas worker Halezinsky. The clerk Querfurth with his goatee beard made a note of this. Then they shook hands. 'All the best, Kamerad,' said Querfurth. 'Look after yourselves,' replied Bertin. And he was amazed to find he had a lump in his throat. It had been a lousy company. For nearly two years he'd been drilled and treated in an increasingly unjust and malicious way, but nonetheless it was his company, a surrogate mother and father, wife and work, home and university. It had fed and clothed him, instructed him and brought him up, it had been a second parental home where the state was the father and Germania the mother, and now he had to leave it and go out into an unknown, uncertain world. A man's eyes might almost fill with tears at the thought. Main thing was nobody saw.

Nobody did see. And when, half an hour later, the shoogly little train on the Meuse line set off taking him to Montmédy, a tanned ASC man stuck his head out of the window and watched the land behind him, which had shaped him in sunshine and rain, summer and winter, day and night, becoming smaller and smaller. What had little Süßmann's last words been before he died? 'To my parents: it was worth it. To Lieutenant Kroysing: it wasn't.' The truth lay somewhere between those two poles, but as a wise man had once noted, not in the middle.

CHAPTER EIGHT

Swansong

IT WAS THE height of June, and the suburb of Ebensee near Nuremberg sparkled in the glow of summer. Here the city touched the old pine and beech woods at the foot of the Franconian part of the Jura hills. Schilfstraße in Ebensee was lined with small villas. From a nearby café came the sound of dance music, modern American tunes called things like the foxtrot or the shimmy.

Two young people strolled along like lovers by the white fence that separated the pavement from the front gardens. The young man was wearing a slightly worn summer suit in a blue-grey material of a cut from before the war. His neck with its prominent Adam's apple rose up from the open collar of a white shirt. His thin cheekbones, slightly sticky out ears and longish hair looked much less out of place in a conventional suit than in uniform. His small eyes peered searchingly through the thick lenses of his new, stronger spectacles. 'Number 26,' he read from the fence opposite. 'It's 28 so it must be the next one. Lene, I'm frightened. I'm not sure I can go in.'

Lenore, in a pale yellow summer dress that came just past her knee, laid her hand protectively on his. 'You don't have to do it. No one's forcing you, Werner. You came here of your own accord. Look over there, the flag's at half mast.'

Werner Bertin looked into the garden of Number 28. A white painted flagpole towered there, and a black, white and red flag hung motionlessly from it. This flag, which for four years he'd seen flying in various countries, from buildings in Skopje and Kaunas, in Lille and Montmédy, in every German street, and which was soon to disappear, had been hoisted in mourning between the cherry tree and the two pine trees on the right and left of the lawn, and scarcely a breeze moved its folds. 'At last someone who marks this day,' he said. 'I'm sure now that it's that house. Can you read what it says on the sign?'

If she shielded her eyes – her wide-brimmed hat hung from her arm – Lenore could decipher the brass sign from across the road: 'It says Kroysing.'

A gaunt man, very tall, with his hands behind his back, came down the path that led from the house to the street, looking as though he often trod that route deep in thought. He appeared for a moment at the fence in a black coat, stiff white collar and black tie, turned round and disappeared round the other side of the house.

Werner Bertin pressed Lenore's hand. 'That's him. Eberhard Kroysing was his double. If only that incessant tootling would stop!'

The date was 29 June 1919. As was the case every Sunday afternoon, people were dancing in the garden pubs and cafés. On the calendar, the day was called 'Peter and Paul' day after the two apostles. That day Germany was celebrating the signing of the Treaty of Versailles, which had taken place the day before. The war was definitively over, and the blockade would soon end too. Soon Bertin and Lenore, and old Herr Kroysing too, would no longer look so pinched. It was a day on which the terrible bloody wounds of the last four years had been declared healed. At the same time, Bertin wished Germany would take it more seriously, be more considered, more collected, more shaken. You felt something of that among the bourgeoisie: there was the flag flying at half mast between black pine trees. But the people danced. They didn't worry about it. No one noticed that a new page had been turned in the earth's destiny. Germany danced. Things could only get better. The shotguns had been thrown into the corner. Everyone was piling into work. People just wanted to forget, rejoice and immerse themselves in the hot days of early summer. After all the years of hardship, grief and horror they had the right to go a bit mad.

The young writer and his wife were on their way to southern Germany to recover in the glorious light of the landscape they loved. But before they disappeared into the mountains, Bertin had decided to look up the two Kroysing brothers' parents. He wanted to tell them how their sons had died, how miserable and pointless their deaths had been, so they might understand it was not some noble lie or bogus heroic sacrifice that had deprived them of the sons who would have supported them in their old age, but brutality and sheer, stupid chance. He'd have to be careful but as a writer he knew how to use words. The poor people shouldn't be left under any illusions. Instead they should be made to join those who wanted to do away with nationalistic jingoism and only allow war against true predators.

And now the flag was flying at half mast, and the man who looked like Eberhard Kroysing as an old man reappeared, his stony face set in bitter lines, walked up to the garden fence, spotted the young couple across the road, shrugged his shoulders grimly, turned and headed back to the house. From the doorway above the front steps an old woman emerged with a handkerchief in her hand. She dabbed her eyes with it, a habit that had clearly become ingrained. 'Alfred,' she cried in a dark voice that held the echo of tears shed long ago, 'it's time for tea.'

The old public official nodded to her, climbed the steps and disappeared inside with her. The windows facing the direction of the music were banged shut. The summer's day sparkled over the red roof of the house, Peter and Paul day, the coming harvest. The corner of the black, white and red flag was almost touching the gravel that surrounded the white mast in a small, yellow circle in the middle of the lawn.

'I can't do it,' said Werner Bertin decisively. 'Come on, let's go to the woods. We're not here to rub salt in old wounds. The government of the republic, once we have a constitution, will expose the truth. Besides, those two won't forget or let other people forget.'

Deep in her heart, Lenore Bertin didn't agree with Werner's decision to shirk this duty. *If you decide to do something, you should do it*, she thought doubtfully. But he was so irritable at the moment that she didn't want to disagree with him. He really belonged in a sanatorium, but he wouldn't hear of it. And so there was nothing left for a wise woman to do but follow the man she loved, who had held out so bravely and still had complete trust in the wisdom of governments, that beloved, foolish boy, that savage heart, into the woods over there, where the magnificent leafy treetops formed a border between the sky and the earth.

'This meadow,' said Bertin, putting his arm round her, 'could be held against two companies from here with one machine gun. They'd never get over that stream down there. And the edge of the woods would make a great emplacement for an anti-aircraft battery.'

The meadow shone blue with lady's smock and crane's bill. At the edge of the woods, flashes of sunlight played on the grey tree trunks. 'That,' said Werner Bertin dreamily, leaning against his wife's shoulder, 'is exactly what the woods at Verdun looked like when we arrived, only much thicker.'

'If only you could leave those woods behind,' said Lenore tenderly. She secretly feared it would be a long time before her friend and husband found his way back from those enchanted woods and their undergrowth into the present, into real life. The war worked on within him, burrowed and seethed, clashed and shrieked. But from the outside – she sighed – no one, thank God, could tell.

Like any other pair of lovers, they wandered off into the woods, through the shadows and the bright greenery, and her yellow summer dress shone through longer than his blue-grey suit.

Afterword

This novel fills the gap between the books *Young Woman of 1914* and *The Case of Sergeant Grischa*, which, together with *The Crowing of a King*, was the original concept for a cycle of novels to be called *The Great War of the White Men*. The novel was sketched out in 1927, begun for the first time in 1928 and for the second time in 1930. Its publication was delayed by the confiscation of my manuscripts and my expulsion from Germany. The steady deterioration of my eyesight complicated final revisions to the freshly dictated manuscript. Unless even worse circumstances intervene, the novel *The Crowing of a King* will conclude the cycle and, much as each part stands on its own, complete an intended whole originally supposed to bear the subtitle of *A Trilogy of the Transition*.

For faithful help in reading the proofs of these books, I owe grateful thanks to my friends Lion Feuchtwanger and Hermann Struck amongst others.

Arnold Zweig
Haifa, Mount Carmel, spring 1935

Characters

In the order of their appearance

PRIVATE WERNER BERTIN, son of a Kreuzberg Jew, a young trainee lawyer and writer now of the German Army Service Corps (ASC).

PRIVATE WILHELM PAHL, from Berlin, a typsetter by trade and a socialist; also of the ASC.

PRIVATE KARL LEBEHDE, in civilian life a Berlin inn-keeper, now of the ASC.

COLONEL STEIN, an old cavalryman, commandant of the Steinbergquell ammunitions depot.

LIEUTENANT BENNDORF, acting captain and adjutant to Colonel Stein.

ACTING LIEUTENANT GRASSNICK, veteran of the Serbian campaign, in command of the labour company attached to the ammunitions depot; known to his subordinates as Panje of Vranje.

ACTING SERGEANT MAJOR GLINSKY, formerly an insurance agent.

PRIVATES OF THE ASC: HILDEBRANDT, a blacksmith; VEHSE, an upholsterer; STRAUSS, a shopkeeper; FANNRICH and REINHOLD.

SPERLICH, an orderly-room clerk.

BRUNO NAUMANN, barber, a socialist.

IGNAZ NAUMANN, the company fool, formerly a packer in a warehouse.

DR. BINDEL, a civilian doctor in uniform.

CORPORAL SCHNEE, from the Sanitary Corps.

SERGEANT BÖHNE, once a postman.

SERGEANT SCHULZ, an ammunitions expert.

SERGEANT CHRISTOPH KROYSING, a Nürnberger, a young poet who stood up against injustice.

AXEL KROG, a Swedish war correspondent, a fervent admirer of France.

LEPAILLE, a French gunner.

WUERFURTH, a clerk.

CORPORAL NÄGLEIN, formerly a farmer.

CORPORAL ALTHANS, a Reservist in possession of a permanent travel pass.

LIEUTENANT EBERHARD KROYSING, Christoph Kroysing's elder brother, by profession a civil engineer, now a sapper and recipient of the Iron Cross, first class.

CAPTAIN ALOIS NIGGL, in civilian life a retired civil servant from Weilheim, Bavaria, now of the ASC and with ambitions for decoration.

MAJOR JANSCH, a Prussian from Berlin, embittered nationalist and anti-Semite, editor of *Army and Fleet Weekly*, now of the ASC.

LIEUTENANT PSALTER, formerly a headmaster in Neuruppen, now of the lorry park.

PROFESSOR CARL GEORG MERTENS, an eminent legal scholar, judge advocate of the court martial at Montmédy.

SEARGEANT PORISCH, Judge Advoate Mertens' deputy.

LANCE CORPORAL SIECK, clerk to the judge advocate.

SERGEANT ERICH SÜSSMANN, a Berlin Jew, a schoolboy in years but a veteran in service.

OTTO SCHNEIDER, a telephone operator.

CORPORAL FRIEDRICH STRUMPF, a switchboard operator, once a park-keeper near Heidelberg.

SERGEANT-MAJOR LUDWIG FEICHT, formerly purser on a Bavarian lake steamer.

LIEUTENANT SIMMERDING, second in command in Captain Niggl's company.

DILLINGER, orderly-room clerk.

LIEUTENANT PAUL SCHANZ, from Russian Poland, now of the artillery.

CORPORAL KARL KILIAN, from Baden, a switchboard operator, once a worker in a tobacco factory.

FATHER BENEDIKT LOCHNER, of the Order of St Francis, a broad-minded representative of the Catholic Church, now serving as field chaplain.

SEERGEANT KNAPPE, an ammunitions expert.

JEAN-FRANCOIS ROUARD, a French painter, now in the French air corps.

PRIVATE PRZYGULLA, formerly a farmhand.

THE CROWN PRINCE OF GERMANY, Commander-in-Chief of the Prussian Army.

LIEUTENANT VON ROGGSTROH, an officer in the Royal Guard Artillery.

SERGEANT KROPP, a peasant from Uckermark.

KRAWIETZ, the company tailor.

SERGEANT BÜTTNER, an industrialist in civilian life.

SERGEANT-MAJOR PFUND, an old regular, embezzler of canteen funds.

STAFF SERGEANT SUSEMIHL, a policeman in civilian life.

STAFF SERGEANT POHL, in civilian life a schoolteacher.

SERGEANT SCHNEEVOIGT, hospital orderly and a barber by trade.

SERGEANT SCHWERDTLEIN, in charge of a construction squad.

SERGEANT ALEXANDER FÜRTH, a Berlin barrister, a Jew, known to his fellow corps members as Pelican, now of the railway transport office.

SERGEANT EMIL BARKOPP, a tavern-keeper from Hamburg, leader of an ill-fated working party.

CORPORAL DIEHL, a primary schoolteacher, clerk to Major Jansch,

KUHLMANN, a messenger.

SISTER KLÄRE, daughter of the well-known Pidderit family of the Rhineland, wife of Colonel Schwersenz, and now a nurse at Dannevoux field hospital.

LIEUTENANT METTNER, a mathematician, now in hospital.

LIEUTENANT FLACHSBAUER, son of a factory owner, now in hospital.

SISTER MARIECHEN, of the Dannevoux hospital unit.

DR POSNANSKI, a Jew from Brandenburg, judge advocate and successor to Professor Mertens; known as Mopsus to fellow corps members.

ADLER, Berlin barrister, clerk to Dr Posnanski.

LIEUTENANT WINFRIED, nephew of his Excellency General von Lychow.

SERGEANT-MAJOR PONT, a master builder from Kalkar on the Rhine.

PECHLER, Dannevoux hospital bath orderly.

DR BAER, Jewish chaplain at Dannevoux hospital.

KELLER, a blind cuirassier, now telephone operator for Dannevoux hospital.

PHILIPPE, pilot of a French bombing plane.

LENORE BERTIN, Werner Bertin's wife.

Translator's note

In completely this translation of Arnold Zweig's *Erziehung vor Verdun*, I was frequently assisted by Eric Sutton's existing translation. Published in the United States in 1936 – just one year after the German publication – Sutton's translation, now out of print, bore the title *Education before Verdun* and has been a rich source for military terminology in particular.

I am also grateful to David Midgley for invaluable assistance with First World War military vocabulary and with some of the trickier nuances in the text, and to Alaric Searle. Thanks are also due to Ingrid Kollak and Titus Kroder for providing a German native speaker's view on certain points.

Some of the terms used in *Erziehung vor Verdun* almost defy translation. I have translated *Feldwebelleutnant* as acting lieutenant. The literal meaning is sergeant major lieutenant, and the term denotes sergeant majors given the command responsibilities of lieutenants due to the heavy losses incurred by the German army.

Also tricky to translate into English are the three categories of reserve forces in the Prussian army: the regular military *Reserve*, the *Landwehr*, roughly equivalent to the Territorial Army, and the *Landsturm*, made up of older men capable of wielding weapons and men not fit for active service. In many cases, I have therefore kept the original German terms of *Landwehr* and *Landsturm* in the English text, as well as the term *Landstürmer*, which denotes a member of the *Landsturm*.

Another problem arises in translating *Erziehung vor Verdun* into English from the fact that the German terms *Kamerad*, a comrade at arms, and *Genosse*, a Communist Party comrade, both translate into English as comrade. I have attempted to clarify the distinction in each instance.

My principal aim with this translation has been to bring Arnold Zweig's magnificent novel of the First World War alive for contemporary English-speaking readers. In particular, I have tried to capture the flavour of the humour, dialect and colloquialisms in the original. For that reason, I have occasionally used non-standard English, particularly Scots, as that is the form of non-standard English with which I am most familiar.

It goes without saying that any errors or omissions in this translation are my responsibility alone.

Fiona Rintoul
Glasgow, April 2014